Black-Eyed Susans

By Julia Heaberlin

Playing Dead

Lie Still

Black-Eyed Susans

Black-Eyed Susans

A Novel of Suspense

JULIA HEABERLIN

PENGUIN BOOKS

PENGUIN BOOKS

UK | USA | Canada | Ireland | Australia
India | New Zealand | South Africa

Penguin Books is part of the Penguin Random House group of companies
whose addresses can be found at global.penguinrandomhouse.com.

First published in the United States by Ballantine Books, an imprint of Random House,
a division of Random House LLC, a Penguin Random House Company, 2015
First published in Great Britain by Michael Joseph, 2015
Published in Penguin Books 2016
002

Set in Garamond MT
Typeset by Palimpsest Book Production Limited, Falkirk, Stirlingshire
Printed in Great Britain by Clays Ltd, St Ives plc

A CIP catalogue record for this book is available from the British Library

ISBN: 978-1-405-92127-5

www.greenpenguin.co.uk

Penguin Random House is committed to a
sustainable future for our business, our readers
and our planet. This book is made from Forest
Stewardship Council® certified paper.

For Sam, my game changer

Prologue

Thirty-two hours of my life are missing.

My best friend, Lydia, tells me to imagine those hours like old clothes in the back of a dark closet. Shut my eyes. Open the door. Move things around. Search.

The things I do remember, I'd rather not. Four freckles. Eyes that aren't black but blue, wide open, two inches from mine. Insects gnawing into a smooth, soft cheek. The grit of the earth in my teeth. Those parts, I remember.

It's my seventeenth birthday, and the candles on my cake are burning.

The little flames are waving at me to hurry up. I'm thinking about the Black-Eyed Susans, lying in freezing metal drawers. How I scrub and scrub but can't wash away their smell no matter how many showers I take.

Be happy.

Make a wish.

I paste on a smile, and focus. Everyone in this room loves me and wants me home.

Hopeful for the same old Tessie.

Never let me remember.

I close my eyes and blow.

PART I
Tessa and Tessie

My mother she killed me,
My father he ate me,
My sister gathered together all my bones,
Tied them in a silken handkerchief,
Laid them beneath the juniper-tree,
Kywitt, kywitt, what a beautiful bird am I!

– Tessie, age 10, reading aloud to her
grandfather from 'The Juniper Tree,' 1988

Tessa, present day

For better or worse, I am walking the crooked path to my childhood.

The house sits topsy-turvy on the crest of a hill, like a kid built it out of blocks and toilet paper rolls. The chimney tilts in a comical direction, and turrets shoot off each side like missiles about to take off. I used to sleep inside one of them on summer nights and pretend I was rocketing through space.

More than my little brother liked, I had climbed out one of the windows onto the tiled roof and inched my scrappy knees toward the widow's peak, grabbing sharp gargoyle ears and window ledges for balance. At the top, I leaned against the curlicued railing to survey the flat, endless Texas landscape and the stars of my kingdom. I played my piccolo to the night birds. The air rustled my thin white cotton nightgown like I was a strange dove alit on the top of a castle. It sounds like a fairy tale, and it was.

My grandfather made his home in this crazy storybook house in the country, but he built it for my brother, Bobby, and me. It wasn't a huge place, but I still have no idea how he could afford it. He presented each of us with a turret, a place where we could hide out from the world whenever we wanted to sneak away. It was his grand gesture, our personal Disney World, to make up for the fact that our mother had died.

Granny tried to get rid of the place shortly after Granddaddy died, but the house didn't sell till years later, when she was lying in the ground between him and their daughter. Nobody wanted it. It was weird, people said. Cursed. Their ugly words made it so.

After I was found, the house had been pasted in all the papers, all over TV. The local newspapers dubbed it Grim's Castle. I never knew if that was a typo. Texans spell things different. For instance, we don't always add the *ly*.

People whispered that my grandfather must have had something to do with my disappearance, with the murder of all the Black-Eyed Susans, because of his freaky house. '*Shades of Michael Jackson and his Neverland Ranch,*' they muttered, even after the state sent a man to Death Row a little over a year later for the crimes. These were the same people who had driven up to the front door every Christmas so their kids could gawk at the lit-up gingerbread house and grab a candy cane from the basket on the front porch.

I press the bell. It no longer plays *Ride of the Valkyries.* I don't know what to expect, so I am a little surprised when the older couple that open the door look perfectly suited to living here. The plump worn-down hausfrau with the kerchief on her head, the sharp nose, and the dust rag in her hand reminds me of the old woman in the shoe.

I stutter out my request. There's an immediate glint of recognition by the woman, a slight softening of her mouth. She locates the small crescent-moon scar under my eye. The woman's eyes say *poor little girl,* even though it's been eighteen years, and I now have a girl of my own.

'I'm Bessie Wermuth,' she says. 'And this is my husband, Herb. Come in, dear.' Herb is scowling and leaning on his cane. Suspicious, I can tell. I don't blame him. I am a stranger, even though he knows exactly who I am. Everyone in a five-hundred-mile radius does. I am the Cartwright girl, dumped once upon a time with a strangled college student and a stack of human bones out past Highway 10, in an abandoned patch of field near the Jenkins property.

I am the star of screaming tabloid headlines and campfire ghost stories.

I am one of the four Black-Eyed Susans. The *lucky* one.

It will only take a few minutes, I promise. Mr Wermuth frowns, but Mrs Wermuth says, *Yes, of course.* It is clear that she makes the decisions about all of the important things, like the height of the grass and what to do with a red-headed, kissed-by-evil waif on their doorstep, asking to be let in.

'We won't be able to go down there with you,' the man grumbles as he opens the door wider.

'Neither of us have been down there too much since we moved in,' Mrs Wermuth says hurriedly. 'Maybe once a year. It's damp. And there's a broken step. A busted hip could do either of us in. Break one little thing at this age, and you're at the Pearly Gates in thirty days or less. If you don't want to die, don't step foot inside a hospital after you turn sixty-five.'

As she makes this grim pronouncement, I am frozen in the great room, flooded with memories, searching for things no longer there. The totem pole that Bobby and I sawed and carved one summer, completely unsupervised, with only one trip to the emergency room. Granddaddy's painting of a tiny mouse riding a handkerchief sailboat in a wicked, boiling ocean.

Now a Thomas Kinkade hangs in its place. The room is

home to two flowered couches and a dizzying display of knickknacks, crowded on shelves and tucked in shadow boxes. German beer steins and candlesticks, a *Little Women* doll set, crystal butterflies and frogs, at least fifty delicately etched English teacups, a porcelain clown with a single black tear rolling down. All of them, I suspect, wondering how in the hell they ended up in the same neighborhood.

The ticking is soothing. Ten antique clocks line one wall, two with twitching cat tails keeping perfect time with each other.

I can understand why Mrs Wermuth chose our house. In her way, she is one of us.

'Here we go,' she says. I follow her obediently, navigating a passageway that snakes off the living room. I used to be able to take its turns in the pitch dark on my roller skates. She is flipping light switches as we go, and I suddenly feel like I am walking to the chamber of my death.

'TV says the execution is in a couple of months.' I jump. This is exactly where my mind is traveling. The scratchy male voice behind me is Mr Wermuth's, full of cigarette smoke.

I pause, swallowing the knot in my throat as I wait for him to ask whether I plan to sit front row and watch my attacker suck in his last breath. Instead, he pats my shoulder awkwardly. 'I wouldn't go. Don't give him another damn second.'

I am wrong about Herb. It wouldn't be the first time I've been wrong, or the last.

My head knocks into an abrupt curve in the wall because I'm still turned toward Herb. 'I'm fine,' I tell Mrs Wermuth quickly. She lifts her hand but hesitates to touch my stinging cheek, because it is just a little too close to the scar, the permanent mark from a garnet ring dangling off a skeletal finger. A gift from a Susan who didn't want me to forget her, ever. I push Mrs Wermuth's hand away gently. 'I forgot that turn was coming up so soon.'

'Crazy damn house,' Herb says under his breath. 'What in the hell is wrong with living in St Pete?' He doesn't seem to expect an answer. The spot on my cheek begins to complain and my scar echoes, a tiny *ping, ping, ping.*

The hallway has settled into a straight line. At the end, an ordinary door. Mrs Wermuth pulls out a skeleton key from her apron pocket and twists it in the lock easily. There used to be twenty-five of those keys, all exactly the same, which could open any door in the place. An odd bit of practicality from my grandfather.

A chilly draft rushes at us. I smell things both dying and growing. I have my first moment of real doubt since I left home an hour ago. Mrs Wermuth reaches up and yanks on a piece of kite string dancing above her head. The bare, dusty lightbulb flickers on.

'Take this.' Mr Wermuth prods me with the small Maglite from his pocket. 'I carry it around for reading. You know where the main light switch is?'

'Yes,' I say automatically. 'Right at the bottom.'

'Watch the sixteenth step,' Mrs Wermuth warns. 'Some critter chewed a hole in it. I always count when I go down. You take as long as you like. I think I'll make all of us a cup of tea and you can tell us a bit of the history of the house after. We'd both find that fascinating. Right, Herb?' Herb grunts. He's thinking of driving a little white ball two hundred yards into Florida's deep blue sea.

I hesitate on the second step, and turn my head, unsure. If anyone shuts this door, I won't be found for a hundred years. I've never had any doubt that death is still eager to catch up with a certain sixteen-year-old girl.

Mrs Wermuth offers a tiny, silly wave. 'I hope you find what you are looking for. It must be important.'

If this is an opening, I don't take it.

I descend noisily, like a kid, jumping over step sixteen. At the bottom, I pull another dangling string, instantly washing the room with a harsh fluorescent glow.

It lights an empty tomb. This used to be a place where things were born, where easels stood with half-finished paintings, and strange, frightening tools hung on peg-boards, where a curtained darkroom off to the side waited to bring photos to life, and dress mannequins held parties in the corners. Bobby and I would swear we had seen them move more than once.

A stack of old chests held ridiculous antique dress-up hats wrapped in tissue paper and my grandmother's wedding dress with exactly 3,002 seed pearls and my grandfather's World War II uniform with the brown spot on the sleeve that Bobby and I were sure was blood. My grandfather was a welder, a farmer, a historian, an artist, an Eagle Scout leader, a morgue photographer, a rifleman, a woodworker, a Republican, a yellow dog Democrat. A poet. He could never make up his mind, which is exactly what people say about me.

He ordered us never to come down here alone, and he never knew we did. But the temptation was too great. We were especially fascinated with a forbidden, dusty black album that held Granddaddy's crime scene photographs from his brief career with the county morgue. A wide-eyed housewife with her brains splattered across her linoleum kitchen floor. A drowned, naked judge pulled to shore by his dog.

I stare at the mold greedily traveling up the brick walls on every side. The black lichen flourishing in a large crack zigzagging across the filthy concrete floor.

No one has loved this place since Granddaddy died. I quickly cross over to the far corner, sliding between the wall and the coal furnace that years ago had been abandoned as a bad idea. Something travels lightly across my ankle. A scorpion, a roach. I don't flinch. Worse things have crawled across my face.

Behind the furnace, it is harder to see. I sweep the light down the wall until I find the grimy brick with the red heart, painted there to fool my brother. He had spied on me one day when I was exploring my options. I run my finger lightly around the edges of the heart three times.

Then I count ten bricks up from the red heart, and five bricks over. Too high for little Bobby to reach. I jam the screwdriver from my pocket into the crumbling mortar, and begin to pry. The first brick topples out, and clatters onto the floor. I work at three other bricks, tugging them out one at a time.

I flash the light into the hole.

Stringy cobwebs, like spin art. At the back, a gray, square lump.

Waiting, for seventeen years, in the crypt I made for it.

Tessie, 1995

'Tessie. Are you listening?'

He is asking stupid questions, like the others.

I glance up from the magazine, open in my lap, that I had conveniently found beside me on the couch. 'I don't see the point.'

I flip a page, just to irritate him. Of course he knows I'm not reading.

'Then why are you here?'

I let the air hang with thick silence. Silence is my only instrument of control in this parade of therapy sessions. Then I say, 'You know why. I am here because my father wants me to be here.' *Because I hated all the others. Because Daddy is so sad, and I can't stand it.* 'My brother says I've changed.' *Too much information. You'd think I'd learn.*

His chair legs squeak on the hardwood floor, as he shifts positions. Ready to pounce. 'Do *you* think you've changed?'

So *obvious.* Disgusted, I flip back to the magazine. The pages are cold and slick and stiff. They smell of cloying perfume. It's the kind of magazine that I suspect is filled with bony, angry girls. I wonder: *Is that what this man sees when he stares at me?* I'd lost twenty pounds in the last year. Most of my track star muscle tone, gone. My right foot is wrapped in a new leaden cast, from the third surgery. Bitterness rises in my lungs like hot steam. I suck in a deep breath. My goal is to feel nothing.

'OK,' he says. 'Dumb question.' I know that he's watching me intently. 'How about this one: Why did you pick me this time?'

I toss the magazine down. I try to remember that he is making an exception, probably doing the district attorney a favor. He rarely treats teenage girls.

'You signed a legal document that said you will not prescribe drugs, that you will not ever, ever publish anything about our sessions or use me for research without my knowledge, that you will not tell a living soul you are treating the surviving Black-Eyed Susan. You told me you won't use hypnosis.'

'Do you trust that I will not do any of those things?'

'No,' I snap back. 'But at least I'll be a millionaire if you do.'

'We have fifteen minutes left,' he says. 'We can use the time however you like.'

'Great.' I pick up the magazine full of bony, angry girls.

Tessa, present day

Two hours after I leave Granddaddy's, William James Hastings III arrives at my house, a 1920s bungalow in Fort Worth with somber black shutters and not a single curve or frill. A jungle of color and life thrives behind my front door, but outside, I choose anonymity.

I've never met the man with the baronial name settling in on my couch. He can't be older than twenty-eight, and he is at least 6'3", with long, loose arms and big hands. His knees bang up against the coffee table. William James Hastings III reminds me more of a professional pitcher in his prime than a lawyer, like his body's awkwardness would disappear the second he picked up a ball. Boyish. Cute. Big nose that makes him just short of handsome. He has brought along a woman in a tailored white jacket, white-collared shirt, and black pants. The type who cares only vaguely about fashion, as professional utility. Short, natural blond hair. Ring-free fingers. Flat, clipped, unpolished nails. Her only adornment is a glittering gold chain with an expensive-looking charm, a familiar squiggly doodle, but I don't have time to think about what it means. She's a cop, maybe, although that doesn't make sense.

The gray lump, still covered in dust and ancient spider threads, sits between us on the coffee table.

'I'm Bill,' he says. 'Not William. And definitely not Willie.' He smiles. I wonder if he's used this line on a jury. I think he needs a better one. 'Tessa, as I said on the phone, we're thrilled that you called. Surprised, but thrilled. I hope you don't mind that Dr Seger – Joanna – tagged along. We don't have any time to waste. Joanna is the forensic scientist excavating the bones of the ... Susans tomorrow. She'd like to take a quick sample of your saliva. For DNA. Because of the issues we face with lost evidence and junk science, she wants to do the swab herself. That is, if you're really serious. Angie never thought –'

I clear my throat. 'I'm serious.' I feel a sudden pang for Angela Rothschild. The tidy silver-haired woman hounded me for the past six years, insisting that Terrell Darcy Goodwin was an innocent man. Picking at each doubt until I was no longer sure.

Angie was a saint, a bulldog, a little bit of a martyr. She'd spent the last half of her life and most of her parents' inheritance freeing prisoners who'd been bullied by the state of Texas into wrongful convictions. More than 1,500 convicted rapists and murderers begged for her services every year, so Angie had to be choosy. She told me that playing God with those calls and letters was the only thing that ever made her consider quitting. I'd been to her office once, the first time she contacted me. It was housed in an old church basement located on an unpleasant side of Dallas known best for its high fatality rate for cops. If her clients couldn't see the light of day or catch a quick Starbucks, she said, then neither could she. Her company in that basement was a coffeepot, three more attorneys who also worked other paying jobs, and as many law students as would sign on.

Angie sat in the same spot on my couch nine months

ago, in jeans and scuffed black cowboy boots, with one of Terrell's letters in her hand. She begged me to read it. She had begged me to do a lot of things, like give one of her expert gurus a shot at retrieving my memory. Now she was dead of a heart attack, found facedown in a pile of documents about Goodwin's case. The reporter who wrote her obituary found that poetic. My guilt in the week since she died has been almost unbearable. Angie, I realized too late, was one of my tethers. One of the few who never gave up on me.

'Is this . . . what you have for us?' Bill stares at the filthy plastic grocery bag from Granddaddy's basement like it is stuffed with gold. It has left a trail of pebbly mortar across the glass, right beside a pink hair band twisted with a strand of my daughter Charlie's auburn hair.

'You said on the phone that you had to go . . . find it,' he says. 'That you'd told Angie about this . . . project . . . but you weren't sure where it was.'

It isn't really a question, and I don't answer.

His eyes wander the living room, strewn with the detritus of an artist and a teenager. 'I'd like to set up a meeting at the office in a few days. After I've . . . examined it. You and I will have to go over all of the old ground for the appeal.' For such a large guy, there is a gentleness about him. I wonder about his courtroom style, if gentleness is his weapon.

'Ready for the swab?' Dr Seger interrupts abruptly, all business, already stretching on latex gloves. Maybe worried that I'll change my mind.

'Sure.' We both stand up. She tickles the inside of my cheek and seals microscopic bits of me in a tube. I know she plans to add my DNA to the collection provided by three other Susans, two of whom still go by the more formal name of Jane Doe. I feel heat emanating from her. Anticipation.

I return my attention to the bag on the table, and Bill. 'This was kind of an experiment suggested by one of my psychiatrists. It might be more valuable for what isn't there than what is.' In other words, I didn't draw a black man who looked like Terrell Darcy Goodwin.

My voice is calm, but my heart is lurching. I am giving Tessie to this man. I hope it is not a mistake.

'Angie . . . she would be so grateful. Is grateful.' Bill crooks a finger up, the Michelangelo kind of gesture that travels up to the sky. I find this comforting: a man who is bombarded by people blocking his path every day – half-decent people clinging stubbornly to their lies and deadly mistakes – and yet he still believes in God. Or, at least, still believes in something.

Dr Seger's phone buzzes in her pocket. She glances at the screen. 'I've got to take this. One of my Ph.D. students. I'll meet you in the car, Bill. Good job, girl. You're doing the right thing.' *Gurrl.* A slight twang. Oklahoma, maybe. I smile automatically.

'Right behind you, Jo.' Bill is moving deliberately, shutting his briefcase, gingerly picking up the bag, in no apparent hurry. His hands grow still when she shuts the door. 'You've just met greatness. Joanna is a mitochondrial DNA genius. She can work goddamn miracles with degraded bones. She rushed to 9/11 and didn't leave for four years. Made history, helping identify thousands of victims out of charred bits. Lived at the YMCA at first. Took communal showers with the homeless. Worked fourteen-hour days. She didn't have to, it wasn't her job, but whenever she could, she sat down and explained the science to grieving families so they could be as sure as she was. She learned a smattering of Spanish so she could try to talk to the families of the Mexican dishwashers and waiters who worked in restaurants in the North Tower. She is one of the best forensic scientists on the planet, who happens to be one of the kindest human beings I've ever met, and she is giving Terrell a chance. I want you to understand the kind of people on our side. Tell me, Tessa, why are you? Why are you suddenly on our side?'

A slight edge has crept into his voice. He is gently telling me not to screw them.

'There are several reasons,' I say unsteadily. 'I can show you one of them.'

'Tessa, I want to know everything.'

'It's better if you see it.'

I lead him down our narrow hall without speaking, past Charlie's messy purple womb, usually pulsing with music, and throw open the door at the end. This wasn't in my plan, not today anyway.

Bill looms like a giant in my bedroom, his head knocking into the antique chandelier dangling with sea glass that Charlie and I scavenged last summer on the gray beaches of Galveston. He ducks away and brushes against the curve of my breast by accident. Apologizes. Embarrassed. For a second, I see this stranger's legs tangled in my sheets. I can't remember a time that I let a man in here.

I watch painfully as Bill absorbs intimate details about me: the cartoonish portrait of Granddaddy's house, gold and silver jewelry littered across my dresser, the close-up of Charlie staring out of lavender eyes, a neat pile of freshly laundered white lace panties on the chair, which I wish to God were tucked in a drawer.

He is already edging himself backward, toward the door, clearly wondering what the hell he has gotten himself into. Whether he has pinned his hopes for poor Terrell Darcy Goodwin on a crazy woman who has led him straight to her bedroom. Bill's expression makes me want to laugh out loud, even though I am not above entertaining a fantasy about an all-American guy with two degrees, when my type runs the opposite direction.

Even though what I'm about to show him keeps me up at night, reading the same paragraph of *Anna Karenina* over and over, listening to every creak of the house and finger of wind, every barefoot midnight step of my daughter, every sweet sleep sound that floats out of her mouth and down the hall.

'Don't worry.' I force lightness into my voice. 'I like my men rich and less altruistic. And you know . . . old enough to grow facial hair. Come over here. Please.'

'Cute.' But I can hear relief. He makes it in two strides. His eyes follow my finger, out the window.

I am not pointing to the sky, but to the dirt, where a nest of black-eyed Susans is still half-alive under the windowsill, teasing me with beady black eyes.

'It is February,' I say quietly. 'Black-eyed Susans only bloom like this in summer.' I pause for this to sink in. 'They were planted three days ago, on my birthday. Someone grew them especially for me, and put them under the window where I sleep.'

* * *

The abandoned field on the Jenkins property was licked to death by fire about two years before the Black-Eyed Susans were dumped there. A reckless match tossed by a lost car on a lonely dirt road cost a destitute old farmer his entire wheat crop and set the stage for the thousands and thousands of yellow flowers that covered the field like a giant, rumpled quilt.

The fire also carved out our grave, an uneven, loping ditch. Black-eyed Susans sprung up and decorated it brazenly long before we arrived. The Susans are a greedy plant, often the first to thrive in scorched, devastated earth. Pretty, but competitive, like cheerleaders. They live to crowd out the others.

One lit match, one careless toss, and our nicknames were embedded in serial killer lore forever.

Bill, still in my bedroom, has shot Joanna a lengthy text, maybe because he doesn't want to answer her questions on the phone in front of me. We meet her outside my window in time to watch her dip a vial into the black speckled dirt. The squiggly charm on her necklace, glinting in the sun, brushes a petal as she bends over. I still can't recall the symbol's meaning. Religious, maybe. Ancient.

'He or she used something besides the dirt in the ground,' Joanna said. 'Probably a common brand of potting soil, and seeds that can be picked up at Lowe's. But you never know. You should call the cops.'

'And tell them someone is planting pretty flowers?' I don't want to sound sarcastic, but there it is.

'It's trespassing,' Bill says. 'Harassment. You know, this doesn't have to be the work of the killer. It could be any crazy who reads the papers.' It is unspoken, but I know. He is uncertain of my mental state. He hopes I have more than this patch of flowers under my window to bolster a judge's belief in Terrell. A little part of him wonders whether I planted the flowers myself.

How much do I tell him?

I suck in a breath. 'Every time I call the cops, it ends up on the Internet. We get calls and letters and Facebook crazies. Presents on the doorstep. Cookies. Bags of dog poop. Cookies *made* of dog poop. At least I hope it's just dog poop. Any attention makes my daughter's life at school a living hell. After a few years of beautiful peace, the execution is stirring everything up again.' Exactly why, for years, I told Angie no and no and *no.* Whatever doubts crept in, I had to push away. In the end, I understood Angie, and Angie understood me. *I will find another way,* she had assured me.

But things were different now. Angie was dead.

He'd stood under my window.

I brush away something whispery threading its way through my hair. I vaguely wonder whether it is a traveler from Granddaddy's basement. I remember sticking my hand blindly into that musty hole a few hours ago, and turn my anger up a notch. 'The look on your faces right now? That mixture of pity and uneasiness and misplaced understanding that I still need to be treated like the traumatized sixteen-year-old girl I used to be? I've been getting that look since I can remember. That's how long I've been protecting myself, and so far, so good. I'm *happy* now. I am not that girl anymore.' I wrap my long brown sweater around me a little more tightly even though the late winter sun is a warm stroke across my face. 'My daughter will be home any minute, and I'd rather she doesn't meet the two of you until I've explained a few things. She doesn't know yet that I called you. I want to keep her life as normal as possible.'

'Tessa.' Joanna ventures a step toward me and stops. 'I get it.'

There is such a terrible weight in her voice. *I get it.* Bombs dropping *one two three* to the bottom of the ocean.

I scan her face. Tiny lines etched by other people's sorrow. Blue-green eyes that have flashed on more horror than I could ever fathom. Smelled it. Touched it, *breathed* it, as it rained down in ashes from the sky.

'Do you?' My voice is soft. 'I hope so. Because I am going to be there when you excavate those two graves.'

My daddy paid for their coffins.

Joanna is rubbing the charm between her fingers, like it is a holy cross.

I suddenly realize that, in her world, it is.

She is wearing a double helix made of gold.

The twisted ladder of life.

A strand of DNA.

Tessie, 1995

One week later. Tuesday, 10 A.M. sharp. I am back on the doctor's plump couch, with company. Oscar rubs his wet nose against my hand reassuringly, then settles in on the floor beside me, alert. He's been mine since last week, and I will go nowhere without him. Not that anyone argues. Oscar, sweet and protective, makes them hopeful.

'Tessie, the trial is in three months. Ninety days away. My most important job right now is to prepare you emotionally. I know the defense attorney, and he's excellent. He's even better when he truly believes he holds the life of an innocent man in his hands, which he does. Do you understand what that means? He will not take it easy on you.'

This time, right down to business.

My hands are folded primly in my lap. I'm wearing a short, blue-plaid pleated skirt, white lacy stockings, and black patent-leather boots. I've never been a prim girl, despite the reddish-gold hair and freckles my wonderfully corny grandfather claimed were fairy dust. Not then, not now. My best friend, Lydia, dressed me today. She burrowed into my messy drawers and closet, because she couldn't stand the fact that I no longer make any effort to match. Lydia is one of the few friends who isn't giving up on me. She is currently taking her fashion cues from the movie *Clueless,* but I haven't seen it.

'OK,' I say. This is, after all, one of two reasons I am sitting here. I am afraid. Ever since they snatched Terrell Darcy Goodwin away from his Denny's Grand Slam breakfast in Ohio eleven months ago and told me I would need to testify, I have counted the days like terrible pills. Today, we are eighty-seven days away, not ninety, but I do not bother to correct him.

'I remember nothing.' I am sticking with this.

'I'm sure the prosecutor has told you that doesn't matter. You're living, breathing evidence. Innocent girl vs. unspeakable monster. So let's just begin with what you do remember. Tessie? *Tessie?* What are you thinking right now, this second? Spit it out . . . don't look away, OK?'

I crane my neck around slowly, gazing at him out of two mossy gray pools of nothingness.

'I remember a crow trying to peck out my eyes,' I say flatly. 'Tell me. What exactly is the point of looking, when you know I can't see you?'

Tessa, present day

Technically, this is their third grave. The two Susans being exhumed tonight in St Mary's Cemetery in Fort Worth were his older kills. Dug up from their first hiding place and tossed in that field with me like chicken bones. Four of us in all, dumped in the same trip. I was thrown on top with a girl named Merry Sullivan, who the coroner determined had been dead for more than a day. I overheard Granddaddy mutter to my father, 'The devil was cleaning out his closets.'

It is midnight, and I am at least three hundred feet away, under a tree. I have darted under the police tape that marks off the site. I wonder who the hell they think is walking a cemetery at this time of night but ghosts. Well, I guess I am.

They've erected a white tent over the two graves, and it glows with pale light, like a paper lantern. There are far more people here than I expected. Bill, of course. I recognize the district attorney from his picture in the paper. There's a balding man beside him in an ill-fitting suit. At least five policemen, and another five human beings dressed like aliens in Tyvek suits, wandering in and out of the tent. I know that the medical examiner is among them. Careers ride on this one.

Did the reporter who wrote Angie's obituary know that his words would pry loose the rusty lever of justice? Create a small public outcry in a state that executes men monthly? Change a judge's mind about exhuming the bones and considering a new trial? Convince me once and for all to dial the phone?

The man in the suit suddenly pivots. I catch the flash of a priest's collar before I duck behind the tree. My eyes sting for a second, struck by this furtive operation and the supreme effort to treat these girls with dignity and respect when no one has a clue who they are, when there is not a reporter in sight.

The girls rising out of the earth tonight were nothing *but* bones when they were transported to that old wheat field eighteen years ago. I was barely alive. They say that Merry had been dead at least thirty hours. By the time the cops got to us, Merry was pretty well scavenged. I tried to protect her, but at some point in the night I passed out. Sometimes, I can still hear the animated conversation of the field rats. I can't tell anybody who loves me these things. It's better if they think I don't remember.

The doctors say my heart saved me. I was born with a heart genetically on the slow side to begin with. Add the fact that I was in peak running condition as one of the nation's top high-school hurdlers. On a normal day, doing homework, eating a hamburger, or painting my nails, my pulse clicked along at a steady thirty-seven beats a minute and crawled as low as twenty-nine at night when I slept. The average heart rate for a teen-ager is about seventy. Daddy had a habit of waking up at two every morning and checking to see if I was breathing, even though a famous Houston cardiologist had told him to relax. For sure, my heart was a bit of a phenomenon, as was my speed. People whispered about the Olympics. Called me the Little Fireball because of my hair and my temper when I ran a bad time or a girl nudged me off a hurdle.

While I fought for life in that grave, the doctors say my heart wound down to around eighteen. An EMT at the scene even mistook me for dead.

The district attorney told the jury that I surprised the Black-Eyed Susan killer, not the other way around. Set off a panic in him, prompted him to get rid of the evidence. That the large bruise on Terrell Darcy Goodwin's gut in the blown-up exhibit photograph, blue and green and yellow tie-dye, was my artwork. People appreciate pretty fantasies like this, where there is a feisty hero, even when there is no factual basis for it.

A dark van is slowly backing up to the tent. O. J. Simpson got off the same year I testified, and he massacred his wife and left his blood behind on her gate. There was no solid DNA evidence against Terrell Darcy Goodwin, except a tattered jacket mired in the mud a mile away with his blood type on the right cuff. The spot of blood was so tiny and degraded they couldn't tackle DNA, still fairly new in criminal court. It was enough for me to hold on to back then, but not anymore. I pray that Joanna will work her high priestess magic, and we will finally know who these two girls are. I'm counting on them to lead all of us to peace.

I turn to go, and my toe catches the edge of something. I pitch forward, instantly breathless, palms out, onto an old broken gravestone. The roots have bullied the marker until it toppled over and broke in half.

Did anyone hear? I glance around quickly. The tent is half-down. Someone is laughing. Shadows moving, none of them my way. I push myself up, hands stinging, brushing off the death and grit clinging to my jeans. I tug my cell phone out of my back pocket, and it casts its friendly light when I press the button. I shine it over the gravestone. A red smear from my hands marks the sleeping lamb guarding over Christina Driskill.

Christina entered the world, and escaped it, on the same day. March 3, 1872.

My mind burrows into the rocky dirt, fighting its way to the small wooden box that rests under my feet, tilted, cracked open, strangled by roots.

I'm thinking of Lydia.

Tessie, 1995

'Do you cry often?' First question. Gentle.

'No,' I say. So much for Lydia's beauty fix of sticking two frozen spoons under my eyes after my little jags.

'Tessie, I want you to tell me the very last thing you saw, before you went blind.' No lingering on my puffy face. Taking up right where we left off last time. *Smart tactic,* I think grudgingly. He actually used the word *blind,* which no one else would dare say to my face except Lydia, who also told me three days ago to get up and wash my hair because it looked like stale cotton candy.

This doctor has already figured out that a warm-up act with me was a complete waste of time.

I saw my mother's face. Beautiful, kind, loving. That's the last perfectly clear image that hung before me, except that my mother has been dead since I was eight, and my eyes were wide open. My mother's face, and then nothing but a shimmering gray ocean. I often think it was kind of God to introduce me to blindness that way.

I clear my throat, determined to say something in today's session, to appear more cooperative, so he will tell Daddy that I am making progress. Daddy, who takes off from his job every Tuesday morning to bring me here. For whatever reason, I don't think this doctor will lie to him, like most of the others. The way this doctor asks his questions is not the same. Neither are my answers, and I'm not sure why.

'There were a bunch of cards on the windowsill in my hospital room,' I say casually. 'One of them had a picture of a pig on the front. Wearing a bow tie and a top hat. It said, "I hope you squeal better soon." The pig – that's the last thing I saw.'

'An unfortunate choice of wording on the card.'

'Ya think?'

'Did anything else bother you about that greeting card?'

'No one could read the signature.' An illegible squiggle, like a wire spring.

'So you didn't know who it was from.'

'A lot of strangers sent cards from all over. And flowers and stuffed animals. There were so many, my father asked them to be sent on to the children's cancer floor.' Eventually, the FBI got a clue and swept everything to a lab. I later worried about what they might have ripped out of a dying kid's hands in return for not a scrap of useful evidence.

The pig held a daisy in his pink hoof. I had left that part out. At sixteen, drugged up in a hospital bed and scared out of my mind, I didn't know the difference between a yellow daisy and a black-eyed Susan.

My cast is itching like crazy, and I reach into the slim gap between my calf and the cast with two fingers. Can't get to the spot on my ankle. Oscar licks my leg with a sandpaper tongue, trying to help.

'OK, maybe that card was the trigger,' the doctor says. 'Maybe not. It's a start. Here's my thinking. We're going to talk about your conversion disorder before we move on to preparing you for court. In the interest of time, there was hope by . . . others . . . that I could work around it. But it is in the way.'

Ya think?

'As far as I'm concerned, time stands still in this room.' He's telling me *no pressure.* That we're sailing together in my gray ocean, and I control the wind. This is the first lie I know he's told me.

Conversion disorder. The nice, fancy name for it.

Freud called it hysterical blindness.

All those expensive tests and nothing physically wrong.

All in her head.

Poor thing doesn't want to see the world.

She will never be the same.

Why do people think I can't hear them?

I tune back in to his voice. I've decided he sounds like Tommy Lee Jones in *The Fugitive.* Rough Texas drawl. Smart as hell, and knows it.

'. . . it's not that uncommon in young females who have endured a trauma like this. What is uncommon is that it's lasted this long. Eleven months.'

Three hundred and twenty-six days, *doctor.* But I don't correct him.

A slight squeak as he shifts in his chair, and Oscar rises up protectively. 'There are exceptions,' he says. 'I once treated a boy, a virtuoso pianist, who had practiced eight hours a day since he was five. He woke up one morning and his hands were frozen. Paralyzed. Couldn't even hold a glass of milk. Doctors couldn't find a cause. He began to wiggle his fingers exactly two years later, to the day.'

The doctor's voice is closer. At my side. Oscar bangs my arm with his nose, to let me know. The doctor is sliding something thin and cool and smooth into my hand. 'Try this,' he says.

A pencil. I grasp it. Dig it deep into the side of my cast. Feel intense, gratifying relief. A slight breeze as the doctor moves away, maybe the flap of his jacket. I'm certain he looks nothing like Tommy Lee Jones. But I can picture Oscar. White as fresh snow. Blue eyes that see everything. Red collar. Sharp little teeth if you bother me.

'Does this piano player know that you talk about him to other patients?' I ask. I can't help myself. The sarcasm is a horsewhip I can't put away. But on our third Tuesday morning together, I have to admit this doctor is starting to get to me. I'm feeling the first pinch of guilt. Like I need to try harder.

'As a matter of fact, yes. I was interviewed for a Cliburn documentary about him. The point is: I believe you will see again.'

'I'm not worried.' I blurt it out.

'That is often a symptom of conversion disorder. A lack of caring about whether you'll ever go back to normal. But, in your case, I don't think that's true.'

His first direct confrontation. He waits silently. I feel my temper flare.

'I know the real reason why you made an exception to see me.' My voice cracks a little when I want it to sound defiant. 'What you have in common with my father. I know you had a daughter who disappeared.'

Tessa, present day

Angie's utilitarian metal desk looks exactly the way I remember, buried in mountains of paper and file folders. Shoved into a corner of an expansive, open basement room at St Stephen's, the stone-and-brick Catholic church that sits defiantly in the 2nd Avenue and Hatcher Street corridor of hell. Smack in the center of a Dallas neighborhood that made a Top 25 FBI list for most dangerous in the nation.

It is high Texas noon outside, but not in here. In here, it is gloomy and timeless, colored by the stains of a violent history, when this church was abandoned for eight years and this room was used as an execution factory for drug dealers.

The first and only time I'd been here, Angie told me that the hopeful young priest who rented her the space whitewashed the walls four times himself. The indentations and bullet holes in the walls, he told her, were going to be permanent, like the nails in the cross. Never forget.

Her desk lamp is the single thing glowing, casting faint light on the unframed print tacked above it. *The Stoning of Saint Stephen.* Rembrandt's first known work, painted at nineteen. I had learned about the chiaroscuro technique in another basement, with my grandfather bent over his easel. Strong lights and heavy shadows. Rembrandt was a master of it. He made sure the brilliance of heaven was opening up for Saint

Stephen, the first Christian martyr, murdered by a mob because evil people told lies about him. Three priests huddle in the upper corner. Watching him die. Doing nothing.

I wonder which came first to the basement: this print or Angie, who decided Saint Stephen's fate was a most appropriate marker for her desk. The edges of the print are soft and furry. It is attached to the pockmarked wall by three scratched yellow thumbtacks and one red one. A small rip on the left side has been repaired with Scotch tape.

Two inches away is another vision of heaven. A drawing on lined notebook paper. Five stick figures with lopsided butterfly wings illuminated by a bright orange sunburst. A child's crooked print tumbles across the sky: ANGIE'S ANGELS.

I learned in Angie's obituary that this drawing was a long-ago gift from the six-year-old daughter of Dominicus Steele, an apprentice plumber accused of raping an SMU coed outside a Fort Worth bar in the '80s. Dominicus was identified by the victim and two of her sorority sisters.

That night, he'd flirted with the victim up close. He was big and black, and a good dancer. The white college girls loved him until they decided he was the guy in the gray hooded sweatshirt running away from their drunk, crumpled friend in the alley. Dominicus was freed by DNA extracted from semen stored for twelve years in an evidence storage unit. Dominicus's mother was the first to speak to reporters in terms of 'Angie's Angels,' and her sweet little moniker stuck.

I'd never describe Angie as an angel. She did whatever she had to. She was a very good liar when she needed to be. I know, because she had lied for Charlie and me.

I take a step, and the hollow sound of my boot echoes on the cheap yellow linoleum that covers up God knows what. The four other desks that are scattered around the floor, in similar states of paper chaos, are also empty. *Where is everybody?*

There's a blue door on the far side of the room that's impossible to miss. I venture over. Knock lightly. Nothing. Maybe I should just hunker down in Angie's chair for a while. Swerve it around on the cranky roller wheels she complained about and stare into Rembrandt's heaven. Ponder the role of the martyr.

Instead, I twist the knob and open the door a crack. Knock again. Hear animated voices. Push the door all the way. A long conference table. Blazing overhead lights. Bill's startled face. Another woman, jumping out of her chair abruptly, knocking over her cup of coffee.

My eyes, traveling down the table, follow the river of amber liquid.

Head thrumming.

Copies of drawings, stretched edge to edge across the scratched surface.

Tessie's drawings.

The real ones. And the ones that aren't.

I am staring at the score, 12–28, scrawled in white chalk on a blackboard. A lopsided Little League game, maybe, or a bad day for the Dallas Cowboys. It is clear from the chart's wording that these are the twelve men who have been freed over the years by Angie and her rotating legal crew, and the twenty-eight who have not.

The woman who tipped over the coffee, introduced to

me as a third-year University of Texas law student named Sheila Dunning, has left us. William quickly swept up the copies of my drawings, tucked them out of the way, and set a fresh mug of hot coffee in front of me. He's apologized multiple times, and I've said over and over, *It's OK, it's OK, I have to see those drawings again sometime* and *I should have knocked louder.*

Sometimes I long for the Tessie in me, who would have just spit out the unvarnished, angry truth: *You're a jerk. You knew I was coming. You knew I hadn't looked at these since I dug them out of a wall.*

'Thanks for driving all the way down here.' He slides into a chair beside me and slaps a new yellow legal pad on the table. He is wearing jeans, Nikes, and a slightly pilled green pullover sweater that is too short for his frame, the curse of a broad-shouldered man. 'Are you still in the mood to do this?'

'Why wouldn't I be?' Tessie, retorting. Still in there, after all.

'We don't have to talk here. In this room.' He gazes at me intently. 'This is our war room. Generally off limits to clients.'

My eyes linger over the walls. Beside the chalkboard, enlarged snapshots of five men. Current cases, I assume. Four of the men are African-American. A young Terrell Darcy Goodwin stars in the center photograph. His arm is tossed around a guy in a red-and-gray high school baseball uniform, a little brother, maybe. Same good looks, wide-spaced eyes, chiseled cheekbones, café latte skin.

On the opposite wall: Crime scenes. Gaping mouths. Blank eyes. Confused limbs. I don't linger.

I flick my head around to a giant erase board that is scribbled with some sort of timeline.

I see my name. Merry's.

I open my mouth to speak and find his eyes glued to my crossed legs and the patch of bare white thigh above my black boots. I keep meaning to let out the hem of this skirt. I scoot my legs under the table. He resumes a professional mask.

'I'm not a client.' I swallow a sip of bitter liquid, read the words on the side of the mug. *Lawyers Get You Off.*

William follows my eyes. Rolls his. 'Most of our cups are dirty. Could use a good washing out.' Joking. Letting the other moment, the curiosity about what's under my skirt, pass.

'I'm fine in here, William.'

'Bill,' he reminds me. 'Only people over seventy get to call me William.'

'Did the exhumation Tuesday go as planned?' I ask. 'They kept it quiet. It didn't even make the papers.'

'You should know the answer to that.'

'You saw me by the tree.'

'That hair of yours is hard to miss, even in the dark.'

So *he's* a liar, too. My hair is down today, long, curling loosely past my shoulders. Still the same burnt color as the sixteen-year-old me. Two nights ago, at the cemetery, it was tucked up tight in my daughter Charlie's black baseball cap.

'You tricked me,' I say. 'Nice.'

I shift uncomfortably in the chair. I'm talking to a lawyer, one I haven't paid a cent to keep my confidences. Sure, he could be the boy next door with those doe-y brown eyes and clean-cut hair and ears that stick out a little and enormous hands that could cover a grapefruit. The funny best friend of the guy you really want, until you realize . . . oh, *shit.*

He grins. 'You look like my little sister does right before she slaps me. In answer to your question, a forensic anthropologist is getting a look at the bones first. Then Jo and her people step in. She would like both of us to watch her techs work the Black-Eyed Susan case next week. Asked me to invite you personally. Kind of as a peace offering since she ordered you not to be present at the exhumation. She really did feel bad about it.'

I shiver slightly. There's no vent, no visible source of heat in here. My father used to say that February in Texas is a cold, bitter lady. March is when she loses her virginity.

'Bones are processed every Monday morning,' he continues. 'Jo had to pull some strings to push the Susans to the head of the line. I can pick you up, if you like. The lab's about twenty minutes from your place.'

'No worry this time about contamination?' This had been Joanna's concern about me officially attending the exhuming of the bodies. She didn't want even the slightest hint of broken protocol.

'We'll be watching the process through a glass window. The new lab is set up as a teaching facility. State-of-the-art. Bones are flown in from all over the world. So are students and scientists who want to see Jo's techniques firsthand.' He smiles tightly and picks up his pen. 'Want to get started? I've got to be somewhere by two. For my job that pays the bills.' A corporate mediator, whatever the hell that is, according to his law firm's website. I wonder where he is hiding his suit.

'Yep. Go ahead.' Spoken much more casually than I felt.

'Your testimony in '95. Has anything changed? Have you remembered anything else in the last seventeen years about the attack or your attacker?'

'No.' I say it firmly. *I am willing to help,* I remind myself, *but only to a point.* I have two teen-agers to protect, the one I was and the one who sleeps in that purple room.

'Just to be sure, I'm going to ask a few specifics anyway, OK?'

I nod.

'Can you describe the face of your attacker?'

'No.'

'Do you remember where you met up with him?'

'No.'

'Do you have any memory of being dumped in that field?'

'No.'

'Do you ever remember seeing our client – Terrell Goodwin – before the day you testified?'

'No. Not to my knowledge.'

'*No* is a nice simple answer,' he says. 'If that's the truth.'

'It is. The truth.'

'Do you remember a single thing that happened in those hours you were missing?'

'No.'

'The last thing you remember is buying . . . tampons . . . at Walgreens?'

'And a Snickers bar. Yes.' The wrapper was found in the grave.

'You've heard your 911 call that night but do not recall making it?'

'Right. Yes.'

'Tessa, I have to ask again. Is there any way you will change your mind and undergo light hypnosis? See if there's anything you can remember from those lost hours? Or examine the drawings you gave me with an expert? If we jog something, anything, loose it might help us get a new hearing in front of the judge.'

'Absolutely no to hypnosis.' I say it quietly. 'I've read enough about it to know that I can be directed to false memories. But examining my drawings from therapy? Yes. I think so. I have no idea whether it will help.'

'Great. Great. I have someone in mind. Someone who has worked with me in the past. I think you'll like her.' I almost laugh. If he only knew how many times I'd heard that.

He lays his pen at a perfect 90-degree angle. Twirls it. Stops it. Twirls it. William knows how to use a big, fat pause. I'm beginning to see that he might be a very clever boy in court.

'There's a reason you're sitting here, Tessa. Something you aren't saying. I really need to know what it is. Because based on those answers, you might still think Terrell Darcy Goodwin is guilty as hell.'

I couldn't sleep last night wondering exactly how I'd answer this question. 'I feel like I hurt . . . Terrell . . . on the stand.' *Slow,* I tell myself. 'That I was manipulated by a lot of people. For years. Angie eventually satisfied me that there is no convincing physical evidence against him. And I showed you the black-eyed Susans. Under my window.' *Still keeping tabs.*

'Yes.' His lips have stretched into a tight line. 'But a judge will write off those flowers to your imagination, or just a random lunatic. He might infer that you did it yourself. Are you prepared for that?'

'Is that what you think? That I'm making it up?'

His gaze is direct, unbothered. Irritating as hell. Maybe *William* doesn't deserve to know all of it. He certainly isn't asking the right question.

I'm beginning to think he planned for me to stumble into this room all along. Slam me back into the past. Poke something sharp into my uncooperative brain.

'My drawings aren't your magic bullet,' I say abruptly. 'Don't pin your hopes on an angry girl with a paintbrush.'

Tessie, 1995

Thursday. Only two days after our last meeting.

The doctor cut the Tuesday session short by twenty minutes, shortly after my outburst. He called twenty-four hours later to reschedule. I don't know whether he was angry about me bringing up his daughter, or just unprepared to hear it. If I've learned anything about psychiatrists in the last year, it's that they don't like surprises from the guests. They want to be the one to scatter the path of stale bread crumbs, even if it leads into a dense forest where you can't see at all.

'Good morning, Tessa.' *Formal.* 'You caught me off guard the other day. To be honest, I wasn't sure how to handle it. For you, or me.'

'I almost didn't come back today. Or ever.' Not really true. For the first time in months, I feel like I own a small shred of power. I blow the bangs out of my eyes. Lydia took me to the mall for a new haircut yesterday. *Cut, cut, cut,* I insisted. I could almost hear my hair fall, soft and sad, to the floor. I wanted to change myself. Look more like a boy. My best friend appraised me critically when it was over. Informed me that I achieved the opposite. Short hair made me prettier, she said. Emphasized my small straight nose that I should thank the Lord Jesus for every day. Drew my eyes out like flying saucers in a big Texas sky. Lydia was practicing her similes for the SAT. She'd announced the very first time we linked arms in second grade that she was going to Princeton. I thought Princeton was a small town filled with eligible princes.

I think the doctor is pacing. Traveling the room. Oscar is not alerting me. He's sleepy, maybe because he got his shots an hour ago. My latest worry is that Daddy considers Oscar a first step to a Seeing Eye dog, and faithful, untrained Oscar will be sent away.

'I'm not surprised you feel that way.' His voice is behind me. 'I should have been straight from the beginning. About my daughter. Even though she has nothing to do with why I took your case.' *His second lie.* 'It was a very long time ago.'

It bothers me, his voice bouncing at me from different places, a game of dodge ball in the dark.

I count two seconds before his chair creaks gently. Not a heavy man, not a skinny one. 'Did your father tell you about my daughter?'

'No.'

'Did you . . . overhear something, then?' His question is almost timid. Like something an insecure normal person would ask. But this is pretty uncharted territory for him, I guess.

'I overhear things all the time,' I evade. 'I guess my other senses are super-enlightened now.' This last part is not actually true at all. All my senses have gone haywire. Granny's recipe for fried green beans with bacon dressing tastes like soggy cigarettes; my sweet little brother's voice is like Aunt Hilda's fake red fingernails scraping glass. I suddenly cry along to country music, which I always secretly thought was for dumb people.

I'm not telling this doctor any of that yet. Let him think

I'm suddenly hyperaware. I'm not about to rat out Lydia, who has read me every word of every story on Terrell Darcy Goodwin and the Black-Eyed Susan investigation that she can get her hands on. Researched every shrink who has tried to tunnel into my brain.

All I know is that when I am lying on Lydia's pink down comforter, with Alanis Morissette moaning, and my best friend reading animatedly from her stack of library printouts . . . those are the minutes and hours that I feel the safest. Lydia is the only one who still treats me exactly the same.

She's relying on some innate seventeen-year-old certainty that I might die if I live in a silent cocoon, curled up and fragile. That handling me with care is not going to make me better.

For some reason, I think this doctor might be the second person to understand. He lost a daughter. He's got to be a close personal friend with pain. I hold out hope for that.

Tessa, present day

I snap off one more picture with my iPhone. Three images in all. I should have done it five days ago, before their stems bowed and their eyes stared dejectedly at the ground.

I've told only Angie the whole story, I think. *Now she's dead.*

I am not fooled by the fainting Susans under my windowsill. I know that each of the thirty-four eyes hoards enough seeds to carpet my whole yard, come spring. I slide on my gardening gloves and pick up the can of herbicide I've retrieved from the garage. I wonder whether he likes to watch this part of the process. I've learned that poison is the best method. Not since I was seventeen have I torn up the Susans by their roots.

A breeze flutters, scattering the spray. I taste it, bitter and metallic.

If I don't hurry, I'm going to be late to pick up Charlie. I smother on one last cancerous coat. I strip off my gloves, leave them with the spray can, run to grab the keys off the kitchen counter, hop in the Jeep, and drive the ten minutes to the freshman gym. Home of the Fighting Colts. Chattering, texting girls stream onto the sidewalk, in ponytails and obscenely tight mandatory red gym shorts that mothers should officially complain about but don't.

The backseat door pops open, startling me, like it does every time. 'Hi, Mom.' Charlie tosses in a blue Nike duffle that always holds smelly surprises and a backpack of books that lands like a chunk of concrete. She jumps in and slams the door.

Smooth, angelic face. Sexy legs. Tight muscles not mature enough to fight back. Innocent, and not. I don't want to be aware of these things, but I've trained myself to see her as he might.

'My laptop sucks,' she says.

'How was school? Practice?'

'I'm starved. Really, Mom. I couldn't print my homework last night. I had to use your computer.'

This beautiful girl, the love of my life, the one I missed all day long, is already firing up my nerves.

'McDonald's?' I ask.

'Surrrrre.'

I've stopped feeling guilty about the after-practice drive-through runs. It doesn't keep my daughter from devouring a healthy full-course dinner two hours later. Charlie eats at least four times a day and remains a tall, slender rail. She has my old runner's appetite and red hair and her father's mood-changing eyes. Purplish is happy; gray is tired. Black is thoroughly pissed off.

Not for the first time, I wish that Charlie's father weren't thousands of miles away on an Army base in Afghanistan. I wish he weren't just a serious fling fifteen years ago that went awry a month before I realized I was pregnant. Not that Charlie seems to care a whit that we never married. Lt. Col. Lucas Cox sends money like clockwork and stays in constant touch. I think a Skype session with Charlie is on tap for tonight.

'We will talk about the computer later, OK?'

No answer. She's texting, I'm sure. I pull out from the

curb and decide to let her decompress from the eight fluorescent-lighted hours she has spent constructing triangular prisms and deconstructing Charlotte Brontë. After Charlie abandoned *Jane Eyre* on the couch last night for Facebook, I noticed that the heroine gazing off the cover was sporting a new mustache and devil horns. *She's so whiny,* Charlie whined this morning, while stuffing her mouth with bacon.

A few minutes later, we roll up to the drive-through.

'What do you want?' I ask her.

'Uhhhh.'

'Charlie, stop with the phone. You need to order.'

'OK.' Cheerful. 'I would like a Big Mac, and a MacBook Pro.'

'Very funny.'

Truth is, I love this about her – the cocky sense of humor and confidence, her ability to make me laugh out loud when I don't want to. I wait until I think Charlie is about halfway through her Big Mac to start The Conversation. In the Jeep, just us, there is always more of a chance my words will end up in her brain.

'I've changed my mind and decided to get involved in the Terrell Goodwin execution,' I say. 'I've spoken with the new attorney on the case. A famous forensic scientist is going to reexamine the evidence. She swabbed my DNA this week.'

A short silence. 'That's good, Mom. You need to be absolutely sure. You've been worrying about this a lot lately. People are getting released on DNA stuff all the time now. Our science teacher told us that Dallas has freed more innocent people from Death Row than almost every other state. People just think we kill everybody.' I hear her crumple up the hamburger wrapper.

'Don't toss that on the floor,' I say automatically. To myself, I think: *Is that because we* have *more innocent people on Death Row?*

'And Angie,' Charlie adds. 'She was nice. She was, like, totally convinced. And she said that none of it was your fault.'

'I'll be in the news again.' Meaning, Charlie won't be immune.

'I've been through it before. My friends will take care of me. I got this, Mom.'

The naivete of it almost makes me want to cry. At the same time, it is hard to believe that Charlie is three years younger than I was when I testified. She seems so much more *prepared.*

I pull into our driveway and switch off the ignition. Charlie is rustling to get her stuff, but I don't turn around. 'Never, *ever* get in a car with someone you don't know. Never walk alone. Don't talk to reporters.' My voice sounds sharper than I'd like in the tiny, closed-up space. 'If I'm not home, turn the security system on as soon as you close the door.'

It's ridiculous to deliver these worn-out instructions for the thousandth time, but I'd become too complacent. I have vowed ever since Angie's wake to know where Charlie is every single second. A few days ago, I turned down a freelance design project in Los Angeles to build a staircase out of old cars and recycled glass. It would have carried our finances for the next two years.

'Mom.' She packs as much teen-age patronization in those three letters as will fit. 'I *got* this.'

Before I can respond, she's tumbling out of the car,

loaded up like a soldier entering battle, jogging to the front door with her house key in hand. She's in the house in seconds. Prepared, like I taught her. *Innocent, and not.*

The question that neither of us ever asks out loud: *But if not him, then who?*

I follow her slowly, fiddling with my phone. I almost trip over the duffle she dumped in the foyer, think about calling out to her, stop myself. I head to the small desk in the living room where my laptop sits, call up the email I just sent to my own address, download, hit print. Listening to it regurgitate a couple of feet away, I think Charlie's right – our house needs a more efficient grasp on technology.

The printer spits out three grainy pictures of wilting flowers. Charlie's door is already closed when I pass by.

A few seconds later, I am on my tiptoes, pulling from the top shelf of my bedroom closet the shoebox boldly marked, *Tax Documents.*

The killer has planted black-eyed Susans for me six times. It didn't matter where I was living. He likes to keep me guessing. I'm sure about this now.

He waited so long between plantings sometimes that, before Angie, I was able to convince myself on most days that the right killer sat in jail. That the first black-eyed Susans were the work of a random stalker, and the other times the whims of the wind.

This box, made for ASICS running shoes, size 7, marked *Tax Documents,* contains the photographs I snapped every time anyway. Just in case.

I set the box on the bed and lift the lid. Right on top, the one taken with my granddaddy's old Polaroid Instant camera.

That first time, right after the trial, I had thought either I was crazy or that black-eyed Susans had suddenly sprung up in October under the live oak in our back yard because of a bizarre weather pattern. Except the ground looked disturbed. I dug up the wildflowers by myself a little frantically with an old kitchen spoon.

I didn't want to tell anybody because life in my house was returning to some semblance of normal. I was done with therapy. Terrell Darcy Goodwin sat in jail. My dad was dating for the first time.

The spoon struck another surprise in the dirt that day – something hard, orange, and plastic. An old prescription bottle. The label ripped off. Childproof cap.

Charlie has turned up her music. It strains through the wall, but can't drown out the words on a scrap of paper curled up in a little orange bottle.

Oh Susan, Susan, lovely dear
My vows shall ever true remain
Let me kiss off that falling tear
I never want to hurt you again
But if you tell, I will make
Lydia
A Susan, too

Tessie, 1995

After he leaves the office, my fingers brush over three stubby charcoal crayons; the cool metal coil binding a drawing pad; a Dixie cup of water; a few brushes, a narrow paint box with a squeaky hinge. The doctor has repeated the order of the paint colors four times, left to right. Black, blue, red, green, yellow, white.

As if what colors I choose will make a significant difference. I am already thinking of swirling the colors to make purple and gray, orange and aqua. The colors of bruises, and sunsets.

This is not the first time I have drawn blind. Right after Mom died, Granddaddy was constantly trying to distract me from grief.

We sat at his old cedar picnic table. He punched a No. 2 pencil through the center of a paper plate, a de facto umbrella, so that I could grasp the pencil but not watch my hand draw. 'Making pictures in your head is primal,' he said. 'You don't need your eyes to do it. Start with the edges.'

I remember the faint blue flower border that etched the paper plate, that my fingers were sticky with sweat and chocolate, but not what I drew that day.

'Memories aren't like compost,' the doctor had said, as he guided me over to his desk. 'They don't decay.'

I knew exactly what he wanted out of this little exercise. The priority was not to cure my blindness. He wanted to know why my ankle shattered into pieces, what implement etched the pink half-moon that hung under my eye. He wanted me to draw *a face.*

He didn't say any of this, but I knew.

'There's infinite storage space up here.' He tapped my head. 'You simply have to dig into every box.'

One more self-help bite from him before he shut the door, and I would have screamed.

I can hear my father outside the door, droning blurry words, like a dull pencil. Oscar has settled into the cave under the desk, his head resting on my cast. Pressure, but nice pressure, like my mother's hand on my back. The doctor's voice floats through the door. They are talking about box scores, like the world is running along just fine.

My head is blank when the charcoal begins to rub insistently against the paper.

The click of the door opening startles me, and I jump, and Oscar jumps, and my pad slides and clunks to the floor. I have no idea how much time has passed, which is new, because ever since I went blind, I can guess the time of day within five minutes. Lydia attributes it to a primitive internal clock, like the one that reminds hibernating animals to wake up in the black isolation of their caves and venture back into the world.

I smell him, the same Tommy cologne that Bobby always liberally sprays on himself at Dillard's. My doctor wears Tommy Hilfiger, sounds like Tommy Lee Jones. Everything Tommy.

'Just checking to see how it's going,' he says.

He is at my side, reaching down, picking up the pad from

the floor, placing it gently on the desk in front of me. My drawings, except for the one on the pad, are ripped out and scattered across his desk. My head pounds, and I press a finger into my right temple like there's a pause button.

'May I?' he asks, which is ridiculous because I'm certain his eyes are already greedily scanning. He picks up a sheet, puts it down, picks up another.

The air is thick with the heat of his disappointment; he's a teacher with a second-rate student who he has hoped will surprise him.

'It's just the first time,' he says. Awkward silence. 'You didn't use any paint.' A hint of reproach?

He stiffens. Leans in closer, tickling my shoulder, turning my pad, which was apparently upside down. 'Who is this?'

'I'm not done.'

'Tessie, who *is* this?'

I had scrubbed the charcoal against the page until it was black. I had dug into his desk drawer for the No. 2 pencil eraser that I used to swirl a chaotic nest of hair around her head. My fingernail carefully scratched out big eyes, delicate cheekbones and nose, full lips rounded into a frightened O.

I thought about *the edges*. No neck anchored her in the blackness. She floated in outer space, a silent, screaming constellation. I had drawn a face, but not the one he wanted.

'It's your daughter.' Why I felt the urge to torture him, I do not know. I could have said it was Lydia. Or my mother. Or me. But I didn't.

I feel a slight whoosh of air as he abruptly draws back. I wonder whether he wants to strike me. Oscar is whining way back in his throat.

'It looks nothing like her.' There is a slight crack in his voice. A picture forms in my head of a perfect black egg with a white hairline fracture.

I know that his reply is inappropriate, even silly. I am a skilled artist at seventeen, but this drawing is surely distorted, even childish. *Of course* it looks nothing like her. I've never met her. *I'm blind.*

He's a doctor. He shouldn't allow me to make any of this personal for him.

When did I become capable of such cruelty?

Tessa, present day

I'm thinking of Lydia as I shove a digger deep into the loose soil under my windowsill, pulling out the poisoned Susans, stacking them in a neat, weedy pile beside me. The metal of the digger is stained with traces of bloody rust, but the shiny part glints in the light filtering out the screen of my bedroom window.

The yellow curtains blow white in the moonlight, billowing and retracting. While I'd waited for Charlie to conk out, I plopped on the couch, flipped on *Jimmy Kimmel Live,* and scratched out a list on the back of a grocery slip, as if that somehow made the contents more harmless.

I wanted to see them neatly written down. Every single place I'd found a patch of black-eyed Susans in the years since the trial. The big question, which I already knew the answer to: *Should I go back to each one of them alone? With Bill? With Joanna? Wouldn't it just waste their time, make them think I was even crazier than they already did?*

It seemed highly unlikely that I'd be able to find things he might have buried for me in the ground all these years later, or that I'd hit the right spot to dig, even with the photographs. Rain gushes, the earth moves.

Now, down on my hands and knees in the inky night, sifting my hand through the dirt, I wonder if I am wrong. I find an errant screw dropped from a worker's hand when the windows were replaced two years ago. A scrap of paper.

The stubborn roots of a vine that appeared like a white bone.

Lydia always knew what to do in these situations. She was the one with the scientific and logical mind, able to shove aside emotion and examine everything with the clinical detachment I didn't possess. The summer we were eight, she stayed inside the lines of her coloring books, while I tried to invent a new color by melting crayons together on the sidewalk in the brutal Texas sun.

In elementary school, I liked to run against the wind for the battle of it; Lydia waited for me cross-legged on a blanket, reading something way too old for her. *The Great Gatsby*. *Hamlet*. *1984*. Afterward, as I lay panting on the ground, she pressed cool fingers to my wrist and counted the beats of my pulse.

I knew that I would not die on Lydia's watch. She's the one who whispered in my ear while I stared at a waxy yellow version of my mother in the casket. *She is not in there.* She was unusually drawn to death, from the beginning.

When we were assigned a world history project on 'a fascinating moment in British history,' two-thirds of Mrs Baker's freshman class wrote about the Beatles. I carefully etched a replica of the medieval London Bridge and pondered the miracle of God that kept the shops and houses crammed on top from crashing into the mighty Thames.

Lydia chose a river of evil so black and swirling you couldn't see the bottom. Mrs Baker asked her to read her report out loud to the class, probably because she knew it would keep us awake at our desks.

I'll never forget Lydia's chilling delivery of her opening lines, stolen from the coroner's report.

The body was lying naked in the middle of the bed, the shoulders flat but the axis of the body inclined to the left side of the bed. The head was turned on the left cheek.

While most of her classmates were contemplating whether 'I Am the Walrus' was just one big John Lennon acid trip, Lydia had buried herself in the story of Jack the Ripper's final victim.

Mary Kelly met her grisly death at the 26 Dorset Street boarding-house, room 13. She was 5'7", twenty-five years old, a buxom prostitute, and owed twenty-seven shillings on her rent.

She was heard singing in her room hours before she died.

It doesn't take a memory expert to figure out why I remember such details so many years later and very little about the medieval London Bridge. Lydia had turned on a British accent during her presentation. At one point, her fist thumped her chest three times in a dramatization of the first knife strikes.

Silly. *Creepy.*

To write that report, Lydia had immersed herself for two weekends in the Texas Christian University library, reading dissertations and nineteenth-century medical reports and essays from self-proclaimed 'Ripperologists.' She tucked it in a plastic binder and told me to flip to the last page before she was supposed to turn it in.

I was gripped by horror porn: a black-and-white photograph of Mary Kelly lying in her flophouse bed, her insides ripped out. I never knew where Lydia found this, in the days before Google. Only that Lydia was always a relentless digger.

Why am I thinking about this now? I rub my hand across my forehead, wiping away sweat, leaving crumbs of dirt. I'm back in the kitchen, my foot on the trashcan pedal, dropping my collection into the trash. And then it hits me.

I had dismissed the scrap of paper because it didn't bear a sadistic poem. Now I'm picking it out of the bin, examining it more closely. It *could* be part of a candy bar wrapper. *Was it the kind of candy bar I bought at Walgreens the night I disappeared? The kind I bought every Tuesday for Roosevelt?*

Roosevelt was a fixture on my Wednesday running route, nicknamed because at straight-up noon every single day, he stood on top of an old red bucket and spouted the entirety of FDR's first inaugural speech.

By the time I flew by on Wednesdays after school, he was always long done with his diatribe. We had worked out a routine. I tossed a Snickers bar, his favorite, into the air without slowing my pace. He never failed to catch it and shoot me a big, toothy grin. It became a ritual of good luck during track season and a pact I kept up when summer started. I never lost a race after meeting Roosevelt.

And so it was decided. Every Tuesday night, I bought a Snickers bar. I didn't buy two or three or four at a time. I didn't buy them on Mondays or Saturdays. I bought one every Tuesday night, and he caught it on Wednesday afternoon, and I won and won and won.

But in those missing hours, I apparently did something I would never, ever consider doing. I ate his candy bar. There were traces of it in my vomit at the hospital.

I was committed to my ritual with Roosevelt. To winning. Did I eat the candy bar that night because I thought that I would never run a race again?

I grab a plastic snack bag out of the pantry shelf and seal the wrapper inside. *Did he touch this? Did he stand under my window, snacking?* My cell phone rings out from the living room couch, disturbing the silence that is everywhere except my chest.

Hastings, William.

'It's late, Bill.' No hello.

'The day got away from me,' he says. 'I just want to be sure you remember to be at the UNT lab tomorrow by 9:45, fifteen minutes before the techs start the process on the bones.'

How could I forget? I want to shout it at him, but instead say: 'I'm driving myself.' This has to be the reason he called. He seems determined to pick me up.

Bill lets a couple of seconds elapse. 'Joanna wouldn't tell me what over the phone, but she says the forensic anthropologist has already found something.'

Tessie, 1995

'How is the drawing at home going?' He asks this before my butt hits the cushion.

'I forgot to bring any of them with me.' A lie. The drawings, nine new ones, are right where I want them – in a red Macy's shirt box in my closet labeled *Xtra Tampons,* sure to dissuade my nosy little brother.

The phone on his desk suddenly buzzes. The emergency buzz, one of my favorite sounds in the world because it sucks minutes away from me.

'I'm sorry, Tessie,' he says. 'Excuse me for just a moment. I've just checked in a patient at the hospital and was expecting a few questions from the nurse.'

The doctor's voice travels over from the other side of the room. I can make out a few words. *Elavil. Klonopin.* Shouldn't he be doing this privately? I'm really trying hard not to hear because I don't want to imagine a person like me on the other end and get emotionally involved. So I focus on other things, like trying to match the doctor's lazy drawl with Lydia's description of him.

It was Lydia's idea. Yesterday, with my blessing, she had hopped the bus to the TCU campus and sneaked into one of the doctor's late afternoon summer classes: *Anastasia Meets Agatha Christie: Exploring the Gray Matter About Amnesia.*

When she told me the class title, I cringed a little. Too gimmicky. But then, I was looking for reasons to be critical.

If Lydia stuck on the big rounded plastic frames she wore when her contacts itched, she could easily disappear into a crowd of college students. Lydia's father told her once that she was one of those people born thirty, and repeated it often, which Lydia carried around like a mortal wound. Me, well . . . I can't tell Lydia but I feel a little uncomfortable around her dad these days.

Through our formative years, Mr Bell concocted a kick-ass chili recipe, and hauled us to the shooting range, and whipped us around Lake Texoma in the unsinkable *Molly* every Labor Day and July 4th. But he was moody and known to strike out. And, since I turned fourteen, his eyes sometimes hesitated in the wrong places. Maybe he was just being more honest than most men greeted with puberty in bloom. Probably better to know, I reasoned, and wear longer shorts at her house.

Last night, after her successful day of spying and some of my dad's leftover Frito pie, Lydia had been in especially good spirits. 'Did you know that Agatha Christie went missing for eleven days in 1926 and no one had a clue where she was?' she had asked me breathlessly, from the corner of my bed.

I had her pictured in the usual position: legs pretzeled into an easy lotus, her pink-flowered Doc Martens lost somewhere on the floor, a hot pink scrunchy holding up a mountain of black hair. Pink was Lydia's color.

A recap of the day's events in the O.J. trial buzzed in our ears as background. It was impossible to get away from it. Daddy didn't like a TV perched on top of my dresser, certainly didn't like a bloody soundtrack, but he had relented instantly when I told him the constant noise made me feel less alone. That I wasn't really listening to it.

It was only a half-lie. I found something soothing about Marcia Clark's methodical voice. How could anyone *not* believe her?

'Agatha kissed her daughter goodnight and disappeared,' Lydia had continued. 'They thought she maybe drowned herself in this pond called the Silent Pool because that's where they found her wrecked car.'

'The Silent Pool?' I was skeptical. It was how anyone sane had to be with Lydia at least part of the time.

'*Really*. You can read it yourself.' She thrust a piece of paper at me. If it had been anyone else, this would have seemed like a mean poke. But it was Lydia. My vision was less gray when she was around. Lighter, like I was splayed flat on the tickly grass, staring up into late summer dusk. I let my fingers grasp her tangible proof that Agatha Christie lived out a page in her novels, as if it were important.

'Anyway, that's where they found her car,' Lydia repeated. 'The other thought was that her a-hole of a cheating husband killed her and abandoned the car there. While all of this was going on, Sir Arthur Conan Doyle even took one of her gloves to a medium to try to figure out where she'd gone. It was on the front of *The New York Times*.' More rustling of paper. 'But she showed up. It turned out she had *amnesia. For eleven days*.'

'This was the focus of his lecture?' It was comforting, and somehow not.

'Uh-huh. I was intrigued by the class title, so I stopped off at the library before. When I got to class, your *doctor* was talking about the etiology of the fugue state and how it's related to dissociative amnesia.'

It would be very hard to live in Lydia's head. I imagined

it blindingly bright and chaotic, like an exploding star. Both sides of her brain constantly at war. Because brilliant, steady Lydia was an addict when it came to murder and celebrities. The O.J. trial, her LSD. Any inane detail got her high. Like the other night, giggling about how O. J. Simpson had asked the cops for a glass of *orange juice* after the Bronco chase, followed up by ten minutes of her railing about the jury not getting the concept of restriction fragment length polymorphism.

'So what happened to her?' Trying to shuttle things along because I was curious, but wanting to know whether my doctor appeared to be a manipulative asshole.

'She was found in a spa hotel under an assumed name. She claimed not to recognize pictures of herself in the newspaper. Some doctors said shc was suicidal, in a psychogenic trance. That's like a fugue state, *thus* the title of your doctor's class.'

'I'd rather think of her as a nice old lady writing cozy mysteries by the fire.'

'I know. It's kind of like finding out that Edna St Vincent Millay slept around and was a morphine addict. Ednas and Agathas should be true to their names.'

I'd laughed, something close to the way I used to, and imagined it drifting under the bedroom door, smoothing out a tight wrinkle in my father's face.

'A mystery novelist with a cheating husband, gone missing. Sounds like a publicity stunt.'

'Some people might say that about you,' my best friend retorted. A rare slip, for her. It had hit its mark, a sharp pain to the right side of my stomach.

'Sorry, Tessie, it just came out. Of course that's not true, *either.* He's the kind of professor you could get a real crush on, you know, because he has that *brain.* He's not a fake.' She sat silently for a second. 'I like him. I think you can trust him. Don't you?'

Smacked again. Fifteen hours later, back on the doctor's couch, I'm fully absorbing the repercussions of this turn of events. Now, Lydia, my objective, loyal friend, would give my doctor the benefit of the doubt. I wondered if she'd been crazy enough to raise her hand. Ask a question. *Get noticed.* I should have thought this through.

The doctor has just excused himself and left the room. The longer he's gone, the darker it gets. You wouldn't think it would make any difference when you're blind, but it does. The air-conditioning is noisily blowing through the vents, but it's harder and harder to breathe. I've drawn my knees up tight and crossed my arms around them. My tongue tastes like a dead trout. There is growing dread that no one will find me and pull me out in time. That I will suffocate in here.

Is this one of your tests, doctor?

The second I decide I can't take it any longer, he strides into the room. His chair creaks with his weight as he settles in. I fight the surge of gratefulness. *You came back.*

'That took longer than I thought. We can make up the time in our next session. We have about a half-hour left. I'd like to talk about your mother this week, if that's OK.'

'That's not why I'm here.' My response is quick. 'I went over and over that years ago. Lots of people have mothers who die.' A fog drools at the corners of my vision. Frenetic pricks of light everywhere, like a swarm of frightened fireflies. New guests in my head. I wonder if this means I am about to faint. *How would I know the difference?* My lips contort, and I almost giggle.

'So you shouldn't mind talking about it,' he says reasonably. 'Catch me up. Where were you the day she died?' *Like you don't already know. Like there isn't a big fat file on your desk that you don't even have to bother to hide from a blind girl.*

My ankle throbs and sends a message to the crescent scar on my face and to the three-inch pink line drawn carefully under my left collarbone. *Can he not see how upset I am? That he should back off?*

The pieces of his face spin around, stubborn, refusing to lock in place. Gray-blue eyes, brown hair, wire-rim glasses. Not at all like Tommy Lee Jones, Lydia had said. Still, no picture falling together for me. No way to draw him blind.

This is the worst session yet, and we are just getting started.

'I was playing in the tree house,' I tell him, while the fireflies do their panicked dance.

Tessa, present day

The first Susan has arrived, bundled in white cloth, like she is dressed for a holy baptism. The woman holding her is covered in head-to-toe white, too, her mouth and nose masked, so that all I can see are brown eyes. They look kind.

She unbinds the cloth and raises Susan carefully up to the window. Most of the small group gathered in the hall on the other side eagerly raise their iPhones. Susan is bathed in brief flashes, like a movie star.

Her skull is a horror show. Her eyes are holes going to the bottom of the ocean. Most of the lower half of her jaw, gone. A few rotten teeth hanging like stalactites in an abandoned cave. It is the emptiness, those two gaping, awful holes that remind me she was once human. That she could once stare back.

Remember? Her hollow, toothless voice bubbles up in my ear. An unspent grenade erupts in my chest. It's a shock, but it shouldn't be. The Susans had been silent for more than a year this time. It had been foolish to think they were gone.

Not now. I imagine my hand clamped over her mouth. I screech out 'The Star-Spangled Banner' in my head.

Bombs bursting in air. Jo is squeezing my arm.

'Sorry I'm late.' I gulp in her quirky normalness. White lab coat, khaki pants, purple Nikes, plastic badge hanging off a skull-and-crossbone-printed lanyard around her neck. A whiff of something chemical, but not unpleasant.

Deep breath. I'm on this side of the glass. This side of hell.

She nods casually to the group. Besides Bill and me, four other people are cleared for this event: three Ph.D. students – one from Oxford, two from the University of North Texas – and a beautiful, unbottled blond scientist from Sweden named Britta.

We'd spent the last fifteen minutes together, strangers pretending we weren't about to observe death at its most sadistic. The students' eyes flicked to me with interest, but no one was asking questions.

Before Jo arrived, we had settled on discussing the three places in Dallas and Fort Worth that Britta should not miss seeing before returning home to her Stockholm lab in two weeks: the Amon Carter for its muscled bronze Russells and Remingtons, and for the beautiful black boy in the newspaper hat; the Kimbell for the silvery light cascading on buxom masterpieces and for the ill-fated young man in the company of wicked sixteenth-century cardsharps; the Sixth Floor Museum, where Oswald angled his rifle, and a wild-eyed conspiracy theorist defiantly roamed the sidewalk, saying, *Nope, not like that.*

As Britta eyes Bill, I am thinking it is more likely she will end up in his bed. I'd gotten a curt smile from him this morning.

'Stephen King researched part of his Kennedy time-travel opus at the Sixth Floor Museum archives,' Bill is telling them.

'Great book,' Jo says. 'King's a genius. But he never really got Texas. And I'm saying that as an Oklahoman. Hi, Bill.

Tessa. Sarita. John and Gretchen. Britta, glad you could make it today. Looks like they are just getting started.'

The skull is now facing us, leering from its spot on the counter. The woman in white is still unwrapping puzzle pieces. A long, pearly leg bone, and then another in much worse shape, like a tree branch snapped off in winter.

'Tammy's in charge today,' Jo says. 'Running the room.' The two exchange a brief wave. Four other women dressed in sterile suits are taking their places in the lab in front of clear glass hoods. The fluorescent light is brutal, and cold.

'Looking into a serial killer's refrigerator,' Bill mutters in my ear.

Jo glances our way, but I can't tell if she heard. 'Each forensic analyst has a specific job,' she explains. 'Margaret will cut a small piece out of the bone. Toneesha will clean it with bleach, ethanol, and water. Jen will pulverize it to a fine powder, from which we extract the DNA. Bessie's only role is to spray down the surfaces as we go, to keep things as sterile as possible. It's protocol. Always.'

Her eyes are focused on the activity behind the window. Jo's in her element. Brilliant, without ego. Empathetic, without cynicism.

I am thinking that Jo remembers every single person by name on both sides of the glass. I am thinking, she could be talking about how to refine sugar.

'Never forget protocol.' Suddenly stern. 'Never get sloppy. Somebody accused me of that once. Worst time of my life.'

She doesn't extrapolate. So far, no talk of the actual case – who these bones represent, why they are special.

'We like the skull and the denser bones, particularly

femurs,' she continues. 'Gives us the longest string of mitochondrial DNA and the best chance at retrieving information on our way to finding out who they are. We're lucky we've got these three specimens, considering the bones have been scavenged and moved at least once.'

The skull is being tucked under one of the hoods. The buzzing of the saw drifts through glass, like it is floating down the street on a lazy Saturday.

When the first Susan returns to the counter, a new one-inch-square hole glares out of the top of her head.

One more degradation in an endless string of them.

I'm sorry, I say silently. But there is no toothless, hollow answer in my head.

The Dremel saw drills a leg bone while the piece of skull is scrubbed raw in the second station. The technicians have forgotten us, slipping into a comfortable rhythm. I don't know what I was expecting, but not this surreal, matter-of-fact routine.

'It must be especially exciting to work on the Black-Eyed Susans,' Sarita says brightly. The student from Oxford. Her voice is British, clipped. Her black heels are too high. 'It must be an honor for these techs. These must be your best.'

I can feel Jo's body go taut as if it is my own. 'To them,' she says. 'And to me, this case . . . these bones . . . are no different than any other bone entrusted to us. Each one represents the same thing. A family, waiting.'

Admonished. All of us.

'Why are there three bones?' Bill shifts the conversation abruptly. 'For two unidentified skeletons? I thought you only tried one bone from a victim at a time.'

'Now, there's the question I've been waiting for.' Still an

edge to Jo's voice. 'The girls' skeletons were ransacked by critters over time. Moved by their killer at least once. The old case file documents foreign soil along with the red clay mixture in that field. So, of course, not every bone was there. Our forensic anthropologist laid out what was exhumed from the two caskets, and counted. He counted three right femurs.'

I hear someone suck in a strangled breath. It takes a second to realize it's me.

'Three skeletons, not two,' Bill whispers, as if I can't do the math.

Five Susans in all, not four. One dead girl named Merry, three gnawed-on nobodies, and me. Another member of my tribe. Another family, waiting.

I'm the one, a Susan says conspiratorially. *I'm the one with the answers.*

Jo shoots me an odd look, even though I know I am the only one who can hear.

Tessie, 1995

I wonder what he is looking at first.

The girl without a mouth. The girl with a red blindfold. The spider's web with the trapped swallowtail. The faceless runner on the beach. The roaring bear, my personal favorite. I'd worked hard on the teeth.

'Did you remember to bring your drawings today?' he had asked first thing.

Anything was preferable to talking about the day of my mother's death. Last time, he might as well have taken a hot poker and stuck it in my belly button.

And what did he learn? That I heard nothing. Saw nothing. That all I remember is a vague image of blood, but that was dead wrong, because the police told me there was no blood. All of it seemed so freakin' off point. Another way to clutter up my head.

So, yes, I brought drawings today. As soon as he asked, I handed Doc a white cardboard poster-mailing tube. It once held the *Pulp Fiction* poster now hanging over Lydia's bed. Lydia had rolled up my drawings carefully after our three-hour session sprawled on the rough Berber of her bedroom floor surrounded by a kindergarten chaos of paper and crayons and markers.

She didn't like my idea when I sprang it on her two days ago, but I begged. More than anyone else, she understood my fear – that someone else would find out my secrets before I did.

So she'd ridden the bus back to the TCU library. Skimmed *The Clinical Application of Projective Drawings. The Childhood Hand That Disturbs.* And, because she was Lydia: *L'Imagination dans la Folie,* which translates to *Imagination in Madness,* some random tome that studied the drawings of insane people in 1846. She had educated me on the principle of the House-Tree-Person test. House, how I see my family. Tree, how I see my world. Person, how I see myself.

When it was all over, the black crayon worn to a flat nub, I thought we'd faked it pretty well. Lydia was even inspired to draw a picture herself, which she described to me as an army of giant black-and-yellow flowers with angry faces.

The doctor is sitting directly across from me, not saying a word. I can hear the crisp rustle of paper as he flips from one sheet to the next.

The silence has to be something they teach all these manipulative bastards.

Finally, he clears his throat. 'Technically excellent, especially since you have no vision. But, mostly, cliché.' No emotion in his words, just a statement of fact.

My scars begin to thrum. Thank God, I didn't give him my real drawings.

'This is why I don't like you.' I speak stiffly.

'I didn't know you didn't like me.'

'You don't *know*? You're like all of the others. You don't give a flip.'

'I give a flip, Tessie. I care very much about what happens to you. So much that I'm not going to lie to you. You obviously spent some time on these drawings. You are a very smart, talented girl. The thing is, I don't believe them.

The angry animal. The girl who has no voice. The idea of running along the ocean's abyss. These Jackson Pollock black and red swirls. They're all just a little too pretty. Too pat. There is no single emotion that connects these drawings to one another. They stand alone. That isn't how trauma works. Whatever emotions you are feeling right now . . . they connect everything.'

His chair creaks as he leans over, placing a sheet in front of me. 'Except for this one. This one is different.'

'Am I supposed to guess?' Trying to be sarcastic. Trying to figure out how he saw through me so fast. Which drawing he found meaningful.

'Can you?' he asks. 'Guess?'

'Are you really going to make me play this game?' I grip Oscar's leash like a lifeline, letting it bite into my flesh. Oscar obediently clambers up. 'I'm going home.'

'You can go home anytime you like. But I think you want to know.'

My stillness says everything.

'Tell me.' I barely croak it out, suffused with rage.

'The field of strangled flowers. Leering. The little girl cowering. It's terrifying. Messy. *Real.*'

Lydia's drawing. She'd spent two hours on it while singing along to Alanis. *Got a plastic smile on a plastic face.*

Lydia used to laugh about the fact that she couldn't even draw Snoopy.

She hadn't told me about the little girl. I wanted to see.

I dropped the leash and scooted myself to the edge of the cushion, words rushing up my throat before I could stop them.

'What would you say if I told you that the main thing

I've been drawing . . .' I suck in a breath. 'Is a curtain. Over and over, until I want to crawl out of my skin?'

'I'd say, it's a start.'

A slightly higher pitch to his voice. Is it hope?

Tessa, present day

I jiggle the key into the first of two locks on the front door. My mind is dwelling on pristine white laboratories and trees made of brittle bones and the fraction of statistical hope that one of the three tiny pieces of dead girl will lead somewhere. All the way home, there was blessed silence from the Susans. While the lock refuses to cooperate, a shadow clobbers into mine, making me gasp.

'What are you so damn jumpy for, Sue?'

Euphemia Outler, right-hand neighbor. Known to me as Effie, to Charlie as *Miss* Effie (despite a marriage or two) and to a few mean boys on the block as Miss Effing Crazy. She is an ex-science professor, a self-employed suburban spy, and an early dementia patient who regularly calls me Sue – not because of my past, but because it is her only daughter's name, the one who lives in New Jersey, who had decided when her mother turned eighty, *What the hell, out of sight, out of mind.*

'Hey, you snuck up on me,' I say. 'How's it going today?'

In her right hand, Effie proffers a small, oblong item wrapped in aluminum foil so crinkled that it could have been reused since the Depression. In her left hand, a vase of flowers, in the tight professional array of a florist. None of the flowers are yellow and black. On her head, the floppy blue-checked sun hat that Charlie and I bought from a beach vendor in Galveston four summers ago as a gift.

Effie's eyes, still those of a provocative teen, peer out of a face toughened by sun.

'I made you some banana bread. Threw some bulgur in it. And I brought in these flowers for you this morning. I saw the guy plop them on your front porch. Thought the wind might blow 'em over. Plus, I've got a problem to discuss with you.'

'That was so nice. Thank you.' I twist the second lock. The deadbolt is a little cranky, too. *Need to take care of that. Maybe add a third lock.* I shove open the door and Effie tramples after me in her battered green Crocs without invitation.

'Let me stick these groceries away.' I avert my eyes from the flowers. 'Go ahead and put the flowers and bread here on the counter, and then you can tell me about your . . . problem. I have iced tea in the fridge. Charlie brewed it last night. Caffeine, sugar, mint, lemon – the works. Charlie stole the mint from your garden after dark.'

'I put bulgur in the bread because I know Charlie especially likes it. And I'll take that tea.'

I am pretty sure my daughter has no idea what bulgur is, but this is likely a step up from last week's offering of oatmeal and carob cookies that Charlie cheerfully likened to eating cow manure.

Effie fancies herself as something of a chef. The problem is, she thinks like a scientist. For instance, deciding it would be a good idea to boil fresh pumpkin for pumpkin pie rather than using a time-tested can of Libby's puree. Chunks and pumpkin strings and *a lot* of canned whipped cream are what I will remember about last year's Thanksgiving dinner. But that's OK: Most Thanksgivings just flow into a dull, pleasant river, and Charlie and I will laugh about that one forever.

'*The New York Times* called bulgur "a wheat to remember,"' Effie informs me. 'They try to make everything so damn profound. I'd stop reading the paper if it weren't for the science section and if I didn't think the crossword puzzles were reviving my dead brain cells. What the hell do they know? Dead isn't necessarily dead. Do you think *they* know a four-letter word for Levantine coffee cup?' *They* generally referred to her neurologist.

'Zarf,' I say automatically.

'Well, you're the damn exception to a damn lot of things.' She wanders from the black granite bar that divides the tiny kitchen from the living room and surveys the industrial Bernina sewing machine on the dining room table, draped like a bride in white tulle. 'What's this week's project? Something else for one of those damn rich ladies?'

I kick the refrigerator door shut. 'For one of those damn rich ladies' little girls. A tutu. For competition. Tulle underpinning, lavender appliqué. Swarovski crystals.'

'Fancy-pantsy. I bet she's paying you a fortune.'

In fact, she isn't paying me a fortune, because it's a sad fact that most damn rich ladies no longer appreciate the cost of things made by exacting, artful hands. Not when everything can be purchased from China with the click of a mouse.

'It's a little side job,' I say. 'The costume designer for a Boston ballet company has asked me to dress the leads for its spring production. I want to make sure I know what I'm doing before I say yes.'

'They'd be lucky to have you. You're getting quite global. I thought you were leaving this week to design a staircase for that crazy actor fellow in California, the one who farts through his movies. Doesn't he want it made out of an old

Camaro or some damn thing? And wasn't Charlie's soldier daddy flying in to stay with her while you were gone? The one who promised to patch that spot on my roof. What's his name? Lucifer?'

'Lucas. That California job's on hold for now.' No explanation, because my past is never discussed. Effie knows about that part of me, or she doesn't. I have no idea and want to keep it like that. Either way, it isn't *important* to her.

I can always tell by the way someone looks at me the first time, like I'm a distressing piece of modern art. As an added piece of luck for me, Effie had mostly cut the newspaper out of her life because it made her think the world was 'going to damn hell in a damn rocket ship.'

That didn't mean she canceled her subscription. During the four years we'd lived in this house, she had dropped *The New York Times* on our stoop with random regularity, unread, minus the puzzle. No iPad crosswords for Effie, despite Charlie's best efforts. Effie was certain the device was controlling her, instead of the other way around.

I nudge her over to the couch. 'Sit. What's the problem?'

'Aren't you going to open the card on those flowers? What's the occasion? Belated birthday?' Her eyes are lit with curiosity.

'No occasion I'm aware of. Did you say you saw who left them?' I drop the question as casually as I can. Flowers always punched a little panic button, because anyone who liked me well enough to send them, wouldn't.

'Cute fellow in a Lilybud's Florist outfit. His shorts hung off his bottom. Gave me an eyeful.'

Effie could have seen that bottom today. Or yesterday. Or a month ago. *Time* is a dull, pleasant river for Miss Effie.

I tap her on the shoulder; I'd need to pick up Charlie from volleyball practice soon and she would be craving something besides bulgur-infused banana bread. 'So what's the problem?' I repeat. 'Shoot.'

'There's a digger snatcher.' She waves a small garden trowel, which I hadn't noticed until now. 'I'm going to take it up with the neighborhood watch.'

'Digger . . . snatcher?'

'I just drove to Walmart to buy this one – $2.99 plus tax. Been going on for six months. I buy a digger, and it disappears. I can't keep buying diggers. Do you know where your digger is? I'm thinking of taking a block digger survey.'

'Um.' I have to think about whether I want to answer. 'Behind the house. I think I left it there when I was . . . doing a little weeding.' Stuck upright in the ground, like a grave marker.

'I'm warning you, you might as well be leaving out a crisp $100 bill.'

'I'll keep an eye out. Do you have a place . . . you regularly put your digger?' I ask this cautiously, knowing that organization is a sensitive topic for Effie.

Things in her house have a way of dancing around: a *Scientific American* on genetic engineering stashed in the freezer, the extra house key taped to the bottom of the butter dish, a bottle of Stoli vodka crammed under the bathroom sink with the rusty can of Comet from 1972.

'Well, back to sorting my seedpods.' Effie stands. 'The grubs ate my beans something terrible last year. I'm going to try putting out a bowl of beer for them this year. I'm sure that's pure bunk but it seems like a happier way to go than me stomping their guts out. I wouldn't mind drowning in a bowl of beer when it's my time.'

I laugh. Reach over and give her a hug. 'Thanks for making my life . . . normal,' I say.

'Honey, I'm a sweaty mess.' She meekly returns my hug. 'Most people think I'm pretty weird.' *Most people* generally meant her daughter.

'Well, I can relate. What kind of person builds staircases for farting actors?' *What kind of person suppresses the flutter in her chest every time the sun goes behind a cloud, afraid she's going blind? Or when she opens a jar of peanut butter? When someone yells 'Susan!' across a playground?*

On her way to the door, Effie pauses. 'Can you send Charlie over in about a half-hour to help me and my hysterical society lady friend move some stuff? I mean, historical. Although she *is* a bit hysterical. These ladies need to get their heads out of their damn bustles, if you get my drift.'

'Of course.' I grin. 'I'll tell Charlie.'

From the stoop, I watch her navigate across the thick carpet of golden brown Bermuda, disappearing into her overgrown front garden until all that's visible is her hat bobbing like a bluebird above a mound of fountain grass.

For sixty-one years, Effie has occupied the frilly yellow house next door, a Queen Anne cottage that, like our 1920s Arts and Crafts bungalow, sits in the middle of Fort Worth's famous historical Fairmount District. Effie can't remember the exact number of paint colors she's slapped on her spindlework and fish scale shingles over time, but she dates things by saying, *When the house was lilac,* or *When the house was in its awful brown period.* Effie still pulls her Cadillac boat out of the garage to attend the neighborhood monthly historic preservation meeting. She revels in dragging Charlie, one eyeball at a time, away from her iPhone and assaulting her with neighborhood history. The trolley once rumbled down our street, which is why it is wider than most of the others. Over on Hemphill, there used to be a fantastical mansion with a life-size windmill on top, until it mysteriously burned to the ground.

When the phone inevitably reasserts its magnetic force on Charlie, Effie just brings out the hard stuff: tales about Butch Cassidy and the Sundance Kid, who lived in Hell's Half Acre only three miles from here, or the creepy, boarded-up pig tunnels that run under the city. 'That's how Judas goats got their name,' Effie asserts. 'By herding pigs to slaughter to spare themselves. Back when, goats herded as many as ten thousand pigs a day through Fort Worth's underground tunnels to their miserable fates in the Stockyards. Like New Yorkers in the subway.'

Generally, when it came down to Effie vs. Twitter, Effie won. 'Kids need a sense of place,' she liked to admonish me. 'A sense that they all aren't living and talking in outer space.'

Back in the kitchen, I firmly root myself in the uncomfortable present, on the one kitchen stool that obediently twirls little half-circles. I sip my tea and stare at the card on the flowers. It begs to be opened. I reach over, tug it off its plastic holder, lift the tiny flap, and pull out a flat cardboard square decorated with a cartoon spray of balloons.

I miss you.
Love, Lydia

The card slips from my hand onto the counter. The corner begins melting into the ring of sweat left by my iced-tea glass. Lydia's name blurs into a purple stain. Not the handwriting I remembered, but maybe it isn't hers. Maybe it is the florist's.

Why would Lydia casually send me flowers? Wouldn't she understand that I'm still in mortal daily combat with them? That I'm hanging on to the bitter shreds of our fight after the trial? We hadn't talked for seventeen years, since her family up and left without a word. The flowers seem like a taunt.

I yank the arrangement out of the vase, splashing my jeans in the process, and slide open the glass door to the back yard. Within seconds, pink Gerbers and purple orchids are scattered on top of the funeral pyre of my compost. I carry the vase to the recycling bin sitting empty outside the two-car garage that backs up along our fence line. Bemoan that Charlie should have taken in the recycling bin two days ago.

No reason to panic and think my monster sent these and signed Lydia's name. I open the gate to the slim ribbon of grass that is our side yard. SpongeBob's squeaky voice wafts from an open window next door. That means the babysitter is inside, not the fussy lawyer parents with matching Tesla sedans.

I learned a long time ago to pay attention to what is usual, and what is not.

To retrieve an encyclopedia from the smallest sound.

I round the corner. No one has planted any more black-eyed Susans under my bedroom windowsill. The ground is smoothed flat and swirled, like a pan of chocolate cake batter. The thing is, I hadn't done any smoothing or swirling.

And my digger is gone.

Tessie, 1995

'If you had three wishes, what would they be?' he repeats.

His latest game.

The curtain had gotten us nowhere last time. I had no clue why I was drawing it. I had told him that it was an ordinary curtain. Still, like there was no breeze. When I didn't bring in my drawings today, he didn't bring it up. He noted my boundaries, unlike the others, but he's irritating me in whole new ways. For instance, now insisting I show up for his little interrogations twice a week.

'Really?' I ask. 'Let me see. Do you want me to say that I wish my mother would come down from her puffy cloud and give me a hug? That I wish I wasn't living in some kind of Edgar Allan Poe poem? That I wish my three-year-old cousin would stop snapping his fingers in my face to see if he can magically make me see? That I wish my father would yell at the TV again? I need a whole lot more wishes than three. How about this: I wish I weren't *answering this stupid question.*'

'Why do you want your father to yell at the TV?' A trace of amusement in his voice. I relax a little. He isn't mad.

'It was his favorite thing. Yelling at Bobby Witt when he makes one of his wild throws. Or walks somebody. Now Dad just sits there like a zombie when the Rangers play.'

'And do you think that's your fault?'

The answer to this is too freakin' obvious.

I wish I'd never met Roosevelt, so I wouldn't have needed to buy a Snickers bar, so I wouldn't have been walking out of that drugstore at 8:03 p.m. on June 21, 1994. I wish I never cared about winning, winning, winning.

'It's interesting that you bring up Poe.' Already moving on.

I'd bite on that one. 'Why?'

'Because most people on that couch who've endured a psychic trauma compare their experiences to something in more current pop culture. Horror movies. Crime shows. I get a lot of Stephen King. And John Paul. When did you start reading Poe?'

I shrug. 'After my grandfather died. I inherited a lot of his books. My best friend and I got into them for a while. We read *Moby-Dick* that summer, too. So don't go there, OK? It doesn't mean anything. I was a happy person before this happened. Don't focus on things that don't mean anything.'

'Poe was mired in his lifelong fear of premature burial,' he persists. 'The reanimation of the dead. His mother died when he was young. Don't you think that could be more than coincidence?'

A hammer is pounding my brain. *How did he know?* Just when I thought he was an idiot, he surprised me. He was always going somewhere.

'Do you want to tell me about it?' he asks.

Oscar picks that moment to readjust himself. He licks my bare knee on the way back down. Aunt Hilda yells at him idiotically all the time, 'No lick! No LICK!' but I love his slobber. And right now, it is like he is saying, *Go ahead, take a chance with this one. I want you to throw the Frisbee to me someday.*

'The college girl from East Texas . . . Merry or Meredith or whatever.' I speak haltingly. 'She was alive when they dumped us in that grave. She *talked* to me. I remember her both ways. Dead and alive.' With eyes like blue diamonds and with eyes like cloudy sea glass. Maggots hanging out in the corners, twitchy pieces of rice.

He doesn't answer immediately. I realize this is not at all what he was expecting.

'And the police have told you that's not possible,' he says slowly. 'That she was already dead when you were in that grave. That she'd likely been dead for hours before you were dumped.'

How carefully my doctor had read everything about this case.

'Yes. But she was *alive* in the field. She was nice. I could feel her breath in my face. She sang. And she was in the church choir, remember?' Begging him to believe me, and I am only telling him the least crazy part. 'She told me her mother's name. She told me all of their mothers' names.'

I wish I remembered them.

Tessa, present day

I am waiting for the morning bomb to go off. Or not. I have made coffee and buttered a piece of bulgur-banana bread, listened to Charlie blast music in the shower, loosely sketched an appliqué design for the tutu, thought about how lucky I am.

Because, make no mistake, I am terrifically lucky. If I ever forget, the Susans remind me, in chorus. And the bread isn't half-bad.

'Mom!' Charlie's shriek carries easily from inside her room. 'Where's my blue jersey?'

I find Charlie in her underwear, hair slapping around like wet red string. She is tossing her room, a rabbit's nest of dirty clothes.

'Which jersey?' I ask patiently. She owns two practice uniforms and four game uniforms. The uniforms were 'required to play,' cost $435, and three of them looked exactly alike to me.

'Blue, blue, blue, didn't you hear me? If I don't have it for the scrimmage, Coach will make me run. He might make the whole team run because of me.' Coach. No last name necessary. Like God.

'Yesterday, he threw Katlyn out of practice for forgetting her red socks. She was so *embarrassed.* And it was just because her mom washed them and accidentally stuck them in her brother's baseball basket. He's on a team called the *Red* Sox. Duh.'

I pull something blue out of the tangle of clothes on the floor. 'Is this it?'

Charlie is now spread-eagled and lying faceup on her unmade bed, deciding whether the world is ending. She cranes her neck slightly in my direction. I note that her backpack is open on the desk, unpacked, biology homework still flayed out. The digital clock on her dresser says nineteen minutes to go before my friend Sasha and her daughter pick her up for school.

'Mom! No! It's the one with the *white* number and that cool edging at the bottom. The *practice* jersey.'

'Yes, I should have read your mind. Have you looked in the washer? Dryer? Floor of the car?'

'Why does this have to happen to *me*?' Still staring at the ceiling. Not moving. I could say, *I'm done. Good luck.* Walk out. When I shouted that very same question of the world at the tender age of sixteen, 'Coach' would have seemed like a wasp to swat. Hard to believe I'd only been two years older than Charlie is now.

The very best thing about landing in that grave? Perspective.

So I peer through this morning's prism: a science test looming in second period, an a-hole of a coach who probably could have used more childhood therapy than I got, and a telltale tampon under my foot.

I consider the clawed tiger on the bed, the one wearing the zebra-printed sports bra – the same tiger that every Sunday night transforms into the girl who voluntarily walks next door to help sort Miss Effie's medicine into her days-of-the-week pill container. The one who pretended her ankle hurt one day last week so the backup setter on her volleyball team would get to play on her birthday.

'It was a really kind gesture,' I had told her that night when she explained why she did not need the ice pack. 'But I'm not sure it was such a good idea.'

Charlie had performed her usual eye roll. 'Mom, you can't let the wrong stuff happen all the time. There is no way Coach would have ever let her play. And she set three points right after that. She's just as good as me. I'm just two inches taller.'

I can't count the times that Charlie has offered me her bits of tempered wisdom along with a little frightening Texas grammar.

'Dry your hair, get dressed, pack up,' I order. 'You have a little over fifteen minutes. I'll find the jersey.'

'What if you don't?' But her legs are in motion, swinging over the side of the bed.

Eight minutes later, I find the jersey behind her hamper. White number 10 on the back, nearly invisible edging along the bottom. Strong odor of sweat and deodorant. Apparently, she'd made a half-hearted effort to put it where it belonged. No wonder we hadn't found it.

I stick it in her duffle by the front door and check for red socks. Two short honks chirp from outside.

Charlie appears. 'Did you find it?'

'Yep.' She looks so perfect to me that it hurts. Damp curls that hadn't been sacrificed to a Chi Ultra flat iron springing up like tiny flames. Lip gloss only, so the freckles are out. Jeans, plain white T-shirt, the St Michael charm that she never takes off nestled in her throat. Her father mailed it last Christmas from overseas, a design from James

Avery, the kingpin of tasteful Christian fashion accessories. He started selling his stuff out of a two-car garage in the Texas Hill Country in 1954. Now, six decades later, his jewelry is both holy and pricey.

But for Charlie, this piece of metal out of a Kerrville factory isn't a status symbol. It is a talisman, a sign that her daddy, in the guise of a sword-carrying saint around her neck, will keep her safe. Keep all of us safe. Lucas had worn the good luck charm as long as I'd known him, a gift from his own mother the first time he went to war.

'You're good to go,' I say. 'You look especially pretty. Good luck on your test.'

She slings the duffle over her shoulder and glances over my breakfast offerings on the table by the door.

'Nice try, but not takin' the booger bread.' She slips the granola bar and the banana into the side pocket of her backpack. Another toot of the horn. Effie will be peering out her living room window at this point.

'This day *sucks.*' Charlie spins out the door, leaving the air charged and a chaotic trail from the bathroom floor to her room.

I catch the slamming screen in time to toss a wave to Sasha, whose face is hidden by the harsh glint of sun off the windshield of the familiar blue minivan. The glass is black, impenetrable. I can't tell if she is waving back.

That doesn't mean I need to run out and check that she isn't bleeding on the ground, out of sight, behind the live oak, tossed out of the vehicle while she waited patiently for Charlie. That a stranger, with all of Effie's stolen diggers stacked in the trunk, isn't necessarily behind the wheel, about to drive my fire-breathing angel off to hell.

I shut the door and lean back against smooth, cool wood. Breathe in deep. Hope that other, more normal moms harbor similar out-of-control thoughts about their children's safety.

I wrap up the rejected slice of Effie's bread, generously lathered in strawberry cream cheese, and stick it in the refrigerator. Lunch, maybe. Wash up my coffee cup and set it to drain.

For the next ten minutes, the erratic whirring of the sewing machine breaks the silence. My foot, pressing the pedal. Fingers manipulating satin. Stop. Start. Stop. Start. The background noise of my childhood before Mama died.

Not the scrape of saw against bone.

My mind is not traveling in a row of tiny perfect stitches. It is skipping, out of order, to the places he has planted black-eyed Susans. My eyes close for a second and the stitches derail and zigzag like a train off track.

The list I'd made a couple of days ago is taped to the bottom of the vegetable drawer. Shades of Miss Effie.

In forty-five minutes, I am pressing the pedal of my Jeep.

Long after Lydia and I broke apart, I had returned to this place. Again and again. Maybe hoping a little bit that she would, too.

Until I stopped.

It is different, and the same. The ducks sail on the shivering glass. Aimless. Waiting for the day's first crust of bread to hit the pond.

My car is slung, alone, by the side of the road. Lydia and I had usually ridden the bus here, from Hemphill to West Seventh.

My feet are soundless on the earth. About here is when they used to pick up speed, ready for takeoff.

Lydia was always talking, laughing, talking while we traveled this path. Telling me what library book she'd dragged along with her dad's soft old green hunting blanket and an already lukewarm can of Diet Dr Pepper.

The Unbearable Lightness of Being.

Diana: Her True Story.

There's a slight breeze rustling things. Half of the leaves on the hackberries and pecans are still trying to make up their minds. Is it winter or not? When Lydia and I walked here, the trees were leafy and thick. They blocked the blazing sun like a tight football huddle, casting a dark, intimate comfort that I wonder if only a Southerner can understand.

Anybody watching would think I was up to no good. If it were two hours later, when bread crusts were flying through the air, parents would tug their children away from the strange lady walking around with the rusty shovel. They might even press the non-emergency police number tucked in their contacts that they'd never used before.

On days like these, I wondered if they'd be right. Whether just two or three brain cells were deciding if I was eligible to join the woman by the tracks who lived in a tent crafted of black garbage bags and old broom handles.

This is why I brought no one with me. Not Jo, who would make no mistakes as she sealed the evidence. Not Bill, who would be worried we should have brought Jo. I am sane, and I am not, and I don't want anyone to know.

What was that Poe quote that Lydia liked so much? *I became insane with long intervals of horrible sanity.*

The ducks and the pond are well behind me now. I hear

the rush of the ocean. Of course, it is not the ocean. It's just what Lydia and I closed our eyes and pretended. The only nearby route to the ocean is the Trinity River, which threads by the park on the other side and flows on for hundreds of miles, all the way to Galveston. *La Santisima Trinidad* – The Most Holy Trinity. Christened by Alonso de León in 1690.

Sense of place, Effie says.

I begin to count the pillars. One, two, three, four. Five. The ocean is above me now. I keep striding, toward a red cow in a purple dunce hat. He's new.

It takes a second to realize that he's a unicorn, not a stupid cow. The mermaid who keeps him company a few feet away has red hair that flows like mine and Charlie's. Her bright green tail floats in a sea of fish with upturned mouths that wouldn't think of biting. Peace, love, understanding.

None of this hopeful art was here all those years ago, when Lydia laid out her blanket under pillar No. 5 of the Lancaster Bridge. Now childlike graffiti covers every single concrete pier of the bridge as far as I can see. The pillars used to be splotched with ugly green paint and strangled with the kind of weedy vines that seem to need nothing to live.

The rush and rumble of traffic overhead.

The knowledge of a secret underground world.

The thrilling fear that all that throbbing chaos could crash down on you at any second, but probably wouldn't.

The worry about what might lurch out of the big thicket of woods nearby.

The same, the same, the same. The same.

I survey the parched dirt floor beneath the behemoth steel and concrete structure. Still unforgiving. Hard and bare. But he didn't plant the black-eyed Susans under the bridge at pillar No. 5, where I used to meet up with Lydia after my runs on the twisty running trails. He planted them *here* – a few feet away, under a large cedar elm at the edge of the woods. They appeared at a time of year when black-eyed Susans flourish, so I couldn't be sure. I just never came back after I found them. I was twenty-four, and Lydia and I had been estranged for seven years.

A slight rustle behind me. I jerk around. A man has emerged from behind the pillar. I grip the shovel, suddenly a weapon.

But he is not a man. He is tall and lanky, but no more than fourteen. Pale skin, slouchy jeans, faded Jack Johnson T-shirt. A black mini-backpack slung over his shoulder. There's a phone with a desert camouflage case clipped at his waist and what I'm pretty sure is a metal detector in his right hand.

'Shouldn't you be in school?' I blurt out.

'I'm home-schooled. What are you doing? You can't take plants out of here. It's still the park. You can only clip their leaves.'

'Shouldn't you be home, then? Being schooled? I'm not sure your mother would like you along this side of the park.' My nerves, no longer on high alert.

'I'm on a scavenger hunt. It's National Botany Celebration Day. Or something. My mom is over at the pond with my sister. Teaching her the wonders of duck vision. They see, like, four times farther than us or something.'

His mother is close by. A *home-schooling* mother who

probably has used the non-emergency police number in her phone many, many times. I have no desire to attract her attention.

There is no evidence of gathered botany anywhere on his person. 'I didn't realize that botanists use metal detectors these days,' I say.

'Funny.' He surveys me while chewing a nail. 'That's a really old shovel.'

He isn't going away.

'What are you doing?' he repeats.

'I'm looking for something that . . . somebody might have left for me when I was younger. I would never steal plants on National Botany Day.'

A mistake. Too friendly. Too truthful. The first light of curiosity in his eyes. He has pushed aside a brown tail of hair so I can see them. He is a nice-looking kid. Cute, even, if he adjusted the angle of his mouth a little more.

'Want me to help? Is there metal in it? A ring or something? I can run my wand. You wouldn't believe the stuff I've found in this park.' He is already at my side, practically stepping on my feet, eager, the red light on his device blinking. Before I realize it, he is casually running the detector along my leg. Then the other one. Now he is roving up, toward my waist.

'Hey. Stop that.' I jump backward.

'Sorry. Just wanted to be sure you weren't carrying. Knife, gun. You'd be surprised who I've met up with around here.'

'What's your name?' I ask. My heart is beating hard, but I'm pretty sure his gadget did not roam high enough to disturb the metal device in my chest.

I'm beginning to wonder about the mother story. About the home-schooling.

'My name's Carl,' he says lazily. 'What's yours?'

'Sue,' I lie.

He takes this brief exchange of names as a sign of collusion. With a professional air, he runs the detector over the area where there is the evidence of my feet trampling the weeds.

'Here?' he asks.

'About. I was going to dig in a two-foot area.' *How do I get out of this? If I leave, he is sure to search on his own.*

'Whatever you're looking for . . . did an old boyfriend leave it?'

I shiver. 'No. Not a boyfriend.'

'The alarm ain't firing. There's nothing here.' He sounds disappointed. 'You want me to dig for you anyway?'

Great. I have become the highlight of National Botany Celebration Day.

'No. I need the exercise. But thank you.'

He leans against a tree, texting. I can only hope it is not about me. In a few minutes, he wanders off without saying goodbye.

A half-hour later, I have hacked through the ancient piping of tree roots and dug a square hole about half the size of a baby crib, and a foot deep.

Carl is right.

There's nothing here.

I can't help but wonder whether he is watching. Not Carl. My monster.

On my knees, I rush to push the crumbly black earth back in place. It now looks like an animal's grave.

My phone chirps, a silly sound, but my heart lurches anyway.

A text. Charlie.

Sorry I was grouchy
Mommy ☺

Charlie has passed her biology test.

I tuck the phone into my pocket and step into the deep shadows under the bridge. I think of the two girls who listened to the drone of traffic and imagined an ocean. Girls who had nothing more important to do than argue whether *Jurassic Park* could really happen and extol the virtues of Sonic drive-ins because they have hands-down the best ice for chewing. All of that, of course, before one of them ended up in a hole and the other one tried to pull her out.

Time to move on.

When I reach the pond, I see a mother kneeling beside a small child with a pink beret. The girl is pointing at a pair of ducks beak to beak in a staring contest.

Her delighted laugh trickles across the pond, rippling the water as it pulls more ducks her way. I see an old crazy quilt spread out behind her. A blue Igloo cooler.

What I don't see is Carl.

Tessie, 1995

He's jabbering.

Blah, blah. Jabber, jabber.

Apparently, it isn't that unusual to experience something paranormal after an *event.*

Other people talk to the dead, too. No big deal. He doesn't say it out loud, but I'm a *cliché.*

'The paranormal experience can happen during the event,' he is saying. 'Or afterward.' *The event. Like it is a royal wedding or the UT–OU football game.* 'The victims who survive sometimes believe that a person who died in the event is still speaking to them.' If he says *event* one more time, I am going to scream. The only thing holding me back is Oscar. He is sleeping, and I don't want to freak him out.

'A patient of mine watched her best friend die in a tubing accident. It was especially traumatic because she never saw her surface the water. They didn't find her body. She was convinced her friend was controlling things in her life from heaven. Ordinary things. Like whether it would rain on her. People in circumstances similar to yours suddenly see ghosts in broad daylight. Predict the future. They believe in omens, so much so that some of them can't leave their houses.'

Circumstances similar to mine? Is he saying that with a straight face? Surely, he is smirking. And, surely, it isn't a good idea right now to hold my head underwater with tangled fishing lines and human-eating tree stumps and silky, streaming strands of another girl's hair. Lydia's dad always warns us about what lies beneath the murky surface of the lake. Makes us wear scratchy nylon lifejackets in 103-degree heat no matter how much we sweat and whine.

'That's crazy,' I say. 'The rain thing. I'm not crazy. It happened. I mean I know *it happened*. She spoke to me.'

I wait for him to say it. *I believe you think it happened, Tessie.* Emphasis on *believe*. Emphasis on *think*.

He doesn't say it. 'Did you think she was alive or dead when she spoke to you?'

'Alive. Dead. I don't know.' I hesitate, deciding how far to go. 'I remember her eyes as really blue, but the paper said they were brown. But then, in my dreams they sometimes change colors.'

'Do you dream often?'

'A little.' *Not* going there.

'Tell me exactly what Meredith said to you.'

'Merry. Her mother calls her Merry.'

'OK, Merry, then. What's the first thing Merry said to you in the grave?'

'She said she was hungry.' My mouth suddenly tastes like stale peanuts. I run my tongue over my teeth, trying not to gag.

'Did you give her something to eat?'

'That isn't important. I don't remember.'

Oh my God, it's like I brushed my teeth with peanut butter. I feel like throwing up. I picture the space around me. If I throw up sideways, I spray the leather couch. Head down, it hits Oscar. Straight across, no holds barred, the doctor gets it.

'Merry was upset that her mother would be worried

about her. So she told me her mother's name. Dawna. With an *a* and a *w*. I remember, like, being frantic about getting to Merry's mother. I wanted more than anything to climb out of there so I could tell her mom that she was safe. But I couldn't move. My head, legs, arms. It was like a truck was crushing my chest.'

I didn't know whether Merry was alive, and I was dead.

'The thing is, I know how to spell her mother's name.' I'm insistent. '*D-a-w-n-a*, not *D-o-n-n-a*. So it must have happened. Otherwise, how would I know?'

'I have to ask you this, Tessie. You mentioned the paper. Has someone been reading you the newspaper reports?'

I don't answer. It would get Lydia in a lot of trouble with Dad. With the lawyers, too, probably, who want me to testify 'untainted' by media chatter. I overheard one of the assistants say, 'If we have to, we can make this blind thing work in our favor.'

I don't want anyone to take Lydia away.

'It is possible that you transposed time,' the doctor says. 'That you know the detail of her mother's name, how it was spelled, but found it out afterward.'

'Is that common, too?' Sarcastic.

'Not *un*common.'

He's checking off all the little crazy boxes, and I'm making a hundred.

The toe of my boot is furiously knocking against the table leg. My foot slips and accidentally kicks Oscar, who lets out a cry. I think that nothing in the past month has felt as awful as this tiny hurt sound from Oscar. I lean down and bury my face in his fur. *So sorry, so sorry.* Oscar immediately slaps his tongue on my arm, the first thing he can reach.

'My Very Energetic Mother Just Served Us Nine Pizzas.' I murmur this into Oscar's warm body again and again, calming Oscar. Calming myself.

'Tessie.' Concern. Not smirking now. He thinks he's pushed me too far. I titter, and it sounds loony. It's weird, because I really feel pretty good today. I just feel bad about kicking Oscar.

I raise my head, and Oscar resettles himself across my feet. His busy tail whacks like a broom against my leg. He's fine. We're fine.

'It's a mnemonic device,' I say. 'For remembering the planetary order.'

'I don't understand.'

'Mercury, Venus, Earth, Mars . . . My Very Energetic Mother . . .'

'I get that. But what does it have to do with Merry?' He's sounding really worried.

'Merry thought we should come up with a code to help me remember the names of the mothers of the other Susans. So I could find them later. Tell them that their girls were OK, too.'

'And it had something to do . . . with the planets?'

'No,' I say impatiently. 'I was repeating the planet thing in the grave, trying to, you know, stay sane. Not black out. Everything was kind of spinning. I could see the stars and stuff.' The moon, a tiny, thin smile. *Don't give up*. 'Anyway, it made Merry think of the idea for a mnemonic device so I wouldn't forget the names of the other mothers. So I wouldn't forget. *N-U-S,* a letter for each mother. Nasty Used Snot. Or something. I remember *snot* was part of it. But I flipped the letters around and made a real word. *SUN.*'

I've shocked him into silence again.

'And the other mothers' names? What are they?'

'I don't remember. Yet.' It pains me to say this out loud. 'Just the three letters. Just *SUN*. But I'm working on it.' Determined. I run through names every night in bed. The *U*'s are the hardest. *Ursula? Uni?* I will not let Merry down. I will find the mother of every single Susan.

The doctor is twisting his mind around this.

I'm not such a cliché anymore.

'There were the bones of two other girls in the grave, not three,' he says finally, as if logic has anything to do with this.

Tessa, present day

The three of us barely fit in the famous Dr Joanna Seger's office. It isn't at all what I expect for a rock star scientist. The large window showcases a lovely view of the Fort Worth skyline, but Jo faces the door, welcoming the living. Her desk, a modern black chunk that almost swallows the whole space, is littered with forensic journals and paper. It reminds me of Angie's desktop in the church basement. The kind of desktop where passion is screwing organization and nobody's making the bed.

The signature piece rising out of the chaos: a Goliath computer running $100,000 worth of software. The HD screen displays a roller coaster of lime green and black bar codes. It's the rare spot of color except for the grinning Mexican death masks and the skeleton bride leering off a shelf like a grisly Barbie. The Mexicans, bless them, have always had a less squeamish, more realistic view of death. I'm guessing Jo can relate.

I'm afraid to peer too closely at what looks like a heart suspended in a glass box, because I'm pretty sure it is a heart suspended in a glass box. Preserved, somehow, with a putty hue. Its dull sheen reminds me of my trip to Dallas with Charlie to tour the Body Worlds exhibit, where dead humans are plasticized in polymer so we can gawk at our complex inner beauty. Charlie fought nightmares for a week after learning that this multi-million-dollar road show might be using corpses of prisoners executed in China.

I'm certain, certain, certain I do not want to know where this heart came from, either.

Lots of commendation plaques on the wall. Is that President Bush's signature?

Bill is scrolling through the email on his phone, ignoring me. He has pushed his chair so far back to accommodate his legs that he is almost in the doorway. My own knees are crammed against the desk, probably turning pink under my cotton skirt.

This is Jo's show, and we are waiting.

She is notched into her little cranny on the other side of the desk with her ear to the phone. She had the chance to say, 'Sit, please,' before it buzzed. 'Uh-huh,' she is saying now, after several minutes of listening. 'Great. Let me know when you've finished up.'

'Very good news,' Jo announces as she replaces the receiver. 'We have successfully extracted mitochondrial DNA from the bones of two of the girls. The femurs. We didn't have luck with the skull. We're going to have to try again, probably with a femur this time, although it was seriously degraded. We'll keep going at it. We won't give up. We'll find the right bone.' She hesitates. 'We've also decided we're going to pull DNA from some other bones. Just to be sure there weren't additional mistakes.'

I can't think about this. More girls. The Susan cacophony in my head is loud enough.

I can, however, appreciate Jo's tenacity. My iPad has been very busy since I witnessed the bone cutting. This high-tech forensic lab might be a well-kept secret in Fort Worth, but not to crime fighters around the world. The building protrudes off Camp Bowie like a silver ship hull, with a cache of grim treasure: baby teeth and skulls and hip bones and jawbones that have traveled across state lines and oceans hoping for a last shot at being identified. This lab gets results when no one else does.

'That's great, Jo.' There is weary relief in Bill's voice.

His tone reminds me that he is pushing a truck of bricks uphill every day with one hand and dragging me behind him with the other. This morning, I'd reluctantly agreed to ride along to meet the 'expert' who is poring over my teenage drawings. The detour to Jo's office was a last-minute surprise, and welcome. I could breathe freely for a few more minutes before I started inspecting the swirls in a curtain for a face. That is, I could breathe if my eyes stopped wandering to that heart in a box.

'That was my boss on the phone,' Jo continues. 'As we speak, the DNA of those two girls is being input into the national missing persons database. I don't want to get your hopes up. It's a useless hunt, obviously, if the families of the victims haven't also placed their DNA into the system for a match. The database wasn't even around when these girls went missing. Their families have to be ones who haven't given up hope, who are still bugging police and on their knees praying every night. You two are most definitely not on a movie set with Angelina Jolie, and please don't forget it.'

I wonder how many times she has repeated this. Hundreds. Thousands.

Her left hand is doodling a drawing on the edge of a magazine. A DNA strand. It has tiny shoes. I think it is jogging. Or dancing.

'Six weeks until D-Day,' Bill says. 'But I've had less at this point with other cases and landed on top. Tell everybody thanks for persevering. Any detail about those girls' identities could provide more reasonable doubt. I want to pile it on at the hearing.'

Jo's hand pauses. 'Tessa, do you know anything about the forensic use of mitochondrial DNA? I'd like you to understand what we do here.'

'A little,' I say. 'It comes only from the maternal side. Mother. Grandmother. I . . . read . . . that you were able to use it to identify the bones of one of John Wayne Gacy's victims thirty years later.'

'Not me specifically, but this lab, yes. William Bundy. Otherwise known as Victim No. 19, because he was the nineteenth victim pulled from the crawl space under Gacy's house in Chicago. That was a very good day for his family. And science.'

John Wayne Gacy. Put to death by lethal injection in 1994, a month and a half before my attack.

Jo's pen is moving again. Dancing DNA guy now has a partner. With high heels. Jo sticks the pen behind her ear. 'Let me give you the twenty-five-cent science lesson I deliver to my sixth-grade tour groups. There are two kinds of DNA in our cells: nuclear and mitochondrial. Nuclear DNA was the kind used way back in the O.J. trial, and, by the way, if you have a scintilla of doubt, they had him dead to rights. But that was a fresh crime scene. For older bones, we have come to depend on mitochondrial DNA, which hangs around longer. It is tougher to extract, but we're getting better all the time. You're exactly right: It remains identical in ancestors for decades. Which makes it perfect for cold cases, like this one. And *really* cold cases, like, say, the Romanovs, where forensic work finally disproved the myth that Princess Anastasia escaped from that cellar where her family was slaughtered. Science was able to prove that anyone who claimed to be her, or descended from her, was a liar. Another great case. It rewrites history.'

I nod. I know plenty about Anastasia. Lydia had been fascinated with all of the romantic conspiracy theories – the ten women who claimed to be the only surviving daughter of Nicholas II and Empress Alexandra, who were executed with their children by the Bolsheviks, like dogs. I'd also watched the convoluted, sanitized, entirely imagined, happily-ever-after Disney version of *Anastasia* while baby-sitting my six-year-old cousin, Ella. 'Are you a princess, too?' Ella had asked when it was over. 'Weren't you the girl who forgot?'

Bill moves restlessly. Impatient. 'What about the hair, Jo?'

'Still in process. A little more red tape than we thought before we got the police to turn it over. Separate evidence box.'

'The hair?' I ask. 'What hair?'

'Do you really still not know the details of the case?' Bill asks impatiently. 'The hair is one of two pieces of physical evidence used to convict Terrell. They found it on the muddy jacket on the farm road.' Muddy jacket. Bloody glove. Suddenly I was back in O.J. Land.

'I've made it a point not to read much about the case,' I say stiffly. His frustration with me hurts. 'It was a long time ago. I was only in that courtroom when I testified. I don't remember a hair.'

Jo is examining me carefully, her pen stilled. 'The hair was red.'

My hair.

'It was brought up at the last minute at trial. The prosecution expert examined it under a microscope and testified that it belonged to you. He was just one hundred percent damn *sure* it came off your head. It was the kind of junk science used back then. It is impossible to match a hair to a specific person by looking at it under a microscope. The only way is through DNA analysis. Which we are now doing.'

Yet . . . only 2 percent of the population has red hair. My grandmother had drilled that into me. First, after she caught me hacking off my orange locks with scissors at age four and then again six years later when I tried to dye it gold by squeezing thirteen lemons over my head and sitting like a piece of salmon in the Texas sun.

Red hair was something else that made me lucky. *Special.*

'I know about the jacket, of course,' I say steadily. 'I know about the ID from the person who saw . . . Terrell . . . hitchhiking by the field. I just didn't know about the hair.' *Or I forgot.*

Bill stands abruptly. 'Maybe you also *don't know* that seventy percent of wrongful convictions overturned on DNA involve eyewitness misidentification. That the jacket found on the road was a size too small for Terrell. And the red hair on the jacket? It was stick straight. If your school pictures are any indication, you looked like you were growing Flamin' Hot Cheetos curls. It could have been a poodle hair, for Christ's sake.'

Poodles *have* curly hair. And I don't think red poodles exist. Although Aunt Hilda once dyed hers blue.

But I understand his anger. The need to lay it on.

I know what he's thinking, although he isn't saying it out loud. The real reason Terrell Darcy Goodwin lost the last seventeen years of his life isn't because of a red hair or a jacket tossed carelessly by the side of the road or a woman who thought she could see in the dark while she was whizzing by in her Mercedes.

The real reason Terrell Darcy Goodwin sits on Death Row is because of the Black-Eyed Susan who testified, scared out of her mind.

Tessie, 1995

I can't wait to tell him.

'I know that last week was rough,' he begins. 'But there are only a couple of months left before the trial begins. That's a very short time to learn what you do or do not know, and help you feel prepared.'

Fifty-nine days, to be exact.

'We should reconsider light hypnosis,' he says. 'I know how you feel about it, but there are things lying in the shadows. Just inches away, Tessie. Inches.'

We had a deal. No drugs. No hypnosis.

My heart is slamming, my breath rapid, like a hot cat on the driveway. Like the time I ran three miles full out in the park last August, and Lydia had to yank the emergency paper bag out of her backpack.

Lydia, always there, always calm. *Breathe. In and out. In and out.* The paper bag, crickling and crackling, puffing and collapsing.

'What do you think?' he persists. 'I've talked with your father about this.'

The silence between this threat and his next sentence is going to kill me. I'm trying to remember where I usually focus my eyes. Down? Up? At his voice? It's important.

'Your father says he won't support hypnosis unless you want it,' he says finally. 'So this is between us.'

I've never loved my father more than this moment. I am

filled with the relief of it, this simple, profound gesture of respect from the man who has watched his flame-haired daughter who believed she could beat the wind shrink to skin and bones and bitterness. My father holds up my future like a banged-up trophy that still means something, no matter how heavy it gets.

He is sitting outside this door, fighting for me. Every single day, fighting for me. I want to run out there and throw myself in his arms. I want to apologize for every silent night, every carefully prepared meal not eaten, every tentative invitation I have refused: to rock on the front porch swing or go for a walk or head up to Dairy Queen for a dipped cone.

'Our goals are the same, Tessie,' the doctor says. 'For you to heal. Justice is part of the package.'

I haven't uttered a word since I walked in the door. And I had planned to say so much. Tears hang in my eyes. What they mean, I don't know. I refuse to let them fall.

'Tessie.' Going in for the kill. Corrupting my name into an order. Reminding me that he knows better than I do.

'This could help you see again,' he says.

Oh.

I want to laugh.

What he doesn't know, what nobody knows yet, is that I already can.

Tessa, present day

I could have lived very happily with the idea of never, ever again. Never again plunking down on a therapist's couch. Never again thinking about my manipulative drawings of the girl running in the sand and the girl without the mouth. Never again fighting this sick feeling that the other person in the room wants to take a paring knife and slowly carve out my secrets.

Dr Nancy Giles almost immediately ushered Bill out the door, politely telling him he would be in the way. Actually it wasn't all that polite. The fact that she is a beautiful gazelle-like creature probably took the edge off. Bill grumbled about being banned in such a little-boy manner that it made me think the two of them had known each other intimately for a long time, although he failed to mention it on the ride over.

My grandfather once told me that God puts pieces in the wrong places to keep us busy solving puzzles, and in the perfect places so that we never forget there is a God. At the time, we were standing on a remote stretch of Big Bend that was like a strange and wondrous moon.

Dr Giles's face may be the human equivalent, a glorious landscape of its own. Velvet brown skin with eyes dropped in like glittering lakes. Her nose, lips, cheekbones – all chiseled by a very talented angel. She understands her beauty and keeps things simple. Hair cropped into a bob. A well-cut blue suit with a skirt that strikes her mid-knee. Gold strings dangle from her ears, with a single large antique pearl at the end of each that dances every time she moves her head. I guess her age to be creeping toward seventy.

Her office, though, is like the favorite fat uncle who wears loud shirts and offers up a slightly smashed Twinkie from his pocket. Walls the color of egg yolk. A red velour couch, with a stuffed elephant plunked in the corner for a pillow. Two comfy plaid chairs. Low-slung shelves shooting out a riot of color, crammed with picture books and Harry Potter and Lemony Snicket, American Girl dolls of every ethnicity, trucks and plastic tools and Mr and Mrs Potato Head. A table topped with a tray of markers and crayons. An iMac at i-am-a-Child level. A refrigerator door riddled with the graffiti of children's awkward, happy signatures. Off to the side, a basket loaded with snacks both forbidden and polyunsaturated, and no mother to smack your hand.

My eyes linger on the framed prints – not your usual doc-in-a-box muted abstractions. Instead, Chagall's magical, musical animals and the loveliest blue ever imagined. Magritte's steam engine shooting out of a fireplace, and his giant green apple, and men in bowler hats floating up like Mary Poppins.

Perfect, I think. If anything is surreal, it is childhood.

'My usual customer is a little younger.' Dr Giles says it with good humor. She has misinterpreted my roving eyes, still on the hunt for my own grim artwork. I tell my nerves to shut up, but they don't. My sweaty hands are probably stickier than the five-year-old who skipped out of the room with a dripping green Popsicle right before I stepped in.

'I'm not sure we can accomplish exactly what William wants, are you?' She has placed herself on the other side of the couch, crossing one knee over the other, her skirt inching up slightly.

Relaxed. Informal.

Or purposeful. Rehearsed.

'William has always set near-impossible goals, even when he was a boy,' she continues. 'The older I get, and the more horrors I've seen, my goals have become . . . less specific. More flexible. More patient. I like to think that is because I am wiser, not tired.'

'And yet . . . he brought me to you,' I say. 'With a deadline. For very specific reasons.'

'And yet he brought you to me.' Her lips curve up again. I realize how easily that smile could melt a child, but I am no longer a child.

'So your plan is *not* for us to look at my drawings together.'

'Do we need them? This is going to disappoint William, but I don't think you wrote the killer's name in the waves in the ocean. Do you?'

'No.' I clear my throat. 'I do not.' I wasn't sure whether this was true. One of the first things I did the night after my sight returned was to examine every swirl of the brush. Just in case. *Who knows what the unconscious mind will paint?* Lydia had asked rather dramatically.

'I find that drawings after a trauma like yours are often widely misinterpreted.' Dr Giles reaches for the stuffed elephant tucked behind her, which is preventing her from leaning back. 'There is a lot attached to the use of color, and the vigor of the pen. But a child may use blood red in his drawing simply because it's his favorite color. The drawing only represents the feeling on that day, at that very moment in time. We all hate our parents on some days, right? A scratchy, angry version of a father doesn't mean he is an abuser, and I'll never testify to things like that. So I use the drawing technique, but mostly as a way to allow young patients to get out their emotions so they don't eat away at them. It is much, much harder to say the words. I'm sure I don't have to tell you that.'

'Dr Giles . . .'

'Please. Nancy.'

'Nancy, then. Not to be rude . . . but why exactly did you take Bill up on this request? If you don't believe there is really anything there to talk about.' *Does she know that more than half of my drawings are faked? Do I need to tell her?*

Jo's chilling, detached lesson on bones, that damn heart in a box, the pink elephant perched beside us who knows way too much about the terrible, terrible things people do – it's about all the reality I can take today.

In an hour and a half, I will be planted in the stands at Charlie's volleyball game, surrounded by weary moms who will scream their throats raw, where the most important thing isn't worrying about the Middle East's urgent signs of Armageddon, or the 150 million orphans in the world, or glaciers melting, or the fate of all the innocent men on Death Row.

It will be whether a ball touches the ground.

Afterward, I will pull a bag of carrot sticks out of the refrigerator, throw four Ham & Cheese Hot Pockets in the microwave, one for me and three for Charlie, toss in a load of clothes, and attach white gauze to lavender silk. These are the pricks of light that have kept me mostly sane, mostly happy, day after day.

'Don't misunderstand me,' Nancy is saying. 'I'm not at all sure your drawings are meaningless. Your case is . . .

complicated. I very much appreciate your permission to view the doctors' notes on your sessions. It was helpful, although the notes from your last doctor were a little sparse. You were blind when you created many of those pictures, correct? Your doctor at the time clearly thought you were faking most of them.' So she knows. Good. 'He also believed that the two of you explored every avenue when it came to figuring out the drawings of the curtain. The drawings that were, essentially, the ones that you declared spontaneous and genuine.'

She glances down at the beeper vibrating at her waist, checks the number, silences it. 'So there are many reasons to discount the drawings. At least that was your doctor's assessment. Would you agree?'

'Yes.' My throat is dry. *Where was this going?* And a random thought, *Should I have ever asked to see the doctor's notes?*

A Susan quickly chimes: *You don't want to know what he said.*

'Of course, it's always a little hard to know exactly what we are faking,' Dr Giles continues. 'The subconscious is busy. The truth tends to creep through. I am, of course, drawn to the curtain. It reminded me of a famous case history that I thought would be worthwhile to share. It's ironic, or a sign if you believe in those, but the girl's name in this other case history is also Tessa. Her name has probably been changed and her story is far different, of course. She was a young girl who had been sexually abused in her home but was far too traumatized to name her abuser. The young girl drew a cutaway picture of her two-story house, so her therapist could see inside. She drew a number of beds on the top floor. The child said the beds were for all the many people living in the house. She drew a living room downstairs, and a kitchen with an oversized teakettle. But instead of asking the girl about the beds, the therapist asked the girl about the teakettle and why it was important. The girl told her that every morning, each member of the house would pour hot water out of that kettle for instant coffee as they left for school or work. So, using the teakettle, the therapist took the little girl through that awful day of the abuse. Tessa remembered, one at a time, who had used the teakettle that morning before leaving the house. The one person remaining, who didn't use it, is the one who stayed alone in the house with her. The abuser. The girl was then able to tell the story of what happened to her.'

Against my will, this woman has mesmerized me.

'I can't know for sure,' she says gently. 'But I believe your ordinary object could be a similarly powerful tool. It belongs somewhere. We need to look around that place. If you like, we can try some exercises.'

My head pounds. I want to say yes, but I'm not sure I can. Nothing, *nothing,* is ever what I expect.

She accurately interprets my silence. 'Not today. But maybe soon?'

'Yes, yes. Soon.'

'May I give you a homework assignment? I would like you to draw the curtain again from memory. Then call me. I'll make time.' She pats my knee. 'Excuse me for a minute.'

She walks toward the closed door at the back of the room. I notice a slight arthritic limp. As the door cracks open, I glimpse her personal refuge – warm light and a large antique desk.

She is back quickly, proffering a business card. Nothing else in her hands. She is not returning my drawings – at least, not today. No cheating.

‘I scribbled my cell number on the bottom,’ she says. ‘I did have one more question before you go, if that’s OK.’

‘Sure.’

‘The drawing of the field. The giant flowers leering like monsters over the two girls.’

Girls. Plural. *Two.*

‘It means nothing,’ I say. ‘I didn’t draw it. A friend of mine did. We drew together. She was in on my . . . deception. My partner in crime.’ I laugh awkwardly.

Nancy shoots me a strange look. ‘Is your friend OK?’

It seems like an unusual question. So many, many years have passed. Why does it matter?

‘I haven’t seen her since we were seniors in high school. She left town before we graduated, right after the trial.’ *She just disappeared.*

‘That must have been hard.’ Every word is careful. ‘To lose a good friend so soon after the trauma.’

‘Yes.’ For more reasons than I want to explain. I am inching toward the door. Lydia is not a place I will go. Not today.

Yet Dr Giles won’t let me leave, not yet.

‘Tessa, I believe the girl who drew that scene, your friend Lydia, was genuinely terrified.’

‘You said there were . . . two girls in that picture. I always thought there was one girl. Bleeding.’ A tiny, tiny red tornado.

‘At first, so did I,’ she says. ‘The shapes are not distinct. But if you look closely, you can see four hands. Two heads. I believe one of the girls is a protector, crouching over the other one. I don’t think that is blood from the attack of the flower monsters. I think the protector has red hair.’

Tessie, 1995

It is hard, pretending not to see. It has been two days. I know that I can't keep it up very long, especially with my dad. I need some time to observe, to analyze body language. To know what everyone is really feeling about me when they think I'm not looking.

The doctor scribbles away at his desk, a scritch-scratching sound that makes me want to scream.

He glances up with a concerned frown to see if I might have changed my mind about talking. Or my pose. Arms crossed, staring straight ahead. I had marched in the room at our appointed time and told him that I was done. Done, done, *done.*

We had a *deal,* I'd reminded him.

No freakin' way was I doing hypnosis, where I float along like a dizzy bluebird and tell him secret things. I set out my rules from *the beginning,* and if it was so easy to erase this one from his mind, what else might he do? Offer up a happy cocktail? I'd read *Prozac Nation.* That girl was sad. So messed up. She wasn't me.

I didn't want to be like her, or Randy, the guy with the locker next to mine, wearing an Alice in Chains T-shirt every day, popping Xanax between classes and sleeping through high school. I had heard that his mother has breast cancer. I don't want to ask, but I am always sure to smile at him when we meet at the lockers. I get it. Randy sent me a cute card at the hospital with a thermometer sticking out of a cat's mouth. He wrote inside, *Sometimes life is so unkind.* I wonder how long it took him to find that lyric. Alanis is plastered inside my locker, so he had to know. He probably couldn't find any Alice in Chains tunes that wouldn't tell me to go kill myself or something.

Lydia had caught on right away. Tiny clues. My Bible on the dresser opened to Isaiah instead of Matthew. The TV ever so slightly more angled toward my spot on the bed. The pink-and-green T-shirt that matched the leggings, and the brown and peach Maybelline eye shadow that I hadn't put on for a year. It wasn't just one thing, she said. It was all of them.

There were surprises, everywhere. My face in the bathroom mirror, for one. Everything about me, more angular. My nose juts out like the notch on my grandfather's old sundial. The half-moon scar under my eye is fading, more pink than red, less noticeable. Dad tentatively suggested a few weeks ago that we could talk to a plastic surgeon if I wanted, but the idea of lying there like Sleeping Beauty while a man with a knife stands over me . . . not ever gonna happen. I would rather people stare.

Oscar is even whiter than I imagined, although maybe that's just because everything seems a little blinding at the moment. He's the first thing I saw at the end of my bed the morning I opened my eyes for real – a pile of dove feathers with a head. I had called out his name softly. When his tongue slapped my nose, I knew for sure I wasn't dreaming.

There was no drama to my sudden transformation. I went to sleep, I woke up, and I could see again. The world had crept back into sharp and excruciating focus.

The doctor's still at it with the scritch-scratching at the

desk. I twitch my eyes over to the clock on the wall. Nine minutes left. Oscar's sleeping at my feet, but his ears are flicking around. Maybe an evil squirrel dream. I kick off my sneaker and run my foot back and forth across his warm back.

The doctor notices my movement, hesitates, and puts down his pen. He makes his way slowly over to the chair across from me. I think again what an excellent job Lydia had done of describing him.

'Tessie, I want to tell you how sorry I am,' he begins. 'I didn't honor our agreement. I pushed you. It is everything a good therapist should *not* do, regardless of the circumstances.'

I greet him with silence but keep my gaze locked over his shoulder. Tears, barely under the surface.

Because there are things I'd still rather not see. My brother's face after my dad talked to him quietly last night about his grades, which used to be straight A's. The medical insurance forms scattered all over the table like someone lost at poker and tossed the deck. The sad, bare state of the refrigerator, weeds choking the cracks in the driveway, tight lines curved around my father's mouth.

All of this, because of me.

I need to keep trying. I want to get better. I can see. Isn't that better?

Didn't this man asking for forgiveness right now probably have something to do with that? Shouldn't I let him score that victory? Don't we all make mistakes?

'What else can I say, Tessie, that might begin to restore your trust in me?'

I think he knows that I can see.

'You can tell me about your daughter,' I say. 'The one you lost.'

Tessa, present day

The tutu is finished.

I steam it gently, even though it doesn't really need it. Charlie makes fun of me and my Rowenta IS6300 Garment Steamer. But Rowenta has probably been my best and most faithful therapist. She pops out of the closet about once a month and never asks a single question. She's mindless. Magic. I borrow her wand and all of the wrinkles disappear. Results are instant, and certain.

Except for today.

Today, a mobile spins in my head, dangled by an unseen hand. I'm transfixed by the pictures whizzing by. Lydia's face is on one. Terrell's is on another. They dance among yellow flowers and black eyes and rusty shovels and plastic hearts. All of them, strung together with brittle bone.

It has been two days since Dr Nancy Giles of Vanderbilt/Oxford/Harvard interpreted Lydia's drawing, right after she had announced in no uncertain terms that she didn't put too much stock in Freudian crap.

Dr Giles thinks something was wrong with *Lydia.* That Lydia perceived *me* as the protector. Which can't be. I never told anyone about the poem he left me in the ground by the live oak. Lydia drew the picture *before* the poem. I would have died without Lydia back then, not the other way around.

I need to see this drawing again, dammit. Why didn't Dr

Giles offer to show it to me? Did she think I was a liar? That I knew something I wasn't telling? As always, as soon as I left a therapist's office, the doubts wriggled out like slimy worms.

I miss you. That's what Lydia wrote on the flowers delivered to my home after all those years of silence. Unless she wasn't the one who sent them. What if they *are* from my monster? What if my silence killed her? What if, because I *didn't* warn her, he carried out the poetic threat so coyly buried by my tree house? *If you tell, I will make Lydia a Susan, too.* What if my denial and stupidity sacrificed both Terrell and her?

Terrell. I think about him all the time now. I wonder if he hates me, if his arms are thick from push-ups on concrete, if he has already thought about his last meal, just in case. Then I remember, he can't ask for a last meal. One of the guys who chained James Byrd Jr. to a pickup and dragged him to death ruined that for everybody. He requested two chicken-fried steaks, a pound of barbecue, a triple-patty bacon cheeseburger, a meat-lover's pizza, an omelet, a bowl of okra, a pint of Blue Bell, peanut-butter fudge with crushed peanuts, and three root beers. It was delivered before his execution. And then he didn't eat it. Texas said, no more.

I can rattle off this menu ordered by a racist freak, but can't remember the day my world blew apart. I can't remember a single thing that will save Terrell.

I glance out to my studio window, glinting at the top of the two-story garage in the corner of the back yard. I should go up there. Shut the blinds. Pull out my pencils and paints, and draw the curtain. Begin my homework.

The garage was renovated from crumbling disaster two years ago. Effie gave the plan her historical stamp of approval.

Blue window boxes and straggly red geraniums for her, Internet and a security system connected to the house for me.

Cheerful. Safe.

The bottom level, which once housed the previous owner's blue 1954 Dodge, is jammed with my table saw and biscuit joiner, router and drills, nail gun and orbital sander, vacuum press and welder. The tools that curve cabinet doors like sand dunes and solder master staircases into a dizzy spiral. Machines that make my muscles ache and reassure me that I can take on a man, or a monster.

The top level was designed just for me. My space. For the quieter arts. It seemed so important – a real home for my drawing table, easels, paints, paintbrushes, and sewing machines. I splurged on a Pottery Barn couch and a Breville tea maker and a Pella picture window so that I could spy into the upper floors of our live oak.

The week after the nail pounding stopped, as I sat and sipped tea bathed in the studio's white, clean, new-smell glory, I realized that I didn't want *my* space. I didn't want isolation, or to miss Charlie's burst through the door after school. So I stuck with the living room. The studio turned into the place my little brother, Bobby, hangs out to write when he visits from his home in Los Angeles twice a year and where Charlie goes on the occasion when every word out of my mouth sets her nerves on fire. *I don't know why, Mom. It's not what you're saying. It's just that you're talking.*

This is the reason that the living room is piled with brocade fabric and designer dress patterns and bead carousels that mingle with Charlie's flip-flops and textbooks and misplaced earrings and itsy-bitsy 'seahorse' rubber bands for braces. Why my daughter and I have an unspoken agreement not to speak about the state of the living room, unless it involves ants and crumbs. We clean it together every other Sunday night. It's a happy place, where we create and argue and refine our love.

The studio is crowded. My ghosts moved in right away, when I did, after the last stroke of linen white on the walls. The Susans feel free to talk as loudly as they want, sometimes arguing like silly girls at a sleepover.

I should climb the steps. Greet them with civility.

Draw the curtain. Find out whether it swings from a window in the mansion in my head where the Susans sleep. *Let them help.*

But I can't. Not yet. I have to dig.

I'm staring into a gaping hole again. This time, a swimming pool, empty except for a chocolate slurry of leaves and rainwater.

Feeling ridiculous. Disappointed. And cold. I pull up the hood of Charlie's Army sweatshirt. It's 5:27. I haven't stood in this place since Charlie and I lived here when she was two. Charlie has already texted the word *hungry* while I was driving the wrong direction on I-30 with a red pickup on my tail, and twenty minutes after that, *home,* and five minutes after that, *cool tutu,* and one minute after that *um?????*

I tried calling back, but no answer. Now the phone in my pocket is buzzing. The sun is dropping lower every second, a big orange ball going somewhere else to play. The apartment windows wink fire with the fading light, so I can't see in. I hope no one is staring down at the hooded figure in the shadows armed with a shovel.

'Why aren't you at Anna's?' I blurt into the phone, instead

of *hello*. 'You are supposed to be at Anna's.' As if that would make it so.

'Her mom got sick,' Charlie says. 'Her dad picked us up. I told him it was OK to bring me home. Where are you? Why didn't you answer my texts?'

'I just tried to call you. I was driving. I got lost. Now I'm on . . . a job. In Dallas. Did you lock the doors?'

'Mom. Food.'

'Order a pizza from Sweet Mama's. There's money in the envelope under the phone. Ask if Paul can deliver it. And look through the peephole before you answer to make sure it's him. And lock the door when he leaves and punch in the code.'

'What's the number?'

'Charlie. You know the security code.'

'Not *that* number. The number for Sweet Mama's.'

This from the girl who last night Googled that Simon Cowell was the young assistant who polished Jack Nicholson's axe in *The Shining*.

'Charlie, really? I'll be on my way home soon. I'm late because . . . I thought I'd remember the way.'

'Why are you whispering?'

'Pizza, Charlie. Peephole. Don't forget.' But Charlie has already hung up.

She'll be fine. Was that me, or a Susan? Which of us would know better?

'Hey.' A man with a weed eater is quickly approaching from the other side of the house. *Busted*. I lean the shovel against a tree, too late. Even at this distance, something about the way he carries himself stirs a memory.

'This is private property!' he shouts. 'What do you think

you're doing here with that shovel at dinnertime?' A drawl mixed with a threat and a reprimand about proper meal-time etiquette. A perfect Texas cocktail.

Because I'm scared of the dark. Because I think there are plenty of people with itchy fingers in this neighborhood who have a gun tucked in a drawer. I know I did.

'I used to live here,' I say.

'The shovel? What's that for?'

I've suddenly figured out who he is, and I'm a little astonished. The handyman. The very same one who worked here more than a decade ago, who swore every day he was quitting. As I recall, he was a distant cousin of the grouchy woman who owned the place, a converted Victorian in East Dallas advertised as *a four-plex with character*. Translated: ornate crown molding that dropped white crumbs in my hair like dandruff, windows requiring Hercules to open them, and hot showers lasting two and a half minutes if I was lucky enough to beat the exercise freak on the first floor who woke up at 5 A.M.

The windows were why I took the place. No one crawling up and in. That, and the listing's promise of *Girls Only*.

'When did the owner take out the parking spaces and dig this swimming pool?' I ask. 'Marvin? Is it Marvin?'

'You remember old Marvin, do ya? Most of the girls do. Pool went in about three years ago. It used to be a gravel lot with numbered signs where everybody had a spot. But then, you'd know that. Now everybody complains they have to fight it out in the street. And Gertie has stopped filling the pool. Says it's not worth the money and that Marvin don't keep the leaves out. Old Marvin's doing the best he can. When did you say you lived here?'

'Ten years ago. Or so.' Vague. I'd forgotten his habit of addressing himself in the third person. It partly explains why he never found another job.

'Ah, the good old days, when these whiney college brats didn't call Marvin at 2 A.M. about how their Apples ain't connectin' to the Universe.'

I shove the laugh back down in my throat and don't correct him. I pull the hood off so I can see better, and instantly realize the mistake. I toss my hair, trying to cover the side of my face with the scar. The toss is enough for Marvin to take renewed interest in me even though I'm in roomy black sweats and running shoes and not wearing a stitch of makeup. It must have been a slow day for him at the Girls Only House, which is the real reason I'm guessing he stays.

'I'm curious,' I say hesitantly. 'Did they find anything when they dug up the pool?'

'Ya mean like a dead body? Whoa, you should see your face. No bodies, sweetheart. Are you missing one?'

'No. No. Of course not.'

Marvin is shaking his head. 'You're just like those damn kids. Or maybe you're a scout for one of those ghost shows?'

'What kids?'

'The sorority that rents the apartment right up there on the left-hand corner every fall, thinking it is haunted. Use it to scare the shit out of their pledges. Drape skeletons dressed in see-through nighties out the window. Invite their rich frat boys and serve black-eyed-pea dip and trashcan punch, the stuff they vomit up on the front porch for me to clean up. Gertie started charging a premium to rent that apartment. But do you think she pays Marvin more? Nope. Marvin just has to suck it up and clean it up.'

'Why do they think . . . there are ghosts?' As soon as the question rolls off my tongue, I regret it. *You know the answer.*

'Because of the girl who lived there a long time ago. The one who got away from the Black-Eyed Susan killer. We didn't even know it was her until a year and a half after she moved in. She was nice enough. Worked at a little design firm downtown. She complained a few times that we wouldn't let her gate up the staircase for her little girl. Gertie said it would take away the old house charm.'

Suddenly, his face freezes.

'Jesus, you're that girl, ain't ya? You're the Susan that lived up there.'

'My name isn't Susan.'

'Shoulda known soon as I saw your red hair. Crap, no one is gonna believe this. Can Marvin take a picture? You're for real, right? Not a ghost?' For a second, he seems to be truly considering this.

Before I can think, the phone is out of his pocket, the button pressed. I am recorded, with flash, for all time, into infinity, about to be passed from phone to Facebook to Twitter to Instagram – Marvin's Universe and beyond.

'Great,' he says to himself, peering at his phone. 'Got the shovel in the background.'

If my monster didn't know already, he will soon.

I am on the hunt.

A light blares from every window as I swing into our driveway around 7. Not a sign that Charlie is scared, I remind myself, just her habit of flipping lights on as she goes and never bothering to turn them off.

I spoke with Charlie about half an hour ago. A pizza with Canadian bacon and black olives had, indeed, been delivered, eaten, and deemed 'solid.' Everything seemed so normal on the other end of the line. Far, far removed from my disturbing encounter with Marvin. So much so that I had stopped at Tom Thumb to fill Charlie's texted list of special requests for her lunch: *yelo cheez, BF (nt honey) ham, Mrs B's white brd, grapes, hummus, pretz, mini Os.*

'I'm home,' I yell, kicking the door closed behind me. The security system is switched on. Check. Charlie had even cleaned up the pizza box from the coffee table in front of the TV, where I assumed she'd been sneaking in a Netflix rerun of something on my waffle-y *I don't really like you to watch shows like that* list.

But no Charlie. No backpack. The TV, warm. I pass through the living room and set the bag of groceries on the counter with my keys.

'Charlie?' Probably in her room, living inside Bose headphones while reluctantly tramping around nineteenth-century England with Jane Austen.

I knock, because Aunt Hilda never did. No answer. I crack her door. Shove it wide open. Bed unmade. *Pride and Prejudice* operating as a coaster for a water bottle. Clothes strewn everywhere. Her underwear drawer dumped on the bed. A streak of mud across the floor.

Pretty much as she left it this morning. But no Charlie.

The rest of the house sweep takes about a minute, plenty of time for sickening waves of panic to roll in. I thrust open the sliding glass doors to the back yard, yelling her name. She's not in the hammock along the back fence line, jerry-rigged from the thick trunk of the live oak to an ancient horse post that Effie had saved from a carpenter's axe. The studio windows gleam black above me; the garage doors are shut tight.

My phone. I need my phone.

I rush back inside and fumble for it in my purse. Clumsily punch in the new security code that I had to choose after the software update yesterday. Locked out. *Shit, shit, shit.* Try the four numbers one more time, slowly. Promise myself that I will never, ever update my phone again. Hit the icon.

And there it is, my one-word, God-sent reprieve.

@ Effie's

In seconds, I am banging wildly on Effie's door. It seems to take forever for her to answer it. She's cloaked in a long white nightgown with lace that strangles her neck. Gray hair, sprung from its usual braided bun, rains down to her waist. I'd peg her as a runaway from Pemberley if she were clutching a candle instead of the largest laminated periodic table I've ever seen.

'What in heaven's name is wrong?' Effie asks.

Be patient, be patient, be patient.

'Is Charlie here?' Breathless.

'Of course she is.' Effie steps aside, and there's my girl, the most beautiful sight in the world, cross-legged on the floor by the coffee table, scribbling in a notebook. I pick up every detail: hair fanned out around her face like red turkey feathers, swept up by a chip clip; the volleyball shorts she's still wearing even though it's 50 degrees outside; the fuzzy pink pig slippers; the chipped gold glitter fingernail polish. Her lips are moving, exaggerated, like a silent film star. *Save me.*

'I was sitting a bit on the front porch swing and I saw a man roaming around our yards,' Effie begins.

Pizza guy, Charlie is mouthing now. Her eyes are rolling and Effie's still chattering while all my brain can do is pound out, *He doesn't have her.*

'. . . I thought about how your car was gone but the lights in the house were on. Got me concerned. I called and Charlie answered and I went right over and got her. I was just helping her with a little early chemistry prep for next year.'

Charlie points to a plate on the coffee table that holds either very burnt or dark chocolate cookies, arranged in a smiley-face pattern. The smiley face is Charlie's work, I'm sure. She picks up two of the cookies and holds them over her face like eyes. Definitely burnt.

Charlie's antics, Effie's sincerity, the inedible cookies. Charlie and I will talk later about breaking one of my hard and fast rules. An @ symbol and a single digital word do not yet replace an old-fashioned, handwritten note and a piece of Scotch tape. Which means I might as well have just stepped out of Pemberley myself.

'That's very considerate of you, Effie,' I say.

'Charlie thinks it was the pizza deliveryman,' Effie says, 'but I thought he had a stealthy air about him. We both know you can't be too careful.'

My mind is basking in a warm cocoon of relief when this registers. Is Effie hinting at what we never talk about? Is she, too, on high alert for my monster?

'You know who I think it was?' Effie asks.

I shake my head, numbly pondering all the things she might say that I don't want Charlie to hear.

'I think,' she says, 'it was the digger snatcher.'

Tessie, 1995

I know a few things about the doctor's daughter now. Her name is Rebecca. She was sixteen. Not because he told me. Because Lydia is a digger.

She disappeared the same year that a madman robbed the world of John Lennon and Alfred Hitchcock died less violently than he deserved. Lydia and I found out that much as we carefully spun the microfiche of a local newspaper until it landed on a two-year-old profile of my doctor, produced right after he won a prestigious international award for research into normal people and paranoia.

Who the hell is normal, Lydia had muttered. Then she spun a few pages and read Hitchcock's obit aloud to me. She was especially riveted by the revelation that he tortured his own daughter during the filming of one of Lydia's favorite movies, *Strangers on a Train.* He stuck her on a Ferris wheel, halted her car at the top, turned off all the lights on the set, and abandoned her all alone in the dark. By the time some crew person brought her down, she was hysterical. Lydia clicked a button on the machine and copied both the doctor's interview and the Hitchcock obit, which she deemed worthy of adding to the personal files of weirdness she kept in the box under her bed.

In fact, on the bus ride home from the library, she was more distracted by the fate of Hitchcock's daughter than by how little she'd learned about Rebecca. *He was a freaking sadist,* she announced, while everyone seated near us stared at my little moon scar.

Rebecca was a single paragraph in the feature story summing up my doctor's life, which makes me unbelievably sad. My guess? He told the reporter that the subject of his daughter's disappearance was off the table.

He certainly made it clear it was off the table for us at our last session. A nice long silence followed my question about Rebecca. So I announced I liked the print of *The Reaper* hanging over his desk. 'My grandfather went through a Winslow Homer wheat period,' I said. And, oh yeah, I'm not blind anymore.

I couldn't tell if he was faking his surprise. The doctor appeared genuinely thrilled about what he declared a 'major, major breakthrough.' He had fiddled around with a silly old-fashioned eye test that involved a pencil and my nose. Asked me to close my eyes and describe his face in the greatest detail possible.

He reassured me again that even though he wouldn't discuss it with me, his daughter had absolutely nothing to do with the Black-Eyed Susan case. I had never asked that, but even if she does, I'm not at all sure at this point I want to know.

It's hard not to be a little happy. I've gained three pounds in five days. My dad and brother squeezed me so hard in a three-way hug when they found out I could see again that I thought my heart would burst in my chest. Aunt Hilda hustled over a three-layer German chocolate cake, gooey with her famous coconut pecan frosting, and I'm pretty sure it was the best thing I've ever eaten.

Last night, a brand-new hardback copy of *The Horse*

Whisperer appeared on my bedside table, in a house where it is unheard of not to wait until a book comes out in paper-back.

The trial is fifty-two days away. That means twelve more sessions or so, if I count a couple extra to wrap things up after the trial. The end is near. I really don't want to drag distractions, like Rebecca, into things. It was kind of a mean thing for me to bring up.

Unfortunately, Rebecca is now Lydia's latest obsession, and she's on a mission to hunt down more about her in other newspapers. Whatever she finds, I tell her, will be meaningless. *Rebecca was pretty, with a lot of friends. She was such a nice girl* and *It was such a nice family* and blah, blah, blah. I don't want to sound cold, but there it is.

I know, because I've read every possible exaggeration about my life since I became a Black-Eyed Susan. My mother died under 'suspicious' circumstances and my grandfather built a creepy house and I am practically perfect. The truth? My mother was struck by a rare stroke, my grandmother was the crazier one, and I am not and never will be a heroine out of a fairy tale. Even though they were all victims first, too. Snow White poisoned. Cinderella enslaved. Rapunzel locked up. Tessie, dumped with bones.

Some monster's twisted fantasy.

Bet the doctor would like me to talk about that, I think, as he settles into his chair.

He smiles. 'Fire away, Tessie.'

Last week, he had agreed to let me lead in this session. He also promised he wouldn't tell my dad I'd faked blindness for a little bit. A promise kept so far. I wondered if he bargained with all of his patients. If this was *appropriate.*

It doesn't matter. Today I am prepared to offer him something real.

'I'm afraid every time the lights dim . . . that I am going blind again,' I say. 'Like when my family went to Olive Garden and some waitress turned the lights down for dinner mood or whatever. Or when my brother shut the living room blinds behind me so he could see the TV better.'

'When this happens, instead of thinking you are going blind again, why don't you just tell yourself emphatically that you aren't?'

'Seriously?' Ay yi yi. My dad was paying for this?

'Because you *want* to see, Tessie. It's not like a little goblin is sitting inside your head manning a light switch. You are in control. Statistically, the chances of this ever happening again are almost nil.'

OK, kind of useful. At least encouraging. Even though chances of this happening to me were almost nil to begin with.

'What else is going on in there?' He taps his skull with a finger.

'I'm worried . . . about O. J. Simpson.'

'What exactly are you worried about?'

'That he might fool the jury and get off.' I don't tell him that Lydia had soaked one of her own red leather gloves in V8 juice, dried it in the sun, and demonstrated how she could spread her hand wide and get the same effect as O.J.

The doctor crosses one long leg over the other. He's much more of a conservative dresser than I'd imagined. Starched white shirt, black dress pants with a stand-up crease, loosened blue tie with tiny red diamonds, black shoes grinning with polish. No wedding ring.

'I think the chances of that happening are also practically zero,' he says. 'You are simply worried that your own attacker will be set free. I'd advise you not to watch any of the O.J. coverage and ratchet things up in your head.'

Aunt Hilda offered this same advice for free, and tempered it by handing me a plate of fried okra fresh out of her skillet while snapping off my TV.

'Tessie, today is supposed to be all your show, but we need to divert for a second. The prosecutor called right before you arrived. He wants to meet one-on-one with you before the trial. I could ask to sit in on the interviews if you'd feel more comfortable. He's thinking about conducting the first interview next Tuesday. We can even do it in our regular session if you like.'

He uncrosses his leg and leans toward me. My stomach wads itself into a hard ball, a roly-poly beetle protecting itself.

'Getting your sight back is huge. Meeting the prosecutor and getting over your fear of the trial is a logical next step. It might even help . . . jog your memory. Think of your brain as a sieve or a colander, with only the tiniest, safest bits getting through at first.'

I'm barely listening to his psycho mumbo-jumbo about kitchen gadgets.

Seven days away.

'I hope you don't mind that I told him the good news,' he says.

'Of course not,' I lie.

I'm thinking about the little bag, packed and ready for months, wedged into the far back corner of my closet.

Wondering if it's too late to run.

Tessa, present day

Charlie and I are playing an old game on the front porch swing. Rain drills steadily on the roof.

We're pretending to be tiny dolls rocking to and fro. A little girl is pushing our swing with her finger. She's locked up her big yellow cat, so he can't paw at us. She's baking a tiny plastic cake for us in the oven, and she's made all the beds and arranged all the tiny dishes in the cabinet. She's used a toothbrush to sweep the carpet. There are no monsters in the closet, because there are no closets.

For just this moment, everything is perfect. Nothing can get to us. We are in the dollhouse.

My daughter's head is warm in my lap. She lies sideways on the front porch swing with me, her knees bent because she isn't three years old anymore with room to spare. I've covered her bare legs with my jacket for when the wind shifts and spits at us between the brick columns.

She wiggles into a more comfortable position and turns her face up to me. Her violet eyes are rimmed with black eyeliner, which makes them even bigger and lovelier, but so much more cynical. Two silver studs are punched in each ear, one slightly smaller than the other.

The eye makeup can be washed off; the extra holes will close up. I try not to get too worked up about these things. She'd just point out the tattoo on my right hip, a butterfly among the scars.

When Charlie's braces come off in three months, that's when I'll worry. 'Mom, you seemed a little crazy last night at Miss Effie's. Like, I know you were worried, but still. I'd never seen you like that. Is it because you're afraid you can't stop that guy from getting executed?'

'Partly.' I fiddle with a lock of her hair, and she allows it. 'Charlie, we've never talked much about what happened to me.'

'You never want to.' A statement, not a reproach.

'I've just never wanted you to be a part of it.' Never wanted her innocence disturbed with more than the straight facts, and a sanitized version of those.

'So you still think about . . . those girls?' Tentative. 'I dreamed about one of them once. Merry. She had a cool name. Someone taped a *People* magazine story to my bike a while back. It was about her mom. She said she wants a front row seat to Terrell Goodwin's execution. Have you decided for sure he didn't do it?'

I will myself to stay put instead of leaping up, to keep my foot pushing firmly and steadily against the concrete floor. A stranger left Charlie a gift. A Susan crept from my head into hers. Worse, she is just telling me about this *now*. I don't want to think that Charlie carries these secrets around because she is afraid to bring them up, and yet I know that is exactly why.

'Yes,' I say. 'Of course I think about those girls. About how they died, and who hurts for them. Especially right now. The forensic scientist I told you about has extracted DNA from the girls' bones. It's a long shot, and involves a lot of luck, but if their families are still looking, maybe we can find out who they are.'

'You would still be looking for me. You would never give up.'

I blink back tears. 'Never, *never*. Honey, do you mind telling me what your dream was about? The one with Su – Merry?'

'We took a walk on this island. She never said anything. It was nice. Not scary.'

Thank you, Merry.

'So you're sure Terrell's innocent?' she asks again.

'Yes, I'm pretty sure. The physical evidence isn't there.' I leave out the seventeen-year trail of black-eyed Susans. The voices in my head, amplifying my doubts.

'Whoever the real killer is, he's not coming back, Mom.' She says it earnestly. 'He was smart enough not to get caught the first time. He isn't going to risk it. And if he was *going* to do anything, it would have happened years ago. Maybe he's in prison for another crime. I've heard that happens all the time.'

My daughter's clearly given this a lot of thought. How could I be so stupid to think her teen-age brain wasn't as wired as Lydia's and mine? I don't tell her one of Jo's shocking statistics – that of 300 active serial killers roaming the United States, most of them will never be caught.

'Listen to me, Charlie. More than anything, I want to give you a normal life. I don't want you to live in fear, but I need you to be very careful right now, until we know what's happening to . . . Terrell. My job is to protect you, and you need to give in and let me for a while.'

Charlie pushes herself up. 'We're, like, more normal than half the people I know. Melissa Childers's mom drove the cheerleaders around one Saturday night and they stuck raw chicken inside mailboxes of these girls they don't like. Like, her mom's mug shot is on Facebook. And Anna's mom didn't get sick the other night when she was supposed to pick us up. She was drunk. Anna says she puts vodka in that Big Gulp Diet Coke in her car cup holder. Kids know things, Mom. You can't hide stuff.' A rare, unfettered stream of information.

'I'm not going to ride with Anna's mom anymore,' Charlie announces.

The swing. Hypnotic. *Keep talking.*

Her phone starts to blare a song I don't recognize. Instantly, Charlie stretches for it.

'Can I spend the night with Marley?'

She's already edging off the swing, away from me.

'I love this place. Nothing like Saturday night at the Flying Fish.' Jo is lifting a giant frosty schooner of beer to her lips. She's sporting old Levi's and a red Oklahoma Sooners T-shirt and the gold DNA charm at her neck that goes with everything.

Bill has just returned from the counter with a basket of fried oysters and hush puppies for us to share. He's loose, in old jeans, more relaxed than I've ever seen him. His shirt is untucked. He needs a haircut. He scoots across a giant schooner of St Pauli Girl for me. His fingers linger longer than they need to, which I decide to chalk up to the beer. This schooner is going to make my drive home a little tricky.

'One size fits all.' He grins and slips in beside Jo on the opposite side of the booth, right below a crowded bulletin board with a photograph of a guy brandishing a fish on steroids.

'Is that for real?' I point at the sea monster, about as long as Charlie.

'It's the Liar's Wall.' Bill pops a hush puppy in his mouth without turning around. 'I've been pushing for one of those in the DA's office for years.'

'That's really not fair,' Jo says, frowning. 'For example, for at least ten years, Dallas County has been a machine at exonerating more people through DNA than just about anyone else.' An echo of Charlie.

'Ah, Jo, you're always getting mired in optimism,' Bill says. 'If I get Terrell a new hearing, then we'll talk.'

The restaurant's picnic tables and booths are loud and packed. A line snakes by us on the way to the counter, a cowboy- and baseball-hat crowd with a Texas fetish for crispy crusts on everything. The state's collective orgasm occurs at the state fair, where even Nutella, Twinkies, and butter get dunked in the fryers.

Almost as soon as Charlie bounced out the door for her sleepover, Bill had texted, asking if I'd join the two of them here for a beer. He didn't say why.

So I hesitated, but not for long. It was either that or a sleepover with the Susans and a bottle of merlot while the thunder rumbled and lightning transformed every tree and bush into a human silhouette. I yanked my rainy day frizz into a ponytail, threw on an old jean jacket, and shot over here in my Jeep, windshield wipers slashing all the way.

Bill and Jo were at least one beer in and engaged in a heated exchange about the Sooners' quarterback when I showed up looking like I'd been making out under a waterfall. Jo tossed me the roll of paper towels on the table to dry my head and wipe off a mascara smudge she pointed out under my left eye. The conversation drifted not toward Terrell but to one of Jo's new cases, the bones of a three- or four-year-old girl that had been discovered in a field in Ohio, and then to me.

'What is it, exactly, that you do for a living?' Bill asks.

'I'm not sure there's a name for it. I'm a . . . problem solver, I guess. People imagine something they've never seen before, and I make it. It can be little, like designing a wedding crown embedded with jewels from a grandmother's ring, or big, like a floating staircase I built for a hotel in Santa Fe. *Sunday Morning* did a piece on the staircase in a series on female craftswomen, which has really helped. The host was classy enough not to mention the Black-Eyed Susan . . . thing. I can pick and choose now. Charge more.'

'Is that your favorite thing you've built so far? The staircase?'

'No. Hands-down my favorite thing is the pumpkin catapult for Charlie's Field Day competition last year. We beat the school's record by sixty feet.' I take another drag on my beer. 'My father had a minor in physics and taught me a few things.' I should have eaten more than two crackers with pimiento cheese for lunch. Bill is looking more boyish than usual in a soft gray T-shirt that clings to taut muscle. I wonder whether he and Swedish Girl have hit it off officially yet.

I decide to shift the spotlight off of me, where it always feels too hot and too bright. I debate whether to ask if they're getting me drunk to deliver bad news. My eyes linger on Jo. She could be anybody tonight – a housekeeper, a bank teller, a first-grade teacher. Her daily relationship with horror is well hidden under that Sooners T-shirt and clear blue eyes that indicate she sleeps pretty well. No one would ever pick her out as the scientist who stood in the middle of hell, running mathematical equations in her head, while the Twin Towers smoked.

'Jo, how do you keep doing what you do . . . day after day?' I ask. 'Not letting it affect you.'

She sets down her beer. 'My gift from God is that I can look at the grotesque and not be grossed out by it. The finger. The guts. But I'm not going to tell you that I don't go home and think about the semen on the Little Mermaid nightgown. Or the bullet in the jaw of the POW that didn't kill the guy. How he must have been tortured. I wonder things like, "Did this young mother live through the airplane crash or did she die right away?" I think about who these people are. When I stop doing that, it's the day I should quit this job.'

The last part sounded a little drunk and also like the most sincere thing I'd ever heard.

'This is the only thing I'm good at,' she says. 'I'm a forensic scientist. It's all I know.'

'You are just too damn nice.' Bill clinks her mug with his. 'I spend most days wanting to punch someone in the face.'

She grins and toasts the air. 'I'm from Oklahoma. We're the nicest people in the world. And we also love to punch people in the face. And, now and then, I have a day like today.'

'If you hadn't noticed, Jo and I are celebrating,' Bill tells me. 'We just wanted to give you a chance to catch up first.'

'And?' I ask. Jo gives him a nod, the OK sign.

'We got a match on one of the DNA samples.'

His words aren't registering. He can't be talking about the Susans. Not this soon.

'We've made an ID on one of the Black-Eyed Susans through the national missing persons database,' Jo confirms matter-of-factly. 'One of the femur extractions.'

'Are you OK, Tessie?' Bill's face is twisted in concern. I don't know if he's realized what he's done. Called me Tessie. This time his hand covers mine and doesn't let go. It stirs yet another feeling I'm not prepared for at the moment. I snatch my fingers away and tuck a wet strand of hair behind my ear.

'I'm . . . fine. Sorry. It's just a shock. After all this time. After everything you said about statistics, I just didn't expect it. Who . . . is she?' *I need to hear her name.*

'Hannah,' Jo says. 'Hannah Stein. Twenty years old. She disappeared from her job as a waitress in Georgetown twenty-five years ago. Her younger brother's a Houston cop now. We got lucky. He insisted that his family enter DNA into the CODIS database a few months ago after he took a required course on missing persons investigations. Hannah's mito-DNA is a match to Rachel and Sharon Stein. Her mom and her sister. Remember, mitochondrial DNA is one hundred percent from the maternal side.'

'If I can prove Terrell was nowhere near Georgetown the day she disappeared . . . well, it will help.' Bill's voice carries a triumphant note.

'There's one thing.' Jo's eyes rest on me carefully. 'The mother wants you to be there.'

'Be where?' This Susan is no longer a pile of teeth and bones and a disembodied voice in my head. Her name is Hannah. She's a shadow darting out into the lightning, about to let me see her face.

'The mother is driving in from Austin with her son so

we can formally give the family the ID. She specifically asked to meet you. She always suspected a cousin of theirs had something to do with Hannah's disappearance. She . . . we . . . the cops . . . want to know if you recognize him.'

'The thing is,' Bill says. 'He's dead.'

Tessie, 1995

Two of them show up in the doctor's office. A man and a woman.

The man is the prosecutor. Mr Vega. Short, compact, around forty. Firm handshake, direct eye contact. Lots of Italian machismo. He reminds me of the football coach who hurled half our school into the gym during an impromptu tornado last year. He walks down the hall, and you know it.

The woman could pass for a high school senior. She seems like she'd be way more at home in something less uptight than whatever Ann Taylor thing she has on. I'm on the couch, and she's sitting where the doctor usually does, tapping her left heel, nervous, like maybe I'm her first big case. She says she's here as a child advocacy therapist, but I'm pretty sure she is mostly a chaperone to make sure I don't accuse the prosecutor of anything creepy.

I'm feeling remarkably who-cares about all of it, because I took two Benadryl an hour ago. This is generally not my thing, but Lydia suggested it when she heard I was meeting the prosecutor for the first time. She pokes down a couple when her parents light off into one of their three-day screaming matches. Once more, Lydia has made the right call. The air is tense and thick, but I'm drifting through it in a cushy bubble.

The doctor isn't happy. First, I haven't begged him to stay.

It just doesn't seem to matter much at the moment and would require some energy on my part to make happen. Mr Vega most definitely wants him out of the room. I am impressed that he has so quickly manipulated the doctor all the way to the doorway of his own office, because the doctor's no slouch in the manipulator department himself.

They are talking in low, urgent tones that carry. The woman, Benita, and I can overhear every word. It's awkward. I can tell she isn't sure what to do, because she's already told me we don't have to talk. I feel sorry for her.

'I like your hair,' I say, because I do. It's black with a few shiny red streaks. I wonder if she does it herself.

'I like your boots,' she says.

It's not like we still aren't listening to every word they're saying.

'Don't ask her any questions that begin with why,' the doctor is instructing the lawyer.

'Just give us about thirty minutes, sir. You have nothing to worry about.' This is the kind of 'sir' that Mr Vega probably also uses with judges and hostile witnesses. I've seen enough of Christopher Darden and Johnnie Cochran at this point.

I feel kind of sorry for the doctor now, too, being tossed out of his own space.

The Benadryl is making me so freaking *nice*.

While this tussle is going on at the door, I decide to give Benita her first test. She's already announced that she's here just for me and to ask her anything. Or ask her nothing. It's entirely up to me. Of course, I've heard this so many times at this point I could vomit. It must be, like, Chapter One in the dysfunctional witness/victim textbook.

'Why is there a problem with asking me questions with the word *why*?' I ask her.

She glances at the prosecutor, who isn't paying attention to us at all. I'm sure she's worried about delivering inside information to a teen-age subject. Probably not addressed in the textbook at all.

'Because it implies that you are to blame,' she answers. 'You know, like "Why did you do such and such?" Or "Why do you think this happened to you?" Mr Vega would not ask you a why question. You are not to blame for anything.'

This interests me. I try to remember if the doctor has ever asked me a why question and decide he hasn't. It never occurred to me that there is doctoring going on by omission, which is bothersome, and a whole new thing to worry about.

The door shuts with a crisp click, and the doctor is on the other side of it. The prosecutor rolls over the doctor's desk chair, facing me intently.

'OK, Tessie. Sorry about that. I am not at all interested in discussing the case today, so you can relax if that's on your mind. We probably won't discuss it next time, either.' He nods at Benita. 'Neither of us believes that it's a good idea to ask you questions about something this traumatic and deeply personal when *we* have no relationship whatso ever with you yet. So first, we'll get to know each other. I also want to assure you that I am completely prepared to go into court with your memory exactly as it is.'

This is not the impression I have from the doctor at all. He's a seesaw, for sure, but always subtly pushing. Sometimes I think he is purposely trying to confuse me.

Now I have to wonder who is telling the truth. It makes

my head hurt. I decide to turn the tables and ask Mr Vega a question. He's clearly a control freak, too.

The Benadryl has set me free. I just don't *care.*

'Why,' I ask, 'are you so sure this man is guilty?'

Tessa, present day

I'm staring at the stupid plastic heart again, half-expecting it to start beating.

It's just Jo and me. I'm the first to arrive even though it took two frantic hours to decide the appropriate outfit to wear to meet Hannah's grieving mother, who probably hopes part of her dead daughter is now living inside me. Of course, it turns out that she *is* living in me, but I don't want to tell her that. It also turns out that the proper outfit for this event is a crocheted sweater, brown leather skirt, boots, and my mother's dangling pearls, which I have never hooked around my neck before today.

'The heart is cool, huh?' Jo pulls it off the shelf, snaps open the box, and hands it to me like it is a rubber dog toy. It *feels* like a rubber dog toy. My instinct to take it was automatic, as is the one to fling it across the room. I hand it back gingerly.

'Is it real?'

'Yes. Preserved through plastination. I did it myself.'

So I wasn't wrong about that part. Still, I can't believe that Jo, my hero, my good guy, is being so cavalier.

'Want to hear the story?' She glances at her watch. This is apparently her idea of a good way to distract me for the next ten minutes.

I shake my head, but her head is bent down while she's placing the heart back in its little customized stand. 'My grandmother and I were driving to my aunt's the night before Thanksgiving on a dark country road in Oklahoma. The deer darted out before I could slam on the brakes.'

A deer. OK. Feeling better.

'It was a nasty clunk,' she continues. 'My grandmother and I were both OK. But I wanted to make sure the deer was dead before we drove off. I wasn't going to leave him on the side of the road dying. But when I got to him, it was pretty clear the car did the job. Before I could decide what to do with the deer, three different pickups had pulled over to the side of the road. Three good ole boys passing by, and all three of them want to take the deer off my hands. I notice one of them has a sharp knife hanging off his belt.'

A distressing turn of events. The heart, back to being a question mark.

'I told the guy with the knife that I'd choose him to keep the deer if he let me borrow his knife. So he hands over the knife and I cut out the deer's heart.'

Grimm's fairy tale, Oklahoma-style. I'm nauseated and relieved at the same time.

'Did these truckers . . . have any idea you are a forensic scientist?' I interject. 'Did they know why you wanted the heart?' *Did you know why you wanted the heart?*

'I don't remember if it came up. They were focused on deer meat.'

'And you brought the heart . . . back to your grandmother in the car and put it . . . where?'

'A cooler.'

'And you brought it to . . . Thanksgiving?' I didn't ask if the pumpkin pie and Cool Whip had to make room.

'My aunt was pretty distressed when she ran out to welcome us and saw the bashed-in hood and blood all over me. We had a good laugh about it.'

There's something else niggling at me. 'How were you going to kill the deer if he was alive?'

'I didn't know. Maybe strangle him with my shoelace. No matter what, he was going to be dead when I left him.'

This is the Jo I know. And another one I didn't.

There's a knock on the door, and a student in a lab coat pokes her head in.

'Dr Jo, the cops are here. I put them in the conference room. The front desk is sending up the family now. Bill called to say that the Stein family has officially rejected his request to be there but wanted to be sure you and Tessa knew the mother is bringing a psychic along with them.'

None of this appears to ruffle Jo in the least. After all, left alone on a black Oklahoma road with her grandmother, three hulking strangers, and a knife, all she's thinking about is cutting out the heart of a deer.

'You ready?' Jo asks me.

Two detectives, one brother cop, one mother, one psychic – all waiting in grim silence around a conference table in a claustrophobic room whose only adornments are a stained coffeepot, a stack of Styrofoam cups, and a brown box of Kleenex that sits untouched in the middle of the table. The fresh-paint smell is so strong it stings my throat. Except for the brother, painfully young and official in full dress uniform, I couldn't in a million years distinguish who was who. No weepy red eyes. No crystal balls or flowing peasant shirts. No other uniforms or badges.

A man in Wrangler's and a tie immediately stands to

shake Jo's hand, as does a woman around fifty, with the most motherly, kind face in the room. Detective No. 1 and Detective No. 2.

I drop into a chair, wishing to be anywhere else on earth.

I turn my attention to the woman across from me, who immediately reaches over to cover my hands. Her hair is stiff with hair spray, and aggravated with bold blond streaks. Her eyes are the bluest I've ever seen. Rachel Stein, I assume. Except I can tell from a frown on Detective No. 2's face that she isn't.

'Ma'am, we've asked that you not participate in this meeting unless asked to. You are here strictly as a courtesy to the family.'

She draws her hands back reluctantly and winks, as if we are on the same team. I am repulsed. I want back whatever she thinks she has snatched out of me with her moist psychic paw.

The detective is droning out introductions while my eyes are now fixed, by process of elimination, on Hannah's mother – a pale, sharp-faced woman in her sixties. Jo had told me she was a middle school English teacher. She has that no-nonsense air about her. Except she brought a psychic.

For a split second, as our eyes meet, I glimpse horror, as if I'd just crawled out of her daughter's grave, like a mud monster.

The Steins have already met the coroner this morning to receive the official identification. Jo's job is strictly to help them believe it beyond a doubt. She is explaining the basics of mitochondrial DNA, the careful lab work, the mind-blowing genetic probabilities, within half a percent, that this is her daughter. It takes about ten minutes.

'Mrs Stein, your daughter has been handled with the greatest of care,' Jo says. 'I am terribly sorry this has happened to your family.'

'Thank you. I appreciate your time with us. I believe this is Hannah.' She directs her gaze to the police. It is obvious she is having a hard time looking at me.

'Tessa.' Detective No. 2, the woman, is speaking. I heard her name but I can't remember it. 'Can I call you Tessa?'

'Of course.' It comes out scratchy, and I clear my throat.

'Since there is some ... speculation ... in the media about whether the right man was convicted for their daughter's death, the Steins are curious if you can pick out a photo of a relative who took an unusual interest in their daughter. A suspect at the time. He is no longer alive, so you don't need to be afraid of any kind of retaliation. They are simply seeking peace of mind. No one wants the wrong man executed.' She says this without rancor, but I wonder what's really in her head.

I suddenly want Bill to be here. I want him to smother my hand with his again. 'That's fine.'

'You remind me of my daughter,' Mrs Stein says. 'Not the red hair, of course. But you give off that same ... free spirit.'

The detective slides two sheets of mug shots flat in front of me. The brother, up until now a silent, poker-straight soldier, leans in. It occurs to me that he wasn't even born when his sister disappeared. He was the recovery baby.

'He was an awful person,' Mrs Stein tells me brokenly. The twelve men on the table swim before me. Bald, white, middle-aged.

'I believe God sent that deer in front of his car.' The

brother's first words are a cold, hard slap. 'Put him in a coma so we could yank the plug. So I didn't have to shoot the bastard myself.'

I'm bewildered. Seriously? A deer? I want to meet Jo's eyes but don't. Too much deer metaphor for one day. Too much coincidence. Too much anger and certainty about God's wrath, when sometimes everything is just pointless.

'I'm sorry,' I say finally. 'I just don't know. There is so much I don't remember.' At the same time, I realize that I am remembering *something*. Fabric. A pattern. I know where I've seen it before, but I don't know what it means.

Impulsively, I reach my hands out to the psychic.

'Do you mind?' I ask the female detective.

'Not if you don't.' Bemused.

Mrs Stein is nodding animatedly, a doll brought to life. Her son is casting me a look of scathing disappointment.

I know I have to do this, whatever I believe. For Hannah. For her mom, eaten by grief. For her brother, who is probably a cop for all the wrong reasons. For her father, who is conspicuously absent.

'Something is coming back to me.' This is exquisitely true. 'There's a curtain. Can you help me see behind it?'

The psychic's sweaty grip tightens. Her nails bite into my flesh. I feel like I'm being consumed by a slobbery shark.

'Of course.' Her eyes glisten like shards of ice, the first thing that reassures people she is special and a window to the netherworld.

'It's a black man,' she says.

I remove my hands carefully and turn to Hannah's mother. Rachel Stein's eyes are not glistening. They are a boggy, open sinkhole, and I don't want to stumble.

'Mrs Stein, I lay in that grave with your daughter. Hannah will forever be a part of me, like we share the same DNA. Her monster is my monster. So please believe me when I say I know exactly what she would tell you right now. She would tell you she loves you. And she would tell you this woman will only hurt you. She's a liar.'

Tessie, 1995

'Are you ready to nail a killer, Tessie?'

Mr Vega is prowling, from desk to window to couch. 'Because you need to be mentally tough. The defense attorney is going to try to screw with your head. I want to make sure you're prepared for his little circus tricks.'

The doctor catches my eye and nods encouragement. He managed not to get kicked out of the room today. Mr Vega and Benita have met with me two more times in the last week, once at a bowling alley and another time at a Starbucks. Mr Vega introduced me to Mocha Frappuccinos and grilled jalapeños on hot dogs. He asked me *why* I like to run and *why* I like to draw and *why* I hated the Yankees so much. I went along with the 'getting to know me' sessions because it was a lot less painful than hanging out on the couch with the doctor. Like Dad said, they were all just doing their jobs.

Things turned for me sometime during disco bowling on lane 16, while the lights flashed psychedelic and pins thundered and Sister Sledge got down. Mr Vega and I were locked in a bowling duel. Benita was keeping score and yelling some crazy Spanish cheer from her high school days. Mr Vega wasn't cutting me any slack, even though I had to get my surgeon's permission to temporarily strip off the boot brace to play. The man about to prosecute my monster threw a spare/strike/spare to win the game, even when I faked a limp at the end.

So maybe he was manipulative and maybe he was genuine and maybe he was a little of both. Regardless, when I sat down on the couch today to officially prepare for the trial, I was in the game – no longer on Mr Vega's team simply because there was no way out. I wanted to win.

'I know every play this guy has.' Mr Vega is still roving the room, like he's already in court.

'He likes to get kids on the yes-no train,' he continues. 'Remember, the less narrative your answers, the less the jury can feel your pain. He will ask you a series of questions, where the answer is positively "yes." So you will answer, yes, yes, yes, yes, yes. Then he will slip in a question that is absolutely a "no" answer, but you'll be on the train, in the "yes" rhythm. You'll say "yes" and when you are immediately flustered and change to "no," he'll ask whether you are confused. And so it begins.'

I nod. This seems easy enough to handle.

'He will throw dates and numbers at you until your head spins. Whenever you are confused, ask him to explain himself again. Every. Single. Time. This makes him look more like a bully.' He steps toward me, and his face goes slack.

'If four times six equals twenty-four and twice that is forty-eight, what is fifty times that plus six?'

I stare at him, disbelieving. Begin to multiply.

He jams his finger in the air. 'Fast, Tessie. Answer.'

'I can't.'

'OK. That feeling right now, numb and slightly panicky? That's it. That's how it's going to feel. Times four.' He is on the prowl again. I'm glad that Oscar isn't here. He'd be going nuts. 'This will be the toughest part. He will insinuate you are hiding things. *Why is it that you can remember buying tampons on the day of the attack but not this man's face? Why did you have a relationship with a crazy homeless man? Why did you run alone every day?*

'I run too fast for most of my friends to keep up,' I protest. 'And Roosevelt isn't that crazy.'

'Uh-uh, Tessie. Don't just *react. Think* about the question. *I always ran in the daylight hours on two routes approved by my father. Roosevelt has been sitting on the same corner for ten years, and is good friends with everyone, including the local cops.* Matter-of-fact. Don't let him get to you. You did nothing wrong.'

'Will he really bring up the . . . tampons?'

'I would bet on it. It's another way to make you uncomfortable. A subtle move that the jury won't notice. The tampons are a fact of life for them. For you, a teen-age girl, they are intimate and embarrassing. Believe me, Dick has no boundaries even when it comes to child victims of sexual abuse.'

His eyes are laser-focused on me again.

'Why did you get suspended from two track meets last year?'

The doctor shifts positions. He wants to interfere. Mr Vega senses it and holds up his hand in his direction, a halt signal. He keeps his eyes trained on me.

Is this the Vega who is pretending, or the real one? Either way, this question really ticks me off. Anger always starts as a little tingle in the roots of my hair, and then spreads like spilled hot water.

'A girl on another track team pushed my friend Denise off a hurdle in a regional meet so she could win in the prelims. If you were watching, and you're not a hurdler, you wouldn't have noticed. But there are certain moves, and I know them.

So I walked over to her after the race and told her that I knew she cheated. She shoved me to the ground. When the track officials ran over, she told them I'd shoved her first. We were both suspended for two meets.'

I straighten up. Level my gaze at him, and just him. Let him know I am mad, but under control. 'It was totally worth it,' I say. 'Because everyone will be watching her now. She won't try it again.'

Nobody speaks. I wonder if they believe me. Everyone else who knows me did. Lydia even wrote an indignant letter to the UIL board. She signed it *Sincerely, Ms. Lydia Frances Bell.*

'Perfect,' Mr Vega says. 'Narrative. Calm. Perfect.' He takes a few steps and places his hand on my shoulder.

The hand on my shoulder – it feels good. Still, it is so hard to know whether I like this man, or whether I just like what he is giving back to me. Power. The thing that my monster snatched away and threw in the gutter at Walgreens.

Mr Vega removes his hand. Picks up his briefcase, on the floor next to Benita. 'A short session, but I think we're done for the day. Benita's going to show you the courtroom at some point. I recommend sitting in every seat. The jury's. The judge's – my personal favorite. I want to wait until closer to the trial to go over your own testimony. We'll see whether you and the doc get any further in that time.'

All of them rise, except for me. I stay planted on the couch. 'Twenty-four hundred and six.'

Mr Vega stops at the door.

'That's my girl,' he says. 'You'll always get to the right answer if you slow down and think about it.'

Tessa, present day

Of course, it's been banging me in the head, ever since I learned her name.

Rachel Stein, Hannah's mother, does not have a first name that begins with *S* or *U* or *N*. She does not fit neatly into the mnemonic device that I've put aside like a crossword puzzle I always planned to finish later. *S-U-N*. The letters that Merry provided while we chatted in the grave, to help me remember the names of all of the mothers and hunt them down.

Ever since the discovery of a third set of bones, I've been thinking that maybe my conversation with Merry wasn't a hallucination. There *were* the bones of three other girls in that grave, not two, just like Merry told me. That couldn't be a coincidence, right?

And yet. The black-and-white, driver's license, DNA certainty of Rachel Stein's name makes me wonder whether I was nuts back then, and just as nuts now. I actually had to restrain myself from peppering Mrs Stein with questions: *Is Rachel your nickname? Your middle name? Did you change your name?*

I couldn't mess with her head anymore – trade the psychic's crazy for my crazy. Hannah's mother drifted out of that hollow conference room as a more haggard spirit than when she entered. *Closure is a myth,* Jo told me afterward. *But there is value in knowing*. Mrs Stein's son had to carefully prop up his mother as they exited. She moved like she was a hundred years old.

Hannah's brother and I made an unspoken pact that he would drop-kick the psychic to her altered universe. She was fuming and tripping at their heels on the way out. As soon as he had heard the word *liar* come out of my mouth, his head popped up and he shot me the most grateful look I'd ever received. As for the psychic . . . well, if I'm not cursed already, I'm sure she finished the job. My scars tingled for an hour afterward.

My Very Energetic Mother Just Served Us Nine Pizzas.

Ever since I left that room, I can't get this string of words out of my head. I imagine Merry punching a button on a jukebox, over and over. Each punch a little firmer, more frustrated. *Remember.*

My boots clunk out a rhythm as I climb the staircase. One step. *My.* Two steps. *Very.* Three steps. *Energetic.* Four steps. *Mother.* At the top, I throw open the door to my studio. Warm, stale air rushes out. I shove the picture window wide open and drink in air that is like an ice-cold tequila shot. A brave blue jay stares me down from his perch on a branch, and I blink first.

I pick up a few pages off the dusty hardwood, remnants of one of Bobby's projects the last time he stayed for a weekend. My sweet, half-doomed little brother. Now he writes for movies that end in numerals and tries to heal himself with holotropic breath-work and a sexy production assistant with a nose ring. He left for college in California and basically never returned except for short visits and funerals, which is probably what I should have done. He even chopped his last name to Wright.

I draw hearts in the dust on my drawing table, until my finger is black. I pick a white tea from the selection in the cabinet and plug in the teakettle. Listen to its friendly hiss. Decide that the old honey in the cabinet smells a little like beer and watch two sugar cubes dissolve to sand in my mug instead. Merry gives the jukebox one last punch with her finger and disappears.

I have always loved this room. I just didn't want to share it with the Susans. Today it seems that I don't have to. I wipe off the drawing table with a paper towel and clip on a piece of paper with a sharp snap that scares the bird into an irritated flutter. I begin to loosely sketch the folds of fabric, a soft sound, like a rat under the floor. I'm in a hurry so I can get to the intricate, important work. A pattern had emerged in my head while I was staring at Mrs Stein's simple cotton blouse. At breasts that sagged with the weight of middle age.

Surprise. I am sketching flowers and it doesn't bother me. An hour floats by. Then another. There are so many, many petals, and a leafy vine that meanders, connecting them all, like a demented family tree. I fill a Dixie cup with water and open up my watercolor box. Blue, pink, and green.

These flowers are not black-eyed Susans.

And these folds of fabric are not a curtain. They were never a curtain.

I'm drawing my mother's apron. You can't see me, but I am underneath, hiding my face. I can feel the cloth tickle my nose and cheeks. It is dark under here, but enough light sifts through the thin cotton that I am not scared. The warm cushion of my mother's body is at my back.

I can't see what is on the other side.

It reminds me of being blind.

Dr Giles is holding my painting gingerly edge to edge because it isn't completely dry.

It's closing time. All the toys and books in the room are tidied up. A couple of table lamps are glowing, but the overhead lighting is flipped off. The elephant is tucked in for the night in a doll bed, the blanket pulled up to his ears.

'So what do you think?' I ask. 'Is the apron the curtain? Does the curtain have nothing to do with me being dumped in that grave? Is it meaningless?' I'm feeling guilty about sounding so urgent.

'Nothing is meaningless,' she says. 'The apron probably represents comfort to you. It would not be a surprise for you to connect some element of your first trauma – the death of your mother – to the other one. Tessa, the most important thing is for you to eliminate the unknown, which is frightening. If you came here and told me you could see the killer behind the curtain, like the Wizard of Oz, well . . . that isn't what you really expected, is it?'

Yes. That is exactly what I expected. I grew up in Oz.

I don't tell her that, though. Or say that this painting of my mother's apron leaves me as unsettled as the blank curtain I drew a hundred times.

Tessie, 1995

'How do you like Mr Vega and Benita?'

Is it my imagination or does the doctor sound a little jealous?

'He's nice,' I say carefully. 'They're both very nice.' Adults make things so complicated. Am I supposed to like the doctor better than them? Is this some kind of contest?

'If you have any questions or concerns, you can let me know. Al Vega can come on a little strong.'

And you don't? 'I'm good right now. But I will for sure if I do.' Lately, this need to reassure him has been taking the place of my desire to annoy the hell out of him. 'I do have a question about . . . something else, though.'

Lydia says it's ridiculous that I'm carrying this fear around and letting it devour me, although she also thinks what's happening *is kind of cool.* 'It isn't just Merry who has spoken to me.'

'What do you mean?' the doctor asks. 'Who else is speaking to you?'

'The other Susans . . . talk to me sometimes. The ones in the grave. Not all the time. I don't think it's a big deal. Lydia just thought I should bring it up.'

'Lydia seems like an extremely sensitive friend.'

'Yes.'

'Well, let's start this way. What's the first thing you remember one of the other . . . Susans . . . saying to you?'

'It was in the hospital. When I first woke up. One of them told me the strawberry Jell-O sucked. And it did. It was sugar-free.'

'And what else?'

'Mostly warnings. Be careful. Like that.' *We told you not to touch the pig-and-daisy card.*

'When they speak, do you think they are trying to control you? Or make you do things you don't want to?'

'No. Of course not. I think, like, they want to help. And I promised to help them. Sort of a pact.' It sounds absolutely insane when I say it out loud. I am rocked by the sudden terror he might convince my father to toss me in a loony bin. I am 100 percent certain that Lydia was wrong about her advice this time.

'So you talk back to them?'

'No. Not usually. I just hear them.' *Careful.*

'And they never suggest that you harm yourself?'

'Are you kidding? What the crap are you talking about? Do you think I'm suicidal? Possessed?' I waggle my fingers on either side of my head, like horns.

'Sorry, Tessie. I have to ask the question.'

'I have never once thought about killing myself.' Defensive. And a lie. 'I have thought about killing *him*.'

'Normal,' he says. 'I'd like to do it myself.' This does not seem at all like something a psychiatrist should say. I don't want to feel warm and gushy about him right now. I want a freaking answer.

'So . . . the voices. Do you think I'm . . . schizophrenic? Maybe borderline?' It occurs to me that I'm opting to be schizophrenic rather than possessed by demons. Lydia absolutely refused to help me research anything about schizophrenia. Whatever knowledge I had about it up to that point was gleaned from Stephen King.

So Oscar and I ventured to the local library on our own. The eighty-five-year-old volunteer who can barely see was on duty so I thought it was safe to ask for her help. She didn't recognize the Cartwright Girl, which is what old people call me instead of a Black-Eyed Susan.

After fifteen minutes, while the checkout line stacked up eight deep, she brought over *An Existential Study in Sanity and Madness, One Flew Over the Cuckoo's Nest,* and a Harlequin romance titled *Kate of Outpatients,* all published in the 1960s. The gist of the one by the existential psychologist was to let crazy people be crazy and stop bothering them. I reshelved it and *Cuckoo* and checked out *Kate of Outpatients.* Lydia and I are taking turns doing dramatic readings from it.

The doctor's gaze is surprisingly kind and steady but he lets the silence stretch. Probably trying to figure out how to deliver the bad news to the poor little girl who's soon going to be rocking and drooling in a room full of checker players.

'You are not a schizophrenic, Tessie. I know there is a set of psychiatrists out there who always think that voices indicate mental illness. There are an equal number of us who don't. Lots of people hear voices. When a spouse or child dies, the people left sometimes talk to them on and off all day, and hear them respond. For the rest of their lives. It doesn't make them dysfunctional. In fact, many of them claim these conversations make their lives better and *more* productive.'

I love this man. *I love this man.* He is not going to lock me up.

'The Susans don't make my life better,' I say. 'I think they are ghosts.'

'As we discussed previously, the paranormal is a normal *temporary* response.'

He isn't getting it. 'How do I get rid of them?' *I don't want to make them mad.*

'How do you think you could get rid of them?'

In this case, my answer is immediate. 'By sending the killer to prison.'

'You are well on the way to doing that.'

'And by finding out who the Susans are. Giving them real names.'

'What if that is not possible?'

'Then I don't know if they'll ever leave me.'

'Tessie, did your mother ever talk to you after she died? Like the Susans do?'

'No. Never.'

'I ask only because you have endured two terrible traumas for someone so young. Your mother's death and the horror of that grave. Part of me thinks you are still grieving for your mother. Tell me, do you remember what you did at the wake?'

My mother *again.* I shrug. 'We ate food people brought over and then my little brother and I played basketball on the driveway.' *I let him win. We played H-O-R-S-E. The score was ten games to two.*

'Children often play the day of the funeral as if it's any other day. It's deceptive. They grieve far longer and more deeply than adults.'

'I don't think so.' I remembered the awful sounds of my dad and aunt weeping, like someone was peeling off my skin.

'Adults grieve harder in the beginning, but they move through it. Kids can get stuck in one stage . . . anger or denial . . . for years. It might be at the root of your symptoms – the memory loss, the blindness, the Susans, the code that you made up in the grave –'

'I'm not stuck,' I interrupt. 'Merry and I didn't *make up* a code in the grave. And I don't want to talk about my mother. She's gone. My problem is strictly with ghosts.'

Tessa, present day

It is only thirteen blocks from where I live now.

Lydia's old house.

It might as well be a hundred miles. I'm standing in front of her childhood home for the first time in years. It is the second place he left black-eyed Susans, and the first time I turned and ran.

Lydia always described her house as a shotgun wedding cake, a two-story beige box with a last-minute white piping of scalloped trim. A lot has changed since our childhood. The icing is crumbling. What used to be a perfectly tended green square of lawn is now black dirt choked by hoodlum weeds. No more wooden stake poked in the ground with WELCOME Y'ALL and a painted yellow sunflower. Lydia told me that her dad ripped the sign out of the ground before I came home from the hospital.

'Hey.' I didn't hear his car pull up, but Bill is suddenly striding toward me, lankier and taller than I remember. Maybe it's because his long legs are extending out of black Nike shorts and expensive athletic shoes. Everything about him is damp – hair, face, neck, arms. A triangle of sweat stains the front of a crimson Harvard T-shirt, so beloved that a few rips don't matter. He finally got a haircut but it's too short for his big ears. I want him to go the hell away. And stay.

'I said not to come,' I protest. 'I thought you were

playing basketball.' I'd regretted my impulsive phone call the second Bill answered. He was out of breath. I wondered whether I had interrupted acrobatic sex with a fellow do-gooding lawyer. He claimed he was playing a pickup game.

'All but over. My fellow law pals and I were getting creamed by a bunch of high-schoolers. Your call was a welcome distraction on the way to my parents' house in Westover Hills, where I've unfortunately committed to dinner. Unless you'd like to invite me over. Or accompany me. So you said you had something to tell me. What's up?'

I promptly burst into tears.

I'm unprepared for this, and by the look on his face, so is Bill. And, yet, the river is flowing like it hasn't since my father died so swiftly four years ago of pancreatic cancer. He hugs me awkwardly, because what's he going to do, which makes me sob harder.

'Oh, hell,' he says. 'I'm too sweaty for this. Here, let's sit.'

He guides me to a sitting position on the curb and curls his arm around my shoulders. The brace of solid muscle, his *kindness,* is waking up every hormone in my body. I need to pull out of this embrace immediately. *No complications.* Instead, my head falls sideways like a rock onto his chest and my shoulders heave.

'Uh, I don't really recommend that you put your nose in that . . . underarm,' he says. But once he realizes how fully committed I am, he pulls me tighter.

After a few seconds, I lift my head slightly and let out a choke. 'Hold on. I'm under control.'

'Yes, you definitely have things under control.' He pushes my head back down but not before I catch something hungry on his face that isn't do-gooding at all.

I raise my chin again. Our lips are two inches apart.

He pulls back. 'You're red all over. Like a plum.'

I giggle and hiccup at the same time. I'm a giggling, hiccuping plum. I tug my skirt down. He averts his eyes and gestures to the house behind us, the one whose address he had plugged into his GPS at my behest only twenty minutes ago. 'What's up with this house? Who lives here?' It is an abrupt, purposeful shift.

God, I'm pitiful. I stand up.

'You, um, need to wipe your nose.'

Utter, *utter* humiliation. I use my sweater because at this point, it doesn't matter. I suck in a deep breath as a test. It doesn't trigger another tsunami. 'Hear me out for a second first,' I say stiffly. 'I think the Black-Eyed Susan killer has been leaving me flowers for years. Not just the other night at my house.'

'What? How *many* other places?'

'Six. If you include under my bedroom window.'

'Are you sure . . .'

'That they aren't just growing up in places like God intended and I'm a lunatic? Of course not. That is why I said, I *think*. The first time, I was only seventeen. It was right after Terrell's conviction. The killer left me a poem buried in an old prescription bottle. I found it when I dug up a little patch of black-eyed Susans, in the back yard of the house over there.' I point four houses down, at a yellow two-story on the opposite side of the street. 'My childhood home. He planted the flowers by my tree house three days after the trial ended.' I watch for the awareness to set in. 'That's right, *after* Terrell was locked up.'

'Go on.'

'The . . . person who left it twisted a warning into a poem called "Black-Eyed Susan" written by an eighteenth-century poet named John Gay. The poem indicated that Lydia would die if I didn't keep my mouth shut.' Bill's face is blank. I don't know whether it's because he doesn't know who the hell John Gay is, or whether he is trying to contain his fury.

'I didn't figure out who John Gay was until about ten years ago. He was most famous for *The Beggar's Opera*. Have you heard of it? Captain Macheath? Polly Peachum? No? Well, more to the point, he also wrote a ballad about a black-eyed girl named Susan sending her lover off to sea. There's some romantic theory that this is how the flower got its name . . .'

I begin to recite softly, as a mower revs up in a nearby back yard.

'Oh Susan, Susan, lovely dear
My vows shall ever true remain
Let me kiss off that falling tear
I never want to hurt you again
But if you tell, I will make Lydia
A Susan, too.'

'Jesus, Tessa. What did your father say?'

'I never told him. You're the first person I have ever told, other than Angie. I just couldn't . . . worry my father any-more.'

'And Lydia?'

'We weren't speaking.'

Bill looks at me curiously.

'I told Angie right before she died,' I continue. 'She was concerned for Charlie and me. At the end, she was considering leaving me completely out of things.'

'Why . . .'

'Why didn't she tell you? Because she was protecting me. I think she was wrong, though. I can't live with knowing I might be part of killing an innocent man. It wasn't a hard decision at seventeen. The trial was over. I wanted everything to go back to normal. I figured it could be just another sick individual who was obsessed with the case. There were plenty of those. Which meant Terrell could still be guilty as hell. The prosecutor, Al Vega, was *sure*. And Lydia . . . I was furious with her, but I certainly didn't want her life in danger.'

'Hold on, OK?'

Bill leaps up and jogs to his car, a small black BMW, three little letters that I think turn normally nice human beings into road demons. He disappears inside his fancy womb for so long, I wonder whether he is listening to Bach and contemplating whether to flip on the ignition and screech off. When he finally emerges, he holds a pen and pad in his left hand. He plops back down on the curb. He's already written some notes, and I glimpse a few of the words.

John Gay. 1995.

'Keep going,' he orders.

'Lately, I've revisited a couple of the places I *think* he left flowers . . . on my own. In no particular order.'

'Whoa. Stop right there. You've been returning to these places. Why in the hell are you doing that?'

'I know, I know. Crazy. You see, after the first time, I

never dug to see if he buried something else for me. It was like I couldn't give him the satisfaction. I couldn't let myself believe that much. I thought it could be some kid's idea of a joke. Or a random freak. We were all over the newspaper, even Lydia.' She always pointed out her name to me. She was thrilled when she made *The New York Times* as *Miss Cartwright's neighbor and confidante.*

'I survived on denial,' I continue. 'And, yes, I realize it's insane to think anything would still be there. And yet, what if? I just thought if I did find something, it might help . . . Terrell.'

And I promised the Susans.

'You're digging? Alone? Have you found anything?'

'Nothing. It's a relief, and it isn't.'

'Why are we here, if your old house is there?'

'This is Lydia's house. Well, it used to be. I found black-eyed Susans here, too, a few weeks after the trial.'

How much should I explain? I'd shown up at the door on a Friday afternoon with a cardboard box of her stuff. I was enacting a ritual goodbye, after our friendship imploded at the end of the trial. She hadn't been at school for a week and a half. The box held two videotapes, *The Last of the Mohicans* and *Cape Fear,* the backup makeup bag she always left in my bathroom, her Mickey Mouse pajamas.

But the house was asleep at three in the afternoon, which was unusual. No cars. The living room shades were drawn for the first time ever. I could have dumped the box and run. Instead, I unlocked the back gate. Curious. When I glimpsed the small sea of yellow flowers, I was even angrier at Lydia, and I hadn't thought that possible. *How could she let them grow?* I couldn't get out of there fast enough. Two weeks later, a For Sale sign went up, and the Bells were gone, like no one was worth a goodbye.

'Let her go,' my father had advised.

'I was in the back yard returning something to Lydia and saw them,' I tell Bill. I place my fingers at my temples and rub in concentric circles. 'It's OK if you think this is stupid. Let's go. I'm sorry I bothered you.'

He stands and yanks me up. Then he surprises me. 'We're here. Might as well check it out.'

We knock three times before a pasty woman with short, frustrated black hair opens the door about six inches. She surveys us like we are Texas liberals and stabs a finger at the sign under the mailbox attached to the porch siding, a slight variation on a familiar plaque to ward off solicitors: WE'RE PISS POOR. WE DON'T VOTE. WE'VE FOUND JESUS. OUR GUN IS LOADED.

Bill ignores her warnings and sticks out his hand. 'Hello, ma'am, I'm William Hastings. My friend Tessa here used to have a very good friend who lived in your house. Tessa has fond childhood memories of playing in the back yard. Would you mind if she took a quick look back there for old times' sake?'

The door opens a little wider, but it's clearly not an invitation. She swivels to shove her foot at a fat yellow cat that can't make up its mind about going out. I'm guessing she's around forty-five, wearing tight jean shorts that are the size she wore two sizes ago. She is carting around a lumpy rear end on skinny legs, and I'm figuring the legs are what she's gauging her weight by as she sits on her ass and sucks down another beer.

No shoes. Band-Aids are wrapped around her big toes. Her breasts are generous flat pancakes, encased in a tank top. A tattoo of red roses snakes from her left shoulder to her elbow. The tattoo clearly required a lot of both time and clenching of teeth.

'Yeah, I mind.' The woman ignores Bill's outstretched hand. She's staring at the scar under my eye. I perceive a fleeting flash of respect in her eyes. She's probably thinking *bar fight*.

'I'm curious, Mrs . . . ?'

'Gibson. Not that it's any of your damn business.'

Bill flashes his courthouse badge.

'I'm just curious, Mrs Gibson, at 5216 Della Court, if you were a no-show to jury duty in the last five years. I have a few friends in the courthouse who would be happy to look that up for us.'

'Son of a bitch,' she fumes. 'Five minutes. That's it. Go around the side by the gate and be sure to shut it when you go. I have a dog.' She spits out the last four words like a threat and slams the door.

'Nice move,' I say.

'It's not my first Mrs Gibson.'

The same old chain link fence is standing guard around back, although several degrees rustier. The horseshoe catch on the side gate requires a good thump from Bill to lift. I think about how Lydia's dad oiled it religiously.

It is a small, crunched yard with too many plastic buildings. A fake-shingled shed is shoved into the right corner, the 'fancy' version with a flower box that was forgotten a long time ago. A filthy white doghouse with a red roof is plopped on the slab of concrete posing as a back porch.

A picnic table used to sit directly under a red oak tree that is now a four-foot stump topped by a statue of a bald eagle with outspread wings. The grass is long and tickly. It creeps up my leg, like a rambling daddy longlegs. Maybe it is. I almost trip over a toy plastic fire truck transformed into a weed planter.

Bill's foot lands in an enormous pile of soft dog poop, and he lets out a loud *'Shit.'*

We halt, and stare more intently at the doghouse. It's big enough for a two-year-old child to sleep in. Bill whistles. A dog starts a serious racket somewhere inside the house, and I wonder if Mrs Gibson is loading her shotgun.

'OK, where?' Bill's tone indicates he may be losing some faith in my treasure hunt. Once again, I regret involving him.

I point to the left side of the yard, at the very back. The weeds are a wild and shaggy carpet, but you can still make out the small hill that Mr Bell used to call the Grassy Knoll. Lydia had inherited that need to nickname things.

Bill follows behind me, dragging his left shoe, trying to scrape off dog poop as he goes. I stop abruptly, lean over, and begin to yank at weeds.

'What the hell are you doing?' He glances back to the house. My weeding efforts have revealed a small metal door planted sideways into the rise of the tiny hill.

The rusty padlock that holds it closed would probably fall apart with a swift kick. I'm tempted.

'It's an old storm cellar from the '30s when the house was built. I don't recall Lydia's family ever using it. Mrs Bell thought they were better off in the bathtub during tornado warnings than hanging out with poisonous spiders and beetles in a black hole.'

'Where were the flowers?'

'Planted across the top. There's always been a layer of dirt above the concrete. Used to be grass.'

'You didn't bring a shovel,' Bill says, almost to himself. He's trying to fit the pieces together, and I'm holding back the big one. 'You think he buried something for you . . . in the storm cellar?'

An image of Charlie flashes into my mind, crammed on a bus with shrieking volleyball girls, headed to Waco.

I'm missing her game for this.

'Yes.' I place two fingers on my wrist and feel my racing pulse, because Lydia always did. 'Last night, I dreamed that Lydia is down there. That the flowers marked her grave.'

Tessie, 1995

'Do you ever have nightmares?'

The doctor's demeanor today, all stiff and formal, suggests he has renewed purpose. I imagine him stabbing at a random page in his Book of Tricks right before I arrived. It is probably thick as a loaf of bread, with crackled yellow pages, a worn red velvet cover, and thousands of useless magic spells.

'Let me think,' I say. I've added this cheerful line to my arsenal of *sure* and *sounds good,* part of my campaign to get off this couch as soon as possible.

I *could* tell him that last night's dream wasn't exactly a nightmare, as my nightmares go, and that his daughter, Rebecca, was the guest star. I was camped out in the grave with the Susans, per usual. Rebecca peered down at us, pale and pretty, in one of my mother's flowered church dresses. She fell to her knees and extended a hand. Her hair, wound in these goofy old-fashioned ringlets, tickled my cheek. Her fingers, when they reached me, were white-hot. I woke up, my arm on fire, choking for air.

I could tell him, but I won't. It seems unkind to bring it up, and I am working on being kinder.

'I dream a lot about the grave.' This is the first time I've admitted this. It also happens to be true. 'The dream is always exactly the same until the end.'

'Are you in the grave? Or hovering above it?'

'For most of the dream, I'm lying in it, waiting.'

'Until someone rescues you?'

'No one ever rescues us.'

'What do you hear?'

A truck engine. Thunder. Bones crackling like firewood. Someone cursing.

'It depends on the ending,' I say.

'If you don't mind, tell me about the different endings.'

'It is pouring rain, and we drown in muddy water. Or snow falls until it covers our faces like a baby blanket, and we can't see.' *Or breathe.* I swig out of the glass of water his secretary always leaves for me. It tastes a little like the lake smells.

'And to be clear . . . *we* means . . . Merry and . . . the bones.'

'It means the Susans.'

'Are there . . . other endings besides those?'

'A farmer doesn't see us and shovels dirt into the hole with his tractor plow. Someone lights a match and drops it inside. A huge black bear decides the hole is the perfect place to hibernate and lies down on top of us. That's one of the nicer endings. All of us just go to sleep. He snores. Anyway, you get the idea.'

'Anything else?'

'Well, sometimes he comes back and finishes the job. Buries us for real.' *With bags and bags of manure.*

'He . . . meaning the killer?'

I don't answer, because once again, it seems obvious.

'Do you ever see a face?' he asks.

Come on, doesn't he think I would have said if I saw his face? Still, I think about his question. Rebecca's is the only face

I've ever seen in this recurring event. She was lovely in her first appearance last night. Big, innocent eyes, dark corkscrew curls, skin like ivory silk.

She looked very much like Lillian Gish, probably because Lydia and I had just rented *Birth of a Nation.*

Lydia says that Lillian Gish loved to play tortured characters, *as a rebellious counter to her devastating beauty.* Lydia knows this because her dad has a huge crush on this actress, even though Lillian Gish is quite dead. She said her dad especially likes the finale of *Way Down East,* where Lillian floats unconscious on an ice floe toward a seething waterfall, while her long hair dangles in the water like a snake. Right after she told me, Lydia said she shouldn't have. That it might provoke more nightmares while I was *in this state.*

It ticked me off. She hardly ever says things like that. It makes me worry. Am I looking in more of a state than usual? Isn't she noticing I'm more cheerful? Aren't I getting better?

Either way, it probably isn't *relevant* to tell the doctor about his daughter showing up in my dream as a silent movie queen, wearing my mother's clothes. It was certainly weird and random, like just about everything else.

'No,' I say. 'I don't see his face.'

Tessa, present day

Once again, I'm in the shadows. Watching.

My body is tucked under the eaves, pressed against the cold, dirty siding, hopefully out of camera range for the television van camped by the curb out front.

I'm trying to steady my nerves by picturing Lydia's yard the way it used to be: green, neat, and shady with two giant clay pots of red and white impatiens on each of the front corners of the flat concrete porch. Always red and white, like the Christmas lights that Mr Bell strung along the front roofline that every single year ended ten bulbs short on one side. It was tradition for my father to comment on it whenever we drove by.

Lucy and Ethel used to live back here. Mr Bell's hunting dogs. When he wasn't around to call them off, their excited claws left little white streaks on my calves. The old boat was usually up on blocks in the back corner, perpetually waiting for July 4th. Lydia and I used to throw off the tarp when Mr Bell wasn't home so we could do our homework and work on our leg tans at the same time.

But there's a circus assembling here today. And I'm responsible for it. My gut cramps. Bill and Jo are staking their reputations on me.

It took three days for Bill to retrieve the judge's permission to dig at Lydia's house and another twenty-four hours to set the time for 2 P.M., which is exactly fourteen minutes from now. The district attorney was surprisingly cooperative, probably because the police are getting killed in the media. A local newspaper editorial criticized the county for 'an embarrassing lack of Texas frontier justice in not identifying the bones of the Black-Eyed Susans and returning them to their families.'

It wasn't a particularly well-written or researched opinion, just fiery, something Southern journalists are good at pulling out of the air on a slow day. But it had worked a little magic on Judge Harold Waters, who still reads newspapers and has presided over the Black-Eyed Susan case from the beginning. He scribbled his signature and handed it down from his perch on top of his favorite cutting horse, Sal.

I barely remember Waters during the trial, just that Al Vega was worried he was too wishy-washy on the death penalty. A few years ago, I saw the judge on CNN giving an eyewitness account of a UFO hovering over Stephenville 'like a twenty-four-hour Super Walmart in the sky.'

'Could have been a worse draw,' Bill had told me.

And so here we are, because of my dream about Lydia, and a judge who believes in flying saucers.

Two uniformed cops are squaring off the back yard with yellow crime tape. Jo is standing on top of the Grassy Knoll with the same female detective who attended the meeting with Hannah's family. A SMU geology professor is rolling by with a high-tech ground-penetrating radar device on wheels that will never in a million years fit through the door to the cellar. It barely fit through the gate. His grim face says he's figured this out.

Jo has told me that GPR is still more theoretical than

practical when searching for old bones underground, but she and Bill decided it couldn't hurt to add to the melodrama. The DA agreed. He'll make hay out of it either way.

The professor is the acknowledged local expert in the complicated task of reading GPR imagery. Still, the ground is not a womb, and Jo tells me he will not be able to discern a skeletal face. He'll be searching for evidence of soil disturbances that would suggest someone dug a grave once upon a time. He might be able to make out a human shape, but it's doubtful. He's mostly part of the show.

The yard is now buzzing with conversations, an impromptu lawn party that's starting to gel. Bill is schmoozing the pretty assistant district attorney assigned to witness this latest crazy turn of events. Her real face is buried under a Southern coat of makeup. I'm calculating the distance between them. Two feet, now one.

Mr and Mrs Gibson are propped up in lawn chairs in their Sunday best Dallas Cowboys T-shirts, smoking like fiends, the only two people who appear to be enjoying themselves. One of them has mowed the weeds for the occasion.

The professor is suddenly making a beeline for them. He shakes their hands. From his wild gesticulating, I've deduced that the professor wants to run his device over both the front and back yards. The Gibsons are vigorously nodding yes.

Are they imagining movie rights? Is that what prompted Mrs Gibson to wash her hair and stick on flip-flops and fresh toe Band-Aids? Is she hoping to add a plaque under her No Soliciting sign that declares this house a historical landmark, like Lizzie Borden's?

The gate clanks behind me, and the back yard suddenly

snaps to attention. Four more people are striding in. Two cops in jeans, hoisting shovels and a metal detector. Two women in CSI protective gear with an unlit lantern and a large camera. Their arrival signals that my tortured wait is almost over.

Across the yard, one of the uniformed cops is already cutting through the lock on the storm cellar. He yanks on the door and it gives way easily. He leaps back and slaps a hand over his nose and mouth, as does every person within ten feet of the door. Even Jo, who told me that on the site of the 9/11 tragedy, she smelled things she will never forget.

Now everything is going too fast. One of the crime scene investigators is busily handing out masks. One of the cops in jeans disappears into the hole like an agile snake. The shovel and lantern are handed down to him. Next, a CSI disappears. The space must be tiny, because everyone else remains aboveground. Eager. Chattering into the hole.

Mr Bell would never let us open that door. *It's nasty down there, girls.*

Empty plastic evidence bags are dropped into the cellar. In fifteen minutes, two of the bags return to the surface, bulging. They are set alongside the back fence.

The CSI pokes her head out from the hole and she beckons for the cop with the metal detector. *In case there is jewelry?* I could tell them that Lydia always wore her grandmother's thin gold wedding band with the pinprick red ruby. I wonder for the hundredth time in four days why the cops couldn't find any of the Bell family in a search of public records. It's as if they sailed off the face of the earth.

Jo is offering her hand to the CSI, covered with muck

and filth, climbing up through the door. The cop with the metal detector descends to take her place. The Gibsons are munching potato chips and passing a plastic tub of ranch dip back and forth. The geologist is methodically rolling his device over the grounds like a wheelbarrow, pausing every now and then to read his screen.

A circus.

Another evidence bag is handed up from the hole. And another and another. All of them are set along the back fence line with the others. In the end, eight black bags, like the bodies of lumpy spiders, their legs ripped off. Finally, both cops emerge, black from the knees down, tearing off latex gloves. The group huddles for a short conversation.

Jo turns and searches the yard until her eyes land on me. She walks toward me, her face twisted with concern, the longest twenty yards of my life.

How could I have left Lydia down there for so long? Why did I not figure this out sooner?

Jo's hand is heavy on my shoulder. 'We didn't find anything, Tessa. We're going to go a little deeper, but they've already dug three feet and struck clay and limestone. It would have taken the killer forever to dig through it. Seems very unlikely that he did.'

'What . . . is in the bags?'

'Someone used the place as a root cellar. It was trashed with broken jars and rotting fruits and vegetables. And a couple of now-dead moles that burrowed in somehow for a last supper. There was plenty of moisture to keep it rancid. Cracks in the concrete.'

'I'm so sorry . . . that I wasted everyone's time.'

Nothing inside me feels that sorry. *Lydia could be alive.*

Those flowers might really be from her. I feel a rising tide of unexpected joy.

'We'll still sift through the contents of those bags, back in the lab. We always knew this was a shot in the dark. Literally. And I like to leave no stone unturned. Or any cliché unturned.' Trying to make me smile.

Behind her, the professor has wheeled his device right below the gaping mouth of the cellar. A small crowd is gathering, including the Gibsons, who've ducked under the crime tape. Someone in the center of the circle gives a shout. The uniforms are pushing everyone back to make room for the cops and their shovels.

The crime scene investigators are talking to the professor like he's an umpire about to make a critical decision. They turn to the cops and dircct how wide to make the hole.

The men nod, and carefully crack the earth.

Tessie, 1995

The doctor is telling me a story about when he was twelve.

I'm sure there's going to be a point, but I wish he'd get to it. Lately, he's been a little all over the place.

I'm annoyed by that smudge on his glasses, by Lydia flushing all of my Benadryl down the toilet last night. *I'm sorry,* she said, but it seemed to be about much more than swirling away those pink pills. Something is going on with Lydia. For the last two weeks, she's been late instead of exactly on time and sometimes cancels on me altogether. She makes vague excuses, her cheeks flush and she rakes her teeth across the pink lip gloss on her bottom lip. She is a terrible liar. Eventually, Lydia will tell me what is wrong, so I don't bug her.

Of course, two sentences into the doctor's tale, I'm wondering if *he's* lying. He says he was a chubby boy and yet he's got all that wiry muscle under the shirt with the collar that stands like a pinned white butterfly. I bumped up against his arm once. It was immovable, concrete, a runner's leg extending from his shoulder.

'I'd come home every day after school to an empty house,' he is saying.

I'm suddenly scared for the boy in an empty house even though he's sitting across from me alive and well with no visible scars.

'Tessie, do you want me to continue? Is this story bothering you?'

'Um, no. Go ahead.'

'In the winter, the house was always dark and cold. So the first thing I did after I unlocked the door, before I put down my books or took off my coat, was walk to the thermostat and turn up the heat. To this day, the thump of the furnace, the smell of heat coming on . . . is the smell of loneliness. Tessie, are you listening?'

'Yes. I'm just trying to figure out your lesson here. I thought you were about to tell me something terrible happened to you.' I'm disappointed. Relieved. Vaguely intrigued.

It occurs to me that I love all of the smells associated with heat. Fireplace smoke drifting my way on a chilly night run, barbecue coals declaring it Saturday afternoon. Sizzling pork chop grease, Banana Boat sunscreen, hot towels tumbled in our old Kenmore dryer. Especially after Mama died, I couldn't get hot enough. I flipped my electric blanket on high so much that it streaked a black scorch mark on the blue fabric and Daddy took it away. I still stretch out by the heating vent in the floor of Mama's walk-in closet and read. I'm not sure I would have survived the last year if I couldn't slam the screen door behind me, sprawl on the back porch lounger, and let the brutal sun fry every black thought to ashes.

'Smell is the sense that is most instantly connected with memory. Do you know anything about Marcel Proust?'

'Am I failing this test if I say no?' I can't wait to tell Lydia that the doctor is pulling a depressed French philosopher with a handlebar mustache out of his bag. It's a big step up. Lydia christened my last therapist Chicken Little after the woman suggested I read *Chicken Soup for the Soul.*

'This isn't a test. There is no way to fail in this room,

Tessie.' His tone is plodding, predictable – and, I realize, a little tired. 'One of Proust's characters recalls an entire event from his childhood after smelling a tea-soaked biscuit. Science has been chasing this theory ever since – that smell retrieves deep memories. The olfactory bulb rests near, and instantly communicates with, the part of our brain that holds the past.'

'So this *is* a test. You are telling me I can retrieve my memory through smell.'

'Maybe. Are there any smells that . . . bother you since the event?'

Peanut butter, peanut butter, *peanut butter*. My dad interrogated Bobby and me last week about why an almost-full jar of Jif was in the trash. Bobby didn't tell on me.

The muscles in my thighs and legs suddenly cramp.

'Tessie, what's happening?'

I can't breathe. I have drawn my knees up to my chin. My fingers are in my ears.

'Why can't I remember? *Why can't I remember?*'

His arm is around me. He's saying something. My head falls onto his shoulder. I feel him stiffen slightly, and then relax. His body is warm, a hot water bottle, like Daddy's. I do not know or care if this is appropriate behavior for a therapist.

He is heat.

Tessa, present day

I spend forty-five minutes in the shower, but it doesn't help. I pace the house. Open the refrigerator, swig out of the orange juice bottle, slam the door shut. Pick up my phone on the counter. Consider calling Charlie. Bill. Jo. Stop myself.

Punch around on Facebook. Stick my daughter's old iPod into the speakers, and turn it way, way up so that Kelly Clarkson full vibrato is massaging my brain. Rearrange the kitchen canisters, the magazines, the mail, Charlie's scattered papers and notebooks. Fold and refold a leftover piece of satin on the floor. Obsess over neat, exacting edges in a house where things usually roll around at the whims of a churlish tide.

I want, *need* to know the contents of the box unearthed seven hours ago near Lydia's storm cellar. From my vantage point under the eaves, I couldn't tell anything other than it was metal, about twelve inches square, and easy for a CSI to carefully lift out with blue latex-covered hands. At that point, the cops began the process of clearing the back yard of extraneous people like me. In the rising clatter of voices, Jo didn't even look my way. Bill and the assistant DA had reappeared and stood together off to the side of the hole, arms crossed, observing.

The knock at the door, three short raps, snaps me to attention. I glance down to see whether I'm decent. The answer is no. Bare legs and feet. The only thing covering me is one of Lucas's old camouflage Army T-shirts that hits about four inches below a patch of lace that Victoria's Secret calls underwear. No bra. I grab a pair of shorts out of the pile of clean clothes on the couch and hurriedly hop into them, one leg at a time.

Two more urgent raps.

The shorts are Charlie's, and they ride high under the T-shirt so that it still appears that I'm wearing nothing. But, good enough.

I thrust my eye up to the peephole. Bill.

He is perfectly framed in the oval, as if he is standing in a tiny, tiny picture from another era. His hair is wet and slicked back. I can almost smell the soap.

I know he is not here to talk about Lydia. We almost kissed on that curb. This silent debate has been going on between us ever since he brushed his head on the Galveston sea glass dangling from the ceiling in my bedroom.

I open the door. He's wearing faded Levi's, and an easy, tentative smile that is going to get me in trouble tonight. I cannot stop staring at his mouth. He's carrying a bottle of wine in each hand. One red, one white. Considerate, because he doesn't know my preference, which is neither. On a night like this, I'm a beer girl all the way. The heat in the few feet between us is unmistakable now, flushing my skin. Pretenses, denials, the fact that I'm a mom of fourteen years and he's probably still getting carded – all of it undeniably stripped away after I fell apart in his arms. Bill has barely said an unnecessary word to me since.

At this moment, we are the same people we were before we sat down on that curb, and two very different ones.

'This isn't a good idea,' I say.

'No,' he says, and I open the door wider.

I have three important rules when it comes to sex.

I have to be in a committed relationship.

It cannot happen in my house, in my bed.

It must be dark.

Bill abandons the wine bottles on the hall table and kicks the door closed without saying anything. He pushes me back against the wall. His body is still chilled with night air, but his fingers and lips on my skin are like drifting flames. My arms are up around his neck, and I'm pressing my body into his, craning my neck up. I have not felt this certain I should be alive in a very long time. It's making me slightly woozy.

He cradles my chin in one hand. His gaze is long enough and deliberate enough to assure me that he knows exactly what he's doing. I think, *If I look away now, if I stop this, it will still be OK, almost like it never happened.* But he bends to kiss me again, and I am lost. I want this intimate dance in my hallway to go on forever. His hands have slipped under my T-shirt and are sliding up my back.

I don't protest when he lifts me and carries me down the hall. I wrap my legs around his waist and keep my mouth on his.

In my room, he sets me down gently. His head brushes the glass again, setting off a trickle of muted music. He strips off my shirt. His shirt. Pulls me down onto my soft, messy sheets. We are instantly coiled, like people who have made love to each other hundreds of times. I close my eyes and swirl to the bottom of the river.

'Tessa, you beautiful girl,' he groans, his breath on my neck. 'You drive me crazy.'

Crazy.

Maybe another one of his lines. Perhaps a last-ditch plea for one of us to come to our senses.

I pull away slightly, but not enough that he can see the scar near my collarbone. He's been too busy so far to notice. I'm always so careful about this. Never too drunk on love or lust to forget. My hand reaches for the switch on the lamp by my bed, and stops. The bulb has cast his face in half-glow, half-shadow. Every cliché pops into my head. Light and dark, life and death, true and false, comedy and tragedy, good and evil, yin and yang.

Golden boy lawyer and girl marked by the devil.

I use one hand to tug at the pins holding up my hair. I know exactly what I'm doing, too. There is a look on his face that I will never forget, that I will hold on to forever, no matter what happens after tonight.

No matter whether we fail Terrell.

No matter whether my monster eats us both alive.

I reach over, and snap off the light.

This is the one rule I will not break tonight.

Sex is the only time I worship the dark.

'This one?' he asks. His finger is tracing the faint line on my ankle, and I shiver.

'From surgery. You know that I broke my ankle . . . that night. Please, come up here.' I tug at his hair, and he ignores me.

'And this?' He's smothering the tiny butterfly above my right hip bone with the tip of his finger.

'An impulse right before the trial,' I say. I'm suddenly flooded with the memory of the exquisite pain of the needle. When I encounter people smothered in tattoos, chattering eagerly about the next one, I understand the addiction.

I only ask to be free. The butterflies are free.

Lydia's voice is ringing in my head. She quoted that line from *Bleak House* to a tattoo artist at a carnival on the state fairgrounds. Lydia was lying facedown on a fresh towel on a metal cot. The flap of the tent was closed, making it an oven. Lydia's jeans were unbuttoned and slightly pulled down over the curve of her smooth white hip. I'd gone first, oddly brave. The wings of my tattoo were stinging, even more as I watched this stranger carve out Lydia's identical twin butterfly.

Bill's fingers are urging me back to the present. He is inching his way up my body slowly, exploring, as if he is clinically gathering evidence for court. It is the first sign in the last hour and a half that my brain is working.

My hair is covering the three-inch line above my left collarbone. He pushes it aside. He *knows.*

'Tell me about this one,' he says.

It is the scar I am the most ashamed of. It *feels* like my monster's work as much as if he'd inked it himself. In reality, he drew none of my scars with his own hand. 'The ER doctors panicked a little the night I was . . . found. Everybody did. The EMT carried me in the emergency room door in his arms, screaming. Later, my cardiologist was furious. He said I would have needed a pacemaker eventually but not that night. Not that soon. They used wires that would be tough to extract so they left it in.' My body stiffens slightly as he nuzzles my neck. This can't be a surprise to him. '*Poor little pacemaker girl.* Al Vega rammed it home on the stand. Don't you remember from the transcript?'

'Yes, but I wanted to hear it from you.'

So Bill *is* on the clock. The love spell is settling like dull party glitter.

'Should we call Jo and ask what was in the box at Lydia's?' Changing the subject. Trying not to sound hurt.

'Trust me, she'll call. Try not to think about it.

'What about Charlie's father?' he asks abruptly. 'Is he in the picture? I like to know when there's competition.'

His question sounds an off note for me. 'Lucas would say no one could compete. He's generally quite full of himself. He's a soldier. His ego keeps him alive.' I touch Bill's cheek. 'We haven't been together for years. Not like this.'

Bill and I are uncomfortably working backward. It's wrong. This is why I generally follow my sensible rules for sex. I'm leaning over to grab for the T-shirt on the floor when it occurs to me that I should adopt another rule: Never wear the Army shirt of one man while making love to another.

'Don't leave,' Bill says softly. 'I'll shut up. Stay with me.' He's yanking me down again, spooning his warm body against my back and tossing the comforter over us. I can't resist the heat.

Sleep isn't coming.

I nestle into Bill's back. Close my eyes and drift.

I'm back in the tent, watching Lydia's butterfly get its wings. The tattoo artist isn't that old. Maybe twenty-five. She's wearing a red, white, and blue halter top that shows a lot of skin. Her back is laced with old white scars, probably from a belt.

A four-word tattoo is flushed defiantly against the damaged canvas.

I am still here.

Tessie, 1995

'Tessie, are you listening?'

Always with the *listening*.

My lips are glued to the pin-striped straw of a Dairy Queen Dr Pepper. The leaves brushing the office window have turned a brilliant red in the last week. I've never seen a tree so lit up in August, like Monet has picked it out and struck a match to it. I figure God is using this tree as a reminder to be grateful that I'm not still blind. But he's a fickle God or I wouldn't have gone blind in the first place.

I rub at a smudge of mascara sweat stinging my eye. Lydia has been obsessed with trying new cosmetics lately, while I am busy trying to be the blur that no one notices. She had experimented on me until she perfected the blend to hide my half-moon scar – Maybelline Fair Stick 10 combined with a tube of something puke green and Cover Girl Neutralizer 730. She wrote all of this down for me, including the order in which I was to apply it, and then she made up herself in my bathroom mirror. She looked amazing when she finished. My dad once said, not meanly, that if Lydia didn't open her mouth, every boy in school would be after her. While she added a layer of clear mascara and smacked on pink lip gloss, she told me all about Erica Jong and the zipless fuck. It is the first time I ever heard her use the f-word and it was like she'd fired a shot that killed our remaining childhood.

'Sex with a stranger,' she had explained. 'No remorse. No guilt.' More and more, I feel like I'm the wheel spinning in the mud, while Lydia's foot is on the gas.

The doctor interrupts my train of thought. 'Tessie, what's with you today? What are you thinking about?'

Zipless fucks. Scar recipes.

'I'm hot. Kind of bored.'

'OK, how about this. What is the emotion you have felt most of the time since you were here two days ago?' *Since you hugged me on the couch and acted like a person?*

'I don't know.' I squirm. I hate this odd habit of his – starting an intimate conversation while standing five feet away.

'I think you feel guilt. Almost all of the time. Ever since the event. We keep skirting around it.'

I suck slowly out of my Styrofoam cup and stare at him. *The event.* Yep, still drives me crazy when he says it.

'Why would I feel guilty?'

'Because you believe you could have prevented what happened to you. Maybe even what happened to Merry.'

'I was sixteen years old. An athlete. I don't know exactly what happened, but I'm sure I could have prevented this if I'd been paying attention. It's not like I'm a two-year-old who could be tossed in a car like a pillow.'

He finally sits down across from me. 'You've hit right on the problem, Tessie. You aren't two or four or ten, Tessie. You are a teen-ager, so you think you're pretty smart. More perceptive than adults, even. Your father. Your teachers. Me. In fact, I hate to tell you, but this is the smartest you will ever feel in your whole life.' Lydia hates the no-socks loafer look on men, and right now, so do I. I stare at his pearly ankle with the bone jutting out and think about how we are just a bunch of ugly parts. I feel so many conflicting emotions about this man. About males in general right now. If he really wanted to get anywhere, he'd ask about *that.*

'Rebecca thought she was smarter, too,' he says.

His daughter's name hits the humid air like a grenade. I'm not bored anymore, if that was his intent.

'There is a reason you feel the need to blame yourself,' he continues. 'From all accounts, you were a very careful girl. If you accept the blame – decide you took a rare misstep – you can reassure yourself this was not a random event. If you blame yourself, you can believe that you are still in control of your universe. You're not. You never will be.'

'And what about you?' I ask. 'I bet you still think your daughter is alive, when she's decomposing in the muck of a river or being snacked on by coyotes. Let me enlighten *you.* Rebecca is dead.'

Tessa, present day

The sunrise is painting the bedroom pink. The best time of day for talking to angels and taking photographs, according to my grandfather. For admiring clouds that drift like feathers off a flamingo, according to Sir Arthur Conan Doyle.

For shoving midnight monsters to the back of the closet.

Bill is sliding a long, skinny leg into his jeans. His back is bare, broad, wired with muscle. It's been a long time since I woke up on a Saturday morning with someone in my bed who wasn't furry or sick. I'm trying to identify the emotion in my gut. Scared, maybe. Hopeful?

Charlie isn't due back on the bus for another couple of hours but she's delivered a series of texts that dinged through a third, lazy round of lovemaking. I'm propped up against the headboard and am thumbing through them, the sheet modestly pulled up to my chest.

> Third place ☹. Coach got ejected. ☺
>
> Forgot need tub of blue hair gel
> for bio lab Monday. Soooorry.
>
> What's for dinner?

Bill's cell phone rings on the bedside table while I'm thinking about where to buy a tub of blue hair gel without returning to 1965. I pick up his phone and toss it over but not before I see the caller ID.

Bone Doc.

My throw across the tumbled comforter falls short, but Bill leans in, catches the phone anyway. Winks.

I remember the first time a man winked at me. Lydia was blowing out eleven candles, one to grow on, while I watched her father's eye open and shut under the ragged brow that never quite filled in after an auto shop accident.

Bone Doc. Jo calling, to divulge the secrets of the box? For hours, even with the distraction of Bill's tongue, my mind has been prying the lid open and slamming it shut.

The box is filled with sand, silky enough to run through my fingers like a waterfall.

It is crammed with girls' jawbones, grinning wickedly at every angle.

It holds a package tied up with glittering black tinsel made of Lydia's hair.

'Hey.' Bill speaks low into the phone and glances back at me. He listens without interrupting for at least a minute. 'Uh-huh. I can reach Tessa.'

He's zipping up his jeans at this point, balancing the phone between his ear and shoulder.

The doctor had taught me in our sessions that I could have waited five years to sleep with this man, and never really known him. The doc was speaking generally, of course. He believed that a person's most profound flaws or virtues emerge in great crisis, or they remain buried forever. I remember leaving his office that day thinking it was sad that ordinary, dull people die all the time without ever knowing they are heroes. All because a girl didn't go under in the lake right in front of them, or a neighbor's house didn't catch fire.

'Be there in about an hour,' Bill is saying.

* * *

Five of us are stuffed into the tiny room, all looking like we'd come off a sleepless night.

Jo, in running shorts and a well-worn T-shirt that says *Pray for Moore, OK.* Bill, wearing the same clothes as the night before. Alice Finkel, the flirtatious assistant district attorney, hiding under a face made up with Mary Kay precision, so desperately interested in Bill that it hurts to watch. Lt. Ellen Myron, in Wrangler's, a gun strapped to her hip.

I concentrate on the three plastic evidence bags, lying in a neat row.

My fingers itch to rip them open and get this grim party rolling.

Lieutenant Myron clears her throat.

'Tessa,' Lieutenant Myron says, 'there were three items recovered from the box exhumed in the back yard of Lydia Bell's childhood home. We're hoping you can identify the items.'

'There were no . . . bones inside?' I ask. *Just tell me, dammit. Tell me you found a piece of Lydia.*

'No. Nothing like that.' Lieutenant Myron flips over one of the bags. I recognize the small book immediately. Gold, frayed cover. A design of yellow flowers with green shoots trickling up toward the title. *Poe's Stories and Poems.*

'Can I pick it up?' I ask.

'No. Don't touch. I'll do it.'

'That's Lydia's,' I confirm. 'I was with her when she bought it. Her dad drove us into Archer City to Larry McMurtry's bookstores.'

Why would Lydia bury this book? After my kidnapping, she probably scourged her room of anything with a yellow flower on it. But Lydia wouldn't be able to completely part with a treasured book. She'd romanticize it like this, in a time capsule to dig up later.

Except she never came back.

Lieutenant Myron sets the book aside and dangles another bag from her thumb and forefinger. 'What about this?'

I swallow hard and peer closer. 'A key? I don't even recognize the random keys in my own junk drawer.'

'So that's a no?'

'That's a no.'

'Worth asking.'

Lieutenant Myron reaches for the third bag. She holds it up, six inches from my eyes.

The room is waiting for me.

Tick, tick, tick.

Can everyone hear that? I don't know if it's my pacemaker, which never makes a sound, or the deer heart trapped in that box.

At ten, I could recite every word of 'The Tell-Tale Heart.' Lydia was better at it, of course. Once, she hid a loud clock under my pillow.

'Tessa?' Bill grips my shoulders. I'm swaying. The ticking is louder. His watch, *dammit,* near my ear. *Tick, tick.* I push his arm away.

'I thought this was lost.' It's the voice of a seething teenager. 'She must have taken it.'

'Who took it?' The lieutenant's voice is sharp.

'Lydia. Lydia took it.'

Tessa, 1995

The doctor is already seated in his chair right by the couch. He doesn't bother to stand up and greet me. I can't tell by his expression if he is still angry after last week, when I spewed that acid about his daughter being eaten by coyotes. He certainly hadn't objected when I just got up and stalked out.

I throw my purse on the floor, flop back on the couch, and cross my legs, hiking the skirt so he can see to China. He's not the slightest bit interested. I could be his eighty-year-old aunt. My face burns hot and angry, but I don't know why. I twist the ring on my finger, wishing it were his neck.

'Your mother,' he says smoothly. 'You found her on the day she died.'

Payback for conjuring his daughter. He's wielding his sharpest knife today. It opens up a place where I store the exquisite pain of missing her. I want to scream, to shatter that pleasant, professional mask that he snaps on with an invisible rubber band. Sometimes I wonder if I died in that hole. If this room is hell's purgatory, and everything else – Daddy, Bobby, Lydia, O.J. the Monster – is part of a dream when the devil lets me sleep. If this judge in a pin-striped shirt is deciding whether to throw me in a locked attic with a bunch of cackling Susans or set me free to haunt our killer for eternity.

'I'm leaving.' I say this yet remain planted on the couch. 'I'm done with your dumb games.'

'That's your decision, Tessie.'

I was in the tree house.

She had called my name from the kitchen window. I thought she wanted me to help with the dishes. She always made a mess. Grease and flour everywhere. Crusted pans. Dirty bowls in the sink. Daddy said it was the price for biscuits that crumbled in your mouth, fudge frosting, fried okra scramble with potatoes and tomatoes that we ate like popcorn, cold, as leftovers.

I was in the tree house. But I ignored her.

'You found her on the kitchen floor.'

My heart bangs against my chest.

'You were eight years old.'

Her face is blue.

'She died of a stroke,' he says.

I pull up the skirt of her apron. Cover her face.

'Are you angry that she isn't here? That she left you?'

I was in the tree house.

I didn't come when she called.

The guilt is roaming free now. Almost unbearable.

'Yes,' I breathe out.

Tessa, present day

The object in the third plastic evidence bag on Jo's desk is tiny, probably never of importance to anyone but me and its first owner, a little girl in a frilly petticoat who is long dead and buried.

When I was fifteen, I found the ring in the bottom of a basket of junk in an antiques store in the Stockyards. It was so caked with filth that I didn't see the inset pearl, like a microscopic spider's egg, until I got it home. The ring fit perfectly on my pinky. The owner of the store told me it was a Victorian child's ring from the 1800s, probably gold-filled, which is why she said she could give it to me for $35, but certainly not the $10 I suggested. Lydia countered to the woman that she wouldn't have known the ring existed if we hadn't wandered in. 'Tessie could have just stuck it in her pocket,' Lydia spewed indignantly, at which point I slid an extra $25 of my Christmas money across the counter and dragged my best friend out the door.

Halfway down the block, Lydia decided that I had purchased the ring against the will of the universe and wanted me to return it. *It's bad luck to wear the jewelry of a dead stranger. Who knows what kind of terrible things happened to the girl who wore it? In Victorian times, children were raised by cruel nannies and saw their parents once a day by appointment. Winston Churchill said he could count the number of times he'd been hugged by his mother.*

By the time we arrived at the bus stop, Lydia was even more insistent, to a higher degree of craziness than usual. She made the leap from the grubby little object on my pinky to the Hope Diamond. *It grew in the ground for 1.1 billion years before it exploded out of the earth and then cursed almost everyone who touched it. Marie Antoinette got her head chopped off and her princess friend was hacked to death with axes and pikes. It even hexed the innocent mailman who delivered it to the Smithsonian. His family died, his leg got crushed, and his house burned down.*

Say what you want about Lydia Frances Bell and her ridiculous chatter, she said things I never forgot. If she were standing here, she'd be alternately dismayed and thrilled to be starring in the kind of morbid tale she devoured and repeated over and over.

The lieutenant is holding the ring so the pearl faces me like a blind eye. Everyone is being courteously silent. The weight of their expectations is suffocating.

'Yes, that was mine,' I affirm. 'It went missing right before I testified at the trial. Lydia thought the ring was bad luck and wanted me to stop wearing it.'

'Why did she think it was bad luck?'

Pearls bring tears. Suicides and insanity, murders and carriage crashes.

'She didn't believe you should wear the jewelry of dead people unless it belonged to someone you once knew. History was important to her.' *And she was right,* a Susan chimes in my ear.

It's true – the ring was on my finger when he threw me in that hole. Everything else I wore that night – my favorite black leggings, Dad's Michigan T-shirt, the cross necklace that Aunt Hilda gave me at my confirmation – disappeared.

The ER doctors cut off every bit of it and handed it over to the police.

The night nurse was the first to notice the ring while checking my IV, a couple of hours after my pacemaker surgery. I could feel her wriggling it off, her fingers floating like feathers across mine. *Shhhhh.* When I woke up, there was a pinched, untanned circle where the ring had been. A month later, at home, I discovered that someone had tucked a hospital Bible into a pocket in my suitcase. When I opened it up, an envelope was taped to Psalm 23, the ring tucked inside.

The first thing I think when I hear the thump is that Charlie has tumbled out of her crib. It takes an instant of consciousness to realize that Charlie has not slept in a crib in thirteen years. She's tangled in the covers beside me, red hair splayed on the aqua pillowcase like she's floating in an ocean. It's coming back to me now: our late-night marathon of *The Walking Dead,* popcorn, and cheddar cheese chips. The antidote to identifying inexplicable objects dug out of your best friend's back yard.

I'd shut off the TV in my bedroom around 1 A.M. That could have been thirty minutes or four hours ago. It's pitch black outside the window. I reach over to touch Charlie's bare shoulder to be sure I'm not dreaming. It feels velvety and cool, but I don't make the usual move to cover her up.

A low hum of chatter, as the Susans gather in my head to confer. I feel for the phone in the bed, where it usually sleeps beside me: 3:33. Charlie's breath is even, and I decide not to wake her. Not yet.

I hear it again. The leaden sound of something dropping,

like the lid of a trunk. It's outside, toward Charlie's room, but definitely not in the house. I slip over to my closet. Drop to my knees to grope around the shoe rack that hangs over the door. Second row up, fourth pocket over. My fingers tighten around my .22. For three years after the trial, this pistol was tucked in my size 2 waistband. I considered a bigger weapon, but I didn't want anyone to see the bulge against my bony hip. Especially not my dad. Lucas secretly taught me to shoot when we weren't sneaking around accidentally making Charlie. He insisted on one thing when he pressed the .22 into my hand for the first time: Go to the gun range like it's a church, at least fifty-two times a year.

I've always hoped it's OK to shoot more than you pray, because that's how it's turned out. Lucas has urged me to trade up for the last ten years, but I can't imagine any gun but this one in my hand.

I shake Charlie's shoulder and she groans. '*Not* morning.'

'I hear something outside,' I whisper. 'Put your slippers on. And this.' I toss over a sweatshirt, hanging out of my hamper.

'For real?'

'For real. Get *up*.'

'Why aren't you calling the police?' The sound is muffled, as she tugs the hoodie over her face.

'Because I don't want us to be on the evening news.'

'Is that your gun? Mom.'

'Please, Charlie, just do what I say. We're going to slip out the back door.'

'That makes no sense. The . . . thing is *out there*. Isn't this why we have an alarm system so freaking sensitive that it goes off every time I turn up Vampire Weekend? Shouldn't we at least look out the window and make sure it's not the garbage truck?'

It's at times like this that I wish I had a daughter who wasn't so wrapped in the confident armor of her beauty and intelligence and athletic grace. Instead, she is just like the Before Tessie. Both insisted strange noises outside the window were teen-age boys with soap and eggs, not monsters with rusty shovels and guns. Most of the time, they were right.

'Charlie, I just need you to do what I say. Follow me.'

Another thump. Now tapping.

'OK, I heard that. Weird.' Charlie is quickening her steps behind me as we navigate the darkened hall and living room. The shades are drawn as usual, but I don't want to flip on any lights.

'Follow our fire drill plan,' I say. 'Go to Miss Effie's. Bang on her back door. Call her house if she doesn't answer. Here's my phone. If I'm not there in five minutes, dial 911.'

'Keep it. I already have my phone. What are you going to do?'

'Don't worry, Charlie. Just go.' *Run.*

I push her out the back door, into utter blackness. The last thing I see is the fleeting deer flash of her pink-and-white polka-dot pajama bottoms between the pine trees that border our properties.

I creep toward the front yard, using my photinia bushes as a shield. The thumping hasn't stopped, just moved inside me, to my chest. The gun is cocked in my hand. I want to be done with him. Tonight. *Forever.* I peer through a branch.

What the hell? Four gray squares are stuck in the middle

of my yard like a row of gravestones. A small shadow hovers beside one of them, bathed in faint light. *A time-traveling Victorian girl searching for her ring?* I blink hard to make her go away. Instead, the shadow rises. The ghost child transforms into a man with a flashlight and a shiny gray nylon sweatshirt.

'Hey!' My reckless scream rips the air.

I make out a Nike swoosh, black hair, a wiry beard, before the man flips off his flashlight and runs.

If he's running, dammit, so am I. Across the yard, down the street. Feet pounding. He's too fast to be my monster. Young legs. Marathon legs. I am still fast, but not this fast. The slippers flop on my heels.

All of a sudden, he slows. Maybe he's stepped in one of our historic potholes. He's taking aim. I raise the .22 in warning just as he presses a car remote, triggering the taillights of a parked sedan. In seconds, a car door slams and he's screeching off. I can't make out the license plate.

I turn back. It's not a cemetery in my yard. I'm staring at crude plywood signs. Hate shimmers off them.

BLACK-EYED BITCH

THOU SHALT NOT KILL

REPENT!!

TERRELL'S BLOOD, YOU'RE HANDS

Just one of the crazies.

I'm not relieved.

I have the sudden, certain feeling I'm being watched.

Charlie.

The house next door, still dark.

My feet tear up the ground to Effie's. I bang hard enough on the front door that something inside clatters to the floor. There's no answer.

I kick off my slippers on the porch and race to the back. I'm thinking of my monster, standing under my window-sill. Of my daughter, in her polka-dot pajamas.

I hurl my fist at Effie's back door. More strangling silence. I survey the back yard, open my mouth again to scream Charlie's name but nothing comes out.

My frantic gaze lands on Effie's rickety garden shed in the back. In seconds, I am yanking open the door, ripping it half off its rusty hinges. Charlie is crouched in the corner by two bags of compost. The phone is pressed to her cheek, half-illuminating her face.

'Mom!' She is in my arms in seconds. A car has screeched to the curb. And another. Siren lights are filtering through the bushes.

A large shape is walking toward us, blinding us with his flashlight.

'I'm a police officer. Did one of you make a 911 call?'

'Yes, I'm Charlie. This is my mom. We're OK.'

I nod, unable to speak. Gruff conversation floats from the front yard.

The policeman's light continues to travel over us. When he's apparently satisfied we aren't hurt or dangerous, he turns it on the shed.

The light trickles like water into the corners, up and down the walls.

He sees nothing out of the ordinary because he thinks what he's seeing is perfectly ordinary.

I'm seeing, but not understanding. I just know it's not ordinary.

Row after row of garden diggers.

They hang neatly in every square inch of space.

Tessie, 1995

'Do you believe in the devil, Tessie?'

Great. Like I don't get enough of this from Aunt Hilda.

'I mean it in a very metaphorical sense. I want to talk about the Black-Eyed Susan killer today. I think it would help when you're testifying to understand him a little better. That he's flesh and blood. Not mythic. Not Bluebeard. Not a troll under the bridge.'

My heart beats a little faster. My hand reflexively moves over the lump above my left breast, the metal chunk under my skin that keeps my heart beating at a minimum of sixty beats a minute. I run a nervous finger on the straight three-inch scar. Lydia is already looking for a bikini with a strap that will cover it up.

'We don't know anything about the creep,' I say stiffly. 'We never will. He isn't talking. His family says he's normal.' I don't ever say his name out loud. *Terrell Darcy Goodwin.*

'I treated a serial killer once,' he says. 'He was the smartest, most calculating person in the room. Could charm a million dollars out of an old lady, and did. He blended in, and stood out. He liked to get to know his victims and use that knowledge to scare them out of their minds.'

'The pig-and-daisy card at the hospital.' Out of nowhere.

'Do you think he sent that to you?' he asks.

'Yes. I think it made me go blind.'

'That's good, Tessie. Excellent progress. Whether he

sent it or not, it was a trigger for you. You control your mind, Tessie. Never forget it.'

I'm nodding. I'm flushing a little, embarrassed by his compliment.

'My patient understood right and wrong, he just didn't care,' he continues. 'He studied carefully how to behave. He was able to simulate empathy because he regularly sat in hospital waiting rooms and observed it. He spent a year selling suits at Brooks Brothers to figure out how to dress and speak. He used the newspaper to manufacture biographies about himself as he moved around. But serial killers make mistakes. This guy did. He carried the remains of his victims in the trunk of his car because he couldn't help himself. The point is, they don't think they are human, but they are.'

'I still don't get . . . the why.'

'No one really knows. Maybe we will never know. For a while, doctors used to think it had something to do with phrenology. How many bumps you had on your skull. My patient turned out to be a cliché. He blamed his mother.'

'Because . . .'

'We're getting a little off track here.'

'Were you trying to cure this guy?' I pester him. *Or were you trying to figure out if he is the one who took your daughter?*

'Yes, against all odds, against all the rules of psychiatry, I was trying to see if that was possible. But it didn't turn out well. He is a psychopath, Tessie. He is perfectly happy the way he is.'

Tessa, present day

Jo has asked me to meet her at Trinity Park, near one of the running trails, about a half-mile away from the duck pond. It seems a little strange. Too close to the bridge. Too much of a coincidence. Did someone besides a home-schooled juvenile delinquent see me digging? Is Bill reporting everything I say to Jo?

The Susans are quiet this morning. It happens that way sometimes, when my paranoia roils into such hurricane force that they can't catch their breath.

My body hasn't stopped jangling since Saturday night when I clutched my gun and pointed it toward the ghostly shape on the front lawn. On Sunday, I tried to rebound and put my daughter's life back in a normal place. I called Bill and told him to please not show up again on my doorstep with alcoholic beverages. That it was a mistake, that we had let overwrought emotion sweep us into the bed, that Swedish Scientist Girl and Assistant DA Girl would be more apt partners for him.

There was sturdy silence before he said: 'We didn't touch the wine. And you're pretty apt.'

Later, Charlie and I had swept the aisles at Walmart in search of blue hair gel, peppercorns, licorice, and lima beans for her 3-D re-creation of an animal cell. She chattered about turning Fruit Roll-Ups into a Golgi body. I listened to soothing snatches of nearby conversation that floated in the fluorescent light like a country western song. *My brother just lost his house* in frozen foods and *God will find a way* by the potato chips and *Daddy's going to kill him* in front of the boxed wine. Soothing, because it seems like very few people at Walmart are pretending that things are OK, or that the world is going to end just because they *aren't* OK. I wheeled my cart through this stew of misfortune and daily kicks-in-the-ass and plain old tenacity. No one at Walmart cared a whit who I was. I arrived home with ten potatoes for $1.99 and churned out my mother's recipe for corn chowder. All of this effort at ordinary seemed to work: Charlie slipped under her fluffy comforter at the end of the night, full of starch and bacon bits and her belief that our bad guy was just a coward of a sign-maker with bad grammar.

Now it's Monday morning, and I want to say no to meeting up with Jo, but I can't. As soon as Charlie leaves for school, I strap on ASICS and yank my hair into a ponytail, every movement angry. I woke up with a deep, persistent need to run, to sweat out every bit of poison. Running is the one thing that always works. I can still manage four miles before my ankle begins to ache, and then two more miles to spite him. But, first, Jo.

The south side of the park is almost deserted when I swing the Jeep beside a shiny silver BMW. It's the only other car in this lot, which serves a small picnic area. I glance inside the BMW as I slam my door shut. A Taco Bell bag and an empty Dr Pepper can are tossed on the floor. A handful of change is mingled in the console with a movie ticket stub. Innocent enough. As I circle behind the car, heading for the path, I glance down at the BMW's license plate: *DNA 4N6.*

OK, so definitely Jo's car. I say it out loud, '*DNA 4N6.*'

4N6? I try again. *DNA Foreign Sex*. Um, probably not, but it's taking my mind off the gun riding at my hip and what things a bone doc might store in the trunk of her car.

On the horizon, a straight black line. The predicted cold front and 30-degree temperature drop by nightfall. A sixtyish woman in pink fast-walks past me, pumping her arms, hurrying away from it. I stop at a homeless man curled into a fetal position, asleep on a concrete picnic table near a shopping cart crammed with useful trash. I stick a $10 bill deep into the empty coffee cup he's clutching. He doesn't move.

I do that whenever I can. For Roosevelt. I made Lydia go visit Roosevelt on his street corner after they found me, because I knew he'd be worried. I never got to say goodbye myself. He was found dead leaning against a tree, like he fell asleep there, a week before the trial.

DNA 4N6. Four-en-six. *Forensics!* I'm an idiot.

I pick up the pace once I see Jo, who is right where she said she'd be – under a landmark live oak rumored to have once been a hanging tree. She's cross-legged on a bench, sipping out of a green neoprene water bottle with a red biohazard sticker. Her black North Face windbreaker bears a *CSI Texas* logo. I'm figuring the bottle and the jacket are high-end graft from a forensic science conference.

'Thanks for meeting me here.' She unfolds her lean legs and pats the bench for me to sit beside her. 'I worked in the lab all weekend and needed some air. I heard about what happened at your house. Have the police caught him?'

'No. I didn't get a good look. There's an anti-death-penalty newsletter that mentions me on a regular basis, so the cops are checking that email list. The editor posted my street address in her last blog that ranted about Terrell's case. I'm not hopeful, though. I've been through this before.'

'It's odd and scary . . . that these people would target you.' She doesn't say it, but I know what she's thinking. *The victim.*

I shrug, used to it. 'The trial was a trigger for a lot of anger. And the jury foreman was very public in saying the case turned on my testimony.' *Even though I was just painting in the scenery.*

She nods sympathetically. I don't really want to talk about what happened Saturday night. It's bad enough that it's rolling on an endless loop in my head: Charlie crouching in the shed under a compulsive array of garden diggers. The police, at my insistence, breaking down Effie's back door. She had drifted off in her La-Z-Boy wearing noise-canceling headphones that she'd ordered off eBay. 'You know, to maybe quiet the voices,' she had told me conspiratorially while a policeman searched her house. For a brief second, I thought she was also hinting at the ones in my own head, but her eyes had been darting around like a feral cat. It seems most likely that Miss Effie's digger snatcher lives under her own roof. So I didn't tell the cops, and I hadn't yet figured out how to bring it up to Effie.

'I thought maybe you could use some good news,' Jo says. 'The red hair on the jacket found near the field? The mitochondrial DNA analysis proves there is a 99.75 percent chance it didn't come off your head. And there is no evidence of Terrell's DNA on the jacket itself.'

'Is it enough to get Terrell a new trial?' I wonder if she's told Bill.

'Maybe. Maybe not. There's a relatively new law in Texas

that allows prisoners to successfully appeal a case when scientific technology can shed light on old evidence. But I talked to Bill this morning. He's been through this wringer before with Death Row clients and he's pretty adamant that a single red hair and a sloppy expert who used junk science aren't going to be enough to convince an appeals court to overturn anything. He wants to throw more than that at the judge. Unfortunately, Terrell only has his mom and sister as alibis for the time Hannah Stein disappeared. And the cops have been unable to draw a line between Merry Sullivan and Hannah. Of course, the cops aren't exactly on Terrell's side – they are mostly focused on getting the girls identified for the families and getting the media off their backs every time the anniversary rolls around. Working at the behest of the district attorney who wants a little TV time. Did you happen to catch his press conference on Hannah?' I can tell she's not expecting an answer. 'Ferreting out the real killer . . . well, that would just be a bonus for *us*.'

The bitterness from her surprises me. 'Sorry.' She grimaces. 'I'm usually the one assuming everyone's doing the best they can. I wish Bill and Angie had pulled me in much sooner.' Her face turns more pensive. 'I'm trying something else in an effort to identify the other two girls. I just don't know if there's time to do it.'

Despite my resolve to pull back from the case, I feel that relentless tug in my gut. *I'm the one with the answers,* a Susan had insisted that day in the lab. Was it the Susan who belonged to the chattering skull? Or the new girl, lost and found in the pile of bones?

'A forensic geologist I know in Galveston is examining the bone evidence,' Jo continues. 'He might – a big might

– be able to narrow down the area or areas where they lived. Then we could check out the cases of missing girls in those places.'

'I've seen websites where you can send in a sample of your DNA and they will decipher your ancestry. Is this anything like that?'

'It is nothing, *nothing* like that. My geologist will use isotope analysis to examine the elements in her bone and try to match it to a region. It's a tool kind of in its infancy stages when it comes to forensic identification. It was first used on a boy whose torso was found floating in the Thames over a decade ago. Scientists were able to trace his origin to Nigeria.'

'And it helped them identify the boy? Catch his killer?'

'No. Not yet. It's a process. When you're trying out new technology, each case is a single step on a million-mile road.' Her voice is softening. 'We are so much a part of the earth, Tessa. Of the ancient past. We store strontium isotopes in our bones, in the same ratio as in the rocks and soil and water and plants and animals where we live. Animals eat the plants and drink the water. Humans eat the animals and plants. The strontium is passed along, all stored in our bones in the same ratio unique to the region.' The simplicity of her explanations always astounds me, and I think what a good professor she must be. 'The problem is, it's a big world. And there is a relatively small database at this point when it comes to identifying geological regions. It's another long shot.'

Jo has fallen silent. It still isn't clear exactly why she's asked me to the park.

'Tell me again how you deal with all of the dead ends,' I

finally say. 'There's just so much futility. Don't you ever think you can't take it anymore?'

'I could ask you the same.'

'But you *choose* this.'

'I'd say it chose me. I've known since I was fourteen this is what I was supposed to do. That's why, when a kid tells me he's going to be a third baseman for the Yankees, I don't doubt him. Did you ever hear about the Girl Scout Murders in Oklahoma?'

'No,' I say, although it stirs a vague memory. Lydia would know.

'Every scientist has a cold case that pulls at them for years. This Girl Scout case is mine. I was in high school when three Girl Scouts were pulled out of their tent in the middle of the night on a campout near Tulsa. They were raped and murdered and left out for show. A local man – who'd been a popular high school football player – was accused, tried, and declared not guilty. DNA evidence was collected at the time, but there was zero technology to examine it. And before you ask, the evidence is now too degraded to be useful. I've used my connections to see every single crime scene photo and read every single word on the police reports and forensic testing. The point is, if I could beam myself back to 1977, I could give those parents some answers. And it's all because scientists in labs keep trying to do futile things. My work is as much in the future as the present.'

'I understand,' I say. 'It's possible there won't be answers in my case. For years. Why exactly did you ask me to the park? Just to update me?' It comes out rudely, which I didn't intend. I'm just so tired.

'No. I wanted to say . . . to make sure that you know that you can always come to me. I don't want you to ever feel alone.'

She's really saying, *Don't dig without me. Not at this park. Not anywhere.*

'Tessa, have you ever thought that maybe I need you, too? That I'm not as tough as you think I am?'

The first whisper of the cold front is stirring the trees.

'Lori, Doris, Michele,' she says softly. 'The names of the dead Girl Scouts. *My* Susans.'

Tessie, 1995

'I'm thinking of not testifying.'

It sounded way more defiant when I practiced in front of the mirror this morning with the toothbrush in my hand and aqua bubbles drizzling out of the corner of my mouth.

I'm NOT testifying, Mr Vega.

There. That's better.

I open my mouth again to say it more emphatically but the district attorney is on his tiger prowl around the office, not the slightest bit interested in what I *think*. The doc is bent over his desk with a pile of folders, certainly listening to every word. He's the master of staying still.

'Did you hear me? I don't think I have anything of value to add. I *don't* have anything to add.' I'm stammering.

Benita offers a sympathetic smile that pretty much says I'm doomed. Both she and Mr Vega are here to review my testimony. This is the first time they want to rehearse the gory details. They've waited this long because Mr Vega wants me to sound as spontaneous as possible. The trial is less than two weeks away, so that's pretty spontaneous.

'Tessie, I know this is hard,' Mr Vega says. 'What we need to do is put the jury in that grave with you. Even if you don't remember details about the killer, you add context. You make it real. For instance, what did it smell like when you were lying there?'

My gag reflex is so strong that even he, the calloused

prosecutor, reacts. I'm sure he did this on purpose, calibrating how this melodrama would play to the jury. I still think he's the good guy. I've just changed my mind. I don't want to testify for him. Cannot, *will not,* sit across from my monster.

'OK, we'll come back to that. Close your eyes. You're in the grave. Turn your head to the left. What do you see?'

I reluctantly turn my head, and there she is. 'Merry.'

'Is she dead?'

I open my eyes and cast them to the doctor for help, but he's busily tapping away on his computer at his desk. *Do I lie? Or tell the prosecutor that dead Merry talked to me? Surely, that would hurt the case.*

If I testify. Which I won't.

'I don't know whether she's dead.' *The truth.* 'Her lips are bluish gray . . . but some girls wear blue lipstick. It's Goth.' I don't know why I said that. Nothing about clarinet-playing, churchgoing Merry was Goth, except when she was lying next to me in a grave like a prop for a horror movie.

'What else?'

'Her eyes are open.' *Things were eating her, except when they weren't.*

'What do you smell?'

I swallow hard. 'Something spoiled.'

'Is it hard to breathe?'

'It's like . . . breathing in a port-a-potty.'

'Are you cold? Hot? As best you can, narrative answers.'

'Sweating. My ankle hurts. I wonder if he chopped off my foot. I want to look but every time I lift my head up, things kind of explode in my head, you know? I'm scared I will faint.'

'Do you call out?'

'I can't. There's dirt in my throat.'

'Keep your eyes closed. Turn your head to the right. What do you see?'

It hurts to turn my head. But it's easier to breathe. 'I see . . . bones. My Pink Lemonade Lip Smacker. The lid is off. I don't know where it is. A Snickers bar. A quarter. From 1978. Three pennies.'

The photograph in my head suddenly animates. Ants crawl in a delirious, sugar-fired frenzy on my lip gloss. A hand stretches out for the Snickers bar. I know it's my hand because it's sprinkled with pink freckles and the nails are short, trimmed, painted neatly blue with Hard Candy Sky polish. The color almost matches Merry's lips. I taste blood and dirt, peanut butter and bile, when I rip open the wrapper with my teeth. The bones of the other Susans chatter encouragement. *Keep up your strength. Stay strong.*

'I remember eating the Snickers bar,' I say. 'I didn't want to.' *But the Susans insisted.*

'I don't remember you mentioning some of this before. Are you recalling other details? Anything about him? His face? Hair color? Anything?' I can't tell by Mr Vega's voice if he thinks this would be good or bad.

Why is this stuff coming back now? No one tells me to, but I shut my eyes again. Turn my face up to the night sky, except there are no stars. The sun is shining. I'm out of the grave. I'm somewhere else, in a light-filled space with Merry and the Susans. Merry sleeps, while the others are whispering, chattering excitedly, making a plan. One of them is bending over me. A ring dangles off her skeleton finger, but the stone is missing. She takes the gold prongs and carves a half-moon on my cheek, and it doesn't hurt at all. There is no blood.

Get him, she says. *Never forget us.*

I know this isn't real, although the lab found my blood type, not Merry's, on the prongs of the ring locked on a Susan's finger bone. They figure, with utmost logic, that I fell on it when I was dumped into the hole.

I have to stop this before I tumble into that hole again and can't ever climb out.

'I'm not testifying. Not for you. Or them.'

Mr Vega tilts his head, ready to fire his next question.

'You heard Tessie.' The doctor has raised his head from the desk. 'This session is over.'

Tessa, present day

I watched until Jo vanished on the path and I was sure she was not coming back. I jogged past the sleeping homeless man curled with his back to the refrigerating wind. Fumbled my way into the Jeep. Locked it. Folded myself forward against the steering wheel and stunned myself by bursting into tears. Here's what kindness and sympathy and an offer of partnership do to me.

I have driven to this office on autopilot, the last place I would have pictured myself this morning. The room is small, white-walled, and slightly chilly. A nervous woman in her thirties sits across from me, eager to start a conversation as soon as I stop pretending to read this magazine and finally make eye contact.

'It's hard, isn't it? When your kid is hurting? My kid is in there right now.' The woman needs something from me. I reluctantly lift my gaze and watch her take it all in. My eyes, red and swollen. The scar. I nod with agreement and empathy, hope that will be it, and return to the headline: *Is it wrong to pay kids to eat their veggies?*

'Dr Giles is terrific . . . if you're here for a first consult for your kid.' She's not going to give up. 'Lily's been going to her for six months. I highly recommend her.'

I carefully close the magazine and tuck it back into the neat arc of reading material on the coffee table. 'I'm the kid,' I say.

The woman's face twists in confusion.

The girl who must be Lily pops out of the closed door, wearing a dizzying array of crayon-esque colors. The right side of her head is attached to a giant sparkly bow. Even with all the effort at distraction, I am drawn to the plain brown innocent eyes.

And the smile. I know that smile because I've worn it, the one that pulls at thirteen muscles and strikes a match for all the other smiles in the room and makes you appear perfectly normal and happy. Except I know Lily's terrified.

Dr Giles isn't far behind Lily and, to her credit, does not act the slightest bit surprised to see me.

'Give me just a second, Tessa, OK? I'll have about twenty minutes before my next appointment.'

'Yes. Certainly.' I feel the flush of heat in my face. This isn't like me, to burst in on people, busy people, without warning. I remind myself that I have not yet paid her a cent.

Dr Giles reaches out a hand to Lily's mother. 'Mrs Tanger, we had an especially good morning. And, Lily, you're going to draw me a picture for next time?' The little girl nods solemnly, and the doctor's eyes meet her mother's in a silent exchange. It's like watching my father's face all over again. *Hope, worry, hope, worry, hope, worry.*

Dr Giles ushers me into the warm jungle of her office. I drop into one of her cushy chairs. I haven't rehearsed what I'm going to say. I think that seeing Lily has sucked the selfish, hot anger out of me, but I'm wrong. My hands are suddenly shaking.

'I want closure.' Each word, staccato. A demand, as if Dr Giles is somehow to blame.

'Closure doesn't exist,' she responds smoothly. 'Just . . . awareness. That you can't ever go back. That you know a truth about life's randomness that most other people don't.'

She leans forward in her chair. 'Maybe you still need to forgive him. I'm sure you've heard this before. Forgiveness is not for him. It is for you.' She might as well be raking her nails on the chalkboard behind her. It's bugging me, the faint ghost of a stick figure still lingering there, half-erased. The happy sun. The flower with a center eye.

'I can't ever imagine forgiving him.' My eyes are still glued to the flower on the chalkboard. I want to take the eraser and scrub away until everything is black. Make it clean.

'Then let's say that there is a way for you to get closure. How do you see that happening? What if he . . . what do you call him?'

'My monster.' My voice is so low, ashamed, that I wonder if she can hear me. *What grown-up, not-crazy woman still talks about monsters?*

'OK. What if your monster opened the door right now and walked right in? Sat down. Confessed everything. You could see his face. Know his name, where he grew up, if his mother loved him, if his dad beat him, whether he was popular in high school, whether he loved his dog or killed his dog. Imagine he sat in that chair right over there, three feet away, and answered *every single one of your questions.* Would it really make any difference? Is there any answer that could satisfy you? Make you feel better?'

I stare at the chair.

The gun feels like a steel cookie cutter against my skin. I itch to fire it dead center into the fabric. Watch the white stuffing explode.

I don't want to have a conversation with my monster. I just want him dead.

Tessie, 1995

'I'm nervous.' Benita's voice is vibrating.

This is an *emergency* session. They've sent Benita in alone to do the dirty work. It's been less than twenty-four hours since I announced that I would not be testifying.

She's wearing no eye makeup, which is a sure sign something is very wrong. She's just as pretty, but now she looks like the hot girl in middle school instead of the hot girl in high school. All I know is, I don't want to be the thing that makes Benita scared. She's been nothing but sweet and kind to me. Like, even her name means *blessed*.

Benita halts abruptly by the window. 'I'm supposed to convince you to testify. Mr Vega and your doctor think we have some sort of young female bond. To be honest, I'm not sure what you should do. I'm thinking about going into my uncle's cabinet-making business.'

Wow. What a backfire.

'They want me to ask you what your worst fear is.' She plops in the doctor's chair and meets my eyes for the first time. 'They told me to sit *here*. Then I'm supposed to convince you that you will never live to regret testifying no matter how hard it is. So if you can tell me what you are most afraid of by going to court, that would be great. So they at least think I tried.'

Tears are brimming in her soft eyes. I'm thinking it's not the first time she's cried this morning. I want to get up and hug her but that might break another ethical code and she's already smashed a few in this room.

'I hear that this defense attorney rips into people until there is nothing left but scraps.' I speak slowly. 'That's a quote my friend Lydia read about Richard Lincoln in the paper. And she overheard her dad tell her mom that everybody calls him Dick the Dick. He might get the jury to think I deserved this. Or that I'm making stuff up.'

'The defense attorney is an asshole,' Benita agrees. She is holding a finger horizontally under each eye, so the tears don't spill.

Without looking at the box, I grab a Kleenex and hand it over. The box is always waiting for me on the little table by my elbow, never an inch out of place. 'And I don't want to be in the room with . . . the guy who did this,' I continue. 'With him staring at me the whole time. I can't imagine anything worse. I don't want him to feel any power over me ever again.'

She dabs at her eyes. 'Neither would I. It seems terrifying.'

'My dad will be there. I don't want to lay out all the details, you know? Thinking about it, *talking* about it, makes me want to throw up. Like, I can see myself throwing up in the witness chair.'

She takes a deep breath. 'I worked on this terrible case during an internship last year. A twelve-year-old girl had been molested by a sixty-five-year-old aunt who couldn't get out of a wheelchair. It was a mess. Her own family was divided about believing the girl.'

She reluctantly shifts her eyes back to me. 'See, you are already wondering yourself. Mr Vega was the prosecutor.

He's brilliant. He had her talk about the details of maneuvering around the wheelchair during . . . the acts. No one doubted her when she got out of that witness chair.'

'So the jury convicted her aunt?'

'Yes. Texas is vicious with child molesters. She'll die in prison.'

'Was the girl glad she testified?'

'I don't know. She was pretty ripped up afterward.' Benita offers me a weak smile. 'I'm thinking selling cabinets would be a lot simpler, you know? They open. They close.'

'Yeah,' I say. 'But you're good at this.'

Tessa, present day

'Why does Obama need to know my damn waistline?'

Effie, in Texas Rangers pajama pants and a pale pink silk blouse with ruffles, is trotting across the lawn, shouting, waving a piece of paper. Charlie and I have just arrived home after an early after-school dinner at the Ol' South Pancake House. Some days, I wonder how long Effie stares out her window before we show up in our driveway, and if that time has any meaning for her. I'm really hoping it doesn't.

I'm sure it's been a long day of trying to remember for both of us. I'm not sure I'm up for Effie. My head hurts despite a confectioners'-sugar fix. She meets us on the porch, breathless, while her finger punches away at the typewritten letter. 'It says right here that he wants me to tell him my weight, waistline, and whether I like to drink and smoke. It's not like we're courting. Although I do like a whiskey on the rocks and a smoke with a handsome black man every good now and then.' A skim of green eye shadow, two rosy circles of blush, and the large fake pearl clips in her ears are dead giveaways that Effie has made it out of the house today. The pearl clips pop out of the drawer for church every Sunday, but the glittering eyelids mean she's been jousting with the ladies of the historical society. Effie regularly declares them 'way too fix-y.'

I prop the door open for Effie. Charlie follows while

carefully balancing a clear plastic box loaded with a sea of blue hair gel and precisely arranged food products.

Effie sniffs the air deliberately.

'It's my 3-D animal cell project,' Charlie tells her. 'Starting to rot.'

'Well, set it on the counter here and let's take a look.' *Animal cell* and *3-D* take the stink out of it for Effie, who lifts the edge of the Saran Wrap cover with enthusiasm. Charlie snatches the offending letter out of Effie's other hand.

'Miss Effie, this letter is from your insurance company.' Charlie begins to skim. 'They're going to give you $100 off your deductible and a $25 Amazon card if you fill out this form and they approve your numbers. They also want your cholesterol.'

'Damn spies, all of them.' She pokes a finger into the blue cesspool. 'Put *1984* on your reading list, Charlie dear. The man was a soothsayer. My waist used to be nineteen inches. Maybe I'll write that in their little chart. And then I'll call the cops and sue for sexual harassment when they send somebody around with a tape measure.' Her finger continues to poke away in the box. 'Hair gel for cytoplasm. Clever girl. What grade did you make on this project?'

'A minus. Which is like, really good for this teacher. The average in her class for this project over her twenty-six-year career is a C plus.'

'Well, I'd say that's the sign of a bad teacher. What was the minus for?'

'The nucleus. I used a clear plastic Christmas ornament from Hobby Lobby.'

'And the nuclear membrane isn't rigid. Hmm. Gotta hand that one to her, I suppose.'

'Should I dump this in the compost, Mom? The jar said the hair gel is all-natural.'

'It seems like more of a biological weapon at this point. I will let you and our neighborhood scientist make the call. I'm going to change into some sweats.' And swig down a couple of aspirin.

I navigate the hall in the dark and flip on my bedroom light. There is a man, sleeping on my bed. Face turned away. And yet his reaction time is still better than mine. I'm looking down, fumbling for the gun in my waistband, and he's already leapt the six feet across the bed, shoved a hand over my mouth, and stifled my scream.

I struggle against him. His other arm is pressing my back against a brutal chest. *Charlie is in the house.*

'Shh. OK?'

I stop squirming. Nod. He releases his grip and I flip away, stumbling. I find myself staring furiously at Charlie's father.

'Jesus, Lucas,' I hiss. 'You scared me. Where in the hell did you come from? Why can't you knock on the door like a normal person?'

He shuts the door. 'I'm sorry. I meant to text as soon as I got here. It was a twenty-nine-hour journey that involved turbulence and an Army pilot who enjoyed it a little too much. The cab dropped me off a couple of hours ago. Your bed was very comfy. I went right to sleep. Might have left some sand in your sheets.' His face is closer to mine than necessary. 'You smell like strawberry crepes.' For a second, I remember what it was like to be wrapped in a burrito of solid Army muscle. And then I feel another little ping for Bill. He'd texted twice today. *How's your day?* About two hours later: *Come on, butterfly girl, talk to me.*

'Why, again, are you here?' Trying to hold my ground in every way.

'I had a disturbing Skype session with Charlie. After your night with a domestic terrorist.'

'Oh.' I sit on the end of the bed. She hadn't mentioned telling her dad, but why wouldn't she?

Lucas plops beside me and tosses his arm around my shoulders. 'I figured I might be needed, but you'd be afraid to ask. Also, I'm trying to be respectful of your parental boundaries. If you don't think I should be here, I'll go. Charlie doesn't have to know. I can slip out the way I came in.'

'Which I assume is through the front door.'

'Well, yeah. You're paranoid about everything but your security code. You should change it more than once every five years.'

'No.'

'No what?'

'No, I don't want you to sneak out. Charlie should know you're here.' *That you'll come for her.*

I knew Lucas. It didn't matter what had just rolled sweetly off his tongue – he wasn't about to go quietly after traversing an ocean for his daughter.

He has dropped his hand to my waist. Distracting. He lifts up the bottom edge of my shirt, lets his finger drift, and tugs out the .22. 'You could use a little practice on your quick draw. You shouldn't carry a gun if you can't get it out of your pants.'

I try to summon up a retort and fail.

'How about a little refresher tomorrow?' he asks.

My head is no longer pounding. If I still believed in them, I'd say this man was a godsend.

Lucas had never once judged my sanity, or told me no.

He slips the gun into my hand. 'Put it up.'

'I need a favor tomorrow morning,' I say.

'Which involves?'

'Digging.'

My bedroom is dark, except for the glow of the iPad. I'm propped against a stack of pillows. A full glass of wine is within reaching distance on the nightstand. Lucas is sprawled snoring on the couch, the contents of his duffle spilled out on the living room floor. Charlie is texting under her covers. The evening's competitive father-daughter game of *Assassin's Creed* was a little too instructional for my comfort. I was relieved when Lucas snapped off the video game about half an hour ago and tucked his teen-ager into bed for the first time in months. She pretended to be too old for tucking in, but we all knew better.

The dark is friendly, for once. The man on our sofa has sifted all of the bad things from the night and stuffed them under his pillow.

Still, I'm not at rest. I'm determined to take a little trip into the past.

I hold the picture in my hand closer to the light, which makes her eyes dance. A trail of Spanish lace spills down her hair and across her shoulders. A tiny locket nestles in her throat. A modern girl transformed into a beautiful antique bride.

I had clipped Benita's wedding picture out of the

newspaper a very long time ago, about two summers after the trial. It contains only the most basic information. In the photo, Benita is beaming up at a very white man with a very white name. The bride's parents are listed as Mr and Mrs Martin Alvarez and the groom's as Mr and Mrs Joseph Smith Sr.

OK, Benita aka Ms. Joe Smith. I type *Benita Smith* into the iPad search bar and click on *Images.* The first twenty-five faces do not belong to my Benita Smith. The twenty-sixth picture is a red Mercedes, and the next is a shopping mall Christmas tree followed by a pearl bracelet and a baby's foot. Farther down, a kitchen pantry with bright red rooster door handles. In case she really did go into her uncle's cabinet business, I click to that page. No luck. I skip through endless, useless Benita Smith story links before I head to Facebook to search for Benita *Alvarez* Smith. Nothing. I delete her maiden name, and the Facebook screen rolls up hundreds of Benita Smiths.

Part of me doesn't want to work too hard at this. *Would she really know something that could help Terrell? Did she overhear something? Suspect something?*

I had let Benita drift out of my life seventeen years ago. There has to be a good reason for that, right? We had met for coffee every Tuesday afternoon for a few months after I testified. The last time, she dropped all official pretenses. She entered the café in tight black jeans and a *Remember Selena* T-shirt, with her six-year-old sister in tow. *Texas Monthly* had made Selena its tragic cover girl that month instead of me, so I was still feeling the naive bliss of being old news.

Not long after Terrell was convicted, Selena's killer had

been sentenced and locked up in Gatesville. She was confined twenty-three hours a day to a tiny cell because of death threats. The Tejano music fans behind bars wanted Yolanda Saldivar to die for her sins. While Benita and I had whispered about that, her sister carefully strung plastic beads onto a shoelace. She had tied the bracelet to my wrist like a purple-and-yellow worm.

I doubt that Benita Alvarez looms boldly in the official records of the Black-Eyed Susans case. If her name is mentioned at all, Bill and Angie would have glanced right over it. She was never interviewed by the media. She didn't testify and only attended the trial on the two days that I took the stand. She was a minor player to everyone but me, drowned out by the thunder of Al Vega – or *Alfonso* as he calls himself now. Mr Vega, 100 percent Italian, picked up the *fonso* to court the Hispanic vote when he ran his first successful race for Texas Attorney General.

When a Terrell Darcy Goodwin question is sprung on him, Mr Vega declares *in no uncertain terms* that he would not try the case any differently today. He sent a birthday card to me when I turned eighteen, and a sympathy card when my father died. On both, he scrawled his name and wrote underneath: *I will always be there for you.* The cynic in me wonders if those words are just part of his regular signature to victims he wrestled into the witness chair. But Tessie? Tessie believes she could pick up the phone and he'd be at her front door in seconds.

I clear the search bar. Hesitate, just for a second. Type. Most of my teen-age angst about my doctor is gone. I'm staring at links to an array of bombastic papers he's written for online blogs and psychiatric journals. There's a new one since I last searched: 'The Colbert Love Affair: Why We See Ourselves in an Imaginary French Conservative Narcissist.'

I clear the search bar and type another name, even more reluctantly. Click on the link at the top for the very first time.

I'm staring at the weekly blog of Richard Lincoln aka Dick the Dick, instantly regretting that I just provided him with a hit, even the tiniest bit of incentive to carry on. Today's post: 'Gasping for air.' It's hard to look away now that I've come this far. Angie always wanted me to talk to him. Thought it might bump something loose. *He's a changed man.*

I can barely stomach the bio, so I skim. *Richard Lincoln, crusader. Nationally renowned death penalty lawyer. Author of* The New York Times *best-selling book,* My Black Eye.

My Black Eye. His confessional, a year after the trial. Whenever I'm in a bookstore, I turn the cover around, even though I've heard that he donates half the profits to the children of prisoners. Because why doesn't he donate all of them?

There's a YouTube video link beside his blog, which my fingers click without my brain's permission. At once, his voice is jarring the silent house, rising and falling like a preacher's, still a saw against my skin. I hurry my finger to turn him down. He's an upright cockroach roving an anonymous stage. *Lincoln-esque,* is how his fans describe him. *I failed Terrell,* he's saying. *I destroyed that girl. The Black-Eyed Susan case was the turning point of my life.*

I can't listen to any more.

He didn't just destroy me. He destroyed my grandparents. The police and Dick the Dick worked in odd concert in that regard. The police ransacked their castle and drove off with my grandfather's beloved truck as evidence. Nobody in Texas took a man's truck unless he was guilty as hell, so even his best and most stalwart farmer friends wondered. It didn't matter that the police said 'whoops' months before the trial. Dick the Dick still hammered away in court. A tabloid screamed, *Could Grampa be the killer?* No, I can't offer *Dick* forgiveness despite the fact that, in the last thirteen years, Richard Lincoln has used DNA evidence to free three innocent men from Texas's Death Row. I pull the cover over the iPad. Nudge a couple of extra pillows to the floor. Slip deeper into sheets rough with sand from a war zone. Squeeze my eyes shut. Imagine the doctor lounging in pajamas covered with ducks in front of a *Colbert* rerun. Hope that Benita's life is strung like a party with purple and yellow beads.

I'm floating at the edge of consciousness when Lydia finds a tiny wormhole.

It's not like I haven't dragged the Internet for her a hundred times. Nothing. Not about her or Mr and Mrs Bell. It's like they are tiptoeing around in invisible ink while everyone else is galloping in screaming neon. The Bells *were* odd. They had little family, and made very few deep connections in town. Both sets of Lydia's grandparents were dead. I retain vague memories of a distant cousin of Mrs Bell's who sent a poinsettia at Christmas. But how could a family simply vanish? How could nobody really care?

Over the years, I've imagined all sorts of outrageous plotlines about their fate. Maybe my monster killed them because Lydia knew something. She was always clipping out articles about the Black-Eyed Susan case and pasting them in a scrapbook she didn't think I knew about. Scribbling notes in the margins in her cramped, intelligent hand. My monster didn't turn the storm cellar into a family mausoleum, but he could have scattered their bones across the West Texas desert.

Or their bodies could be lying miles and miles under the sea with ocean garbage. The whole family could have bounced off on a spontaneous vacation and sunk to the bottom of the Bermuda Triangle in a wayward craft piloted by Mr Bell. He was always forgetting to buy a boating permit. They could have slipped, undocumented, under the waves.

My most logical theory was witness protection. Someone had to plant the For Sale sign. Mr Bell dealt in recycled auto parts with Mexican mafia types in the salvage yards. He rushed off in the middle of the night all the time to meet them. Lydia had shown me his drawer full of hundred-dollar bills.

I do know this. If another family on the block had quietly slipped out of town right after the trial, and Lydia was the one speculating, she'd suggest that the father was the Black-Eyed Susan killer. His wife and daughter were in on it. They were spooked by my survival and now travel from town to town, changing their names as they go, killing girls.

That's exactly the kind of story Lydia would have made up when we were under the blanket with our flashlights, and she was scaring the crap out of me.

Tessie, 1995

October third, nineteen hundred and ninety-five, 1 P.M.

O.J. was set free an hour ago, which makes me sick to my stomach.

In mere minutes, if I don't screw this up, I will be, too.

This is my last session. The doctor is recommending a follow-up every six months for the next two years, and, *of course,* I should call before then if I'm ever feeling any distress. He's taking a sabbatical in China, so he won't be around, but he will recommend someone *perfect for me.* In fact, he already has someone in mind. There's a little transfer paperwork to fill out, but he'll take care of that before he leaves. *How lucky,* he says, *that the trial only lasted a month.* That the jury took only one day to reach a verdict.

Everyone is beaming. The doctor. My dad. I'm beaming back because otherwise I might explode. *Almost free, almost free, almost free.*

'I want to say again how brave you were to testify,' the doctor says. 'You held your own. The bottom line: Because of you, a killer is on Death Row.'

'Yes. It's a relief.' A lie. The only thing that's a relief is the news that my doctor is moving to China.

He's sitting there, so smug. I can't let him get away with it. I won't forgive myself.

'Dad, can you just give us one second alone to say goodbye?'

'Sure. Of course.' He plants a kiss on my head. Shakes the doctor's hand.

Dad doesn't pull the door shut hard enough when he leaves, so the doc gets up to close the two-inch gap. *Click*. Doctor-client confidentiality and all.

'Why wouldn't you ever talk about Rebecca?' I ask, before he sits down.

'Tessie, it's very painful. Surely you can understand that. And it would have been unprofessional of me to do so. I shouldn't have even said what I did. You need to let this go. It can't be a part of our professional relationship.'

'Which is ending. Right now.'

'Yes, but that doesn't matter. You are still my patient until you walk out that door.'

'I saw you with her.'

'You're really beginning to worry me, Tessie.' And, in fact, his face does look worried. 'You were right. My daughter is most likely dead. She isn't . . . talking to you, is she? Like the Susans?'

'I'm not talking about your daughter.'

'Then I have no idea what you mean,' he says.

I don't say it out loud, because what's the point?

We both know he's lying.

'See you around,' I say.

PART II
Countdown

'According to the *L.A. Times,* Attorney General
John Ashcroft wants to take "a harder stance"
on the death penalty. What's a harder stance on the
death penalty? We're already killing the guy. How
do you take a harder stance on the death penalty?
What, are you going to tickle him first? Give him
itching powder? Put a thumbtack
on the electric chair?' – Jay Leno

– Tessa, listening to *The Tonight Show* in bed, 2004

September 1995

MR VEGA: I know that this has been a very difficult day of testifying, Tessie. I appreciate your willingness to speak for all of the victims and I know the jury does, too. I have just one more question for now. What was the worst part of lying in that grave?

MS. CARTWRIGHT: Knowing that if I gave up and died, my father and little brother would have to live without knowing what happened. That they would think things were more horrible than they were. I wanted to tell them that it wasn't that bad.

MR VEGA: You were lying near-comatose with a shattered ankle in a grave with a dead girl and the bones of other victims – and you wanted to tell your family that it wasn't that bad?

MS. CARTWRIGHT: Well, it was bad. But imagining what happened for the rest of your life is worse. You know, letting your mind fill all that in, like, a million different ways. That's what I thought about a lot . . . how they'd have to do that. When the rescuers came, I was, like, so relieved that I could tell my dad it wasn't that bad.

29 days until the execution

In a month, Terrell's coffin, black and shiny as a new Mustang, will be hitched on a wagon to the back of a John Deere tractor. He will sink into the ground with the bodies of thousands of rapists and killers rotting in the Captain Joe Byrd Cemetery. Most of these men lived violently on the surface but they are interred on a pretty little hill in East Texas summoned out of Walt Whitman's dreams. These were men officially unclaimed in death. In Terrell's case, people claim him, *love* him – they just don't have the money to bury him. The state of Texas will do that with $2,000 of taxpayer money and surprising grace.

Inmates will rumble that tractor. They will be his pallbearers and bow their heads. They will chisel out his stone. Stencil on his inmate number. Maybe misspell his name.

They will use a shovel like the one in my hand.

My stomach churns for Terrell as I stare at the patch of black earth that my grandfather used to till behind his fairy tale house. At the very place where, twelve years ago on a hot July day, I found a suspicious patch of black-eyed Susans. It is the last place I'd ever want to dig for a gift from my monster, and so that's what I've done. Left it for last. My stomach boiled in a sick stew that day, too.

I was twenty-two. Aunt Hilda and I had banged a For Sale sign onto the front lawn a few hours earlier. Granny had died eight months before. She was buried beside her daughter and husband in a small country cemetery, eight miles down the road from their fantastical house.

That day, I'd gone outside to breathe after opening a drawer in Granny's jewelry box and sucking in a powerful hit of her church perfume. Charlie was almost three, and she'd slammed the screen door to the back porch ahead of me a few minutes earlier. When I opened the door, my beaming daughter stood several feet from the bottom of the steps, hands behind her back. She thrust out the handful of black-eyed Susans that she was strangling in her sweaty fist. Behind her, a hundred feet away, their sisters danced in flouncy yellow skirts – pretty little bullies hanging out near a row of sickly beans and a bonsai-like fig tree.

I poured a pot of boiling water into their eyes while Charlie stared from the porch. When my aunt called out from the house and asked what I was doing, I told her I was getting rid of a vicious pile of fire ants, which was just a bonus. *Don't want Charlie to get stung.* A few ants were already carting the dead away on their backs.

I'm jolted back to the present as Herb Wermuth lets the screen door slam behind him. It echoes like a tinny symbol. More than a decade later, it's his castle, not my grandfather's. He's gone inside, abandoning Lucas and me with little instruction to the devious winter sun and the garden that he says his wife, Bessie, chews up with a tiller twice a year. *Good luck finding anything.* Herb has made it clear he couldn't care less where we are digging as long as it is not for a dead body and the media isn't involved. He did ask us to try to get our business done before his wife returned in a couple of hours from a session with her new personal trainer.

At first, when we showed up on his front porch, Herb hadn't been so accommodating. 'I listen to the news,' he'd said grimly. 'After all this time, you're not sure they got the right killer. You're working with his lawyer.' His eyes had raked over the shovel hanging from my hand. 'Do you actually think one of his girls is buried out back?'

'No, no, of course not.' I had rushed to reassure him while hiding my revulsion at the use of the pronoun. *His*. Like the monster owns us. Owns me. 'The cops would be here if that was the case. As I said, I've just always thought that it was possible that the mon . . . killer buried . . . something for me in the garden.'

Herb couldn't hide it on his face – he believes, like most people around here, that the Cartwright girl had never been right in the head again.

'You've got to promise,' he insisted. 'No media. I got rid of some tabloid photographer yesterday asking to snap a picture of the room where the Black-Eyed Susan slept. And some guy called the other day from *Texas Monthly* wanting permission to get a portrait of you in front of the house. Said you hadn't called him back. It's so bad I'm taking Bessie to a condo in Florida until this execution thing passes over.'

'No media.' Lucas had responded firmly. 'Tessa only needs to ease her mind.' Patronizing. It sent a trickle of annoyance up my neck, but it did the trick for Herb. He even retrieved a shiny new shovel out of the garage for Lucas.

So Herb has left us to it. Except Lucas and I haven't budged since the screen door ricocheted on its hinges a minute ago. Instead of investigating the garden, Lucas is casting watchful eyes up the walls and windows of my grandfather's mythical house. He has never been here before, even though it's just an hour's drive from Fort Worth. By the time Lucas and I were wrestling in the backseats of cars, my grandfather was half-blind and permanently propped in bed.

It is comforting to know that Lucas is so focused. Protecting me from my monster, even if he has always believed, no matter what I say, that the monster is mostly confined to my head.

The house has cast a cool, dark arm across my shoulders. I know this house like it is my own body, and it knows me. Every hidden crevice, every crooked tooth, every false front. Every clever trick from my grandfather's imagination.

I start a little when Lucas steps beside me, armed with his shovel and ready to go.

The Susan times her warning to my first squishy step into the soil.

Maybe he did bury one of our sisters here.

If it weren't for the fig tree standing there like an arthritic crone, I wouldn't know where to dig. The garden is twice as large as when my grandmother grew her precise rows of Early Girl tomatoes and Kentucky Wonder beans and orange habanero peppers, which she turned to jelly that ran on my tongue like lava. This morning, other than the fig tree climbing out of it, the plot is a flat brown rectangle.

I used to stand in this garden and pretend. The blackbirds stringing across the sky were really wicked witches on brooms. The distant fringes of wheat were the blond bangs of a sleeping giant. The black, mountainous clouds on the horizon were the magical kind that could twirl me to Oz. The exceptions were brutal summer days when there was no movement. No color. Nothingness so infinite and dull it made my heart ache. Before the monster, I would always rather be scared than bored.

'This is a very open area, Tessa,' Lucas observes. 'Anyone who looked out a window on the west side of the house could have seen him plant the flowers. That's pretty brazen for a guy you think has managed to fool everybody into thinking he doesn't exist.' He shades his eyes to look up. 'Is that a naked woman up there on the roof? Never mind. It is.'

'She's a replica of *The Little Mermaid* statue that gazes over the harbor in Copenhagen,' I say. 'The Hans Christian Andersen one – not the Disney version.'

'I get that. Definitely not G-rated.'

'My grandfather cast it himself. He had to rent a crane to lift it up there.' I take three carefully measured steps north from the fig tree. 'About here,' I say.

Lucas thrusts the glistening metal of Herb's shovel with crisp, clean determination into the dirt. My own rusty shovel is leaning against a tree. I've brought a stack of newspapers, an old metal sieve from the kitchen, and a pair of work gloves. I plunk myself down and begin to sift through the first chunks of overturned soil. I hear Jo's voice in my head insisting that *this isn't the way*.

I glance up, and for a second, see a little Charlie on the porch. I blink, and she's gone.

It isn't long before Lucas has stripped off his shirt. I keep sifting, averting my eyes from the muscles rippling across his back.

'Tell me a story,' he says.

'Really? Now?' A black bug is skittering down my jeans. I blink, and it's gone.

'Sure,' Lucas says. 'I miss your stories. Tell me all about the girl up there on the roof with the nice boobs.'

I pull out a rough piece of old metal. Think about how many layers to leave out of a multi-layered fable. Lucas has a short attention span. I know that he is just trying to distract me.

'A long time ago, a mermaid fell madly in love with a prince she rescued from the sea. But they were from different worlds.'

'I'm already sensing an unhappy ending. She looks lonely up there.'

'The prince didn't know it was the mermaid who rescued him.' I pause from breaking apart a large chunk of soil. 'She had kissed him and laid him on the beach, unconscious, and swum back out to sea. But she desperately wanted to be with him. So she swallowed a witch's potion that burned away her beautiful singing voice but in return carved out two human legs. The witch told the mermaid that she would be the most graceful dancer on earth, yet every single step would feel like she was walking on knives. The mermaid didn't care. She sought out the prince and danced for him, mute, unable to speak her love. He was mesmerized. So she danced and danced for him, even though it was excruciating.'

'This is a horrible story.'

'There's lovely imagery when it's read aloud. It loses a lot in my retelling.' I raise my eyes to the window in the turret of my old bedroom. The partly drawn shade makes it appear like a half-closed eye. I imagine the muffled sound of my grandfather reciting on the other side of the stained glass. *An ocean as blue as the prettiest cornflower. Icebergs like pearls. The sky, a bell of glass.*

'And did this a-hole of a prince love her back?' Lucas asks.

'No. Which means the mermaid was cursed to die unless she stabbed the prince and let his blood drip on her feet, fusing her legs back into fins.'

At this point, I stop. Lucas has already produced an impressive hole the circumference of a small plastic swimming pool and about as deep. I'm way behind on sifting through his piles of earth. All I have to show for my efforts are a stack of rocks, the ribbon of rusted metal, and two plastic pansy markers.

Lucas drops the shovel and falls to his knees beside me. 'Need some help?' he asks. I know him well enough to translate. He thinks this is futile. My heart isn't really in it, either.

I hear the creak of a door opening, punctuated by a noisy slam. Bessie Wermuth is trotting our way in fire-engine-red workout gear that clings to two narrow inner tubes of fat around her waist. She's carrying tall yellow Tupperware cups chunked with ice and amber liquid.

'Good morning, Tessa.' She beams. 'So nice to see you and . . . your friend.'

'I'm Lucas, ma'am. Let me help you with those glasses.' He picks one and swallows a quarter of it in the first swig. 'Delicious tea. Thank you.'

Bessie's eyes are fastened on Lucas's snake tattoo, which starts around his belly button and disappears into his jeans.

‘Have you found anything yet?’ She raises her eyes from Lucas’s belt buckle.

‘A few fossils, a plastic plant marker, a rusty piece of metal.’

Bessie barely acknowledges my stash. ‘I wanted to tell you about my box. Herb said he didn’t tell you about my box.’

‘Your box?’ A curl of uneasiness.

‘It’s a bunch of junk, really,’ she says. ‘I’ve even labeled it, *Stuff Nobody Wants But Mom.* You know, so my kids don’t have to add it to the crap they’re cleaning out when we die. There might be something in there you’re interested in, though.’

The sweat under my arms is icy. *What is wrong with me? It’s just Stuff Nobody Wants.*

‘I’m going inside to get it,’ she says. ‘I couldn’t carry the box and the tea. Meet me at the picnic table.’

‘Are you all right? You don’t look right.’ Lucas pulls me up. ‘We need a little break anyway.’

‘Yes. Fine.’ I don’t say what I’m thinking – that I have a bad feeling about Bessie and her relentless tilling. We walk thirty yards and plant ourselves on the bench of an old picnic table slopped carelessly with green paint.

Lucas nods toward the house. ‘Here she comes.’

Bessie is hauling an old U-Haul box across the yard, breathing with furious intention. Lucas jumps up and meets her halfway, relieving her of the box. He sets it in front of me, but I don’t reach. I’m mesmerized by Bessie’s large bold print, which says exactly what she declared it did, thereby assuring that this will be the one box her grieving, surely sentimental kids will never throw away no matter what.

'This holds all the odds and ends I've found on the outdoor property since we moved in.' Bessie pops open flaps. 'Useless archaeology, really. Except the old bottles. I got those on the kitchen windowsill. But if it comes out of the earth and isn't wriggling or biting me, I keep it in here. I don't organize it by year or location. It's all dumped together. So I have no idea what came out of the garden and what got kicked up by the mower.'

Lucas is bending over the box, pawing through it.

'Just dump it,' Bessie says. 'Can't hurt anything. Then Tessa can see, too.'

Before I can prepare, the contents are rolling recklessly across the table. Wire springs and rusty nails, an old, half-crushed yellow-and-red-striped Dr Pepper can, and a blue Matchbox car with no wheels. A tiny tin for Bayer aspirin, a chewed dog bone, a large white rock streaked with gold, a broken arrowhead, fossils of cephalopods that once skulked around with tentacles and eyes like cameras.

Lucas is fingering through pieces of broken red glass. He's pushed aside a tiny brown object with a point.

'This is a tooth,' he says.

'That's what I thought!' Bessie exclaims. 'Herb told me it was a candy corn.'

But I'm staring at something that lies all alone at the edge of the table.

'I think that was Lydia's.' The words catch in my throat.

'Spooky.' Bessie picks up the little pink barrette, frowns at it. I pull off my gloves and take it with unsteady fingers.

'What do you think it means?' she wants to know. 'Do you figure it's a clue?' Bessie isn't breathing fast because she's old, or because Lucas is a sweaty god. Bessie is a junkie. She's probably devoured everything ever written on the Black-Eyed Susans. *How could I not have seen this?* She bought my grandfather's house when no one else would. She apparently knows exactly who Lydia is without explanation.

Lucas has placed his hand on my shoulder. 'We'll borrow the tooth and the . . . hair thing, if that's OK,' he tells Bessie.

'Of course, of course. Whatever Herb and I can do.'

I rub my finger absently over the yellow smiley face etched into the plastic. *This means nothing,* I scold myself. It was probably tugged out of Lydia's hair by a cornstalk during a game of hide-and-seek back when we thought monsters were imaginary.

And yet. The pink barrette with the smiley face. The Victorian ring, the Poe book, the key. *Why do I feel like Lydia is the one playing a game with me, planned cunningly in advance?*

Lucas scans my face, and there's no discussion of whether to sift through the rest of the dirt.

I look up. On the roof, the flash of two girls. One with fiery red hair. I blink, and they're gone.

Lydia's barrette is wrapped in a tissue in my purse. The tooth is in Lucas's pocket. About fifteen miles down the road, Lucas clears his throat and breaks the silence. 'Are you going to tell me what happened to that mermaid chick?'

My passenger window swims with blue and brown. The Texas sky, a bell of glass; the rolling farmland, once buried under an unfathomable sea. *Sun so powerful that the mermaid was often obliged to dive under the water to cool her burning face.*

I still my grandfather's voice. Place my hands on burning cheeks. Turn to Lucas's profile, a rock to cling to.

'The mermaid can't bring herself to murder the prince,' I say. 'She throws herself into the sea, sacrificing herself, and dissolves into sea foam. But a miracle happens – her spirit floats above the water. She has transformed into a daughter of the air. She can now earn her immortal soul and go to live with God.'

Daughters of the air. Like us, like us, like us, breathe the Susans.

'The Baptist in your grandfather must have loved that one,' Lucas says.

'Not really. Baptists believe you can't earn heaven. The only way to save yourself is to repent. Then you're good to go, even if you turn sweet mermaids to sea foam.'

Or girls to bones.

September 1995

MR LINCOLN: Tessie, do you love your grandfather?

MS. CARTWRIGHT: Yes. Of course.

MR LINCOLN: It would be very hard to think something terrible about him, right?

MR VEGA: Objection.

JUDGE WATERS: I'll give you a little leeway here, Mr Lincoln, but not much.

MR LINCOLN: Did the police search your grandfather's house the day after you were found?

MS. CARTWRIGHT: Yes. But he let them.

MR LINCOLN: Did they take anything away?

MS. CARTWRIGHT: Some of his art. A shovel. His truck. But they gave it all back.

MR LINCOLN: And the shovel had just been washed, correct?

MS. CARTWRIGHT: Yes, my grandmother had run the hose over it the day before.

MR LINCOLN: Where is your grandfather today?

MS. CARTWRIGHT: He's home with my grandmother. He's sick. He had a stroke.

MR LINCOLN: He had a stroke about two weeks after you were found, right?

MS. CARTWRIGHT: Yes. He was very upset about . . . me. He wanted to hunt down whoever did this and kill him. He said the death penalty wasn't good enough.

MR LINCOLN: He told you that?

MS. CARTWRIGHT: I overheard him talking to my aunt.

MR LINCOLN: Interesting.

MS. CARTWRIGHT: No one thought I could hear while I was blind.

MR LINCOLN: I'd like to get to your episode of blindness a little later. Did you ever think your grandfather was odd?

MR VEGA: Objection. Tessie's grandfather isn't on trial here.

MR LINCOLN: Judge, I'm almost done with this line of questioning.

JUDGE WATERS: You can answer the question, Ms. Cartwright.

MS. CARTWRIGHT: I'm not sure what he means.

MR LINCOLN: Your grandfather painted some grisly images, didn't he?

MS. CARTWRIGHT: I mean, yes, when he was imitating Salvador Dalí or Picasso or something. He was an artist. He experimented all the time.

MR LINCOLN: Did he ever tell you scary stories?

MS. CARTWRIGHT: He read fairy tales to me when I was little.

MR LINCOLN: The Robber Bridegroom who kidnaps a girl, chops her up, and turns her to stew? The Girl Without Hands, whose own father cuts them off?

MR VEGA: Oh, come on, your honor.

MS. CARTWRIGHT: Her hands grow back. Seven years later, her hands grow back.

26 days until the execution

I wonder if Jo is in a freezing lab scraping enamel off a tooth that looks like a candy corn while I fold and stack clothes still warm from the dryer. If Terrell is sitting on his rock hard cot, composing his last words, drinking water that tastes like raw turnips, while I sip my $12 pinot and decide to throw out Charlie's pink socks with the hole in the left heel. If Lydia is out there somewhere laughing at me, or missing me, or up in heaven pestering dead authors while her body rots in a place only my monster knows about. I wonder if the tooth from the ground at Granddaddy's could be hers.

For three days, I debated about whether to turn the tooth over to Jo. I couldn't explain to Lucas why I waited. It made perfect sense to try every unlikely thing, to hold nothing back unless what I really wanted was *not to know.* Jo had met us in the parking lot of the North Texas Health Science Center a few hours ago. She was still wearing white shoe covers from the lab. She had listened in taut silence to my rambling about drowning black-eyed Susans in boiling water and a box of useless objects that no one cared about but Bessie. I didn't mention Lydia's pink barrette with the smiley face. Jo accepted the tooth from Lucas. Said little in return.

I wonder if Jo will forgive me for not bringing her with us, although it doesn't seem all that important right now. Nothing does. Numbness grips me, a slow-acting poison that drugs the Susans to sleep and yet still allows my hands to build perfectly tidy little towers of clothes. Clothes that have mingled intimately in the washer – Lucas's Army underwear, Charlie's flannel pajamas with the pink cotton-candy sheep, my neon running shorts.

Lucas is slugging a beer at the end of the couch, watching CNN and rolling his briefs into tiny eggrolls, Army Ranger-style, then aiming and tossing them at my head, my butt, whatever is a good target. We're pretending to be just fine while the clock ticks the seconds off my sanity. Because after Terrell dies, then what?

Keep folding. The doorbell rings, and Lucas is up, opening the door. Probably Effie dropping off a food bomb. I glance at my watch: 4:22 P.M. – a couple of hours before I have to pick up Charlie from practice.

'Is Tessa home?' A nerve, plucked like a guitar string, as soon as I hear his voice.

Lucas's feet are planted deliberately, blocking my view of the door. 'And this would be regarding what?' The drawl pulls out every bit of the West Texas in him. In slow motion, I see Lucas's left hand, the support hand, casually rise and rest on his upper chest. The fingers on his right hand, clinching. The ready position for the fastest way to yank a gun out of your pants. He'd demonstrated for me in the back yard not an hour before.

'Lucas!' I jolt myself away from the couch, toppling three of the piles. 'This is Bill, the lawyer I've told you about who is handling Terrell's appeal. Angie's friend.' All I can see beyond Lucas is the tip of a Boston Red Sox cap. I'm behind Lucas, pushing uselessly against hard muscle. I feel around his waist for a gun that isn't there. His movements a few seconds ago, just the reflex of a wary man. I realize that while Bill can't see my face, he has a perfect view of my hand curled intimately near Lucas's crotch.

Old resentment flushes heat into my face. This macho idiocy from Lucas is the primary reason we were drawn to each other when I was a scared, hormonal eighteen-year-old, and the primary reason we broke up. He descended from a generation of men who sent hearts skittering in terror with the one-two clunk of their boots. Who lived life like everyone was about to quick-draw. Lucas leaps eagerly at cat screeches, car backfires, knocks on the door. He's a good man and a terrific soldier, the best, but as an everyday life partner, he electrocutes the roots of every hair on my skin.

'Lucas, *move.*' I shove a little harder.

Lucas steps aside slightly so I can wriggle beside him.

'Bill, Lucas,' I say. 'Lucas, Bill.'

Bill sticks out a hand. Lucas ignores it. 'Hello there, Bill. I've been wanting to meet you. I've been wanting to ask how involving Tessa at this very late date is a good thing. Don't you think it's time to step away? Ride off in your BMW out there? Give Tessa and my daughter the peace they deserve?'

For a moment, I'm speechless. I had no idea Lucas was pulsing with this kind of anger. We were melting down, every one of us. I step firmly onto the porch. 'Lucas. Butt out of this, OK? Whatever I'm doing, it's my call. Bill isn't forcing me.'

I shut the door in Lucas's face, not for the first time. 'You can wipe off that expression, Bill.' Not exactly what I meant to say. Not, *I miss you.*

'So that's your soldier?' Bill asks.

'If you mean Charlie's father, yes.'

'He's living here?'

'On a short leave. Long story, but Charlie was scared after that night of the . . . vandal. She Skyped Lucas about it and shortly after that he showed up on my doorstep. He has an understanding boss and was overdue for a leave to visit Charlie anyway. I didn't invite him, but I'm not sorry he came. He's on . . . the couch.'

'That doesn't seem like a very long story.' Bill's voice is cool. 'If you're still in love with him, just say so.'

My arms are crossed tight against my thin sweater. I have no interest in inviting Bill inside and refereeing between the two of them.

'This isn't a conversation . . . we need to have,' I say. 'You and me . . . we can't be a thing. We slept together for the wrong reasons. It's not like me to do something that impulsive. *I'm not that girl.*'

'You didn't answer the question.' I meet his eyes. Flinch. The intensity is almost unbearable. Lucas had never looked at me like that. Lucas was all hands and instinct.

'I'm not in love with Lucas. He's a good guy. You just caught him at a bad moment.' Already I'm wondering if Bill's laser gaze is for real, or if it's method acting with an on/off switch. Useful for withering a witness, or stripping a girl down to her scars.

Lydia had always sworn no one could reach her vagina with his eyes but Paul Newman, 'Even though he's ancient.' She hadn't met Bill. I wouldn't *want* her to meet Bill. To tarnish this, whatever *this* is.

Why am I thinking about Lydia right now?

Bill plunks himself down in the swing, clearly not going anywhere. I reluctantly position myself on the other end. For the first time, I notice a large manila envelope about two inches thick, in his hand.

'What's that?' I ask.

'I brought you something. Have you ever read any of your testimony from the trial?'

'It never occurred to me.' A lie. I'd thought about it plenty. The jury ogling me like I was an alien and the sketch artist scratching long, swift pencil strokes for my hair. My father, sitting in the front row of a packed room, petrified for me, and Terrell, in a cheap blue tie with gold stripes, keeping his eyes glued to a blank piece of notebook paper in front of him, the one for his notes. He never once looked at me or took a note. The jury interpreted it as guilt.

So did I.

'I've pulled out a few sections for you,' Bill says.

'Why?'

'Because you feel such guilt about your testimony.' Bill halts the swing abruptly. He taps the envelope that now rests between us. 'Please read this. It might help. You are not the reason Terrell sits in prison.'

I cross my arms tighter. 'Maybe you're just thinking that the more I take myself back there, the more I might remember something that would help Terrell.'

'Is there something wrong with that?'

My heart begins to pound, hating this. 'No. Of course not.'

He pushes himself up and the swing bounces and jerks in protest. 'Jo told me about the tooth. I wish you'd let us know you were going to your grandfather's. I wish you weren't so intent on shutting me out. Are you planning to dig somewhere else?' He's stilling the swing with his hand while I get up.

'No. It was the last place. Is Jo . . . mad?'

'You'd have to ask her.'

He's moving away, bristling with frustration. At life. At me. I grab the envelope off the swing and follow him to the steps. 'Tell me the truth. Is there any hope at all for Terrell?'

He starts to step off the porch before swiveling halfway around, almost knocking me back. I am already there, only inches away. 'There are a few more appeals to file,' he says. 'I'm driving to Huntsville to see him for the last time next week.'

I grip his arm. 'The last time? That doesn't sound good. Will you tell Terrell . . . that I'm still trying very hard to remember?'

Bill's eyes are glued to my fingernails gripping his sweatshirt, always unpolished and cut short, still crumbed with dirt from my grandfather's garden. 'Why don't you tell him yourself?'

'You can't be serious! I'd be one of the last people he'd want to see.'

Bill removes my hand deliberately. He might as well have shoved me down.

'It isn't my idea,' he says. 'It's his.'

'Doesn't Terrell . . . hate me?'

'Terrell is not a hater, Tessa. Not bitter. He's one of the most remarkable men I've ever met. He believes you have it the worst. For a long time, he said he could hear your weeping at night over the other sounds of Death Row. He says a prayer for you before he goes to sleep. He's told me not to push you.'

Terrell has heard me crying on Death Row. I'm keeping him awake. I'm an echo in his head, like the Susans are in mine.

'Why in the hell didn't you tell me this before?'

'There's no human touch. Can you imagine that? Twenty-three hours a day in a tiny cage with a narrow slot for food. A tiny Plexiglas window that's so high he has to ball up his mattress and stand on it to see out, for a fuzzy view of nothing. One hour a day to briskly walk around another small cage for exercise. Every second to think about dying. You know what he says is the worst part? More than the sounds of men screaming, or trying to choke themselves, or arguing over imaginary chess games, or incessantly tapping typewriters? The smell. The stench of fear and hopelessness oozing from five hundred men. Terrell never takes deep breaths on Death Row. He thinks he might suffocate or go insane if he does. I can't swig a deep breath without thinking of Terrell. Why didn't I tell you before, Tessa? Because you have enough to carry around.'

He taps the envelope I'm holding. 'Read this.'

He doesn't wave goodbye as he backs out of the driveway.

When I walk inside, Lucas is facing the door, leaning against the back of the couch, dragging on his beer. Waiting. 'What's wrong?' He's already restacked the piles of clothes that toppled over, a Lucas-style apology. 'What did he want?'

'Nothing important. I think I'm going to take a nap before I pick up Charlie.'

'You're sleeping with him.' A statement, not a question.

'I'm going to take a nap.' I brush past him toward the hall.

'He could be using you, Tess.'

I close my bedroom door and slide down its back to the floor. Lucas is still calling after me. Tears prick at the corners of my eyes.

I run my nail under the flap of the envelope and pull out the tidy stack of court documents.

Bill might not think Tessie's guilty. But I know she is.

September 1995

MR LINCOLN: Tessie, would you say that you played unusual games as a child?

MS. CARTWRIGHT: I'm not sure what you mean.

MR LINCOLN: Let me put it this way. You have a pretty big imagination, right?

MS. CARTWRIGHT: I guess so. Yes.

MR LINCOLN: Did you ever play a game called Anne Boleyn?

MS. CARTWRIGHT: Yes.

MR LINCOLN: Did you ever play a game called Amelia Earhart?

MS. CARTWRIGHT: Yes.

MR LINCOLN: Did you ever play a game called Marie Antoinette? Did you lay your head on a tree stump and let someone pretend to lop off your head?

MR VEGA: Your honor, once more, Mr Lincoln's questioning is simply designed to distract the jury from anything meaningful and from the man who sits in that chair on trial.

MR LINCOLN: On the contrary, your honor, I'm trying to help the jury understand the environment where Tessa grew up. I find that very meaningful.

MR VEGA: In that case, let me enter into the record that Tessa also played checkers, dolls, tea party, thumb wars, and Red Rover.

JUDGE WATERS: Mr Vega, sit down. You're bugging me. I'll let you know when you're bugging me, Mr Lincoln, but you're close.

MR LINCOLN: Thank you, your honor. Tessa, would you like a drink of water before we continue?

MS. CARTWRIGHT: No.

MR LINCOLN: Did you ever play Buried Treasure?

MS. CARTWRIGHT: Yes.

MR LINCOLN: Did you ever play Jack the Ripper?

MR VEGA: Your honor . . .

MS. CARTWRIGHT: Yes. No. We started the game but I didn't like it.

MR LINCOLN: We, meaning you and your best friend, Lydia Bell, whom you mentioned earlier?

MS. CARTWRIGHT: Yes. And my brother. And other kids in the neighborhood who were around. It was a super-hot day. A bunch of us were bored. But none of the girls wanted to be the victims after one of the boys brought out a ketchup bottle. Maybe it was Lydia. We decided to do a Kool-Aid stand instead.

MR VEGA: Your honor, I used to dissect live tadpoles by the river when I was six. What does that say about me? I'd like to remind him and the jury that Tessa is the victim here. It's been a very long day for this witness already.

MR LINCOLN: Mr Vega, I have a really good answer for your tadpole question. But right now, I just want to note that Tessie's childhood involved games about violent deaths, missing people, and buried objects. That art imitated life long before she was found in the grave. Why is that?

MR VEGA: Jesus Christ, you are actually testifying. Are you calling what happened to Tessa 'art'? Are you suggesting it was some kind of divine karma? You're a son of a bitch.

JUDGE WATERS: Up here, boys.

19 days until the execution

Terrell and I are not breathing the same air. That's the first thing I think. I wonder how many puckered lips of mothers and lovers have kissed the cloudy window that divides us.

The first thing I *feel* is shame. Until this moment, I've never really examined his face. Not in the courtroom when he was twenty feet away, not on the television when it blared our names like a celebrity marriage, not in a grainy image in the newspaper.

His eyes are bloodshot holes. His skin is shiny black paint. Pockmarked. A line drawn by a knife drizzles like milk down his chin. I stare at his scar and he stares at mine. More than a minute passes before he reaches for the phone on his side of the wall. He gestures for me to do the same.

I pick it up and press it hard against my ear so Terrell Darcy Goodwin can't see my hand shaking. He sits in a tiny cubicle on the other side of the glass. The small vent above my head is pumping cold air and drying my throat into brittle paper.

'Billy said you'd come,' he says.

'Billy?' I croak out involuntarily.

'Yeah, he hates that. But somebody's got to give him shit, don't you think?'

Terrell, loosening me up. I attempt a smile.

'How did you get yours?' My fingernail raking my chin

eels like the soft edge of a knife, the taunt before a killer draws blood.

'I got this scar by making the wrong friends when I was thirteen,' Terrell says easily. 'I stepped off God's path early on. Here I am.'

Two minutes in, the conversation already at God.

'Do you believe in our savior Jesus Christ?' he asks.

'Sometimes.'

'Well, Jesus and I've gotten real close in here. Jesus and I have plenty of time every day to chat about how I screwed up my life. How I screwed up my family's life. My daughters, my son, my wife will all be paying the price for a night I got high again and didn't know where I was.' His forehead is now almost touching the glass. 'Look, it took guts for you to come here and we don't have much time. I got something to say. I need to cross you off my list. You need to accept that my dying isn't your fault. I don't want to die being anybody's burden, OK?'

'I shouldn't have testified,' I protest. 'I didn't remember anything. I was just a prop. It was all hocus-pocus. The jury couldn't look at me without seeing their daughters.'

'And the big black boogeyman who got her.' Astonishingly, he says this without rancor. 'I had to let go of that years ago. It ate me alive. Every night, I hear the ones who've gone crazy. They chatter away to folks who aren't there. That, or they're so quiet for weeks you wonder if their brains just flew out of their heads and there's a big hole there. I made up my mind not to go crazy like that. I meditate. Read the Bible and Mr Martin Luther King. Play a lot of chess in my head. Work on my case. Write my kids.'

He's trying to reassure *me*. 'Terrell, I thought years ago

you might be innocent. And I did nothing. You have every right to hate me.'

'If you can't remember, why are you so sure it wasn't me who took you that night?'

'The killer keeps planting black-eyed Susans for me. The first time was three days after you were convicted.' I offer Terrell a pretend smile. 'It's OK if you think I'm crazy. I would.' *I do.*

'I don't think you're crazy. Evil sneaks up on little cat feet. *It sits looking over harbor and city on silent haunches.* I know that ain't the way the poem goes. It's supposed to be fog on little cat feet. Fog. Evil. It works either way. You usually can't see the headlights comin' at you until it's too late.'

I blink away the image of this giant on a cot reciting a Carl Sandburg poem, trying not to listen to men scratching up the walls like cats.

'When I first saw you,' Terrell is saying, 'you were sitting in the box in that pretty blue dress, shaking so hard I thought you might shatter to pieces. I saw my daughters sitting there.'

'That's why you didn't look at me,' I say slowly. There had been such debating back and forth over The Blue Dress. Everyone had an opinion. Mr Vega, Benita, the doctor, Lydia, even Aunt Hilda. The lace was itchy, but I never told anybody. When I testified, I had to casually flick my hand at my neck and my shoulders to make sure I wasn't really crawling with bugs. The Blue Dress was nothing Tessie would ever wear in real life. *The hem should hit her just slightly above the knees so the jury can see the brace on her ankle. Not too sexy. She's going to wear the brace, right? Can we gather in the waist to emphasize that she's still pretty much skin and bones? The color makes her look a little bit yellow, but I think that's good.*

'I wasn't going to make it worse for you.' Terrell's voice brings me back. He's grinning. 'I'm a pretty ugly man.'

A guard rattles the cage at Terrell's back. 'Gotta go, Terrell. Closing early.'

'A man's going down tonight,' Terrell tells me matter-of-factly. 'The Row's always extra-tense when a man's going down. This is the second time this month.' Terrell is rising while he speaks into the receiver. His broad body fills the window, softer and rounder than I expected. 'It took real guts for you to come here, Tessie. I know you're tied up about this. Remember what I said. When I die, let it go.'

My stomach dances with sudden panic. *This is it.*

The words are boiling up in a desperate rush. 'I'm going to testify again if they'll give you a hearing. Bill is a terrific lawyer. He really believes there is . . . some hope. Especially now, with the DNA results on the red hair. It's not mine, of course.' I pull a copper strand over my ear.

Terrell knows every bit of this already. Bill has already spent an hour with him. He's nearby, finishing up the habeas appeal on his laptop. All the other things Bill hoped might come through to bolster the appeal haven't.

'Yeah, Billy's a good boy. Never met a more Lord-guided man who doesn't believe one inch in the Lord. I've still got a little time to change his mind.' Terrell winks. 'Take care of yourself, Tessie. Let it go.' And he hangs up.

I'm frozen to the plastic chair. It seems like everything has been neatly decided with that final click of the receiver. Terrell's fate. Mine.

He leans over and touches a finger to the glass in a direct

line with my moon scar. It begins to throb. A Susan, tapping. *He's too good to be true, too good to be true.*

His mouth is moving. I'm panicking. I can't hear through the glass.

He repeats it a second time, carefully forming the words.

'You know who it is.'

Bill didn't want to bring me here tonight, but I insisted. We are only a few hundred yards from the infamous Death House unit known as 'The Walls,' where Terrell informed me just hours earlier that a man was going down. The Walls is a quaint, stately old building too tired to sigh. It's been witnessing death by rope and electricity, gunfire and poison, for more than a century.

Next door, there's a small white frame house with a neatly covered barbecue grill on the front porch. Embracing the other side, a church.

Terrell is lying in his cell a few miles away in the Wynne Unit on Death Row, about to put away his reading. Bill has told me that even with lockdown and lights out, Terrell will know before we do if tonight's execution has been carried out.

When I ask how that can be, he shrugs. The prisoners have their ways.

Tiny ice pellets crackle on my jacket. I pull up my hood. We won't be allowed inside. We are merely voyeurs.

I've breathed in the dust of my premature grave, but I've never felt anything as oppressive as the weight of this air. It's as if a dying factory threw up death, spewing plumes of grief and misery, hope and inevitability. The hope is what makes it seethe. I wonder how far I'd have to run to get away from this toxic cloud. Where its filmy edges end. Two blocks from the death chamber? A mile? If I peered down from space, would it be smothering the whole town?

Huntsville is a mythical place that I had all wrong. In my mind, Huntsville was a single house of horrors. A giant slab of concrete in the middle of nowhere where the state of Texas locks up Things that deserve to die. Where stuff happens that you don't ever, ever need to know about unless it's on a big screen with Tom Hanks.

That's what Lydia's father, a big fan of Tom Hanks and the revengeful philosophy of Deuteronomy, always told us.

I was badly misinformed. Huntsville is not just one badass prison but seven scattered around the area. The death house that looms in front of us in the waning light doesn't sit in the middle of nowhere.

It's a 150-year-old redbrick building with a clock tower where time has literally stopped. It's located two blocks off the quaint courthouse square, in the middle of town. People are downing chicken-fried steak and strawberry cake right now at the city's best restaurant, within easy eyesight of The Walls.

The cops are casually roping off the front of the prison with crime scene tape. We are within shouting distance of a windowless corner of the building, where the execution will take place.

I'm trying not to let Bill know how bothered I am by all of this matter-of-fact efficiency. It started right away, when Bill easily slid his car into a spot at the side of the brick prison wall and shouted up to the guard on the roof to ask if it was OK to park there. She shouted back, 'Sure,' like it was a middle school basketball game.

The Fors and the Againsts are obediently positioning themselves on opposite sides of the building, with four hundred yards between them, fighters in a ring who will never meet.

So civilized. So uncivilized. *So casual.*

A few Texas Rangers stand idly by, watching the small but slowly gathering crowd. No one appears concerned there will be trouble. Two Spanish television crews are setting up for live shots, while the rest of the press corps is composed of dark heads in a lit building across from the prison. A group of Mexican women are kneeling beside a blown-up portrait of the condemned, singing in Spanish. Two-thirds of the anti-death-penalty crowd is Mexican. The other third is mostly white, old, resigned, and quiet.

Tonight, a Mexican national is going to be executed for pumping three bullets into the head of a Houston cop. And then, in nineteen days, it's Terrell. And then a guy who hit his pizza delivery girl in the head with a baseball bat, and then a man who participated in the gang rape and murder of a mentally challenged girl on a lonely road. And on and on.

Every few minutes or so, Blue Knights are rounding the corners on their Harleys. They are former police officers avenging their own, who would maybe like to push the syringe themselves. I watch them position themselves on the far side of the prison, the pro side, near the execution chamber. The police and guards have sprung to life, and are directing them to park a little farther away.

'Are you sure you want to be here?' Bill asks one more time. We are hovering in a little bit of no-man's-land, in between both camps. 'I'm not sure there's a point.'

Of course there's a point. The point is, I don't know what I believe. I just know what I want to believe.

I don't say it, though. The less emotion, the better. We agreed to an uneasy détente as soon as I called and asked him to please take me with him to Huntsville to meet Terrell. I promised I wouldn't flake out. My eyes drift across the street to a man holding a battery-operated Christmas candle. He's leaning against a railing backed up to a gas station billboard that tells newly sprung prisoners to cash their checks *here*. He's comfortably packaged between two women with the peaceful countenance of nuns, and two men, all riding past sixty.

Bill follows my gaze. 'That's Dennis. He never misses. Sometimes, he's the only guy out here.'

'I thought there would be more people. Where are all the people who scream on Facebook?'

'On the couch. Screaming.'

'When will it start?'

'The execution?' He glances at his watch. 'It's eight now. Probably in about fifteen minutes. Usually, it's set for six and it's done by seven. There was a delay tonight while the federal court was debating a last-minute appeal that the condemned was mentally deficient.' He gestures back across the street. 'Dennis and that core group of four over there show up more as a vigil than protest. I mean, at this point, the writing's on the wall. Dennis is the one who always stays until the bitter end, even on the rare occasion when appeals go on until midnight. He waits until the family of the executed walks out. Wants them to know someone is out here for them.'

I picture it – a skinny old Santa, his Christmas candle, a lonely corner by a Stop sign, and the night.

'The woman with the bullhorn is Gloria.' He redirects my attention to the sign-wielding protesters in the street, who are oddly silent. No chanting. 'She's a fixture, too. She pretty much believes everyone on Death Row is innocent. Of course, most of them are guilty as hell. She's much beloved for dedication, however. She'll start counting it down soon.'

'Where are the families now?'

'The family of the victim, if any of them want to be there, is already inside the prison. The family of the prisoner is in the building across the street. I've heard Gutierrez has asked his mother not to watch. Whoever *is* witnessing for him will walk across with a few reporters as soon as all appeals have expired. That's the high sign.' He is directing my eyes under the clock tower, where there are steps that lead up and inside.

A young television reporter in a brand-new blue suit and a bright lavender camera-ready tie has appeared to my right. He's thrusting his microphone into the face of a woman carrying a sign that declares the governor is a serial killer. The camera casts eerie light on both of their faces.

The protester's shoulders are hunched in an arthritic mountain. She's traveling on red cowboy boots anyway. She drawls her answers to the reporter a little cynically, as if she's seen a hundred of him. *Yes, the lights of the whole town used to dim for a second every time a prisoner was electrocuted. Yes, this is a typical crowd. Yes, Karla Faye Tucker was the biggest zoo, being a woman. Someone on the square even advertised 'Killer Prices.'*

The reporter cuts her off abruptly.

Bill nudges my shoulder. Gloria has raised the bullhorn to her lips.

Shadows are moving across the street. Ice keeps shooting out of the sky.

The air suddenly vibrates with the roar of a hundred angry tigers, so loud and so fierce that it rattles my brain, the balls of my feet, the pit of my stomach.

The thunderous noise drowns out Gloria shouting into her bullhorn and the hymn of the women, whose mouths continue to open and close like hungry birds.

The Blue Knights are revving their motorcycles in unison, so he can hear.

Kill him.

September 1995

MR VEGA: Will you please state your full name for the record?

MR BOYD: Ural Russell Boyd. People call me You-All. Ever since I played basketball in high school. The cheerleaders turned it into one of their yells.

MR VEGA: How would you like me to address you today?

MR BOYD: You-All's fine. I'm a little nervous.

MR VEGA: No need to be nervous. You're doing just fine. You own four hundred acres of land approximately fifteen miles northwest of Fort Worth, correct?

MR BOYD: Yes, sir. In my family for sixty years. But everybody still calls it the Jenkins property.

MR VEGA: Will you please tell us what happened on the morning of June 23, 1994?

MR BOYD: Yes, sir. My hound dog went missing. We were supposed to go bird hunting that morning real early. When I couldn't find him, I set out with Ramona.

MR LINCOLN: Ramona is . . . ?

MR BOYD: My daughter's horse. Ramona was the most in the mood for a ride that morning.

MR LINCOLN: And what happened after that?

MR BOYD: Almost right away I heard Harley start to howl near the west pasture. I thought maybe he met a copperhead. I've had some problems with copperheads.

MR VEGA: You followed his howl?

MR BOYD: Yes, sir. Once he started he wouldn't stop. I think he felt the vibration of Ramona's hooves and could feel us coming. He's a real smart dog.

MR LINCOLN: Approximately what time was this?

MR BOYD: About 4:30 A.M.

MR LINCOLN: How long did it take to find Harley?

MR BOYD: Ten minutes. It was dark. He was at the far corner of the property, about a half-mile off the highway. He was keeping watch.

MR VEGA: What was he keeping watch over?

MR BOYD: Two dead girls. I didn't know that the one girl was alive. She didn't look alive.

MR VEGA: Will you please describe to the jury exactly what you saw when you came upon the grave?

MR BOYD: First, I flashed my light on Harley. He was flat down in a bunch of flowers in a ditch. He didn't move. I didn't see the hand at first because his nose was lying on it. I knew it was a girl's hand because of the blue fingernail polish. Sir, I'd like to take a minute.

MR VEGA: Certainly.

MR BOYD: (inaudible)

MR VEGA: Take all the time you need.

MR BOYD: It was a bad moment. My daughter picks those flowers all the time. I hadn't checked her bed before I left the house.

18 days until the execution

While Bill and I waited for Manuel Abel Gutierrez to die, a light freezing rain had transformed the highway home into a ribbon of glistening ice. It's the kind of storm that Yankees make fun of on Facebook with a picture of a spilled cup of ice on the sidewalk that shuts down schools or a cartoon that depicts massive car pileups with one culprit snowflake. It would be funny, if a tenth of an inch of ice in Texas wasn't deadly.

Bill had announced six minutes onto I-45 that he wasn't about to skate the four-hour trek back, and swung the car around. So here we are, locked in a Victorian ice castle two blocks from the death chamber and its dissipating cloud. We were lucky that Mrs Munson, the eighty-seven-year-old B&B proprietor, picked up her phone at 11:26 P.M. Every other hotel that lined the highway was booked solid, their parking lots crammed with cars frosted like petits fours.

Bill is running the water in his bathroom. The sound rushes through the wall and under the one-inch gap beneath the connecting door. Mrs Munson had called up to us three times as we climbed the stairs to say that the whole house was replumbed and wired with central heat, as if we might not understand the $300 price tag per room. I bounce lightly on the bed, running my fingers over the path of tiny stitches of red and yellow tulip quilt. I want to tell Mrs Munson that her accommodations are worth every penny.

Lydia would love this room with the cheery lemon walls and the grim faces of dead people staring off the dresser. The iron lamp with a gold-fringed shade that glows like a tiny fire. The ice chips clicking against the window, chattering teeth.

She would lie on this bed and construct a doomed romance for the gauzy antique wedding dress that hangs like a ghost in the half-open wardrobe, and a more terrifying tale about the door to another dimension that hides in the shadows behind it. Maybe she'd combine the stories into one. This night would race ahead, a splendid, radiant adventure. We would be girls again, before monsters and devastating words, our imaginations locked together.

There's a short knock on the connecting door.

'Come on in, Bill,' I say immediately.

Bill hesitates on the threshold, dressed in jeans and a T-shirt that must have been hidden under his button-down. 'I found toothbrushes in a cabinet in my bathroom. Want one?' I slide off the bed and walk over.

'Thanks.' I pick blue over yellow. 'I could use a glass of wine, too. Maybe a shot of tequila.'

'I don't think that's stocked in the bathroom cabinet. I'm getting a bottle of water from the little fridge in the hall. Want one?'

'Sure.'

He disappears into his room before I can tell him to use my door to the outside hall. We are being so very polite. Earlier tonight, before we headed to the execution, Bill had punched a button on his computer and officially filed Terrell's habeas corpus appeal with the federal court. It emphasizes the 'junk science' DNA results on the red hair, the overwhelming statistics on faulty witness ID, and a statement from me, the living victim who thinks the real Black-Eyed Susan killer might still be stalking her and is willing to testify to it.

No mention of mysterious black-eyed Susan plantings or a buried book of Poe in Lydia's back yard or a tooth in an old U-Haul box.

I have wished, more than once, that I had kept the sick piece of poetry I found under my tree house instead of ripping it to shreds and throwing away the pill bottle it came in. It might have been impossible to retrieve DNA or fingerprints from the paper or plastic all these years later, but it was tangible proof that I wasn't making it up.

Bill's habeas petition is far short of what he wanted to file at this point, but he is hoping it is enough for the judge to grant a hearing. He's hoping that Jo will shake more loose from the bones in the meantime.

'Here you go,' Bill says. 'I see you've got cable TV, too. It's just a little hard to see around these tree trunk bedposts. Did you reach Lucas?'

'It's all good. He's got it covered. Charlie's asleep.'

'Can I sit down for a second?'

'Sure.'

He pulls the straight-back chair from beside the dresser and sits on a needlepointed seat of roses. I reassume my position on the corner of the bed.

'You asked the other day if there's hope,' Bill says. 'After today . . . I just think it's better if I'm honest. I think it is likely that Terrell is going to die. He's on a runaway train. I know today was tough. Meeting Terrell. The execution. It doesn't matter how you feel about the death penalty. I was all for the death penalty five years ago and it's just as fucking grim either way.'

I'm stunned by this admission. I had never imagined him with a single doubt.

'Two things happened for me to change my mind. The duh lawyer moment when I realized that you're never going to find a rich white guy on that gurney. And the Angie moment. She made me get to know a couple of guys on Death Row. Guilty ones, like a guy who broke in to a back yard high on meth and shot an elderly woman sitting in the garden in her wheelchair, so he could run inside and steal her purse. Angie didn't think I could do this job to her satisfaction until I understood that it wasn't just about proving innocence. That I needed to be all in. To understand that men on Death Row were human beings who did horrible things but that didn't mean *they* were horrible things. The men that I've met who are sitting on Death Row are not the same men who committed those crimes. They are sober. Born again. Repentant. Or bat-shit crazy.' He eases back in the chair. 'Occasionally, but not often, innocent.'

I wonder how long he's been holding in this speech and why he chose tonight to give it. 'I don't know where I am on the death penalty,' I say. 'I'm just . . . not . . . there.' *I have promises to keep.*

'And Terrell?'

'I can't talk about Terrell.'

He nods. 'I'll let you get some sleep.'

As soon as he shuts the door between us, I'm desperate to wash away everything about this day. I enter a bathroom both bygone and modernly appointed, strip off all of my clothes, and lay them on the counter. I dread putting them on in the morning. They're tainted by death. But I'd brought nothing else in my backpack – just a couple of PowerBars, a water bottle, a spool of silk thread and needles for an experiment in lace-making. And, at the last minute, I'd tossed the testimony inside, mostly in case Bill asked if I'd read it. I hadn't. I'd opened the envelope, pulled out the papers, and stuck them right back in.

I push aside the shower curtain and crank the knob. The hot water responds, silky, hot, and immediate. I wash everything three times before stepping onto slick white subway tile and reluctantly tugging on the day's underwear and a white cotton tank that had been my ineffective effort at winter layering. I towel-dry my hair into a frenzy of curls, too exhausted to use the expensive ceramic blow dryer on the counter.

I slip into chilly sheets, shivering, trying not to think about the grieving mother who raced to a morgue tonight. Who hoped, for the first time in years, to touch the body of her son, a killer, while it was still warm.

At 4:02 A.M., my eyes pop open. I'm gasping for breath as if someone just snatched a pillow from my face.

Lydia.

Cool light streams through the windows. The winter storm, asleep. My mind, racing.

To Charlie, safe at home, tangled in her comforter. I picture her breathing softly, in and out, and I breathe in rhythm with her. To Lydia, holding the paper bag to my face after a race, telling me to *breathe,* and I do. In and out.

Lydia, Lydia, Lydia. She's invaded this room. The old

Lydia, who checked my pulse, and the other one, who is scratching to get out of Bill's envelope in my backpack.

Did I just miss the clues? Or are all of us just one betrayal, even one sentence, away from never speaking to each other again? I always, always defended my best friend. Even Granddaddy, a fan of her rabid imagination, wasn't completely sure.

He asked once: 'What do you see in Lydia?'

'She's like no one else,' I had replied, a little defensively. 'And loyal.'

She changed in the month before the trial. The old Lydia made fun of the push-up Wonderbra. She stuck her hands under her breasts, arranged them into little mountains and mocked the Eva Herzigova billboards. *Look me in the eyes and tell me that you love me.* She cocked her knee, planted her hands on her hips, thrust out her chest, and drawled: *Who cares if it's a bad hair day?*

The new Lydia *bought* a Wonderbra and strapped it on. She complained that all high school boys wanted was a blank slate to draw their pencil on. Her grades dipped into the A minuses. She renounced Dr Peppers and Sonic cheese tots, and worst of all, she stopped her incessant, encyclopedic chatter. I knew I should press her, but I was trapped in my own head.

Old Lydia kept all of my secrets.

New Lydia told my secrets to the world.

I'm standing over his bed. The covers are a rumpled drift, like snow is falling through the ceiling. Bill is facing the other way. His body, rising and falling, slow and steady.

It isn't like me to do this, I think, as I shed my T-shirt and it falls soundlessly to the floor. I don't play games. I'm not impulsive. *I'm not that girl.* I lift up the quilt and slide in. Press my bare skin against the heat of his back. His breathing stills. He waits pregnant seconds before turning over to face me. He's left a few inches of distance between us.

'Hey,' he says. It's too dark to read his expression.

This was a mistake, I think. He's already mentally moved on. He's reaching out now to push me away.

Instead, his finger travels my cheek, the side without the scar. I'm suddenly aware that my face is wet.

'You OK?' His voice, husky. He's being chivalrous, offering me a last chance to escape, even as I make a naked present of myself in his bed.

'I'm not that kind of girl.' I lean in. Drift my tongue along his ear.

'Thank God,' he replies, and tugs me to him.

A bird's distress call slices the silence and jars me awake. It's a high-pitched plea from a branch by the window. *Why is my world frozen? Where did everybody go?*

I crawl out of bed, away from the delicious heat of Bill's body. His breathing, rhythmic.

I shut the connecting door, back on my side of it. I relive the intimacy of what just happened. Things I didn't do unless I was in love. *How can I ever be sure his attraction is to me, and not the shiny glitter of Black-Eyed Susan?*

My red North Face jacket drips like blood off the closet doorknob. A fresh white orchid is stuck all alone in a slim vase, even though no one knew I was coming. A young woman in the antique frame on the dresser gazes at me coolly as if I have no place in her room.

She's just a girl in this picture, about Charlie's age. A

thick, migraine-inducing braid is roped around her head. I imagine her with loosened braids and a little of Charlie's MAC eye makeup. I pick up the picture and flip it over.

Mary Jane Whitford, born May 6, 1918, died March 16, 1934, when a convict roaming the sugarcane fields stepped in front of her carriage and startled the horses.

A tourist attraction. Like me.

It makes sense that Lydia would come to me here, in this room, embroidered like a doily in the dark fabric of this town. Where I'm reminded by a pretty girl in braids that we don't get to choose.

I almost died three hours ago on I-45, halfway between Huntsville and Corsicana. What an ironic end that would have been – the lone survivor of the Black-Eyed Susan killer taken out by an eighteen-wheeler packed with baked goods. A truck driver a hundred feet in front of our car had skidded on a patch of ice into a perfect jackknife. If skidding were an Olympic sport, he'd win. All I could think for six seconds, while Bill and I hurled toward a picture of a giant pink confetti-sprinkled donut, was, *Is it all going to come down to this?*

Instead, it came down to me completely rethinking BMWs. Their drivers act superior for a reason.

Lucas is opening my front door before I can, a good thing because I don't remember the new security code he insisted on, and a bad thing because Bill is still in the driveway making sure I get inside safely. I turn to wave but Bill is already backing the BMW onto the street. I hope he believed me when I said I wasn't sleeping with Lucas.

Breakfast at the B&B was a little awkward. Bill sat across from me, at a table formally appointed with fragile crystal and an array of silverware, while Mrs Munson sat at the head of the table and chattered on about how prisoners carved the intricate detail on the cupboard behind us. It was impossible to resist the work of art placed in front of us by Mrs Munson's daughter, a Dutch baby pancake with a strawberry fan on top and a spritz of powdered sugar.

Maybe Bill was upset that he woke up alone in bed. Later, in the car, we each seemed to be waiting for the other to bring up those thirty intimate minutes. It almost seemed like a dream conjured by a house that missed the noise and meaning of its old life – the people who wed on its lawn, gave birth in its beds, lay dead in their coffins in the front parlor. Except I can still feel his handprints on my skin.

After Bill avoided the near-accident, the silence in the car grew even more awkward. As if Bill was exhausted from saving lives.

Because I'm distracted by such boy-girl worries, still wearing death like a coat, still delirious not to *be* a Dutch baby pancake, it takes a second to register the expression on Lucas's face.

'Welcome home.' He seems uneasy. He's pulling the backpack off my shoulder as I walk the few steps into the living room.

'What's wrong?' I ask.

'Someone leaked your . . . feeling . . . that the Black-Eyed Susan killer has planted flowers for you over the years. A few quack experts on TV are chiming in on your mental state. There's a shadowy picture going around of a woman with a shovel at the old Victorian house where you used to live. It's supposed to be you. Well, it *is* you. But it's hard to tell.'

'When did you find this out?'

'Why don't you sit down?'

'I've been sitting for hours.'

Lucas examines my face carefully. 'Charlie texted me. It's all over Twitter and Instagram.'

'Shit. Shit, shit, *shit.*'

He hesitates. 'I had to turn off the ringer on the phone. Why do you even have a landline?'

'Is it OK if we don't talk about this right now? It doesn't really matter, does it? Terrell's going to die. It's impossible to protect Charlie.' I've moved over to the kitchen island, where Lucas has stacked the mail. He's behind me, rubbing my shoulders. Kind. Concerned. But not helping. His fingers are grinding the death that clings to these clothes into my skin.

I try to be casual as I move away. 'What's this?' I'm fingering an opened cardboard box. A new paperback lies next to it on the counter.

'That came in the mail yesterday. Charlie opened the box because she thought it was *Catch-22* and wanted to get going on it for an English class. She says she asked you to order it a week ago?'

'I forgot. I didn't order *Catch-22*. Or any other books.'

'Your name is on the address label.' He turns the box over so I can see.

'Where's the receipt?' I'm staring at the book cover. A filmy image of half-spirit, half girl rising out of a rocky sea. *Beautiful Ghost* by Rose Mylett.

Rose Mylett. The name stirs something unpleasant at the back of my brain.

Lucas reaches inside the box. 'Here's the receipt. It looks like it was a gift. There's a message. *Hope you enjoy.* Nothing else.'

Hope you enjoy. Ordinary words that crawl like three spiders up my back.

'Are you OK?' he asks.

'Sure,' I say dully. 'It's just a book. A gift. I need to get these clothes off.'

'One more thing. Your friend Jo dropped by for a second. You need to give her a call. That geochemist friend of hers is coming to town, the one who's been working on the Susan bones. She wants you to meet him. Oh, and that tooth from your grandfather's yard? It's from a coyote.'

Twenty minutes until Charlie gets home from school. A little longer before Lucas returns from his hunt for *Catch-22* and coffee with a 'new friend' – Lucas code for 'female.'

There's no time to dry my hair. I wrap the belt of my robe more tightly around my waist, ransack Charlie's drawer for some fuzzy socks, and plant myself on her unmade bed with my laptop. It had found a happy home in her sheets during my absence.

I am suffused with manic energy, pulsed back to life by the shower and the certainty that Rose Mylett means something. Her name is an insistent drill in my skull, more important than me, as the Grim Reaperette, skipping across Twitter right now, or calling Jo to hear about more hopeless efforts to pull names from dust. Those bones are stubborn.

I get an immediate hit. The first Rose Mylett that pops up isn't a true crime writer. The image on my screen isn't of an airbrushed author trying to look smart and beautiful and ten years younger.

This Rose Mylett is very dead. Murdered in 1888. A purported victim of Jack the Ripper. A prostitute also known as Catherine, Drunk Lizzie, and Fair Alice. She was wearing a lilac apron, a red flannel petticoat, and blue-and-red-striped socks when she was found with the imprint of a string around her neck.

For a second, I'm fourteen again, in the second row, smearing on Pink Lemonade Lip Smacker, listening to Lydia's Jack the Ripper report that instilled nightmares in half of our class.

My fingers are still working in the present. They skip to the next page and, four links down, find *Rose Mylett, author, Beautiful Ghost, What Elizabeth Bates is trying to tell us about her murder fifty years later.* Yep, the same book as the one sitting on my kitchen counter. I read the plot summary quickly. This crime rings no bells whatsoever – the tale of a young English royal who vanished off the rugged coast of North Devon on her honeymoon – 184 reviews, 4.6 stars. Published five years ago in the U.K. That .4 off of perfect would eat at Lydia. There's no author bio. No other book by Rose Mylett. The site does politely suggest, 'If you like this author, you might also like these books by Annie Farmer and Elizabeth Stride.' I Google quickly even though I already know. Two more Ripper victims. Clever, clever Lydia.

This has to be Lydia, right? Sending me flowers. Mail-ordering a book for my reading pleasure.

Still walking the earth after all. Still sticking her nose in evil. Stealing her pseudonyms off of pitiful dead whores. Making money off of excruciating sorrow. For some ungodly reason, she's messing with me.

Why are you suddenly back, Lydia?

I snap the laptop shut.

My daughter is coming home.

For a few precious moments, I bask in the Bohemian essence of Charlie: the black chalkboard wall she painted herself last summer, now scribbled with Stephen Colbert quotes and skilled graffiti from her friends; her collection of moon-and-stars ornaments that hang on fishing line thumbtacked to the ceiling; the array of candles in various stages of melted life on the windowsill. The trophies she's stuffed into the top shelf of her closet because they are 'braggy.'

I'm hurriedly spilling detergent into the washing machine when I hear the click of the key in the lock.

'Mom?'

'In the laundry room!' I yell back. Three clunks. Her backpack, hitting the floor. One shoe off, and then the other. *Good sounds.*

Charlie wriggles her arms around me from behind just as I'm about to drop the lid on clothes that will probably never feel clean again.

'Why is it so freaking cold outside?' she asks. Not *Why are you such a freak? The kind of mom who ends up on Twitter?* I pull Charlie's arms tighter.

'I missed you,' Charlie says. 'What are we eating?' She releases me from our backward hug. I decide to throw some extra Biz into the washer.

'I missed you, too. I'm thinking of making eggala.'

'Awesome.' Eggala, short for egg a la goldenrod, our go-to comfort food. Hard-boiled egg whites chopped into a white sauce, slathered over white toast, sprinkled with powdery yolk. Lots of salt and pepper. Dr Pepper on the side. Aunt Hilda made it once a week for me when I was blind.

'I'm sorry about . . . today,' I say.

'No big deal. My friends don't believe it. They are starting a campaign against it. Make some bacon, OK? Hey, don't start the washer. I've got a ton of volleyball clothes. People forgot shi – stuff all week and Coach kept making us run. *Everything* stinks. Plus, some guy's mom is *losing it* because he has this scabby thing going on with his foot. These people in Star Wars suits cleaned all the locker rooms and now every person in school smells like Lysol. Well, the guys smell like Lysol *and* Axe.'

'Hmm, not good.' I shut the lid. 'Don't worry, I'll wash another load of your clothes after this.'

'But there's hardly anything in there,' she protests. 'I'll go get the rest of it right now. I can't forget anything tomorrow. The team can't *take* any more running.'

She's already stripped off her clothes. She's standing there in her bra, panties, and knee-high socks, the cheerful, melodramatic all-American girl. Fourteen years ago, she was the adorable pink package with red fuzz sent to a teenage girl named Tessie so she'd agree to stay on the earth.

'That's OK.' I shut the washer lid firmly. 'I don't want these clothes to bleed on yours.'

I'm lying and telling the truth.

* * *

I'm in my pajamas when I remember to call Jo. She picks up on the first ring.

'Tessa?' she asks eagerly.

'I'm so sorry I didn't call sooner.'

'It's OK. I talked to Bill. He told me about your trip. Ice and sorrow and no tequila. Sounds grueling. Can you drop by my office tomorrow?'

'Yes. Sure.' My response is immediate even though all I really want is to lock the front door and never come out.

'I wanted to give you a heads-up before we meet because this will be part of his presentation.' Jo is rushing the words. 'I've held something back from you because it just seemed . . . like a little too much. You know? A week and a half ago, one of my Ph.D. students was finishing up cataloging the remains of the Susans from the two caskets we exhumed. There was a lot of detritus, as you might imagine. Dirt, clay, dust, bits of bone. I just wanted to make sure every last piece of it was recorded after we figured out the original coroner missed that there was a third right femur. In fact, we're looking back at some of the other cold cases he worked and have found other mistakes.'

'Just spit it out, Jo,' I say.

'My student had a hunch about a tiny piece of cartilage. I confirmed that hunch. The cartilage came from a fetus. One of the two unidentified girls was pregnant with a baby girl. We just tested the baby's DNA against Terrell's. There's a 99.6 percent chance he isn't the father. We're throwing the baby's DNA into criminal databases. Maybe we'll get a hit. A new lead.'

Of course Terrell isn't a match.

I'm counting in my head. Six girls in that grave. Merry

and me. Hannah makes three. Two more unidentified se
of bones. And now a little girl. One of them is buzzing
awake in my head, reminding me, just in case I forgot.

I'm the one with the answers.

September 1995

MR VEGA: Tessie, can you tell us a little about Black-Eyed Susan glitter?

MS. CARTWRIGHT: It's hard to explain. My friend Lydia came up with the name for it.

MR VEGA: Just do your best. Maybe you could start by telling us about the time you stood outside in the middle of a bad storm and your father couldn't get you to come in.

MS. CARTWRIGHT: I was thinking that if I stood out there long enough the rain would wash out all the Black-Eyed Susan glitter.

MR VEGA: Can you see this glitter?

MS. CARTWRIGHT: No.

MR VEGA: And when did you first notice it?

MS. CARTWRIGHT: The day I got home from the hospital. Again, I can't see it. For a while, I decided it was in my conditioner. In the Ivory soap. In the detergent we put in the washer. I decided that's why I could never get it out.

MR VEGA: Do you have glitter on you now?

MS. CARTWRIGHT: Just a little. The worst time, it was in the Parmesan cheese I put on my spaghetti. I threw up all night.

17 days until the execution

There are no Susan bones on Jo's conference table. Just that lonely brown Kleenex box. My heart feels like someone hammered a nail into it.

I was worried I would be late for Jo's meeting, but it's apparent as I open the door to the conference room that everyone else is even later. The room is empty except for the table and chairs, unless you count the requiem of pain that Hannah's mother and brother left behind. If there were a black light to reveal grief and anger, it would surely be streaked in graffiti, Dalí-like, on these walls. Not only sucked from Hannah's family, but all of the others who sat here waiting for their loved ones to be reduced to the stubborn rules of science.

The door clicks shut behind me. The fluorescent glare feels like it's restricting the flow of blood to my head. I slide into the chair where Hannah's brother sat at attention in his dress blues not so long ago and, for a few minutes, try not to think.

The door opens, and all of them spill into the conference room at once. Bill; Lieutenant Myron; Jo; and her Russian friend, Dr Igor Aristov, the genius from Galveston.

'Igor, as in Igor Stravinsky,' Jo had told me last night on the phone, knowing that I was, of course, imagining the hunchbacked Frankenstein one and not the one who composed *The Rite of Spring*.

This Igor, though, is not hunched, or wearing a black hood, or creeping me out with white golf ball eyes. He is tall and fit, wearing khakis and a red Polo. His eyes are warm and hazel. Fine wrinkles run out of the corner of his eyes and stop short. There are the tiniest shreds of gray at his temples.

He immediately crosses the room to take my hand first. 'You must be Tessa. It is a pleasure.' His accent is thick as paste, and most women would want him to say their names over and to never let go of their hands. Not me. I'm only in this room as a conciliatory gesture to Jo. I don't want to hear Igor's maybes and ifs. Unless this lab genius is about to pull a miracle out of his ass, I need to listen to Bill. I need to come to terms with Terrell's fate.

Lieutenant Myron is the first to slide into a chair. I wonder if I look as raw as she does. 'Everybody, sit,' Jo says. 'We're going to make this as quick as possible. Ellen had a rough night.'

'A cop and his bride of six months,' Lieutenant Myron explains. 'He fired a shot into her face for every month of marriage. Go ahead, Jo.'

Jo nods. Her hands are agitated with no place to go. I've never seen her this visibly on edge. 'Usually,' she says, 'I will send Igor samples of powder from the bones and he emails his findings to me. But that's white paper between two scientists. I want the three of you to hear everything straight from his mouth just in case some detail tickles your brain.' She is careful not to look at me. It is obvious I am the one whose brain needs the most tickling.

Igor has settled himself at the head of the table. 'I am a geochemist. A forensic geologist. Do any of you understand the basics of isotope analysis?

'I will keep it as simple as possible,' Igor continues, without waiting for an answer. 'I will refer to each case as Susan One and Susan Two. I received samples from the femur of Susan One and from the skull and teeth of Susan Two. I also received a scraping from a fetus that belongs to Susan Two. I was able to determine that one of the women lived much of her life in Tennessee, and the other was most certainly from Mexico.'

'What?' Bill's surprise pops the tension in the room. 'How can you possibly know that?'

Igor shifts a level gaze to Bill. 'Your bones absorb the distinct chemical markers in the soil where you live. Some of it has retained the same ratio of elements – oxygen, lead, zinc, et cetera – for hundreds of thousands of years, all the way back to when rivers and mountains formed. And then there are more modern markers. It's easy to tell that Susan One is American, not European, because America and Europe used different refinery sources for leaded gas.'

'We're soaking crap from the air into our bones?' Lieutenant Myron is pressing forward, suddenly engaged. 'Regardless, we don't use leaded gas for cars anymore.'

'It doesn't matter,' he replies patiently. 'The residue from leaded gas, even though it's been banned for years, still clings to our soil and soaks into our bones. Susan One's markers also indicate that for a significant portion of her life she lived near a specific set of mines, probably near Knoxville, Tennessee. I can't tell you how long exactly. Or specifically where she died. I might have been able to if I had a rib bone. Ribs are constantly growing and remodeling and absorbing the environment. We can usually use them to guess at a victim's residency for the last eight to te years of life. And, of course, a lot of the bones were lost so the grave only provided random puzzle pieces.'

'Mexico. Tennessee.' Bill's eyes are trained on Lieutenant Myron. 'Your killer could be a traveler. Terrell was a homebody.'

'He's not *my* killer.' Lieutenant Myron's sarcasm gets zero reaction from Bill, who continues tapping notes into his phone.

'Come on, guys, let him talk,' Jo says.

'It doesn't bother me,' Igor says. 'It's thrilling to be out of the lab, frankly. To meet you, especially, Tessa. I rarely meet any victims. It makes my science . . . alive. And this case is particularly interesting. I was able to discern even more from Susan Two and her unborn fetus. Susan Two's bones reflect a corn-based diet and the elements of volcanic soil. If I could hazard a guess, I'd say she was born in or near Mexico City. I concur with Jo that she was in her early twenties when she died.'

'What else?' Bill asks.

Igor lays his palms flat on the table. 'There was only one skull in that grave, which belonged to Susan Two. I asked Jo to send me scrapings of very specific teeth because the teeth can give us a timeline.' His voice, so far in college lecture mode, has picked up a little excitement. 'It's fascinating, really, what this science reveals. As children, we put things in our mouths. The teeth enamel absorbs the dust. The first molar forms when a person is three, and freezes the isotope signal for that period of time. So I can say that Susan Two's first molar tells us she was living in Mexico as a toddler. The incisors close at age x to seven. The chemical markers in one of her incisors ndicate she was still living in Mexico. The third molar's signal shuts down in the teen-age years. For Susan Two, still Mexico. After that, I don't know. Sometime in her late teens or early twenties, she moved, or was kidnapped.'

'This is remarkable.' Lieutenant Myron glances around the table. 'Isn't this remarkable?' I can't tell whether she is genuinely engaged or giddy from lack of sleep and a steady diet of savagery.

'How are you certain she left Mexico alive?' Bill asks. 'We know the bones were moved at least once because they didn't originate in that field of flowers where Tessa was dumped.' He flicks a look up at me, as if remembering I'm in the room. 'Sorry, Tessa. My point is, maybe her bones were simply moved across the border.'

'Her baby tells that part of the story,' Igor says quickly. 'This young woman lived in Texas for at least the last few months leading up to her death. I know this because fetal bones are the most current marker we can get. They were still developing and therefore still absorbing the current environment at the time of death.'

Lieutenant Myron shoves fingers through her uprooted hair. 'If she was an illegal immigrant, or kidnapped, that makes our job nearly impossible. Her family wouldn't want to reveal its illegal status and certainly wouldn't stick their DNA in a database. If they thought a drug cartel grabbed their daughter, there's even less of a chance – they wouldn't want to piss them off. Those guys hang headless bodies from bridges. The family would need to protect their other daughters if they have them.'

Jo nods her head in agreement. 'She's right. I've worked

on some of the bones of girls and women who have been murdered and buried in the desert near Juarez. Talked to the families. They're scared shitless. There are hundreds of girls in that desert. More every year.'

'I can only share my science.' Igor shrugs. 'And, frankly, I drummed up a lot more than is usual in cold cases like this. This is a fairly new strategy in forensic science. We are lucky these women lived in places where we have established soil databases. My dream is that we can map out a good portion of the geological world in the next decade, but it's spotty as hell at the moment.'

Bill's face is inscrutable, but I know what he's thinking. It's too late for this. Someday, science may give the Susans back their names, but not in time for Terrell.

It's Lieutenant Myron who jumps up, newly animated. She walks over and gives Bill a playful punch in the shoulder. 'Cheer up. You're one of those Texans who believes in evolution, aren't you?' She turns to the rest of us.

'We'll get busy with missing person and newspaper databases,' she says. 'In an hour, we'll be looking for missing girls in their late teens or early twenties from Tennessee and Mexico that fit our time frames. I'm most hopeful on the Tennessee angle. Good job, Dr Frankenstein. This is something real. Y'all think I don't care? I care. I just like real.'

She wouldn't want to be in my head. I'm wondering why none of the Susans speak to me in Spanish.

I enter the house quietly and see my Death Row clothes folded and stacked neatly on a kitchen chair. I wonder if Charlie or Lucas alienated them from the others; it's a toss-up as to which one sees through me better.

Charlie's volleyball clothes are piled on the coffee table. A vacuum cleaner has swallowed up the popcorn crumbs in front of the couch. Lucas has been taking care of the mundane, important details of my life while I've been trying to fathom how we are so deeply connected to the earth and wind that it is cooked into our bones.

I have no problem believing Dr Igor. It wasn't exactly science, but there was a period when I believed that if someone brushed my shoulder by accident or shook my hand that black-eyed Susan pollen would rub off like a sticky curse. People had thought I was obsessive-compulsive because I ignored outstretched hands. I was just protecting them.

I'm a big girl now. I offer strangers the firm grip of my grandfather and swallow my daughter in a hug twice a day and let friends take a sip from my Route 44 Sonic iced tea, all without breaking out in a sweat. That doesn't mean *Black-Eyed Susan* isn't still who I am. It's a brand. Like *schizophrenic. Fat. ADD.*

Lucas rises briefly from the couch, then falls back down when he sees me. He's already asleep again, a soldier grabbing zzz's while he can, so I don't call out for Charlie. She's probably in her room doing her complicated dance. Jane Austen, calculus, Snapchat. Repeat.

It's at moments like these that I find it hard to explain to myself and to Charlie why Lucas and I don't work as a permanent team. How many lieutenant colonels would fold girls' underwear? I smell potato soup gurgling in the Crockpot because that is about the sum total of Lucas's dinner repertoire. Potatoes, onions, milk, salt, pepper, butter. Bacon bits, for Charlie. If pressed, he can also kick out a pretty mean bologna and mustard sandwich.

Normal always tries to cuddle up with me but I tend to push it away. My mother was making brownies one second and then she was dead on the kitchen floor. That is my baseline for normal. After that, it's a very jagged graph.

I set my purse on the kitchen counter. *Beautiful Ghost* has been shoved off to the side with some unopened mail. I want to read it, and I can't bear to touch it. It will hold answers about Lydia I can't fathom knowing, or I'll prick my finger on its paper and fall into a cursed sleep. My fingers absently examine the foil-wrapped brick on the counter, which wasn't there this morning. The scrawl on the masking tape label declares it to be *Effie's Carob Fig Bread Surprise.* Almost all of Effie's recipes have the word *Surprise* tacked to the end, and if they don't, they should.

I wonder if her daughter is next door right now trying to politely chew and swallow. As I pulled in the driveway, I noted the Ford Focus with New Jersey plates parked at Effie's. She had told me last week in excited tones that her daughter was venturing down South for a visit. I discounted it, thinking she was confused with the time that Sue made that false promise a year ago, or even three years ago. I don't know what her arrival means after years of staying away, but I hope it's good for Effie. Maybe Sue got a peek of the digger snatcher who lives in Effie's brain, too. He's a first-class thief all right, just not the kind Effie thinks. The sight of all those diggers lined up in a row still sends a chill through me.

I toss an afghan over Lucas and decide to check on Charlie. Her bedroom door is shut tight. I knock. No response. I knock again a little harder before turning the knob. The white lights strung around the ceiling are twinkling, a sign she was planning to be camped out here for a while. But no Charlie.

A slight noise on the other side of the wall, in my room. A sniffle? Is she sick? Seeking comfort in my bed while I'm off on a field trip with the Susans? Guilt washes over me. Lucas should have called to let me know. Maybe the flu shot didn't take, or her allergies are acting up, or Coach scratched her fragile teen-age heart with an offhand remark.

No. Not sick. Charlie's cross-legged on my bed like Lydia used to be, her curls falling forward, intent on what she's reading. There's a frenzy of paper everywhere, littering the bed, the old antique rug on the floor. My backpack rests against the pillow behind her. It's unzipped for the first time since I returned from Huntsville. I want to scream *No,* but it's way too late.

Charlie's cheeks are slick with tears. 'I was looking for a highlighter.'

She holds up a piece of paper.

I know in that instant that our relationship will never be the same.

'Is this why you won't eat Snickers bars?' she asks.

Before I can utter a word, Lucas is there. He's holding out my phone, which I'd left on the kitchen counter with my purse.

'It's Jo. She says that you have to come back to her office. Immediately.'

September 1995

MR LINCOLN: Lydia . . . I can call you Lydia, right?

MS. BELL: Yes.

MR LINCOLN: Exactly how long have you known Tessa Cartwright?

MS. BELL: Since second grade. Our desks were in alphabetical order. Tessie's aunt used to say that God made out that seating chart.

MR LINCOLN: And you've been best friends since? For ten years?

MS. BELL: Yes.

MR LINCOLN: So when Tessie went missing you must have been terrified?

MS. BELL: I had a really bad feeling right away. We had like a secret way of letting each other know we were OK. We'd call the other one and let the phone ring twice. And then we'd wait five minutes and let the phone ring twice again. It was kind of a silly thing we did when we were little. But I stayed home and waited.

MR LINCOLN: Tessie didn't call? And you never left the house?

MS. BELL: No. Well, I left for about ten minutes to check her tree house.

MR LINCOLN: Check the tree house for . . . Tessa?

MS. BELL: We used to leave notes in this little crack.

MR LINCOLN: And there was no note?

MS. BELL: No note.

MR LINCOLN: Were your father and mother home during this period of waiting while Tessa was missing?

MS. BELL: Yes. My mom was. My dad had some emergency at work. A car's engine exploded or something. He came home later.

MR LINCOLN: Yes, we'll get back to that. In an earlier deposition, you mentioned that you have had nightmares since Tessa's attack. Is that right?

MS. BELL: Yes. But not as terrible as Tessie's.

MR LINCOLN: Can you describe some of yours?

MS. BELL: There's really just one. I get it practically every night. I'm standing on the bottom of the lake. It's cliché. Freud wouldn't be too interested, you know?

MR LINCOLN: Is Tessie in this dream?

MS. BELL: No. I can see my face but it's not my face. My father is reaching his hand down from his boat. He was always freaked one of us was going to go under. Anyway, his college ring falls into the water and starts sinking. He was always freaked about that happening, too, and never wore it on the boat. He went to Ohio State for a year. He's really proud of that. He loves that ring. He bought it at some garage sale.

MR LINCOLN: I know this is hard but try to keep your answers just a bit simpler, OK? Tell me this: Was Tessa ever afraid of your father?

16 days until the execution

This time, I'm not the first one there. It's a little past midnight. The Kleenex box on the conference room table has been disturbed. Moved to the very far edge of the table. Jo is pulling on latex gloves. She'd told me on the phone that I needed to drive over, *now*, but I couldn't leave Charlie in a paper bed of my testimony. We had to talk. Charlie is a little Tessie, sometimes. Too quick to reassure adults that she's OK.

Jo wouldn't tell me *why* I had to come. It was maddening. *Drive carefully*, she urged. Once I unwrapped myself from Charlie, I drove at warp speed, through two red light cameras, wondering what waited for me. My monster in handcuffs. More Susan skeletons grinning in ugly glee.

There is one other person in the room. A young girl by the window who is very much alive. A silky black ponytail trails down her back. She is gazing out the window at silvery trees, lit by pale moonlight, on the lawn of the Modern Art Museum across the street. Two stainless steel trees, their branches intricately, tediously soldered, pulling toward each other as if by magnetic force. That is how I feel about this girl, as if she can't turn toward me fast enough. When she does, I have an immediate impression of familiarity. Of longing.

'This young woman is Aurora Leigh,' Jo says. 'She says she is Lydia Bell's daughter.'

It's not like it wouldn't have been my first guess. The hair is darker, the skin even more ivory, but the eyes, full of dreamy blue intelligence, unmistakable.

And her name. Aurora Leigh. The epic heroine of Lydia's favorite poem.

'Hello, Aurora,' I say. I'm trying to tamp down the words being silently pelted at Aurora by the Susans. *Liar,* screams one. *Imposter.*

Jo is drumming her fingers on the table, drawing my attention back. 'Aurora went to the police station first. They called Lieutenant Myron, who is off duty. She told the front desk to call me.'

'I was making a scene.' Aurora plops into the nearest chair and drops a handful of crumpled tissue onto the table. Her nose is shiny and red and pierced by a tiny silver ring. Her lovely eyes are bloodshot. 'I'm sorry. I'm calmer now.'

'You sit, too, Tessa.' She turns to Aurora. 'Do you want me to explain?' She touches Aurora's shoulder, and she flinches.

'No,' says Aurora. 'That's OK. I'll do it. I'm OK. Really. I just wanted someone to listen to me. You listened.' She turns to me with eagerness. 'I saw a story on Fox about the box that was dug up. It's my mom's stuff. It belongs to me.'

'But I explained to Aurora that it is still evidence,' Jo says. 'That she can maybe get it back later.'

'I don't want it later. I want to see it now.' Matter-of-fact and petulant at the same time. Reminds me of Charlie. This girl couldn't be more than two years older. Sixteen. Seventeen, at most.

'I didn't know Lydia had a daughter.' My voice sounds surprisingly calm. 'Where is your mother right now?'

'I've never met her.' Aurora's words are an assault. Accusatory, even.

Jo forms her face into a professional mask. 'Aurora tells me she has lived with her grandparents since she was born. Mr and Mrs Bell. Although Aurora says she just learned that they changed their last name. They told her that her mother was dead and they had no idea who her father was. She had no reason to doubt them. Then her grandmother died. Her grandfather had a stroke last year and was moved to a full-term care facility. Aurora has been living with a foster family in Florida. I've already called them to let them know she's OK.'

'So . . .' I begin.

'So a lawyer cleaned out her grandparents' safe deposit box a month ago. Birth certificates. Tax documents. It's all there in Aurora's bag.' She points to a stuffed, pink-flowered tote.

'They lied to me. Every single day, they lied to me. I'm not Aurora Leigh Green. I'm Aurora Leigh Bell.' Aurora pulls out another Kleenex. 'I was saving money for a private investigator. I was Googling around in the meantime. It freaked me out when Lydia Bell's name came up a couple of times. You know, in those Black-Eyed Susan stories. But I didn't know if it was the same Lydia Bell. I didn't want it to be. And then I saw that story about the police digging at my grandparents' old house. They said their real names on the air. So I knew. I couldn't wait anymore. I stole some money out of my foster mom's purse for the bus.' Tears are lurking again. 'She's going to kill me. She probably won't take me back. She's not that bad really.'

'She's just happy that you're OK, Aurora. Remember, I

talked to her and she told you not to worry.' Jo, reassuring. 'Aurora is worried that her mother was a victim of the Black-Eyed Susan killer and that's the reason her grandparents went into hiding. I told her there is absolutely no evidence that she was. I explained that you could tell her the most about her mother. What she was like. Who she was dating.'

I open my mouth, and close it.

As far as I knew, Lydia only made it as far as third base one time, with our school's star third baseman. Lydia reveled in the literalness of it. She even told me she was considering similar conquests with the first and second basemen. It made me ache for her. When it came to Lydia, boys just wanted a cheap thrill: to meet a beautiful, crazy girl in the dark and hope she didn't bring an axe.

Aurora's face is twisting with impatience. Here she is, defiant, flesh and blood evidence that I never dreamed existed. I feel ineptly unable to answer without hurting her. Aurora's eyes are incandescent holes despite the harsh light of the conference room. Even with the nose ring and a scowl, she's a stunning replica of her mother.

'Jo, why are you gloved?' I ask.

'I was about to swab Aurora's DNA. I told her I can't give her the evidence, but I can run her DNA through all of the databases.'

'So that maybe she can find my father. That was blank on my birth certificate.' Aurora is so hopeful. Innocent. 'Maybe he didn't know about me.'

'How old are you?' I ask.

'Sixteen.'

So Lydia was pregnant when she hurtled out of town.

The picture is a little clearer. Why the Bells might flee. Mrs Bell believed brides should bring their hymens to the altar intact. Sperms and eggs instantly make microscopic people. A pregnant daughter would be the ultimate humiliation in her world. Abortion, not an option. But changing their names?

'Jo says you were best friends.' Lydia's daughter is begging me. For anything.

Aurora's arrival seems a little too pat.

She might be telling the truth. Or she might be a pawn of her mother's.

'She was loyal,' I lie. 'Like no one else.'

September 1995

MS. BELL: No. Tessie is not afraid of my dad. He could be a little mean after a few beers but he never bothered Tessie. She was so tough sometimes. Stood up for everybody. One time I told her that I could never handle it if I'd been the one to wake up in that grave. Don't get me wrong. She's messed up. Or maybe she's just mortal now like the rest of us. But I'd be totally nuts. And you know what she said? She said, that's why it happened to me and not you. Not to make me feel guilty or anything, or be martyr-y, just because she really can't stand to see anybody else hurt. You need to know something . . . Tessie is the best.

MR LINCOLN: Again, try to keep your answers short and confine them to my questions. I'm sure Mr Vega has told you this, too.

MR VEGA: I'm not objecting.

MR LINCOLN: Lydia, let me ask you this. Are you ever afraid of your dad?

MS. BELL: Only sometimes. When he drinks. But he's getting help for that now.

MR LINCOLN: Lydia, your dream sounds pretty scary to me. At the bottom of a lake with no one coming to your rescue.

MS. BELL: I never said that no one comes to the rescue. My dad always dives in after me.

MR LINCOLN: Interesting that you never mentioned that ending when I took your deposition. How can you be sure your father wasn't going for that college ring he loved so much?

MR VEGA: OK, your honor, now I'm objecting.

12 days until the execution

'Reconstructing memory doesn't work this way,' Dr Giles says. 'It's not a magic act. And I'm not the expert on light hypnosis. I've told you that.'

I'm staring down the same empty velour chair as last time, the one where Dr Giles suggested I picture my monster and give him a pop quiz. There's a frizzy blond Barbie nestled in the corner, her arms confirming a touchdown. 'So tell me how it works,' I beg.

'Some therapists use the imagery of a rope or ladder. Or tell you to watch a painful event from above, as a voyeur. There's a famous quote – that traumatic memory is a series of still snapshots or a silent movie and the role of therapy is to find the music and words.'

'So, let's find the music,' I say. '*And* the pictures. I pick . . . watching from above. Let's make my movie.'

I don't tell her about Aurora, who is safely back in Florida with her foster mom.

I don't tell her that I'm giving Lydia the starring role today. She always wanted it, and I was always snatching it away. I was the little girl with the dead mommy. I was the Black-Eyed Susan.

I'm hoping Lydia will appear in that chair and tell me something I don't know. She usually does.

'If you really want to try hypnosis, I'll recommend

another therapist. I'm not on board here. This is not what I do. I thought you understood this.'

'I don't want another therapist.'

My forehead begins to sweat. I'm hanging from the ceiling, a bat in the dark.

There I am. In the back of the parking lot. Tying my Adidas shoe with the pink laces that were in my Christmas stocking. Glancing up. There's Merry, gagged with something, pressing her face against a backseat window of a blue van. Me, running. Clinging to a sticky pay phone. Praying the silhouette turning the ignition in the van didn't see me. Sudden, excruciating pain in my ankle. Concrete slamming up. His face, looming. Strong arms, lifting me. Black.

'Tessa. Are you seeing something?'

Not now. I can't stop the movie to talk. I want more. I close my eyes into a light so bright it burns. There's Lydia, dancing with the Susans. Pushing them off the floor. Voguing to Madonna in my kitchen. Brushing my hair until my scalp tingles. Imitating Coach Winkle's sex talk: *Every time you think about doing it, I want a picture of my head to pop up. I'll be saying: 'Genital warts, genital warts!'*

Images, smashing into my brain. Lydia's drawing of the red-haired girl and the angry flowers. Mr Bell, drunk. The dogs yipping and spinning in crazy circles. Mrs Bell crying. Lydia and I pedaling our bikes to my house with our bodies slung low and forward, feet churning as fast as they can. Mr Bell's Ford Mustang breathing like a nasty dragon in the driveway while we hide in the flower garden. My father talking to him in calm tones on the porch. Sending him away. It was one night, and a hundred nights.

Me, the protector. A sob catches in my throat.

Cut. New scene. Here comes the doctor. Right on cue. I've seen this part of the movie before. There's Lydia. And over there, under that tree, are Oscar and me. Such a pretty campus to take a walk. If I'd let Oscar tug me the other way, I never would have seen them.

The camera weaves in close. I can almost read the titles of the library books crammed in Lydia's arms. Lydia, the pretend college girl. Yammering up at the doctor in her usual, earnest frenzy. The doctor, hurried, trying to be polite, looking like he wants nothing more than to get away.

September 1995

MR LINCOLN: Your honor, permission to treat the witness as hostile. I've been patient but I'm in the home stretch here. This witness has skirted around my last five questions.

JUDGE WATERS: Mr Lincoln, I see nothing hostile about a hundred-pound girl wearing glasses unless it's that her IQ is larger than yours.

MR LINCOLN: Objection . . . to you . . . your honor.

JUDGE WATERS: Ms. Bell. You need to answer. Did Tessie lie about anything related to this case?

MS. BELL: Yes, your honor.

MR LINCOLN: OK, let's go over this one more time. Tessie lied about the drawings?

MS. BELL: Yes.

MR LINCOLN: And she lied about when she could see again?

MS. BELL: Yes.

MR LINCOLN: And before the attack, she lied about where she was going running?

MS. BELL: Yes. Sometimes.

MR LINCOLN: And your father also lied about where he was going sometimes?

MR VEGA: Your honor, objection.

9 days until the execution

A little more than a week before Terrell is scheduled to die, and I'm cleaning out Effie's freezer.

The judge rejected Terrell's habeas corpus appeal five hours ago, news leached to the bottom of my stomach. Bill delivered the announcement by phone. I could barely listen after I heard the word *rejected.* Something about how the judge felt it was *a tough call* but there was *no convincing evidence* that Terrell was innocent and the jury got it wrong.

It's not like the police aren't still plugging away with Igor's new theories. They've turned up sixty-eight names, all females in their late teens to early twenties from Mexico and Tennessee who went missing in the mid-to-late '80s – Jo's best estimate on the age of the bones.

The problem is, that list of sixty-eight translates to hundreds of searches for family members who have moved or died or who don't answer their phones or who simply won't give up their DNA to help identify the Susans. At least fifteen people contacted by the police are family members still listed as suspects in some of those cases. Some of them are probably killers, just not the one we're looking for. Eleven girls on the list turned out to be runaways found alive but never removed from the missing persons database. It's a slog that could take months or years, all of it surmised from an ancient code from the earth. It seems impossible. I can't even figure out the best way to scrape purple Popsicle juice out of Effie's freezer.

'Effie, keep or toss?' I know the answer – it's been my mantra for the last hour – but I'm asking anyway. I'm holding up a plastic bag that contains the battered paperback copy of *Lonesome Dove.* Gus McCrae and Pea Eye Parker had been freezing to death for years behind several foil-wrapped items furry with ice crystals. Those have solidly hit the trashcan outside without Effie's knowledge.

'Keep,' Effie admonishes me. 'Certainly. *Lonesome Dove* is my favorite book of all time. I put it in there so I'd know where it was.' I'm never sure with Effie if these explanations are truth or cover-up.

Two days after Terrell is scheduled to die, Effie is moving to live with her daughter in New Jersey. I can barely breathe thinking about the absence of Effie's spirit in this house, but here I am, helping my friend load her life into boxes. At least that was the plan.

So far, she has not relinquished her hold on anything, including four iron skillets that are almost exactly alike except for the stories fried into their black history. In one, Effie made her husband's favorite Blueberry Surprise pancakes on the day he died. The skillet with the slightly rusted handle belonged to her mother. Effie almost came to blows over it post-funeral with a sister *who can't cook a lick.* The other two leave the best, crispest *almost burnt* crust on okra and cornbread, and *you always have to have two pans of okra.*

Effie is rather elegantly sprawled on the kitchen floor in a pair of old red silk pajamas, looking like an old Hollywood diva, if that's possible sitting on yellowed black-and-white linoleum surrounded by sixty years of pots and pans. The kitchen, like the rest of the house, is a wreck. She has spent the last three days yanking every single thing out of the cabinets, shelves, and closets and tossing it onto the beds, the floor, the tables, any available open space. The effect is that of a tornado hitting an antiques store.

'Sue, you're awfully quiet. Is it that damn Terrell Goodwin business?'

My fork stops its scraping. My head emerges from the freezer. Effie called me Sue, her daughter's name, while asking me the most pointed question of our relationship.

'Don't look so surprised. My mind's not that far gone, hon. I thought you might finally bring it up after the police broke down my door that night and ripped off my earphones. But you didn't, and that's fine. It's not even a smidgen of who you are, honey. Who you are – well, I'm going to miss who you are something terrible. And Charlie. I want to see that girl grow up. She's going to teach me to do that Sky-hype thing. Did I tell you that Sue's fiancé and I had a real good talk last night? He's fifth-generation New Jersey Italian. He told me it's always been an honor and privilege in his family to take care of the old. At least that's what I think he said. I couldn't understand half the conversation. I thought he had a speech impediment for the first fifteen minutes.'

I laugh because I've listened to Effie rattle off fluent French in her East Texas drawl, and it wasn't as pretty as a Hoboken accent. It's a slightly uneasy laugh, because I'm not interested in any heartfelt, tell-all goodbye with Effie. I'm going to leave her dreams alone. I don't want her to see my eyes dilate into black holes or for her to walk endless fields of yellow flowers that hold the scent of death. I don't want her to wake up still smelling it.

I'm relieved when my phone begins to buzz somewhere

near a counter of jumbled spices. I dig it out from under yellowed directions for a Sunbeam Percolator and a recipe for Doc's Gay Salad. I have no memory of placing my phone under anything; it's like the kitchen is turning into some form of kudzu and growing over itself.

Jo's name is on the screen. An instant sense of dread, pickled with hope.

'Hello,' I say.

'Hi, Tessa. Bill told me he let you know about the judge's ruling. Sucks.'

'Yes, he called.' I want to say more, but there's Effie.

'I'm a little worried about Bill. He looks like he hasn't slept for days. I've never seen him quite like this with a case. I think it's all tied up in his grief for Angie. Like he can't let her down.'

If I start to feel something for Bill or Terrell right now, I will feel everything. I already sense the hot well building behind my eyes.

'There's another reason I'm calling,' Jo continues. 'The cops got the guy who stuck those signs in your yard. He was caught vandalizing the lawn of a Catholic priest in Boerne. I thought you might want to get a restraining order. He's free on bond. His name is Jared Lester. He'll probably end up with a severe fine and community service instead of jail time.'

'OK. Thanks. I'll think about it.' *I'll think about not purposely pissing him off right now.*

'One more thing. He claims, rather proudly, that he planted the black-eyed Susans under your windowsill several weeks ago. I've checked, and the potting soil in his garage has the same basic signature as what I sampled from your yard that day. I don't think he's lying. He brought it up voluntarily in the police interview. Here's the deal. He's only twenty-three.' Meaning, not my monster. I do the math. He was five when I was tossed in that grave.

Effie's eying my throat, where my pulse drums. One of my tears drops onto the yellowed coffeepot instructions with the cartoon percolator with a Mr Kool-Aid face. I begin to methodically stand the spices into efficient lines.

How long has Jo known? Long enough that the police have caught this man, interviewed him, and set his bail. Long enough to run tests on potting soil.

I should give Jo a break, of course. As she ran that test, she had to know the outcome couldn't reassure me that much.

My monster is still out there.

This time, the door opens, and it's me on the other side wanting in.

I search his face, and my heart cracks.

I silently beg him to see all of me. The Black-Eyed Susan who talks to dead people, and the artist with the half-moon scar who tortures paint and thread to make sure beauty exists somewhere inside her. The mother who named her daughter Charlie after her father's favorite Texas knuckle-ball pitcher, and the runner who has never stopped running.

'You look like hell,' I say.

'What are you doing here?' As he says this, Bill is pulling me across the threshold into his arms.

We haven't spoken much or texted in the last several days. Bill doesn't appear to have showered for most of them. I don't mind. He smells alive. His chin scrapes my cheek like sandpaper. Our lips connect and, for a very long time, that's all there is.

'This is a bad idea,' he says, breaking us apart.

'That's my line.'

'Seriously. I'm running on fumes. Let me get you a beer and we'll talk.'

'I'm so sorry about Terrell,' I say, following him inside. 'Sorry for everything.' My words, inadequate.

'Yes. Me, too.' His voice is grim.

'I didn't mean to be so short on the phone. I was just . . . shocked.'

He shrugs. 'Next stop, U.S. Court of Appeals. A bunch of buffoons with rubber stamps. The habeas appeal was our real shot. Have a seat and I'll be back with your beer.'

He disappears through an archway, leaving me to glean what I can from the first encounter with his living space. I scour the art on the walls the way other people surreptitiously peer at bookshelves and CD collections. Or used to anyway. A few decent modern prints with reds, greens, and golds. Nothing that provides insight into Bill's soul, and if it does, I don't want that to pop my bubble.

I pick out a buttery white leather chair and wonder a little too late if I'd gotten a nice young law intern named Kayley into trouble by bullying her for Bill's home address. When I showed up in Angie's basement, Kayley dripped as much exhaustion as Bill. I wore her down with my red eyes, driver's license, and a rambling dissertation on Saint Stephen, still being stoned to death over Angie's shrine of a desk. Kayley spent much of the dissertation time trying not to gape at my scar, openly impressed that she was meeting the myth.

All of which led me to this 1960s-era converted garage, which I'm sure is worth about $600,000 plus. It nests in the winding waterways and trees of Turtle Creek, a famous, wealthy old Dallas neighborhood where Indians used to camp. I love the play of light on hardwoods, the gracious white brick fireplace with a grate covered in ash, even the concentric coffee rings near the open laptop on the coffee table. The art, not so much. It matches these pillows.

Bill appears with two St Pauli Girls in his hands. I want to think this means he took note of my favorite beer and stocked it.

'In case you're wondering,' he says, gesturing with his beer, 'I'm a squatter. My dad enjoys flipping town homes after retirement, which I guess is better than playing baccarat at Choctaw. My mother decorates. So I'm just here making it look lived in until it sells.' He takes a swig and settles on the couch directly across from me.

'I have to confess,' he says. 'Kayley called to warn me you were coming.'

'So you could get your gun out.' I smile.

'Well, it wouldn't be the first time,' he says.

I switch the subject back to Terrell. 'How many times have you won a reprieve in a death penalty case?'

'A reprieve? Five or six. That's the real goal most of the time. To extend life as long as possible, because if you're sitting on Death Row in Texas, you are most likely going to die on that gurney. I've only worked one case with a Capra-esque ending. Angie was the lead. I don't do this full time. But you know that.'

'That one time . . . you must have been . . . elated,' I say.

'*Elated* isn't exactly the right word. It doesn't change that the victim died a horrible death. There's a family out there who might always feel like we set a killer free. So I'd say, more like very, very, very relieved. Angie insisted we did our high-fiving in private.' Bill pats the side of the couch. 'Come here. You're too far away.'

I get up very slowly. He pulls me down into his arms and drags a kiss along my mouth. 'Lie down.'

'I thought this wasn't a good idea.'

'This is a very good idea. We're going to sleep.'

The fierce pounding rocks both of us upright and fully awake.

Bill jumps from the couch, leaving me gracelessly sprawled against the pillows. He's already peering through the peephole before my feet touch the floor. In a second, I'm beside him. 'Go into the kitchen,' he orders, 'if you want to keep us a secret.'

I don't budge, and he turns the knob.

I'm blinded by lime green. A ski jacket meant to stand out to rescue helicopters on a snowy slope. Jo's head is sticking out of it. She pushes her way into the room like she's been here before.

She's quickly figuring out what my presence means. 'Tessa? Why . . . ?' She shakes her head. 'Oh, never mind. It doesn't matter. You should know, too.'

'Know what?' I'm awkwardly smoothing my hair.

'About Aurora.'

'Is something wrong? Is she hurt?' *Or dead?*

'No, no. It's her DNA. We found a match. It's bizarre.'

'Come on, Jo. What's up?' Bill, impatient. Watching my face.

'We have a DNA match from Aurora to the fetal bone from the Black-Eyed Susan grave. They shared the same father. They would have been half-sisters.'

'A DNA match to . . . Lydia's daughter?' Bill is asking the incredulous words while I'm trying to catch up. To let go of the picture of Lydia and a high school boy in a naked tangle.

Lydia slept with the killer. Or she was raped.

I'm the one with the answers, a Susan whispers.

Bill's phone begins to bleat. He pulls it out of his pocket, annoyed, and glances at the screen. His face is suddenly locked down.

'I have to take this.' He points a finger at Jo and me. 'Hold off saying more until I'm off the phone.'

Jo guides me by my elbow back to the couch. The Susans are whispering very low, like the wind humming through that tiny hole in my tree house.

That night, the Susans come to me in my sleep. They are frenzied, running around, a blur of youthful limbs and bright swirling skirts, more alive than I've ever seen them. They are searching for my monster in every nook and cranny as if their mansion in my head is about to explode. As if it is for the very last time.

They are shouting and cursing at each other, at me.

Wake up, Tessie! they are shrieking. *Lydia knows something!* They are spreading out like Army men. Opening and slamming closet doors, tearing off bedcovers, dusting cobwebs off chandeliers, ripping weeds out of the garden. Merry, sweet Merry, is falling to her knees to beg God's mercy.

A Susan calls out. *Over here! I've found the monster!* She's telling me to *hurry, hurry, hurry* because she can't hold him down for long.

I teeter on the edge of consciousness. The Susan is planted on top of him, her red skirt swirled over his body like blood. She is using every last bit of strength to twist his neck around so that I can see. A worm is gyrating out of his mouth. His face is caked with mud.

I wake up sobbing.

My monster is still wearing a mask. And Lydia knows exactly who he is.

September 1995

MR LINCOLN: I think we're all done, Ms. Bell. Thank you for your testimony. I'm sorry it's been a difficult day for you.

MS. BELL: It wasn't difficult. I have one more thing. It's about Tessie's journal.

MR LINCOLN: I wasn't aware she had a journal.

MR VEGA: Objection. I know nothing about this journal. It is not in evidence, your honor, and I don't see its relevance.

JUDGE WATERS: Mr Lincoln?

MR LINCOLN: I'm thinking.

JUDGE WATERS: Well, while you're thinking, I'm going to ask the witness a few questions.

MR VEGA: Objection. I believe you are overstepping a little here, your honor. We only have this witness's word that it exists.

MR LINCOLN: I believe I have to object as well, your honor. I'm walking a ledge just like Mr Vega here, not knowing its contents.

JUDGE WATERS: Thank you for your united interest in pursuing the truth, gentlemen. Look at me, Ms. Bell. I need you to speak very generally. Did you bring up the journal because you think there is something in it pertinent to this trial?

MS. BELL: Most of it was running times, personal stuff. Sometimes she'd read to me from it. A fairy tale she made up. Or show me a little sketch she did. Or . . .

JUDGE WATERS: Hold on, Ms. Bell. Did Ms. Cartwright let you read her journal?

MS. BELL: Not exactly. When she was acting funny, I would, though. And I'd go through her purse or drawers to make sure she wasn't hoarding Benadryl and stuff. That's what best friends do.

JUDGE WATERS: Ms. Bell, I need you to answer my question with a yes or a no. Do you believe there is something in the journal that is pertinent to this trial?

MS. BELL: That's hard to say but, you know, like, I wonder. I never read the whole thing. I skimmed. We used to do our journals together. It was one of our things.

JUDGE WATERS: Do you know where Tessie's journal is?

MS. BELL: Yes.

JUDGE WATERS: And where is that?

MS. BELL: I gave it to her psychiatrist.

JUDGE WATERS: And why did you do that?

MS. BELL: Because it had a picture she drew when she was blind of a red-haired mermaid jumping off her grandfather's roof. You know, killing herself.

PART III
Tessa and Lydia

Flowers are restful to look at. They have neither emotions nor conflicts.

– Lydia, age 15, reading the words of Sigmund Freud while lounging on her father's boat, 1993

Tessa, present day

1:46 a.m.

Effie is standing on my front porch holding a lumpy brown package. Her flimsy robe is billowing out behind her. The neighborhood is dead asleep, except for us and a few street-lights. Before she knocked, I was wide awake trying to read *The Goldfinch* but thinking about Terrell.

Three days left.

'I forgot to give you this earlier.' Effie plops the package into my arms. 'I saw some girl in a purple dress drop it off. Or maybe it was a handsome man in a suit. Anyway, I saw it on your front porch this afternoon. Or yesterday. Or maybe a week ago. I thought I should bring it in for you.'

'Thank you,' I say, distracted.

Tessie scrawled on the front. No stamp. No return address. It feels squishy, with something stiff in the middle.

Don't open it. A Susan, warning me.

I cast my eyes past Effie, onto the dark lawn. I survey the lumps of bushes crouching between our property lines. The shadows dancing to a tuneless rhythm on the driveway.

Charlie is at a sleepover. Lucas is on an overnight date. Bill is at the Days Inn in Huntsville because Terrell begged him.

Effie is already floating back across the yard.

Lydia, age 16

43 Hours After the Attack

This is not my best friend.

This is a thing, with a Bozo the Clown wig and a slack face and tubes running everywhere like an insane water park except the water is yellow and red.

I'm holding Tessie's hand and squeezing it, timing every squeeze by my watch, because her Aunt Hilda told me to. *About every minute,* she said. *We want her to know we're here.* I'm trying not to squeeze the part of her hand where the bandage is turning a little pink. I overheard a nurse say Tessie's fingernails were ripped out, like she was trying to claw her way out of a grave. They had to pick yellow flower petals out of the gash in her head.

'It can take like eighteen months for toenails to grow back,' I say loudly, because Aunt Hilda said to keep talking because *we don't know what she can hear* and because I'd already reassured Tessie that her fingernails will only take six months.

As soon as I heard Tessie was missing, I threw up. After twelve hours, I knew for sure something evil got her. I started writing what I'd say at the funeral. I wrote how I wouldn't ever again feel her fingers braiding my hair or see her draw a lovely thing in about thirty seconds or watch her face go animal when she runs. People would have cried when they heard it.

I was going to quote Chaucer and Jesus and promise I'd devote my entire life to looking for her killer. I was going to stand at that pulpit in the Baptist church and throw out a warning to the killer in case he was listening because killers usually are. Instead of saying *Peace be with you,* people were going to flip around in their pews and give each other jumpy stares and wonder from now on what exactly was living next door to them. There's a knife in every kitchen drawer, pillows on every bed, anti-freeze in every garage. Weapons everywhere, people, and we're ready to blow. That would be my message.

Tessie thinks humans are basically good. I don't. I'm dying to ask if she thinks evil is an aberration now, but I don't want her to think I'm rubbing it in.

The monitor over the bed is screeching for the hundredth time, and I jump, but Tessie doesn't move. I feel like my hand is squeezing a piece of mozzarella cheese. It hits me full blast for like the tenth time that she'll never be the same. There's a bandage on her face that's hiding something. She might not be pretty anymore, or funny, or get all my literary references, or be the only person on earth who doesn't think I'm a total ghoul. Even my dad calls me Morticia sometimes.

The beeping *won't stop.* I punch the call button *again.* A nurse swings open the door, asking me if an adult is coming back in soon. Like *I'm* a problem.

I don't want to be dispatched to the waiting room again. There are a million people in there. And Tessie's track coach was driving me crazy. Repeating how lucky it is that the *calvary* got to Tessie in time. *Calvary is where Jesus died on the cross, you moron.* I tell the story to Tessie again, even though I already did a few minutes ago.

Tessie's eyelids flutter. Except her Aunt Hilda warned me her eyes do that regularly. It doesn't mean she's waking up.

I picked out Tessie in second grade, the instant I sat down at the desk next to hers.

I squeeze her hand. 'It's OK to come back. I won't let him get you.'

Tessa, present day

1:51 a.m.

I close the door. Finger in the security code.

Turn around and almost stop breathing.

Merry's face is pressed into the mirror's reflection on the wall.

She's trapped on the other side of the glass, just like the night she pressed her face against the car window in the drugstore parking lot. How much effort it must have taken for her to throw herself up from the backseat, half-dead, half-drugged, gagged with a blue scarf, one last-ditch effort to hope that someone like me would happen along to rescue her. Of all the Susans in my head, Merry's the least needy, the least accusing. The most guilty.

It's OK, I say softly, walking toward her. *It is not your fault. I'm the one who's sorry. I should have saved you.*

By the time I press my palm flat against the glass, Merry's already gone, replaced by a pale woman with messy red hair, green eyes, and a gold squiggly charm in the hollow of her throat. My breath fogs the mirror, and I disappear, too.

Merry has shown up twice before. She appeared in the doctor's office window when I was seventeen, five days after I got my sight back. Four years ago, she sang 'I'll Fly Away' in the back row of the church choir at my father's funeral.

I walk over to the kitchen drawer, pull out a knife, and slice it across the package.

The Susans, a rising hum in my head.

Lydia, age 16

6 Months Before the Trial

I'm pounding on the door and yelling Tessie's name.

She's locked me out. I'm stuck in her stupid pink fairy tale bedroom that was fine *when we were ten.* I woke up and she wasn't in bed and now I can't get the door to the terrace open. I *told* her I didn't want her out there alone tonight because she's blind and it's dangerous and I've been left in charge. But, really, it's because I think she might jump off her grandfather's roof.

Today was another Sad Day. She's had twenty-six in a row. I mark a smiley face on my calendar every day she smiles *once.* No one else is marking smiley faces on a calendar and yet if Tessie kills herself tonight, it will be the fault of Lydia Frances Bell.

Lydia was never a good influence. Lydia's morbid. Lydia might have given Tessie a little push.

I put my ear on the door. Still alive. She's playing something dirge-y on her flute. It takes a lot of breath to blow a flute. I wouldn't want to stand too close and get a whiff. She hasn't brushed her teeth for six days. No one but me is counting *that* number, either. One life lesson of the Tessie thing is that it's harder to love people when they smell. Of course, there are a lot of good parts, too. It's cool to be called her *fairy tale friend* by *People* magazine. And I feel a secret, tickly thrill all the time now, the same as when I'm staring into the ocean and thinking about how deep and black it goes, and what lurks on the bottom. I *like* walking around inside a terrible novel, *living* it, getting up every day to write a new page, even if people always see Tessie as the main character.

The door is budging a little, so I bang my hip into it a little harder. It was her grandparents' stupid idea, not mine, to bring her to their castle for the weekend. Of course, they crashed at 9:30 and are half-deaf.

Surely she wouldn't jump because of that Frida Kahlo remark I made at dinner. Her grandmother had given me a dirty look. I mean, it was her grandfather who brought it up.

He was telling Tessie about how Frida Kahlo had painted in bed after the terrible bus accident when she was eighteen that left her frozen in a body cast. Frida's mother made this special easel for her bed. So Tessie's grandfather asked her if she'd like him to make something like it for her. He was trying to inspire her, but it seems to me the lesson there is that a random bus accident screwed up Frida Kahlo pretty much for life, just like Tessie's going to be. And all I *said* was that it was a good thing Kahlo killed herself because she was literally painting herself to death. I thought it was funny. Like, how many Frida Kahlo faces can the world take?

The door suddenly gives way, and I stumble onto the terrace. She's sitting on the ledge with her back to me, wearing her grandfather's extra-large white Hanes T-shirt, looking like Casper the Friendly Ghost. She forgot her nightgown on our little overnight trip, so she borrowed the shirt out of her grandfather's drawer.

There are much better ways to kill yourself, I am thinking. *And I wouldn't wear that.*

Maybe I should let her jump. It just pops in my head.

If she did, she'd probably just end up in a wheelchair because she's just that lucky. Or unlucky. It's such a freaky line. All this hard work to bring her back to life when I'm pretty sure she wishes she'd gone to sleep in that grave and never woken up.

I'm really, really pissed off tonight. More than usual. I'm *crying.* I'm not sure how long I can keep this up. All those stories in the newspaper, and yet the ugly, real story is never told.

She's still playing the stupid flute. It makes *me* want to jump.

'Please get off the ledge,' I choke out. *'Please.'*

Tessa, present day

1:54 a.m.

I reach into the package and tug out a plastic bag.

A shirt is inside.

Crusted with blood.

I recognize it.

Lydia, age 17

10 Weeks Before the Trial

I could draw *twenty* smiley faces in my calendar today.

My mom just brought us freezing cans of Coke with straws, and Chips Ahoy on a plate. She said it was good to hear us laughing so much again. I locked the door after that. It was Tessie's idea to draw these fake pictures for her new doctor, a big shocker, because it's more like the kind of thing *I* would come up with. Tessie was never a big liar but I've never had a problem if it's a means to an end. She told me she's not ready to let this new doctor peer into her soul. The soul thing was just her mimicking the doctor she got stuck with right before this one. That idiot told her she could cure her blindness if she jumped off the high dive and opened her eyes underwater. I've never seen Tessie's dad so mad as when I told him. *He might as well be suggesting she kill herself!*

Tessie's wearing these white nerdy pajamas with lace that her Aunt Hilda gave her. If she could see, she wouldn't be caught dead in them. But she can't, and it's kind of sweet. They make her look all innocent, like the world isn't ending.

'Do you have the black marker?' Tessie's asking.

'Yes.' I perfect a grimace on a flower and hand it over.

For once, I'm not embarrassed to draw in the same room as Tessie. She had to go blind for that to happen.

Everything she draws is always so *perfect.* I like this picture. I definitely draw better when Tessie's no competition.

Still, I'm thinking this picture's a little *literal.* A field of monster flowers. A girl cowering. It needs *drama.*

I add another girl right on top of the other one. Scratch in some red. Are the girls fighting to the death? Is one killing the other? Are the poor little flowers actually just worried and trying to make it stop?

Ha-ha. Let him wonder.

Tessa, present day

2:03 a.m.

My eyes are glued to the brown stain on the pink shirt. My shirt. She borrowed it from me a very long time ago and never returned it.

It's a lot of blood.

Not for the first time, I'm numbly contemplating the idea of Lydia, murdered.

Lydia was fond of ketchup, I remind myself. Of corn syrup and red dye, manipulation and guessing games.

There's something else in the package.

A college-ruled notebook. I recognize it, too. There used to be a whole box of them.

A date is scribbled on the front of this one. And a name.

The *L* curls up on the end, like a cat's tail. I'd seen her write that *L* a hundred times.

My hand hovers between the notebook and my cell phone.

Deciding how to play.

Lydia, age 17

3 Weeks Before the Trial

'I'm Lydia Frances Bell,' I introduce myself, wishing I hadn't added the *Frances.* Or used the *Lydia,* which I never felt was my true name. I'm more of an Audriana or Violetta or Dahlia. I should have given him a fake name. Tessie would say it was stupid to introduce myself to him in the first place. She'd be mad. I told her I was just going to sit in her doctor's class one time to observe and not even raise my hand. I've come twice since then. Tessie is driving me freaking crazy. Last night, she nearly tore my head off when I made myself a peanut butter sandwich and brought it to her room. I mean, get over it. It's a *sandwich.*

Today is the first time I signed up for his office hours. I feel as fully prepared as I can be. I've researched everything I can about him. I've read his lecture series *From Marilyn Monroe to Eva Braun: History's Most Powerful Bimbos.* I *devoured* the case study of that girl who survived being buried alive by her stepdad, which got everyone all into him being Tessie's therapist when his name appeared on the list of candidates. He's been a visiting professor at *three* Ivy League schools. He *never* teaches anything with 101 in the title. I couldn't find much personal, so that was a bummer, and *nothing* about his missing daughter, but I'm sure he's a private man and is totally devoted to his life's work.

'I'm so glad you dropped by, Lydia,' he's saying. 'I've seen you sitting in the front row.' His smile is a draught of sunshine. He makes me *think* in Keats.

I lay down my *copious* notes on his last lecture, about the dark triad of personality, so he can see right away what a good student I am. He asks me whether I agree with Machiavelli that we are not helpless at the hands of bad luck. It was apparently a rhetorical question, because he's still talking. I love the sound of his voice rolling over all those four-syllable words. I feel like he is having sex with my brain.

I have ten brilliant questions all set to impress him, and I haven't asked a single one.

He has rolled his chair over from behind the desk. His knee is pressing against my leg in this delicious pleasure-pain thing. I can barely *think* with his knee on mine and yet he acts like it's not even there.

I know I need to tell him I'm the Lydia who is Tessie's best friend, but not when he's looking at me like that.

Next time.

Tessa, present day

2:24 a.m.

I'm whipping through the pages. They're brutal. Nicking me, stabbing me, kicking me in the gut. Blowing me a few kisses. Love and resentment, all mixed up.

A whole other Lydia going on when I was sixteen years old. A picture behind a picture. I flash back to that night on the terrace when I thought we dredged up everything. Every unspoken pebble of anger. Every benign tumor that had been growing since our friendship began – the tumors that live under the skin of every relationship until the unforgivable moment that changes their chemistry forever.

I was wrong. There was so much more.

I'm trying to reconcile the girl in this notebook with the one who gave me back my breath with a brown paper bag. Who hugged me all night when my mother died, and braided my hair when I was blind. Who read me breathless poetry. Who wrote notes in Edgar Allan Poe's favorite cipher, with invisible ink made from lemon juice, and stuck them in a crack in my tree house for me to find the next day. So I could hold her words up to the sun.

I feel sick.

The phone rings. I jump up, knocking over a bottle of water.

Lydia's ink begins to blur.

I blot frantically at the pages.

The phone shrills again. Insistent.

I stare at the Caller ID.

Outler, Euphemia.

At least a quarter of the pages left. I don't know how Lydia's story ends. Or how quickly my time with the journal will be up. I have to figure, very, very soon.

I pick up the receiver.

'Sue? Sue?' Full-on Effie panic.

She lowers her voice.

'I think the damn digger snatcher is here.'

Lydia, age 17

2 Days After the Trial

Tessie is *screaming* at me.

You gave my diary to the doctor? You rifle through my things?

'I had to give jurors the full picture.' Good grief, she is freaking *out*. I thought she'd get it. 'I gave him the diary to *protect* you. I testified to all that stuff to help convict Terrell.'

'Yeah, right. You had to tell them I didn't bathe? That you found lice in my hair? That I stole painkillers out of Aunt Hilda's medicine cabinet?'

'I'm sorry I said the boys call you Suzy Scarface. That was a very unfortunate headline.'

'Do they really call me that, Lydia?' Tessie looks like she's about to cry. But I can't give in. She always wants things both ways.

'You testified for *you*,' Tessie is saying. 'So *you* could be a star.'

We're standing on her grandfather's terrace like we have a million times before. She's shaking, she's so freaking mad at me. But, like, I'm getting madder by the second, too. *Doesn't she understand everything I've done for her?* She's yelling, and I'm yelling right back, the catfight of the century. Finally, she doesn't have a comeback. There's just silence and black night and us, breathing hard.

'I saw you with the doctor.' Her tone creeps me out.

'What are you talking about?' Of course, I *know* what she's talking about. *But which time? How much does she know?* I take a stab. 'You mean the time I gave him your diary?'

'I guess. I was walking Oscar at the college. What did you think you were doing, Lydia? *Get out.*'

Her grandmother is suddenly at my back, clawing my shoulder, wheezing a little, because she had to climb all those stairs. She never liked me much. 'Girls – '

'Get out, Lydia,' Tessie sobs. *'Getoutgetoutgetout.'*

Tessa, present day

2:29 a.m.

I'm crossing the yard, running. Barefoot. It feels like a dream. A starry night above my head. A sweet, drifting perfume, nauseating.

Shadows hang off every tree, ready to smother me. I focus on the light trickling out of Effie's kitchen window. On the cold steel in my hand. On the idea of Effie, alone with a monster. The one eating her brain, the one who turned girls to bones, the one who used to brush my hair and secretly despise my weakness. Maybe all three.

Waiting for me. Using Effie as bait.

What is that on the ground? I bend and brush my fingers on the grass. Confetti. It litters a path between my house and Effie's. I rub the bits of paper between my fingers. Watch the pieces tumble and float downward like brilliant abstract thoughts.

It isn't confetti.

The grass is littered with black-eyed Susans.

Someone has ripped off their body parts and left me a trail.

I'm gasping, sucking at air that is evaporating.

Van Gogh's sky is spinning above me.

My head is exploding with images, and settles on one.

He has finally wiped the mud off his face.

My monster. The Black-Eyed Susan killer.

He's clean, and shaved. Smiling.

The Susans yip with joy. *That's him that's him that's him!*

I can feel his arm trapped around my shoulder. Smell the cologne on his suit coat.

Hear his lazy, reassuring drawl.

If you had three wishes, Tessie, what would they be?

Lydia, age 17

3 Days After the Trial

We made love twice. He's already on the edge of the bed.

'I'm going to take a shower, sweetheart,' he says. 'Then I'm going to have to run. So pack up, OK?'

Sweetheart. Like I'm a 1940s thing on the side. How about getting a little more mythological? Calling me Eurydice? Or Isolde? I'm thinking that Lydia Frances Bell deserves better right now than scratchy sheets and *pack up* and *sweetheart.*

The shower is already running.

I slip naked out of bed, shivering. He always keeps it freezing in his apartment. He doesn't like the noise of the furnace coming on and off. *Whatever.* I grab his shirt off the floor and slip my arms into it. Flap the long sleeves like a bird. It's his last day at school before his China sabbatical. He says Tessie doesn't ever need to know we slept together, which is, like, *huge.* I'm thinking she'll get over the testimony stuff. I give her a month.

These packing boxes are freaking everywhere.

Maybe I'll explore. Find a memento he won't miss.

I stick my hands in the pockets of his old man suits. I wish he'd let me dress him. His shirts are way too starchy. They scratch my neck. I thumb through a stack of textbooks that would bore the crap out of me. I rove around in his boxer shorts drawer. Ordinary, ordinary, ordinary.

The shower's still running.

I open and shut more empty drawers. Check out the freezer.

Thumb through a pile of mail. Geez, even Tessie leaves me better surprises.

I almost didn't bother to open the cabinet under the kitchen sink.

That's where I found them.

Straggly yellow flowers with black eyes, sitting in the dark.

Tessa, present day

2:34 a.m.

I'm kneeling. Staring at a petal stuck to my hand. Pulsing with rage.

At him. At myself, for knowing all along but being too afraid to see.

At Lydia.

I don't know how much time has passed. Seconds? Minutes? The light still glows steadily from Effie's kitchen.

You control your mind, Tessie. The doctor. In my head. Leering. Mocking.

I will myself to stand.

Petals are everywhere, glued to my knees, to the soles of my bare feet.

I reach down to brush them off.

They are not petals.

They are tiny, twisted scraps of Kleenex. Fragments of tissue that have disintegrated in the washer. The ones constantly nesting in the pockets of Effie's robes and sweaters.

This is Effie's trail. It leads to her front door, miles away from the grave where Tessie went to sleep.

Except Tessie is waking up. The old Tessie, who outran boys, who beat a plodding heart, who risked scabs and bones and scars, *who did not lose* because her dead mother cheered her across the finish line.

I see Tessie crouched on a track in blinding sunlight. Heat rises in visible waves. Her eyes are down. To finish first, she will spend the least amount of time possible in the air, over the hurdles.

Her fingertips are poised on gritty dirt.

Mine are twisting Effie's doorknob.

Both of us, ready for the gun to go off.

Lydia, age 17

10 Days After the Trial

He's like a serial killer Mr Darcy, offering me his hand so that I can step into the boat bobbing away off the ratty dock. We took this wiggly little path down from the cabin to get here. His idea, the rental cabin. Our special goodbye night, he says, before he takes off for China or wherever he's really going. This place is remote as hell. I wonder if he brought other girls here. Or does he choose a new spot every time? Everything's black. The water, the sky, the forest of trees behind us. And what about that tarp in the bottom of the boat? Does he really think that Lydia Bell is this stupid? Of course, I'm stepping into a boat with a serial killer but that's what you have to do when there's no real evidence and you're the very last hope.

'Careful,' he warns as I step down. 'Want to drive?' While I sit, he's yanking the outboard string, having a little trouble getting it all revved up. I could offer advice but I don't.

'No, thanks,' I say. 'I'd be scared. I'm just going to sit back and look at the moon if I can find it. I have a flashlight. Maybe I'll read to you.' I wave the book in my hand, *The Ultimate Book of Love Poems: Browning to Yeats,* even though I have a photographic memory and I've read this book a billion times.

'I didn't know anything was capable of scaring you,' he

teases. *Hmm,* I'm thinking, *the scared thing might have been too much.*

'You're going to love it out here on the lake in the dark,' he's saying. 'Just your style. Wait to read until we get to a good spot. I'll cut the motor and we can drift a little. Drink a little wine.'

He's about two miles out, slowing the boat down, when I flick on my flashlight, open the book, and begin. '"You love me. You love me *not.*"'

The words get lost in the noise of the engine.

'What?' Impatient. 'I told you not to read yet.'

I go silent, which is hard.

He kills the motor in the middle of the lake.

I'm prepared, of course. Ten questions are typed out in my head, numbered one under the other. I shut the book.

Question No. 1: 'Did you kill those girls?'

'What girls, sweetie?'

'Did you think I wouldn't love you anymore? That I would tell?'

'Lydia. Stop.'

'Did you know who I was that very first day in your office? That I was Tessie's best friend?' I want him to say *no.* I want him to *explain.*

It's hard to see his face in the dark. His body remains perfectly relaxed. 'Sweetheart, of course I knew. I know everything about you and Tessie. You are fucked-up little girls.'

I'm watching his hands, fiddling with a coiled rope.

It's official. Lydia Frances Bell loved a serial killer.

My heart is pounding pretty hard, which is to be expected. I keep my eyes on the rope. 'Where are you really going on that plane?'

'Surely your big brain has better questions than this, Lydia. But to answer . . . I'm not sure yet.'

'I have ten questions total.'

'Fire away.'

'Do you really have a daughter named Rebecca?'

'I do not.' He's grinning.

'No family? No friends?'

'Unnecessary, don't you think?'

'My other three questions don't matter.'

My fingers curl around Daddy's gun in my coat pocket.

'I'm pregnant,' I say.

The gun, now aimed at his chest.

Blood drooling out of his shoulder instead.

I didn't even hear it go off. A gunshot on the lake sounds like the sky is cracking. Like it might rain shards of glass. That's what Tessie used to say.

I steady my hand.

'Wait, sweetheart.' He's pleading with me. 'We can work this out. You and I, we're the same.'

Tessa, present day

2:44 a.m.

The foyer, dark.

'Effie?' I call out.

'In the kitchen, Sue.' Her voice traveling over from the next room. Lilting. Her panic erased. I smell something burnt.

I wonder if it's gunpowder. If my neighbor has shot her digger snatcher dead with that little pearl-handled revolver she keeps loaded in her bedside table against my wishes.

You can do this. For Charlie.

I round the corner.

It is an ordinary tableau.

And a chilling one.

Lydia, a very alive, *blond* Lydia, seated at the table.

Effie, beaming and placing a blue-flowered china plate in front of her.

'There you are!' Effie enthuses. 'False alarm! It wasn't the digger snatcher after all. It was just Liz here. Which is a real treat.'

Lydia, smiling. Not buried in an anonymous grave. Not broken. Not sorry. A part of everything.

Her lips are slashed with bright red. I see the tiny, tiny black birthmark on her upper lip that one boy teased her was a tick. She'd held her hand over her mouth for a week.

Her left leg is crossed over the right knee at a slightly odd angle. She used to sit just like that one summer to hide a mark from her dad's belt buckle. It became a habit she couldn't break.

I knew her habits. I knew secrets that made her howl. I could tear her to shreds.

Lydia watches me carefully. Still not saying a word.

My gun clatters to the floor.

I don't move. Because that was my move.

'You dropped something, honey,' Effie is saying. 'Aren't you going to pick it up? You might remember me talking about Liz. She's the researcher from the national historical society who visits me now and again. She stored some of her boxes of Fort Worth research in my shed not that long ago. She visits societies all over the nation!'

I remember. *Boxes, taped tightly shut. Charlie, helping Effie and a strange woman lug them to the shed.*

'Liz came over tonight to get something she needs out of them, and didn't want to wake me,' Effie continues. 'I told her it was best not to skulk around here in Texas. She spends most of her time in more civilized places like Washington and London, isn't that right?'

Lydia, this *dyed,* smiling, nodding Lydia, has been insinuating herself into Effie's life. Pretending to be someone she isn't. Spying, like she always did. *Watching me. Watching Charlie. Delivering her diary to my doorstep. Returning my shirt, soaked in red. Playing her little games.*

'Where is he?' I hiss at Lydia.

It was Lydia who always told me not to say the doctor's name out loud. *Seize control. Limit his power.*

'The digger snatcher isn't here, honey.' Effie, trying to

clear things up. 'Like I mentioned, it was Liz in the back yard. We were just discussing that little Mudgett man from Chicago who tried to build one of his murder castles downtown. Liz knows *everything* about old Fort Worth. I agree with her that a plaque should be erected on that lot where he planned his slaughterhouse for girls.'

'I'm sure she knows all about serial killers.' I can't tear my eyes off her. The brilliant, familiar eyes. Expensive tortoiseshell glasses. Hair tied up in a chic, messy knot. A chunky Breitling leather watch hugging her wrist. A plain wide band of hammered silver on her right hand.

'He's dead, Tessie.' The first words Lydia has uttered to me in seventeen years. Her voice, triumphant. 'I killed him.'

'Of course he's dead,' Effie prattles. 'Mr Mudgett died in prison in 1896. He was hanged at Moyamensing, Liz. You just told me a second ago that he twitched for fifteen minutes.'

Lydia, age 17

I press the trigger four times.

Simple as that for a fucked-up Texas girl.

I crawl over him to the wheel.

It takes eleven minutes to whip around the lake in the dark and find Dumbo. My marker. The large tree on the west shore with a single branch that curves up like an elephant's trunk.

This is the creepiest spot in the lake. Dead Man's Triangle. Good fishing, but if people go under here, they often don't pop back up. I've driven a boat around this lake since I could see over the front and my father was a drunk, which means pretty much since the day I was born. Daddy and I had our best times on this lake. I gutted the fish without throwing up, and he swilled vodka out of Coke cans and always did.

My mind is *so quiet.* Like, quieter than it's ever been. It's weird. I stop the motor. Drift for a second. Better get back to business. It isn't that hard to push him out of the boat. *Plop.* He sinks in less than a minute. I don't feel a thing, watching him go under. I toss in the old book I found under his kitchen sink with the black-eyed Susans and the Cascade. *Rebecca* by Daphne du Maurier. Blood had soaked the brittle binding, or I would have kept it. That book was my No. 8, 9, and 10 questions, but he was about to lasso me with that freaking rope.

It takes no time to motor back, yank up the tarp in the boat, and collect all our stuff around the cabin. *Be out by 11 a.m.,* the notice on the back of the door instructs me. *Make sure the boat is properly docked. Leave the cabin key on the table.*

My teeth are chattering and my hands and feet are numb when I stick his key in the ignition, but I'm feeling pretty good about myself. I drive around to the Lake Texoma State Park camping area and dump the tarp and his suitcase in two giant garbage bins on either end.

I'm halfway to the rental place to return his car when I run out of gas.

Tessie, present day

2:52 a.m.

My monster's dead.

My best friend's alive, folding a white napkin into a tidy point.

So why do I feel this terrifying urge to run?

To scream at Effie.

Run.

Lydia, age 17

I thought Daddy was going to kill me. He had to pick me up at a Whataburger in Sherman. I had walked four miles. There was blood on my face and clothes. I told the woman behind the counter that it was a burst packet of ketchup when I asked if I could use the phone. Daddy is smarter than that.

He broke me just like he always does. I was so tired. I could barely move. He didn't have to threaten much. I wish I could have called Tessie.

Daddy said a lot of things on the way home. *You have no proof he was the killer. Under no circumstances will you have an abortion. Jesus Christ, Lydia. Jesus Christ.*

I overheard him make a call to two of his salvage yard pals. He was paying them to gas up the doctor's rental car and return it.

No matter how hard I try, I can't get warm.

It seems like a million years ago that I stood behind a shed and watched him bury flowers under Tessie's tree house.

Now my parents are on the couch making a plan and I'm out here in my back yard doing a little burying of my own. I'm calling it the little box of Bad Things. The key to the cabin that I forgot to leave on the counter. Tessie's ring that I stole and stuck in a corner of my jewelry box because it was bad luck for her. My favorite Edgar Allan Poe book, because I thought I heard it ticking tonight on the shelf and I wasn't going to live with that the rest of my life. I'm not *ever* going to be crazy like Tessie.

Tessa, present day

2:53 a.m.

She's crazy. *Lydia is crazy.*

When should I have known? As soon as she sat down beside me in second grade with her red glitter pencils sharpened like ice picks?

She's prattling now, like Lydia always does when she tells the truth, about Keats and the sky cracking over the lake and how *the last thing I saw of him was a bald spot like a big mosquito bite* and then *black, black, black.*

The doctor. My monster. Her lover.

At the bottom of the lake. The one where I taught Charlie to slalom. She probably skied right over him.

He was always dead.

Relief, flooding me. Realization, rocking me to hell.

I'm the one who kept my monster alive.

My best friend let that happen. Let me suffer. Let Terrell pay for what he did not do.

Lydia, a greedy flower. More like a black-eyed Susan than any of the girls in that grave. Controlling. Thriving in devastated soil.

'I watched him plant black-eyed Susans under your tree house four hours after we made love for the last time,' Lydia is saying smoothly. 'I found them in little plastic pots under his cabinet and then I followed him and watched him dig the hole. You don't have to hit *me* over the head.' She giggles.

He will never touch my daughter, I'm thinking.

He is bones.

Lydia loved him.

'You look strange, dear,' Effie says. 'Tired. You should sit.'

'The flowers . . . ?' I stutter at Lydia.

'Yes?' Impatient. Waiting for something.

Gratitude. Lydia's waiting for gratitude. I strain against a flood of anger and disbelief. She held my sanity hostage for seventeen years and would like to be thanked for it. I feel a rabid urge to slap her, to tear at her shiny fake hair, to scream *why* until Effie's old house shakes on its foundation.

Lydia is already restless, and I need to be sure. 'Lydia,' I start again. 'If he's dead . . . who kept planting black-eyed Susans for me all these years?'

Her eyes steady on mine. 'Are you accusing me? How should I know? They're just *flowers,* Tessie. Are you still freaked out by a PB and J, too?'

'Liz's job has not a thing to do with planting,' Effie interjects. 'It's Marjory Schwab over at the garden society who's in charge of wildflowers. And it's Blanche something who provides the sandwiches. Or maybe her name is Gladys. And it's Liz, not Lydia, dear.'

'It's OK, Effie,' I say.

Lydia dabs a napkin at her lips. More pretend. She hasn't taken a bite of whatever Effie lump is on the plate in front of her. 'I know you're mad, Tessie. But perfect murders don't just *happen.* Timing is everything. It was very O.J. of me to keep my shirt, don't you think?'

'That's . . . *his* blood on the shirt,' I say slowly. 'The night you killed him.'

'Did you not finish the journal?' she demands. 'I gave you forty-five minutes.'

My mind is shutting her out. Focusing like a laser on the one thing that is still important. That can still be fixed. *Terrell.*

The doctor's blood on the pink shirt. The fetus in the grave. Aurora's DNA.

All connected. Science that could help free Terrell. If Lydia is telling the truth, the blood on that shirt links them all. The doctor not only fathered Lydia's daughter, but the child of a murdered Black-Eyed Susan.

'Aren't you going to ask me why I'm here?' Lydia sounds plaintive, just like she did at ten and twelve and sixteen. 'I have three years of research about the doctor out there in the shed. Colleges he taught at. Girls who disappeared while he was there. Circumstantial, but it ties up pretty nicely. And we'll get them to drag the lake, of course. And I'll let them interview me but I'll be too devastated to share *everything.*' She's giddy with her Lydia-ness. 'I showed up *for a reason,* Tessie. The last-minute stay will be a fantastic way to end my new book. Even if they kill him, I'm a hero for trying. The book's all about the *other* surviving Black-Eyed Susan. *Me.* I tell it like a modern feminist fairy tale. You'll love it. The point being, the monster gets it in the ass.'

'I'm beginning to think you are not with the historical society,' Effie says.

Lydia is sticking her fork into a piece of Effie's cake. It's almost to her lips.

I don't stop her.

For the first time in a long time, I feel hope. Like a cool wind has whistled my head clean.

The monster, 1995

October third, nineteen hundred and ninety-five, 1 P.M.

Cheers to O.J., who just walked out of court a free man.

It's our final session. Tessie's got that telltale flush in her cheeks. She's upset.

Her itty-bitty scar stands out on her tan like a new moon in a sky of freckles. No makeup covering it up today. I like that. A sign of restored confidence. The nuclear emerald eyes are sharp and focused. That glorious copper hair is pulled back flat against her skull like she's about to run a race. The muscles in her face are taut and purposeful, not a limp bag hanging off bone like the first day she walked in here. She's still biting her nails but she's painted them carefully with a lovely lavender polish.

I want to tell her so many things.

How I intended to tear her apart, but it was much, much more thrilling to put her back together.

How Rebecca was both a flippant lie I told a lazy reporter and a metaphor for everything. Rebecca is the ghost who kept me company on the worst night of my life. She is every wife and daughter I will never have and every special girl who sat down in my class, lifted her eyes, and did not glimpse her fate.

I want to tell Tessie that sometimes – many times – I am sorry.

I want to finish that story I started about the sad boy who walked to a lonely house after school and turned on the heat.

Tessie had been worried about that boy, I could tell. When she's sad, her face always crinkles prettily, like origami.

That boy's mother always left a horrible surprise for him to find while she was at work. A dead baby bird on his pillow. A live water moccasin in the toilet. A cat turd in the Twinkies box. Gags, *she called them.*

The Saturday night that he put twenty crushed pills into his mother's cheap red wine, she fell asleep on page 136 of Rebecca. *Daphne du Maurier. She pronounced it* doomayer, *like the fat clod she was.*

He had plumped up her pillow, flipped on the air conditioner to high in the middle of winter, and read the whole book before he called the police and told them she'd been suicidal for months.

'I saw you with her.' Tessie is taunting me.

I want to put my hand on Tessie's knee to stop its jackhammering.

I want to place that well-thumbed book in her hand.

I want to tell her that red flowers, not yellow ones, had a special meaning for Rebecca.

I want to tell her that very soon, I'm going to run my finger over the butterfly tattoo on her hip. The one just like Lydia's.

Epilogue

Imagination, of course, can open any door – turn the key and let terror walk right in.

– Lydia, age 16, reading *In Cold Blood* under the bridge in Trinity Park, waiting for Tessie to finish her run, ten days before the attack, 1994

Tessa

One at a time, the pieces have come forward, like shy girls stepping up to dance.

Lydia admitted to a cold-blooded killing and to a relationship with the doctor, but never to planting the black-eyed Susans in her back yard or at my old apartment or nestled by my grandmother's dead tomato vines or under the bridge that roared like an ocean.

If that's true, the doctor planted flowers exactly once, the first time. The wind and a death penalty nut were responsible for the rest. I allowed a diabolical gardener to live in my head for more than a decade. Like the Brothers Grimm, I ascribed power to an ordinary, innocent object. Oh, the hell that can be wrought from a hand mirror. A single pea. A one-eyed flower.

I remembered the T-shirt Merry was wearing, one morning while I watched Charlie eat Frosted Cheerios out of a yellow cereal bowl that used to be my mother's. *Welcome to CAMP SUNSHINE,* the shirt read, except the dirt and the blood obliterated everything but the *SUN. S-U-N.* My desperate mnemonic device naming the mothers of those girls was just a brain chip gone haywire. *A survival tool,* Dr Giles says.

Dr Giles tries to convince me every other session that the Susans in my head weren't real. I'll never believe her. The Susans are about as real as it gets. I used to lie awake at night imagining my mind as my grandfather's house, with passageways and dark rooms seeking a candle and Susans sleeping and waking in all of the many beds. Now the moon is pouring like melted butter through those windows. The floors are swept. The beds are made. The closets emptied.

The Susans have flown from my head, but only because I kept my promises. That was my grandfather's one survival tip if I ever found myself trapped in a fairy tale. Keep your promises. Bad things happen if you don't.

The bones of the two other Susans in that grave have been officially identified as Carmen Rivera, a Mexican foreign exchange student at University of Texas, and Grace Neely, a cognitive studies major at Vanderbilt. The earth's code turned out to be remarkably accurate. Eight other unidentified girls in morgues in three states have been linked to Lydia's meticulous research.

To my relief, Benita Alvarez Smith does not peer out of any picture lineup except the one in her church's directory. Lucas tracked her down for me. She's a happily married mother of two in Laredo who's meeting me for coffee when she's in Fort Worth next month to visit her parents.

The best part, of course, is Terrell. Lydia's encyclopedic research set Terrell free. That, and the DNA match between her shirt and the fetus, created enough reasonable doubt for a state court to halt the execution and release Terrell six weeks later. I was worried that three days wouldn't be enough time to brake the Texas death train. Bill declared that, on Death Row, three days is an eternity.

So now Terrell is tearing out hearts on talk shows, reassuring people about a purposeful life, God, forgiveness, all the things that should not fall out of the mouth of a man who was the innocent victim of a racist system. Off camera, Terrell confines himself to one room, keeps the shades drawn, sleeps best on the couch, so far unable to wean himself from claustrophobia.

He's also collecting $1 million in compensation from the state of Texas and a guaranteed $80,000 annuity every year for life. Who knew that the state that executed the most people also was the most generous in compensating for its errors?

Charlie and I miss Effie. She Skypes us in pink plastic curlers, mails food bricks without regard to the cost of postage, keeps up the good fight with her gremlins. The new owners next door painted her house a non-historical Notre Dame blue and gold. The three tiny human terrors they brought with them have ripped out every bit of Effie's landscaping. Charlie politely refuses to babysit for a standing offer of $20 an hour.

Jo continues her battle with a never-ending supply of monsters, throwing on her white lab coat every day and grinding up the bones of the lost. We've become running buddies, and more. The night before Lydia's grand appearance, she had dropped by. She unfastened her gold DNA charm necklace and looped it around my neck like an amulet of protection.

I spend a lot more time than I'd like to admit thinking about Lydia Frances Bell aka Elizabeth Stride aka Rose Mylett. She makes her home in England, where she lives with her two cats, Pippin and Zelda. At least that's what it says in the bio on the back of her *New York Times* bestseller, *The Secret Susan*. Charlie is reading Lydia's book on the sly. *Let her do it,* Dr Giles insists.

Charlie and Aurora text regularly. They started following each other on Facebook after the media coverage that threw all of us into a boiling soup for two months. *Aurora's had a sucky life, and I haven't,* Charlie tells me, as if defending the relationship. *She wants to be a nurse. Her foster parents just bought her an old yellow Bug. She's still hoping her mom will pick up the phone and call.*

Their relationship makes me happy, and uneasy.

My gaze is stretching as far as it can over the sloshing, murky Gulf. I'm thinking about how to paint it. With dark, reckless abstract strokes? With a brilliant Jesus sky resurrecting everything that lives under the surface?

Jesus isn't a sunburst today. There was a shark attack an hour ago, so there are only a few spots of brave color in the water. It's cloudy. The water is leaden and impenetrable, like it often is in Galveston even when the sun is shining. The sand is littered with seaweed that makes it feel like you are walking barefoot on a thousand snakes.

My daughter and I return to this rickety rental house for a week every summer anyway. The hard, chunky sand is perfect for castle building. The sunsets are worth every second of still watching. At night, you can plunk down on the seawall and count the fish jumping out of the water in the moonlight. It's an island, ugly and beautiful, with a history as deep and dark and quirky as ours.

For the first time, we tentatively invited company. Bill may drop by this weekend. I'm on the deck, watching Charlie run along the water's edge with her friend Anna, whose mom has been whisked to a three-month rehab for her Big Gulp Diet Coke and vodka habit. No one passing by would guess that anything tugs at either of these teen-agers. They are kicking at the surf, laughing, their chatter mixing it up with the seagulls.

Reminding me of two other girls.

Before Lydia hopped a plane, she told the police a serpentine and wholly convincing tale about the night she took out the Black-Eyed Susan killer. Self-defense. Rape. Manipulation by her parents. The police have never considered filing charges. When they stumbled across the same online psychological journal pieces I did, written under the doctor's name, Lydia freely admitted penning them herself. 'It made me feel less like his victim to use his name,' she told them. 'I can't explain it.' So they even let her off the hook for that.

Anti-death-penalty advocates are still trying to goad Terrell into suing her. The female talk show hosts who chatter in silly tribal circles don't like that Lydia cashed in. Domestic violence groups remain staunchly behind her. She was a teen-age girl sexually manipulated by a killer. *Either that,* I think, *or the other way around.* Much has been made about the doctor's cleverness. The risks he took to thwart the process. His ability to fool a district attorney and a devoted father. The way he snaked onto a list of doctor candidates so I'd choose him myself.

I lock my rage in a place I go less and less often. I use the tricks he taught me. When I do let him crawl into my head, he is very much alive. Sitting under that Winslow Homer painting with his legs stretched out, waiting for me. Slithering in the dark along the lake bottom. They've dragged parts of Lake Texoma with high tech equipment three times now, unearthing the skulls of a fifty-something unidentified woman and a two-year-old boy who went under last fall, but not the remains of a monster.

Of course, it makes me wonder.

If almost every word out of Lydia's mouth was a lie.

If her pockets are full of seeds.

If Lydia and I are really finished.

Just in case, I hold on to a final weapon. Her diary. I've curled her notebook into my old hidey-hole in the wall of my grandfather's basement. I won't hesitate to pry open that tomb if I need to. Bring all of her darkness and vanity up to the light. Let Lydia's own words vanquish her. Strip her back down to the pale, weird little girl no one wanted to play with but me.

I do go to sleep certain about one thing.

Wherever Lydia is, alone with her pen or lying on soft sands or stretched out in a field of flowers, the Susans are quietly building their new mansion in her head, brick by brick.

The End

Look, you shoot off a guy's head with his pants down, believe me, Texas ain't the place you want to get caught.

– Lydia and Tessie, 14, watching *Thelma and Louise*,
hanging out the back of a pickup
at the Brazos Drive-in, 1992

Acknowledgments

This book took an army of kind, brilliant human beings – scientists, therapists, and legal experts – who generously advised me about cutting-edge DNA science, the impact of psychic trauma on teen-agers, and the slow path to a Texas execution.

Mitochondrial DNA whiz and Oklahoma girl **Rhonda Roby** consulted on *Black-Eyed Susans* over text, phone, email, and beer. She also shared her profound experiences identifying victims of serial killers, the Vietnam War, Pinochet, plane crashes, and 9/11. She stood with some of the best scientists in the world at Ground Zero in the days after the attack, and spent years getting answers for families. Her personality, expertise, and humanity are woven throughout this book. And that crazy deer story? It's true. Rhonda now works a dream job as a professor at the J. Craig Venter Institute.

The University of North Texas Center for Human Identification in Fort Worth is represented with a little fictional license, but not much. Its mission, under **Arthur Eisenberg,** is beyond imagining – to put names to unidentified bones when no one else can. Law enforcement agencies from all over the world send their coldest cases here. And, yes, UNTCHI did identify one of the unidentified victims of serial killer John Wayne Gacy thirty-three years after his remains were dug out of a crawl space under a Chicago house.

George Dimitrov Kamenov, a geochemist at the University of Florida, opened my mind to the miracle of isotope analysis and its current use in solving crimes and identifying old bones. He made me understand, more than anyone ever has, that we *are* the earth. George also inspired one of my favorite twists.

Nancy Giles, a longtime children's therapist, provided intricate detail about how both good and bad therapists operate and a reading list of psychiatric textbooks (*Shattered Assumptions, Too Scared to Cry, Trauma and Recovery*) that changed the course of this book. I was also aided by her son, **Robert Giles III,** an expert with the Child Assistance Program in the Judge Advocate General's Corps for the U.S. Navy, and his wife, **Kelly Giles,** a therapist who has dedicated a good portion of her life to treating abused children. Nancy's husband, **Bob Giles,** a two-time Pulitzer Prize-winning editor and former boss of mine, believed in me early in my journalism career. He's a big reason why I eventually had the crazy confidence to write a book.

David Dow, a renowned Texas death penalty attorney, jumped right into the imaginary plot of my book and told me how he'd handle the case. What I didn't expect is that he'd end up feeding the philosophical core of one of my characters. His memoir, *The Autobiography of an Execution,* is unforgettable, and I highly recommend it no matter how you feel about the death penalty.

One of David's former Death Row clients, **Anthony Graves,** took time out of a precious day of freedom to chat with me on the phone and share his experiences as an innocent man behind bars. He spent eighteen years in prison, falsely accused of killing a family of six. Now free, he operates with a spiritual confidence that makes most of us puny by comparison. Check out his tireless advocacy at www .anthonybelieves.com.

Dennis Longmire, a professor at Sam Houston State University, has shown up for years as a steadfast regular at Texas executions. He holds a battery-operated Christmas candle. One chilly night in front of the Texas Death House, he and other regulars explained the matter-of-fact reality of executions to me. **John Moritz,** a former *Fort Worth Star-Telegram* reporter who witnessed more than a dozen executions, provided additional detail.

The mother-daughter team of **Mary and Mary Clegg,** who run the Whistler bed and breakfast just blocks away from the infamous Walls Unit, revealed the softer side of Huntsville, Texas. I took a little fictional license with the ghosts of their beautiful ancestral home, but they did serve me the most delicious Dutch baby pancake I ever ate. Anyone who stops in Huntsville, don't miss the Marys.

I'd also like to note an article by **Cathy A. Malchiodi** about the use of art intervention with traumatized children. She detailed the case of little 'Tessa' and a dollhouse, which I've included as an anecdote in this book.

Laura Gaydosh Combs led me to information on fetal bones.

Black-Eyed Susans is fiction, but it was important to me that the forensic science, the role of therapy in psychic trauma, and the legal path of Texas executions be rooted in truth. If there are any mistakes or flights of fancy, they are mine.

I'd also like to thank:

Christopher Kelly, a phenomenal friend and writer

who is a critic when I need one and a shoulder to cry on when I don't.

Kirstin Herrera, the only pal I know who would take me up on a grim invitation to stand outside the Texas death chamber on the night of an execution.

Christina Kowal, for handing me the Big Mac line from the backseat and for inhabiting part of Charlie. Also her mom, dear cuz **Melissa.**

Sam Kaskovich, my son, for drawing mustaches on Jane Eyre, thinking trophies are braggy, and operating with such faith and kindness. This book is passionately dedicated to him.

Kay Schnurman, who makes magic out of thread and steel and was the inspiration for Tessa's artistic side.

Chuck and Sue Heaberlin, my parents, who must wonder why all this dark stuff jumps from my head to paper, but are proud of me anyway.

At Random House, a village: **Kate Miciak,** my editor, a bulldog and a poet who executes the best line edits on the planet; **Jennifer Hershey,** an early champion of *Black-Eyed Susans;* **Libby McGuire; Rachel Kind** and her foreign rights team; my rockin' publicist, **Lindsey Kennedy**. And the people who save me from my errors and turn a book into a beautiful package: production editor **Loren Noveck,** copy editor **Pam Feinstein,** production manager **Angela McNally,** text designer **Dana Leigh Blanchette,** and cover designers **Lee Motley** and **Belina Huey.**

Also, **Kathy Harris** for an early copy edit.

Maxine Hitchcock at Michael Joseph/Penguin UK, for her enthusiastic support of this book and my career.

Danielle Perez. I won't forget. Thank you.

Steve Kaskovich, my husband, therapist, and early reader. The luckiest day of my life was when he threw those Mardi Gras beads across a newsroom and then asked me out until I said yes.

Garland E. Wilson, artist, morgue photographer, singer, and storyteller. He was the best grandfather a girl could have. I miss your creepy basement.

And, finally and most emphatically of all, my agent, **Pam Ahearn,** who was there at every twist and turn of these pages. She never stopped believing in this book or in me. I will be forever grateful.

About the Author

Julia Heaberlin grew up in Decatur, Texas, a small town that sits under a big sky. It provided a dreamy girl with a great library, a character behind every door, and as many secrets as she'd find anyplace else. An award-winning journalist, she has worked as an editor at the *Fort Worth Star-Telegram, The Dallas Morning News,* and *The Detroit News. Black-Eyed Susans* is her third psychological thriller set in Texas. She lives near Dallas/Fort Worth with her husband and has a son who attends the University of Texas at Austin. She is currently at work on her next novel of suspense.

Reading Group Discussion Questions

Contains Plot Spoilers

1. Tess is not always truthful, especially when she is younger. How reliable is she as a narrator? Did you completely trust her version of events?

2. Discuss the ways in which Tess's relationship with her daughter is affected by her traumatic past and how it manifests itself in their day-to-day life. Are there ways in which she has been made a better mother because of this?

3. Though called Tessie as a teenager she switches to Tess as an adult. Discuss the reasons behind this change.

4. Tessie pretends to be blind long after her eyesight has returned. Discuss what sight and blindness represent in the novel.

5. As the years pass, Tess still has a blank in her memory from the time surrounding the attack. Do you think that she could have accessed these memories if she had tried hard enough?

6. Discuss the representations of friendship in the novel. Is there always an element of power play and how does that affect Tess and Lydia?

7. In the aftermath of the 'event' the people around Tessie were doing all they could to help her. Do you think that they went about this in the right way? Was there anything more that could have been done?

8. Tessie and Lydia make 'fake' drawings to show her therapist. Though she was consciously trying to deceive, do these drawings still say something about the workings of Tessie's mind? What does Lydia's drawing say about her?

9. Discuss the role of the 'Susans'. Are they a creation of Tess's mind and, if so, why does she do this? What do they represent?

10. Though he never saw death row, the real killer was still fatally punished for his crimes. What is the novel trying to say about the death penalty? Is the author taking one side of the debate or merely opening it up for questioning?

11. Charlie's father is in the army and therefore can only occasionally visit. Is there significance in Tess's choice in men?

12. Though Terrell is at risk of being put to death, it still takes Tess many years to own up to her doubts about his guilt. Is everyone in the novel guilty of some crime? Are there any truly good people here?

Now an exclusive look behind the scenes at some of Julia Heaberlin's chilling research for *Black-Eyed Susans* . . .

As part of her research for Black-Eyed Susans, *Julia Heaberlin stood outside the Texas death house during an execution. She also spoke with Anthony Graves, an innocent man who spent more than a decade on Death Row. Here, she recounts those experiences along with her perspective on the death penalty. Heaberlin is also an award-winning journalist.*

Everything quivers. The trees, the grass, the birds. The ribs in my chest, the balls of my feet. The air, brittle with chill and death even before the thundering noise began. I feel like I am about to explode from the inside out.

When people ask me what it is like to stand outside the Texas death chamber while a prisoner is being executed, this is what I remember first. The man executed that particular night was Edgar Tamayo, a Mexican national who shot a Houston cop three times in the back of the head. The terrible sound was the revving of motorcycles from the nearly two dozen retired police officers parked as close to Edgar Tamayo as they could get. They demanded that he hear the guttural protest of their motors through the walls as the needle was going in. Kill him, roared the motorcycles. Kill him.

And make no mistake, Edgar Tamayo, his family, and the witnesses he chose, could hear.

It is easy to stand only yards away from the tiny, nondescript room in Huntsville, Texas, that is the busiest execution factory in the United States. Since 1982, my state has killed more than 525 prisoners. The death chamber is housed on the corner of 'The Walls,' a historic, friendly looking prison with a green area and a clock tower. In Texas, executions have been performed by rope, poison and electricity for almost 200 years. The Walls unit sits in the middle of town a few blocks off the quaint square. There is a barbecue grill on the front porch of the white frame house next door, and an old neighbourhood stretches out beyond it.

Within sight of the walls, while men die, people are munching on pie and chicken-fried steak at the best restaurant in town. They don't mean anything by it; it's a matter of routine. Back when the electric chair was used, the lights of the whole town used to shiver when the executioner flipped the switch. If the townsfolk who live here don't work for the prison system – seven sprawling units in all – their parents probably did, or their grandparents. The history here is deep and bloody. Clyde Barrow, one half of Bonnie and Clyde, the most famous and romantic outlaw couple in US history, did time here in 1930. He was repeatedly raped in Eastham prison, still nicknamed The Ham. Barrow took an axe to two toes in an attempt to get transferred to a place more forgiving.

Sometimes, I take my mind back to the night of Edgar Tamayo's death. Survey the scene. On that night, and most execution nights, the screaming politicians and social-media fanatics are far from the town of about 40,000 in the piney woods of East Texas. The crowd I'm with is small, mostly Hispanic. Two beautiful Mexican TV reporters are brilliant stars in the dark, illuminated by camera lights, one in a brand-new purple tie, another in bright red lipstick. Mexico, despite its on-going battle with corruption and brutal cartels, is anti-death penalty. The government is vigorously protesting the execution of one of its own on our soil.

A group of mourners kneel by Edgar's picture and sing, their mouths opening and closing like birds. Gloria, who runs a straggly group of regular, vocal protesters, chants through her bullhorn that an innocent man is about to die, even though he is not innocent at all. Some of them hold signs that declare Rick Perry a serial killer (279 people were executed during his time as governor). Another group of five men and women, all white, all older, weigh down a street corner. Most of them make the drive from Houston to as many executions as they can. They come not to yell but to be present for the family of the executed. On the coldest nights, the most stalwart, a criminal justice professor in Huntsville, stands by the stop sign alone with his battery-operated Christmas candle until the family of the executed walks out the door. He is tired and cynical and understandably does not want to talk much. He has been talking to tourists like me for ever.

The whole thing is so banal. So efficient. Everyone here knows where to be. The pros are on one side of the building, the cons on the other. The Texas troopers wandering around don't expect trouble. The execution process usually starts at six, is done by seven, although tonight is going long. Legendary Texas death penalty lawyer David Dow says he doesn't mean to be flip when he speaks a truth: 'Killing people is like most anything else; the more you do it, the better you get. If killing people were like playing the violin, Texas would have been selling out Carnegie Hall years ago.'

Ice starts to fall. I re-examine why I am here and why I have not been here before. I am writing a novel, a story meant to entertain. I showed up out of convenience, curiosity and a desire to be authentic in my book. I had casually Googled the Texas execution schedule two months before: should I pick the woman who helped a group torture and murder a mentally ill man for his life insurance? The man who ate the doughnuts and breakfast tacos that he ordered after beating the delivery woman with a baseball bat? A boyfriend who repeatedly stabbed and killed the married woman he was sleeping with and her daughter and three-year-old grandson? A guy who kidnapped a young Houston couple, raped the woman and then killed them both?

In the end, I picked Edgar, and so we were united. The day of his death fit into my schedule. I asked a friend to come with me. We chattered and ate sour gummies and red liquorice on the three-hour ride from Dallas to East Texas. We booked at a lovely bed-and-breakfast only a few blocks from the Death House.

I am horrified as I write that last paragraph.

I was raised by a woman who gave spiders a free ride out of the kitchen on a newspaper. There was no death penalty in our house. I was a sensitive kid who didn't believe my God would send anyone to hell. I couldn't stomach violent movies, much less the barbaric concept of it being legal to kill someone. As I grew older, I was further shaped by intellectual reasoning – that the death penalty is part of a racist and unfair system. I protested by voting for candidates who believed as I did.

When I arrived back home from Huntsville, the experience began to shape my story, my characters, in ways I didn't plan. I poured out a chapter I feared my editor would cut entirely. She never touched a word.

The lawyer, so important to this part of the story, sprang to life.

Tessa, my heroine, would not cooperate. She was conflicted about the death penalty no matter how much I tried to convince her otherwise.

How can you know how I feel, she asked me, if you've never experienced something this terrible? If evil hasn't ripped out a staggering piece of who you are?

Don't preach, she told me. Let me be who I am.

*

Evenings like this are a routine fact of life in Huntsville, but they are becoming far less common in the United States, where the death penalty appears to be slowly dying itself amid growing concerns over its fairness, cost and morality.

The number of executions in America has been steadily falling this century, from a high of ninety-eight in 1999 to twenty-eight in 2015. Similarly, fewer convicts are being sent to Death Row each year as more juries opt for the sentence of life without parole, even for the most heinous crimes. Last year, the young man who shot up a Colorado movie theatre, killing twelve and wounding seventy, was spared a death sentence.

According to the Death Penalty Information Center, only forty-nine new death sentences were handed out in 2015, the lowest number since the 1970s. Even Texas, which led the US in executions last year with thirteen, only added two new inmates to Death Row.

Seven states have voted to abolish the death penalty since 2007 (thirty-one states out of fifty still have it) and several others have issued moratoriums, including Pennsylvania, Washington and Oregon. California, which has more inmates on Death Row (746 as of last year) than any other state, has not executed anyone since 2006 due to various legal challenges to the system.

There are several reasons behind the growing hesitance to use capital punishment.

The emergence of DNA technology has led to highly publicized exonerations and concerns that states may execute innocent men and women. The cost of fighting lengthy appeals, sometimes lasting a decade, is straining state and local governments. Facing pressure from European nations and religious groups, some manufacturers stopped supplying drugs used in lethal injections, causing a shortage and prompting states to try new ones. This has resulted in some grisly episodes during executions, such as with inmates in Arizona and Ohio reportedly left gasping for air instead of being sedated.

This year, the Supreme Court was asked once again to declare the practice unconstitutional. Last year, the Court voted five to four to allow Oklahoma to proceed with lethal injections despite having experienced problems with its drugs. In a long dissent, Justice Stephen Breyer invited challenges, arguing that capital punishment likely violates the Eighth Amendment prohibiting 'cruel and unusual punishment'.

Even so, business at the Texas death chamber moves on. As the year began, nine executions were scheduled for 2016.

*

David Dow, a Texas death penalty lawyer who has represented more than 100 men on Death Row, helped me navigate the slow march to a Texas execution in *Black-Eyed Susans.* He kindly agreed to drop himself into my plot and tell me how he'd handle the case. Dow is the author of the acclaimed *The Autobiography of an Execution*, a poignant memoir of his life as a death penalty attorney and a heart-rending tale whichever side of the line you stand on. His philosophy became part of the heart and soul of one of my characters.

I learned that the goal of a death penalty attorney is primarily to extend life. The appeals process drags on for years, costing the government far more than paying for a criminal to live out his life in prison. Dow personally believes the main argument for abolishing the death penalty is that it is part of a racist and unfair system, not because there are hundreds of innocent men about to be executed. Most of the prisoners on Death Row are guilty as hell. That said, Dow is the founder and director of Texas's oldest innocence project, the Texas Innocence Network, which uses law students at the University of Houston to investigate claims from the condemned. And Dow himself has helped exonerate two clients, including Anthony Graves, who spent more than eighteen years in prison, most in solitary confinement on Death Row.

I interviewed Anthony one sunny afternoon. I was on the phone, sitting at my kitchen table, glancing out at the shimmering aqua of our pool. I felt a bit guilty that I was taking minutes from one of Anthony's precious days of freedom while he told me one of the worst things about living on Texas Death Row was that he didn't want to breathe. He didn't want to suck in air that smelled of the sweat and desperation of men condemned to die, locked in tiny cells for twenty-three hours a day with no hope of human touch. The smell is indescribable, he told me, like nothing in the outside world. He told me how prisoners play imaginary games of chess in their heads. How he somehow hung on to hope while those around him went crazy.

Graves had spent almost two decades in prison, twelve of those years on Death Row. He was convicted of walking into a house in Somerville, Texas, in 1992, helping slaughter a family of six and then setting the house on fire. While many men placed on Texas Death Row are unequivocally guilty of horrors – one killed his daughters, aged six and nine, during a custody visit while their mother heard the shots on the other end of the phone – Anthony was one of the innocent ones.

The real killer had decided to implicate Graves at random in an unsuccessful effort to save himself, admitting in a sworn statement right before his own execution that he had lied. Despite a lack of evidence, it took years and countless lawyer hours for Graves to be freed and for Charles Sebesta, the district attorney who withheld evidence and used false testimony, to be disbarred. Now? Now Anthony travels around the country, telling people his story, fighting for reform. Now he is remarkably grateful, even forgiving. Now he breathes deeply. He talks to a thriller-writer and journalist like me and asks politely if, in return, I would please mention his website and foundation whenever I can (www.anthonygravesfoundation.org). The wheel continues to turn. Graves, so unjustly accused himself, was named to the non-profit governmental board of the Houston Forensic Science Center, which oversees the city's crime lab.

When I started this novel, I was a journalist who wanted my fiction to be authentic. After I talked to these two men, I wanted to be a more authentic person.

Sometimes, my mind drifts back to the scene outside the Death House.

The furious motorcycles. The men gunning them for one of their own, Guy Gaddis, a twenty-four-year-old cop who left behind a pregnant wife. He was two-and-a-half years on the job. A war veteran.

The roaring of engines drowned out the singing of the mourners and filled every molecule of air.

It was hard to breathe.

If you enjoyed

Black Eyed Susans

then you'll love these:

DISCLAIMER
Renée Knight

THE SILENCE OF THE LAMBS
Thomas Harris

POST MORTEM
Patricia Cornwell

GONE GIRL
Gillian Flynn

THE GIRL ON THE TRAIN
Paula Hawkins

THE ENCHANTED
Rene Denfeld

You might also enjoy the *Serial* podcasts and the documentary series *Making a Murderer*